CW01619868

Journey from Darkness

No se permite la reproducción total o parcial de este libro, ni su incorporación a un sistema informático, ni su transmisión en cualquier forma o cualquier medio, sea este electrónico, mecánico, por fotocopia, por grabación u otros métodos, sin el permiso previo y por escrito de los titulares del copyright.

Luke Darracott. *Hikikomori. Journey from Darkness*
Primera edición: febrero de 2025

ISBN: 978-84-129617-2-0
Depósito legal: M-1217-2025

© Luke Darracott, 2025
© Imagen portada: Wayne Kehoe. De esta portada, maqueta y edición: Editorial Ybernia, S. C., 2025
Imágenes capítulos y divisores de secciones: Hamonshū, Mori Yūzan (Smithsonian Libraries, Internet Archive, dominio público)

Impreso en Italia por 4graph
Printed in Italy by 4graph

Luke Darracott

Hikikomori

Journey from Darkness

Ybernia

Ame futte chikatamaru
雨降って地固まる

When it rains, earth hardens.

- Japanese proverb

CONTENTS

Author's Introduction

Adding an author's introduction to one's novel can smack a little of pretension, which it does, it will and is something I endorse, because I am bit...pretentious that is.

I shall avoid wallowing in self-love and reflective musings as to the artistic 'why' that this novel came to be, but for some it might come out of leftfield a touch so I feel at least a perfunctory prologue from me might help set it up a little.

For many years I have been involved in the world of travel and gastronomy, namely wine, and namely on top of that previous namely, all things Spain related.

My Madrid-based adult life eating and drinking too much, getting sunburned in the sierras and lounging around ancient villages and absurd landscapes aside, I have always had an obsession with Japan; a country that could almost be the diametric opposite of the boisterous Mediterranean lands of Iberia.

Since I was boy, he writes whilst playing the small violin to nobody, my brain was filled with the usual tropes that so often shoot their tendrils into the souls of the westerners and bring them in: samurai, technology, Akira Kurosawa, anime and manga, swords and violence, politeness and neon. I was just another stereotypical little European boy dreaming Blade Runner dreams and hitting sticks against trees in the park.

I even took up karate for a couple of years in an ill-fated attempt to get closer to the world of artistic fighting that I saw in the Asian cinema that became my obsession — one I still have to this day. I found that the Koreans, the Chinese and the Japanese had a way of making violence beautiful.

Then university came, and the obligatory dive into the wonderful world of Haruki Murakami, foreshadowing a 'see you in a decade' addiction to Japanese literature of all kinds.

All this is to give the impression that, short of dressing up as cartoon characters and going to conventions, which I applaud, I was as much a weeb as you could get. This, along with the added gastronomic dependency created by falling in love with their cuisine, led me to be labelled a 'Japanophile'.

We come then to the apogee of my Japanophilic career: in 2019, a few months prior to a world-stopping virus, I finally visited Japan.

In the decade preceding this trip I had been writing and taking photos and making travel videos. I had published two books about travel in Spain and visited Iceland — my other childhood obsession, but for wildly different reasons — where having had my fill of volcanic photography, planned to write a flurry of travelogues or, who knows, even a book.

That didn't pan out.

Despite my brain melting out of my eyes every day in that country, I had too much on my plate to write another book.

Then I opened a wine shop, a rather successful one at that, in the centre of Spain's capital, and free time became a luxury I wouldn't be privy to.

That visit to Japan, much like the trip to Iceland, had the rare result of not only meeting my expectations, but pounding them into dust and challenging me not to be breathlessly impressed every second of every day. The neon was more luminous, the sushi fresher, the ramen naughtier, the people more polite, and the temples more beautiful than I could have ever imagined.

Was I seeing the superficial? Yes of course.

Was I still seeing Japan? Yes of course.

There's nothing wrong with seeing a country as a temporary traveller. Each day was a new town, a new shrine, a hike through a valley, a hidden restaurant. But of course, it's only the surface being scratched. So, after scooping my mind off the floor and pouring it back into my head I returned to Madrid life, the three weeks spent roaming the country frozen as a perfect tangible memory.

Then some little contagious sub-microscopic agent went and put the world on hold for a couple of years. The lockdowns and quarantines in Spain were fierce and we were housebound for a long time.

I was allowed, owing to the fact the country viewed wine as food, and necessary, to leave my house and go to my shop to process orders. But apart from that, and occasionally delivering wines in the zombie streets, bedecked in latex gloves and what felt like fifteen masks, I was at home. Alone.

I got a teacher and started learning Japanese. I did about a year, both online and masked up in person, before finances and the rearing head of work meant I had neither time nor money. But I did achieve the initial N5 qualification, the exam taken in summer, mouths covered, with a startling number of other sweating students at various stages of their studies.

In short, I got good at telling people what I had for dinner and what I'd like to do on holiday. The aim was always to have a better level for when I finally got back to Japan, so I hoped to move onto the N4 at the end of that same year.

I didn't.

Life got in the way, my bank account, jittery as it was being a small business owner during a pandemic, was shivering and as the months passed and Japan remained closed off still, a viral spectre of the Tokugawa floating in the air, my triumphant return to Nippon with nicely formed sentences flowing out of my mouth seemed a rather distant proposition.

So, by 2023 I was left with a burning desire to return, a capacity to recall some language and the ability to read *hiragana* and *katakana* and about 30 *kanji*. Not much else.

Around the time I was learning Japanese in my little pandemic apartment, staring out the window and remembering what it was like to be crammed into tapas bars, I also submitted stories to a monthly short-story competition in Australia called 'Furious Fiction'. Every month they emitted a few keys words or a place or a topic and you had a couple of days to produce a 500-word short story.

My friend Dave, because we all have a mate called Dave in the UK, was really into it and so, in a moment of literary bonding, I joined in a couple of times. One of my stories was about a shut in, a *Hikikomori* who, in a time of crisis, would find the impetus to finally leave his flat. Dave said it sounded like the start of a larger story. And that little seedling of an idea was the start of mine. A fleshed out version of the submission to Oz would eventually become Chapter One of the book.

What followed was extensive research, fuelled by my aforementioned obsession, into both Japan, the phenomenon of Hikikomori and the country's folklore.

A couple of final notes: the names are presented in the western format FIRST NAME + SECOND NAME, though it is the reverse in Japan itself; when a Japanese word is first mentioned it will be italicised and thereafter not; despite my research I do not claim to be an academic, so should there be any historical or cultural error I can but apologise. Regarding the many Japanese words used in the book, many of the regularly used ones and indeed ones I think were important to include, can be found with their meanings in a short glossary at the back of the book.

I won't say much more at the risk of removing the reason to read the rest of this book, but safe to say this project has swallowed me up over the last couple of years and made me fall ever more in love with Japan and feel more connected to it. At the same time, I have learned more about its shortcomings, which has helped dispel a little of the starry-eyed fangirl aspect of my interest and see her more as the complex country she really is.

Anyway, that's enough from me, if you've even bothered to get this far. So, from an Englishman, living in Iberia, and dreaming of the land of the Rising Sun, please enjoy.

- Luke Darracott, 2024

Character List

People:
Natsuo Hirawa - Our hero, a social recluse living in Kochi
Akihiro Hirawa - Natsuo's salaryman father
Yui Hirawa - Natsuo's meek mother

Captain Tanaka - the local policeman in Tosashimizu
Mayu - Captain Tanaka's wife
Mr Shi - lifesaving man-with-a-van delivery river
Mina - old lady who really believes in folklore
Ichika Jinja - bar-owning exorcist

Shinjiro Kenji - owner of the Yuzuya Ryokan
Yuki - mysterious employee of the Yuzuya Ryokan

Akari Naganohara - itako shaman
Abe no Semei - head of the Bureau of Divination and magic user

Yōkai:
Sōjōbō - venerable chief tengu
Kaneda/Kuzu-no-Ha - kitsune at the Eiheiji temple
Nurarihyon - gourd-headed *yōkai* leader
Hozaki - hell's best sake brewer
Yashima-no-Hage-tanuki - eccentric and heroic tanuki
Shuten dōji - powerful oni leader
Ibaraki - Shuten dōji's lieutenant

Gods:
Enma Daiō - King of the Underworld
Izanagi - heavenly creator god, brother of Izanami
Izanami - heavenly creator goddess, sister of Izanagi
Amaterasu - chief goddess of the sun
Susanoo - tempestuous god of storms, brother of Amaterasu

Chapter One: Hikikomori
引きこもり

Acute and total social withdrawal from society.

This was the fifth typhoon to strike Kochi. The normal summer – long, sultry days when the air shimmered like gel and the buzz of the crickets hummed in the ears – never arrived. To Natsuo Hirawa it seemed the world had dimmed. Clear skies had given way to a tempestuous grey roof and the world was wild and angry.

Wind, rain, flooding, evacuations, deaths.
He couldn't bear it anymore.
But then he didn't have to.
Natsuo hadn't left his home in thirteen years.
Thirteen years, rent-free, in a small family home on a quiet street in a suburb of a peaceful town on the south coast of Shikoku, which itself was a somewhat forgotten place on the south side of the Inland Sea. Gas, electricity, and water were all paid for by parents he never saw; a father and mother he had no contact with.

They had never understood that he wanted to be different. His *otousan*, Akihiro Hirawa, the nebulous, off-the-shelf salaryman who looked like every other middle-aged Japanese man who fell in line and disappeared into the masses on his way home and whose eyes had long lost whatever fire they may have once had. His *okaasan*, Yui Hirawa, the doting, gentle and submissive housewife who would, at any given minute on any given day be found making *dashi*, hand cleaning clothes, slicing fish, or washing what were apparently eternally dirty pots and pans.

Natsuo had once read that wives did seven times more housework than their husbands. Something like a pathetic half an hour versus four and a half hours per day. He believed it and it sickened him.

Every day when he got back from school, he would find his mother toiling away in some corner of the house. Natsuo had always wondered how she continually found something to do. He swore there was never enough mess or enough eating or enough anything going on in that hushed house to warrant so much work. But there she would be as he came home calling '*Tadaima*!' in his little jet-black button-up, long-sleeved uniform, slipping off his shoes in the *genkan* and putting on his slippers. She'd call back an '*Okaeri*' from somewhere in the house but never rush to welcome him home.

His father would arrive hours later, sometimes so much later that Natsuo would be asleep already. If it was a day when Akihiro returned after he had gone to bed, Natsuo would note the beer-scented spectre of his father the morning after. If Natsuo was still awake when his father came home, it was as if the man in front of him who bore the official title 'father' wasn't even there. He'd be sat on the tatami mat floor, cross-legged, one elbow on the table as he massaged his tired forehead, the other arm loose in his lap and clutching a glass of beer or sake. A man defeated. A man devoid of spark.

But still a man of tradition who expected everything that was happening: wife doing 'wife' work, child at school, father spending all day every day pleasing his bosses by his mere presence as opposed to the output or quality of the work itself.

When his parents were together it was a masterclass in wordless communication, a perfection of the art form of understandable silence. He smoked and drank and deflated like a tired old engine while she fussed around him. Natsuo began to find the lack of laughter, smiles, real emotion, and even sound deafening. He started to find solace in his room.

Evenings and days all blended into one continuous methodological parade. Up, breakfast, school, home, dinner, bed. His parents never showed much interest in his affairs, never asked after friends or plans. He always thought it was as if they were on autopilot. Going through the motions. Rarely angry, rarely happy, everything just ticking along as it was 'supposed' to be. His whole life was a grey sludge with no distinguishing features.

It wasn't just that Natsuo's anger and frustration were targeted at his parents; it was Japanese society as a whole. Since he was old enough to watch television and understand how to use the internet he had been swamped by colour and noise from other countries.

American and British television shows, Korean YouTube personalities, music from all around the world, and later, he had learned of the casual emotion and sexuality of various European countries. But it wasn't like that in his country, his town, his house. His was a colourless, sexless world.

In Japan sexuality and individualism were pushed to the margins of daily life, not embraced. Quirks and fetishes that wouldn't be given a second thought in France or Australia might have you labelled as a *hentai*, a pervert.

If you dressed differently, coloured your hair so that it wasn't black like everyone else's, even took up interests that veered on the side of kooky, the majority of traditional society thought you were odd at the very least or profoundly warped and perverse at the other extreme.

He could never take the pressure of having to conform to what he saw as a black and white society; one where you were simply a number, a faceless nothing, part of the masses. But then Natsuo didn't exactly show any signs of great potential to the contrary. He was just a quiet kid to most and suffered and crumbled accordingly.

He was bullied a lot at school; sometimes physically. Nothing lasting. The worst were the teachers, especially one man at his high school who had taken an intense dislike to Natsuo almost on day one. He bemoaned the boy's fragility, his weak nature, his 'lack of spirit'; and he often asked the boys to read works by writers like Yukio Mishima to see how to really be. He would pick on Natsuo in class, using him as an example to the other teenagers of how not to be. It wasn't unheard of for Natsuo to have pieces of chalk or rolled up balls of paper thrown at him.

And every time this happened, he burrowed further into himself, occasionally lashing out only to get pushed over, punched, and laughed at by the stronger boys. His parents took no notice of this. They just presumed it was a phase many of the milder kids all went through. That he'd be fine in the end and come out stronger.

He didn't.

Natsuo stopped attending classes for a while. There was no legal requirement to attend school after all, so initially his parents just let it happen, thinking that after a few days he'd get bored and want to go back. Hoping that everything would just sort itself out.

It didn't.

His father sometimes shouted at him but was never violent. Natsuo at least escaped that fate that so many young children hadn't. But he could feel the ever-present disappointment emanating from everyone around him. That was enough. No child should have to carry that burden.

A month passed and he became what the Japanese Education Ministry referred to as a *futoko.* A drop out.

'In the old days they were called *tokokyohi.*' Natsuo overheard his father telling his mother one night, cradling a bottle of beer. 'It was considered a mental problem to not attend school!'

I'm mad?...

He lashed out; stopped school, stopped life, stopped feeling. As far as Natsuo was concerned he was being raised in an environment where his personality didn't exist. It was missing. He would often be immature and destructive at home.

Looking back, he was never proud of that part of his life. He probably acted worse towards his mother because she was the weaker of the two. But at the same time, he resented her for never sticking up for him, never listening, never intervening. He had smashed doors and shojis, plant pots and even once had ripped out his father's bonsai tree in the garden.

After a couple of years, it was clear that nothing was going to change. His parents had gradually come to terms with what he was and glumly recognised him as a Hikikomori. With this came an enormous personal shame to the family that would be muttered and rumoured around as it caught speed like wildfire.

His parents had thus absconded to the natal home down the coast in Tosashimizu. They had all given up on each other. But out of a warped sense of familial duty, despite the public shame, Natsuo's parents still gave him money every month to exist. Shame but also pride. A familiar yin and yang.

Most of that money was spent on drugs. Thienotriazolodiazepine for sleeping and maprotiline and escitalopram for depression. Over the years he would often discover new ones with intriguing names; paroxetine, fluvoxamine, sertraline, mirtazapine, bupropion, which meant that there was often a collection of three-quarter finished packets of pills strewn around the house.

Once or twice, he had thought about suicide. He thought it would make him better, make him happier; by just removing himself. But he was too cowardly for that. Or brave.

The only problem he ever really faced were power cuts, and these past weeks had seen him spend many nights in darkness; the flat now permeated with the smell of cheap cup noodles, tomato-encrusted pizza boxes and beer malt.

It was easier now to be a Hikikomori. He had everything he needed at the push of a button. Natsuo was never a big eater anyway, but when he needed anything, he just pressed little images on his phone and sustenance would arrive. His existence was held in the balance thanks to screens and apps. He would tell the delivery person to leave it at the door and that was that. Impersonally and technologically sustained.

Natsuo often wondered what it would have been like before the modern advances and breakthroughs.

He remembered the story of a 37-year-old man in Iwate prefecture in the early '90s who was completely dependent on his parents despite hating them and living in seclusion right next to them in the same house. They would, as was fairly common, just bring him food and leave it outside his bedroom door. The man's mother fell ill one day and following that, his father had an accident and was left bed-ridden. The man didn't know how to look after himself at all. How to cook, how to clean. He lost hope and had no idea how to keep on living. One day he killed his father in front of his sick mother and then committed suicide. He believed it was the best and only way out.

Natsuo also often wondered if that was one of the reasons his parents had left the house. Maybe they were scared they'd be next.

Thanks to his tablet and phone, he would never reach that point at least. Small miracles of the 21st century.

He couldn't stand it. He blamed himself for being different; blamed his parents for not understanding. He became afraid of society, fearful of meeting people. Natsuo was sure they all despised him. The negative emotions had risen up and swarmed his brain; a warped, self-inflicted pressure drowning him. Jealous of happiness and terrified of conformity.

He couldn't leave his house.

So, after that couple of years of violent outbursts and infantile behaviour his parents abandoned him.

Then his father died, leaving his poor mother alone. But still, he couldn't leave.

He wasn't stupid. He knew what he was.

Natsuo had once attended a support meeting, one of those held monthly by a local do-gooder in his sixties. A sweet man who had dedicated his retirement to helping coax Hikikomori out back into the wild.

There were four other men there, two were around his age, one was in his late twenties. They shuffled into a small portable building in the garden in front of the do-gooder's house that had been laid out with plastic chairs and some low tables.

They were offered tea and mochi. Everyone accepted dutifully with a nod of the head as they sat down, hands on knees or hugging themselves, rubbing their arms, eyes darting around, looking at the floor, trying not to make contact.

'Sumimasen,' said the old man to Natsuo, 'would you like an orange? I grow them in my garden. Here, take one.'

Natsuo mumbled thank you and took one.

On the low table there were brochures from a group of 'reformed recluses' who wanted to help people like Natsuo. He started to read it. Maybe this could be it, the way he could be understood, accepted.

They had monthly and weekly events of differing levels of interaction and numbers of people. Natsuo had never had a group of friends, so this could be the start of something.

Then the old man asked everyone, if they wanted, to share their stories. Natsuo snapped out of his daydream and was thrust back to the awkwardness and embarrassment of the now. He tried to burn through the floor just by staring at it.

He managed just two visits. And every so often when the man came round to check on him, knocking on his door, he'd turn off the lights and hide in his room. It was the first kindness he had been shown for a long time, but he still couldn't bear dealing with the world and after a few months of sporadic check-ups the man gave up.

Although it was directly Natsuo's fault, he just felt even more deeply abandoned. His parents, his classmates, his teachers, even a person invested in helping people like him ultimately gave up. Months or years later he felt rather sorry for the man and wondered about his oranges.

As a teenager Natsuo buried himself in a world of manga comics and anime shows. *Natsume's Book Of Friends, I Am A Hero, Naruto, Inuyashiki, My Hero Academia, Vagabond, Mushishi;* his walls were a library of ink-lined tales of heroism, monsters and magic, do-gooders and vanquished villains.

Natsuo liked to lose himself to stories of characters he could never hope to be like in mythical lands far more colourful and exciting than his provincial island life could ever hope to be.

When his father died Natsuo felt near to nothing. All the emotion and drama on show in the pages of his books and the animated frames of his shows had not manifested in him. His father had left so little mark on Natsuo that his removal from the world barely registered inside him.

'A heart attack' he had read on the back of the little postcard sent by his mother. She had found him one morning in the same pose from the night before; sat on the floor behind the low table, head slumped on his chest, a half-full beer glass still in his hand. As if he were sleeping. A quiet departure from a quiet life.

The first years of his hibernation were spent in his cramped childhood room, but since his parents had left, he had the whole house to himself. His bedroom had become frozen in time; a snapshot of the life of a kid that never grew up.

His thirtieth birthday was around the corner and even Natsuo, in whose lifetime had almost lost all meaning, understood the strangeness of spending almost half a life inside a house.

The present. And a day that played out like almost every other day.

He woke up whenever his eyes decided to, no point in having an alarm set, and went to make some green tea. He always started his day with green tea, but regularly skipped eating. Living a life in slow motion meant he rarely had an appetite. He would put the television on and watch the news. Despite not leaving the house he wasn't ignorant of the goings-on in the world. Once again, the screen crackled with rolling news about the typhoons, the rains, the floods. It amazed him how many hours of news could be milked out of weather.

On one channel was a man in a black suit and tie pointing at various places on a map sliced up with arrows and isobars and question marks. On another was a special meteorological report explaining how nobody in the weather world could understand what was causing such a rapid, near-constant succession of typhoons to hit Japan. Five had hit Shikoku in the south, but Japan had seemingly been struck at various angles up and down the country for nearly two months by differing strength tropical storms. This just didn't happen. The experts said it couldn't. Natsuo switched to a 24/7 anime channel.

Whenever his stomach started grumbling, he would shuffle to the kitchen, boil water, and have a cup noodle with more green tea. At some point he would bore of the television and sit cross-legged on the tatami mat in his room reading comics, go back to sleep, or just lie back and stare at the ceiling.

He did cook sometimes. Omelettes, rice, teriyaki chicken and other simple one pot dishes. Though Natsuo had no real interest in food, he had picked up things from cooking shows and videos online. He wasn't so dead inside that he couldn't appreciate taste. But more often than not he ordered delivery food.

The other rooms of the house were untouched by his years of residence. Very much a lingering homage to the Hirawa family. The living room was a perfect square almost exclusively covered in bookshelves, which, in turn, were filled to bursting with books, notepads, papers, trinkets and family photos. There was no wall space and everything was covered in dust.

In the corner was the *butsudan*. The small shrine cabinet had been in the family for generations and was peppered with incense sticks and photos of Natsuo's forebears. It was the only part of the house he took any real care of.

The family home was situated on a street in Fukuichō neighbourhood in west Kochi near a rising bank of low green hills. It could have been anywhere in Japan as far as Natsuo was concerned. All the homes were smart, two-storey grey or brown buildings, neatly kept, each one with cars and bicycles unattended out the front. No rubbish was usually to be found anywhere on the street, though during these stormy days pot plants and shrubs had been blown all over the place and the community rubbish receptacles had been blasted open. It was an utterly pleasant and utterly nondescript place to live. Never offending nor ever exciting.

Though he never left the house, there was still a small, now rather overgrown, garden out back. He would often sit on the floor with the sliding living room doors open and look at the plants and trees and buzzing insects. The only joy he got from the world was nature. Other days he'd stretch and breathe and walk around for exercise. Sometimes he'd hear neighbours coming out to work in their gardens and he would scurry back inside for fear of being seen and talked to. It embarrassed him to run away like that, but it was as if he had no choice.

Over the years his suicidal thoughts had almost disappeared. It seemed almost too much effort even to kill himself. But, in lieu of fully eradicating his own life, he instead took to drinking beer, and quite often a little too much. Not quite an adequate substitution. It wasn't that he was trying to get drunk, it was just convenience. An inebriation of inertia. So as a result, his house at the end of every week would be an absolute pigsty of cans of Kirin and Asahi, until he remembered to take out the rubbish. He hated this part most and would creep out under the cover of darkness in order not to be seen.

Due to the weather, he hadn't been out in the garden or taken the rubbish out in weeks. The wind rattled the doors and the rain was a constant drum on the roof. In the brief interludes between storms the world was grey, sodden and wet.

I'll just wait until it dries off...

But it never did. So, the disorder increased.

TV and Internet were his only windows to the world. A kaleidoscope of misery usually.

Cape Ashizuri has been hit hard by this typhoon and yesterday we detected another is approaching.

Natsuo stirred, pushing empty bottles and crisp packets off the table to get the remote to turn the volume up. Cape Ashizuri was west along the coast where his mother lived. It was the headland-cragged southern tip of the Ashizuri-Uwakai National Park. A beautiful and underpopulated place about a two-and-a-half-hour drive from Kochi where Natsuo had spent weekends and holidays as a young boy. It was all gorges and limestone cliffs that had been carved out by the Pacific and her winds.

He used to like walking up into the hills alone, losing himself to a wooded world of secret paths and forgotten shrines and temples. Or he'd follow the Nishino or Kagumi rivers, hopping from boulder to boulder throwing sticks into the water and trying to catch fish.

The area was used to rough weather but not this.

Most at risk are Shimanto, Kuroshio and Tosashimizu. Evacuations are underway.

He lay back in the glow of the TV screen.

Natsuo had not seen his mother for over a decade, but at this news something shifted. Something long lost, some spark of emotion had fired in a place deep down, long barren and greyed. The prospect of her possible lonely demise had moved something in him. The small kid, young Natsuo, before the bullying, before his removal from the world, called out.

'Okaasan,' he whispered.

Tosashimizu was a little harbour town, somewhat sheltered by a small hill jutting out into the ocean, but in no way prepared to withstand a slew of Pacific cyclones. The family home was an old, two-floor expansive wooden building that was almost right on the seafront. The only thing that protected them, in a place that never really needed to be protected, was a small sea-defence comprised of enormous haphazardly shaped boulders, and a line of fisherman's homes, cafés, liquor stores and port authority buildings.

In the face of an unending cycle of storms, this would do little.

To make matters worse, as was so common in Japan, the village was surrounded by those ubiquitous fuzzy green hills and wild rivers. The risk of landslides and flooding would increase.

Japan was a country where people were used to living with the constant risk of destruction and death and disaster at the hands of Mother Nature. Scattered over the country were more than a hundred active volcanoes and about five thousand earthquakes glimmered through the earth every year with almost two hundred of those being the kind that shakes the house.

At school all the children were trained in what to do in the event of a disaster like this. Add to that the risk of tsunami and you had a people used to giving up their mortality to the elements.

In 2011 a magnitude 9 megathrust earthquake punched up from the bowels of the planet forty-five miles off northeast Japan. The resulting waves screamed landward and bulldozed through civilisation. It was the fourth most powerful earthquake ever recorded but it was the tsunami that brought both the fear and the chaos.

Waves dozens of metres high reached as far as six miles inland and wiped away everything in their path as easily as a person passes their hand through sand. As well as a nuclear meltdown, thousands of displaced people, billions of yen of damage and general carnage, about twenty thousand people had perished.

Since then, the earthquake sirens and storm warnings always sent a spike of fear running down the spine. One thing is to read about something, hear it at school or learn about it in a museum. The other thing is to have it happen during your lifetime.

Over the course of his mother's life, she would have read about in the papers, heard about it on the radio, later seen it on the television and occasionally experienced first-hand around twenty major disasters resulting in great loss of life.

Now she was in danger Natsuo no longer felt confused and drowsy with years of being shut inside. He was still her son. And she still his mother. Only now she was older and defenceless.

A moment of lightness and clarity broke through the cloying fug in which he had been living. A decade of hiding from the world; of shutting himself off. Something more primal and base had bubbled up to the surface. Familial protection and love.

He looked out the window at the squally skies, rain whipping through the cable-filled streets pockmarked by broken umbrellas.

'Mother...I'm coming.'

The decision to go to Tosashimizu on foot was almost instantaneous. The local buses down the coastal E56 road weren't running and Natsuo had no desire to hitchhike. He hadn't left his house properly in over ten years. He wasn't prepared to start jumping into cars with strangers.

It was about 140 km from Kochi to his parents' house on the coast. Natsuo reckoned on it taking him about five or six days if he did about 25 km a day. He would simply follow the gentle undulating coastal roads. As soon as the rains had passed through, he would leave. The current typhoon had calmed down to light gusts and sheet rain, so his departure seemed imminent. At night he planned to simply sleep in bus shelters, backstreets or *haikyos*. All over the country were abandoned buildings: hotels, factories, schools, even whole villages. Gutted, over-grown with vegetation and graffiti, these haikyos had been left to be taken over by nature. A post-apocalyptic vision of what the future might hold as well as the crumbled memories of what once was.

In the meantime, he collected various items for his typhoon kit. From an early age every young Japanese child was taught what to do in times of crisis; how to best get through the angry throes of mother nature. If you had to leave your house, you had to be prepared.

He knew that in the cupboard under the stairs there was an old rucksack that contained his family's disaster survival pack: first aid kit, plastic bags, torch, batteries, towel, small pillow, water bottle, toothbrush. All he really needed was to stock up on food for the trip.

He wandered into the kitchen and checked the cupboards. Apart from a few cup noodles and soup packets, the only useful item was a packet of Meito chocolate biscuits, a few Kit Kats with the flavours he didn't like: green tea, cappuccino, 'Tokyo banana' and wasabi, and a bag of strawberry mochi. He stuffed them all in the bag and then opened a delivery app to place an order at the Family Mart grocery store down the road.

Your order has been submitted!
1 bag apples - 450¥
2 onigiri tamago - 155¥ x 2
2 onigiri zakutto rayu - 140¥ x 2
2 onigiri spicy tuna - 180¥ x 2
2 onigiri umeboshi - 130¥ x 2
1 pack mochifuwa pancakes - 380¥
3 cheesecake sponge - 125¥ x 3
1 bag bananas - 525¥
2 bag yakitori - 106¥ x 2
2 can peanuts - 295¥ x 2
1 pack yōkan - 208¥
3 azuki dorayaki - 100¥ x 3

Natsuo had no concept of what he would need for almost a week of walking through squally weather. He had decided to pack things that were small, individually wrapped and needed no cooking. In the worst case scenario he supposed he would just have to go into a shop and brave purchasing something in person.

Forty minutes later the delivery driver pulled up in a van and ran through the rain in a waterproof jacket. The intercom buzzed and Natsuo stuck his eye to the peephole.

'Family Mart, I have your order.'

'Thank you very much; just leave it on the doorstep.'

'It's going to get wet.'

'On the doorstep is fine. *Arigato gozaimasu.*'

The delivery man shrugged, left the two plastic bags in a puddle by the door and ran back to his van. When the little Family Mart branded kei car drove off, Natsuo quickly opened the door, snatched the two bags, and sealed himself off from the world again.

Next, he rooted around and found his father's sturdy old walking boots. As Natsuo had grown from teenager to man having not bothered to leave the house, he had never needed his own pair. Fortunately, those of his father more or less fit. He took a large navy-blue cover-all poncho and then picked out two or three t-shirts and trousers as well as a selection of underwear. He was surprised how much space he still had left in the bag but decided not to fall into the trap of choosing capricious or unnecessary items just to fulfil the human wish for completion and symmetry.

With everything prepared he simply sat back down on the sofa and turned on the television. The beauty of having nothing to do in one's life meant that when a task presented itself, he could invest 100% of his time and energy into it until said task was completed.

It took him just a couple of hours of an afternoon to ready himself for his expedition through typhoon season.

According to data collected from the Japan Meteorological Agency for the Kyushu, Shikoku and western Kansai regions, Typhoon Minata has finally abated. Locals can sadly however only expect a brief period of peace. The JMA has noticed another

supercell gathering in the Philippine Sea and is expected to make its way north, hitting the south coast in four or five days. In other news Hokkaido is still being ravaged by Typhoon Gustav...

'Kuso...' Natsuo cursed to himself through gritted teeth.

He would never make it to Tosashimizu in time to beat the next typhoon if he started walking now, but then he wasn't prepared to just keep waiting. He was geared up and finally ready to leave his house after his long reclusion.

At least he had four days before it would strike land.

By the time the typhoon made landfall he should be nearing the small city of Shimanto; so he at least may have more opportunity to find somewhere to shelter during the worst of it.

Whatever happens, Natsuo thought to himself, I'm leaving at first light tomorrow morning.

A strange noise. A bizarre ringing. Something clawing at Natsuo. His dream. He was walking through fog, a wet fog, following a shadow. He tried to catch up to the shadow, but it was constantly out of reach. He called out to it, but there was no answer. The noise rang from the heavens; high above the fog was a piercing rhythmic siren. Through the dim greyness ahead of him he pushed ahead. The figure in the fog was almost within his grasp. Finally, he reached it and caught it by what must have been its shoulder. It spun round. The body of a man in a suit. But the face. What a terrible face! Bright red, with a long straight nose, two slender fangs jutting out from the lower jaw, a dark brown flowing beard and moustache. The shrill siren got louder and louder. The fog around the figure then started to shine golden and shimmer and bubble. Then two large feathered wings arched gracefully out from behind the besuited being. The stern and piercing gaze of its eyes fixed Natsuo dead. He fell backwards and couldn't look away. The noise in the sky got so loud that he clasped his ears and closed his eyes.

Natsuo then came to. The sound, one he had not heard for years, an alarm clock. The rest was a bad dream. He grumbled to himself, 'well if you will read comics into the night...'. It was six o'clock in the morning. He showered, made a green tea, had some toast, took a last look at the family shrine and got ready to leave.

Quietly he opened the front door. It wasn't raining and the world was still. A faint idea of daylight had gently lifted the sky from black to dark grey. Natsuo stood, bag in his hand and black cap pulled tight over his eyes, on the threshold to the house. He breathed deeply and heavily, feeling a little dizzy; like he was at the top of a roller coaster.

'Okaasan...'

Natsuo took a step forward and locked the door behind him. He slung his backpack over one shoulder and walked nervously the few steps to the road, took out his phone to look at the map once more, and turned right.

It had taken a mother in peril during a cascade of natural disasters to wrench Natsuo away from the family property once and for all. Riding the bizarre euphoria, which he took to be bravery, Natsuo started down the road fast and focused, his gaze set dead ahead.

'*Ohaio gozaimasu*!' A voice came through the air. Natsuo yelped and froze like a startled deer. He had not even reached the end of the street, barely fifty metres, when a small old man with a prune-like, shrivelled-up face had wished him a good morning. He dropped his bag and started to run back to the house.

No, no, no, I can't do this, he screamed to himself, his soul somersaulting inside his stomach, as he scrambled around his pockets for the house key.

He arrived, wheezing, at the door and made to unlock it. But as the key made contact with the lock he stopped. Something above him, or within him, wouldn't let him go any further.

His mind was telling him to go inside. Go inside where it's safe. No people. No worries. Just curl up in bed away from the world. Have a warm tea and watch the story unfold on a screen. Why are you putting yourself at risk for some old lady who doesn't love you? Why all this for a woman who left you? Go inside and be safe.

But another wordless power stopped him.

His hand dropped and he put the key away. Natsuo was never going to make it to his mother if he couldn't even stand the greetings of a neighbour.

When he got back to his bag, he found it untouched and the old man gone.

Probably thought I was crazy. Natsuo smiled grimly.

About an hour later he arrived at Kagami River and the edge of Kochi city. Apart from faceless, anonymous cars passing him, he barely saw any people. Even the people he did see paid him no heed. In a place where nobody knows anyone anybody can be invisible. With this small boost of confidence Natsuo readjusted his backpack, walked down to the river path and started to make his way south to the coast.

Chapter Two: Bōken
冒険

Adventure.

Natsuo spent his first night southwest of Tosa in the storeroom of the Kameizumi sake brewery. Instead of heading immediately to the coast his phone had told him the quickest route would be due west along the Hage river. This had the added advantage of taking Natsuo past some beautiful fields of sunflowers that had somehow still managed to brave the fierce typhoon winds. He presumed the broad, flat valley had been somewhat protected by the Hasukeyama mountains that rose up, cutting it off from the sea. If those yellow petals could withstand a typhoon he was hopeful that his mother would have no problem.

The storeroom door to the building had seemingly been blasted open by the storm winds and so he had slipped in during the evening. Rice harvest wasn't until the fall so the typhoons coupled with the lack of chaos in the brewery itself meant that it was very quiet. He slept surprisingly well on a few empty rice bags and was surrounded by empty sake barrels, prettified by kanji, colourful brushstrokes, and bound up with white rope.

He made sure he was up again at first light. Natsuo had no desire to interact with other people and even less to be caught sleeping rough by the owners of the brewery.

The room smelled musty of yeast and old wet rice. Natsuo opened the door slowly and peeked out. Still grim and grey but no rain at least. He opened the bag of dorayaki and nibbled away at the small pancake, enjoying the sweet-savoury taste of the red beans. His first breakfast away from his house since he was a school kid. Given that this may well be the first day that the Kameizumi workers could actually do anything productive in the brewery he didn't want to linger in case they caught him on their grounds.

As far as a day's walk went, Natsuo's was one without any real challenge or interest. A quiet valley floor road surrounded on all sides by patchwork fields of wheat and rice. He had planned a twenty kilometre or so day, hoping to stop just after Susaki town where there would be less people. The rains had yet to come, which meant the predictions made by the bespectacled man reading the weather were holding true for the moment. It should only take him four or five hours, which for someone who hadn't walked more than the distance to and from the garden or kitchen for more than ten years, was quite an expedition. He was heartened by his mission, however, and was secretly proud of himself. Proud of having summoned up the courage, as slight as it may be, to leave his house. Proud to be doing something heroic.

That pride would be shaken and tested a mere couple of hours into his walk.

Natsuo reached Susaki around 10:30 in the morning. He felt fit and strong and thought he might even carry on to Tosa-Kure, another two and half hours down the coast. He was beginning to feel comfortable outside. Nobody talked to him. Hiking and rambling were fairly popular pastimes in Japan, so he didn't look out of place. No one cared he was there. As long as he didn't make eye contact, he just breezed through the villages. There was always a flutter of butterflies in his stomach when he approached a larger settlement, but he was seemingly quite good at being ignored.

Just south from Susaki, acting as a backbone for the tiny hamlet of Awa, was an attractive and empty beach. He decided to sit in front of the surf and eat a pickled plum rice ball. He laid out the towel and sat down on the damp dark sand. All along the shoreline were pieces of branches, seaweed and some debris washed in by the storms. But nonetheless Natsuo still regarded the scene with a sense of peace. He listened to the gentle lapping of the waves as they spilled up the sand and disappeared in a gentle fizz of white foam. He couldn't really see the horizon; it was lost to a fuzz of sheet-grey under a dark sky, though he guessed what was coming. Natsuo checked the weather bulletin on his phone. Typhoon Nōken was on course to make landfall in a day or so.

An average typhoon had winds of around 120 to 145 kmh. They were very strong but one could still just about walk if need be; to find cover or get out of the way of aerial debris. The fastest winds were at the eyewall; the internal part of the typhoon that span round the calm eye of the storm. The eye was often only about 30-65 km across compared to the hundreds of potential kilometres that the whole cyclone embodied. Wind speeds of up to 290 kmh or more were not uncommon in the strongest storms.

Natsuo decided he had better check tomorrow as to what strength the storm was forecasted to be. If the authorities deemed it a category 4 or 5, he would have to simply take cover somewhere during the worst gusts and wait it out. If he was lucky, he could cover ground in the early part of the storm as the outer arms that spun slower touched land, and perhaps a quick burst should the eye pass over his location.

Natsuo started to have a pang of regret. His mind zoomed out to look down on him, sat on a muddy beach by himself and about to walk through a tropical storm. What the hell was he doing? Then the fear set in. The romantic notion of do-goodery and heroism were fading fast as the very real concept of personal risk and threat to life set in. He drew his legs up to his chest and nestled his chin on his knees as he looked out across the surf.

'Young man!' said a body that slumped down next to Natsuo. In his daydreaming he hadn't noticed the man approach. He stunk of alcohol and wore a crumpled black suit, his tie half undone around his open white shirt, round cheeks shining and glowing red. Natsuo froze and said nothing. 'What a lovely morning...' he snorted.

Taking Natsuo's silence as a sign to carry on, the drunken businessman continued.

'Can you believe it...' the man burped, 'fifteen years of servitude...'

Natsuo remained quiet.

'Go in...seven in the morning...only one there during these storms... then fired without a warning!' The man started laughing. 'Can you imagine firing someone at breakfast time?'

Natsuo joined the simply aligned dots in his head and concluded the man must have stumbled out of the Poem cafe on the other side of the road from the beach. *But why did he have to come up to me?* He thought to himself. *Why now? Why at all?*

'What you got there?' said the man, his hot breath stinging Natsuo's right cheek. 'Oh! Mochifuwa pancakes! Give me one pleeease!'

Still no response. Frozen. The man put a hand around Natsuo's shoulder.

'Come on, just one. I deserve it. I lost my job. Don't be cruel.' The man started to weep uncontrollably.

Natsuo made to get up. He couldn't respond and didn't know what to do, what to say. This was his first real interaction with a person since school. He just knew he needed to not be there.

The man's hand tightened a little.

'Hey. Don't go. Where are you going? Can't you at least show me a little pity.' He slurred, eyes watery and nose dribbling.

Natsuo couldn't stand it anymore and got up quickly and started to walk away down the beach. He sensed the man getting up and start to follow him, his voice tinged with anger now.

'What's all this young man? Hey! I'm talking to you. Say something.'

The next thing he felt was a tugging at his back. The drunk man was clumsily holding onto the rucksack by one of the cords.

'I just wanted a fucking pancake.' The man spat irately.

Natsuo was panicking so he spun round, dislodging the man and threw the whole plastic bag of food at him. The businessman fell back onto the sand, covered by snacks, and started laughing. Natsuo turned and ran.

A few minutes later he stopped and keeled over onto a grassy bank breathing heavily and wrenching. Flooded with endorphins. He still had his bag but, in his fear and anguish, he had tossed away most of his food. The only edibles left were apples, bananas and the bag of peanuts. All the rice balls, pancakes and other items were in the bag he had hurled at his pursuer. Holding his head in his hands he began to whimper.

Natsuo spent his second night in a campground in Kure. Unbeknownst to him, the road from Awa passed through mountain tunnels. He decided against taking his life into his hands and instead took the more circuitous road that followed the coast: hillside to his immediate right, road, and the ocean to his immediate left. The scrappy land abutted a scruffy little beach and was located between the isolated town hall and a cooking school. He positioned himself at the east end of the beach near the school and lay down with his bag under his head.

Natsuo fought the urge to cry and was grimly glad that he had no other recourse but to carry on. He was only about fifty kilometres from the self-made cocoon that was his home, but he felt, here by this isolated little nothingness of what was barely a village, looking out at the ever-darkening sea horizon, that he may as well be in another country.

He ate two apples and a handful of peanuts. His stomach gurgled but he couldn't risk eating any more. His desire to not interact with people seemed stronger than that most base of desires: hunger. He reckoned he could stretch what he had another day. Natsuo closed his eyes and tried to just focus on the sound of the lapping waves.

He was in the eye of the storm. Natsuo was standing on the peak of a solitary mountain. He could see the wooded hillsides sloping down away from him but nothing else. Around him the wall of clouds rotated, hissing and whistling. He stood in a perfect column of calmness within white wispy violence. What was this? The typhoon already? Why was he here on a hilltop?

There was a shapeless form sliding through the swirling walls of cloud. It flittered left and right. A shadow. Sometimes darker, sometimes lighter. Then a red smudge appeared and a light. A hole then punched through the towering, gyrating column of cloud and out into the open calm of the eye, trailing a wispy tail of mist behind it, was the red-faced, long-nosed winged being. This time no longer in a suit, it wore a green tunic that exposed a bright crimson chest. Brown trousers cut off just under the knee, red legs and sandals with scarlet toes. A long sword hung from its waist and seemed to be tied-to by a blood-red bow. It swooped low down the mountain out of sight, then arched up to land directly in front of him. Natsuo staggered back and shielded himself with his arms, but nothing happened. The monster didn't move, but his burning eyes once again bore into him. The creature first pointed to the floor. Natsuo could understand that it meant to highlight the hill they were on, but the reason evaded him as the devil remained silent. It then, without taking its eyes off Natsuo's, pointed at the now rapidly approaching walls of the typhoon.

What did it mean? What was this creature? What was the significance of the solitary mountain or its link to the typhoon?

'What do you want?' Natsuo screamed at the creature over the now howling gale winds. He felt no wind but the eye of the storm was almost past and the whirling walls of the maelstrom almost upon him. 'Who are you?' He screamed again, but his calls were lost to the winds as the typhoon gusts covered him and everything and all the world went dark.

Natsuo awoke with rain hitting his cheeks and water pooling in his eyes. He arched up onto his elbows and saw that the typhoon was now making landfall. The first rains would get heavier and then be accompanied by winds that would steadily increase in anger and ferocity. He had to make as much headway as he could. Eating a soggy apple, he put on his cover-all poncho and set off.

Fortunately, the route planner took him inland somewhat along Route 56; so thanks to the hills he would get a little protection from the worst of the early winds. The road was beautiful. The first couple of hours it seemingly hovered halfway up the hillside of the south-facing side of the Osakatani river valley. He imagined what it would be like on a blue day. One thing Natsuo hadn't realised was that there were a couple of short tunnels to walk through, but given the weather forecast and the isolation there were barely any vehicles on the road. He was glad of the few minutes of respite that each hole through the hill afforded.

At the Nanako pass Natsuo came down out of the hills joining the house-scattered lonely road along the Niida river. He planned to follow this for as long as he could or for however long the weather let him. It was a quiet road and carried on languorously through flooded rice-paddies. Backed a way off from the road, and hiding in the treeline of the low hills, were large wooden houses and little mossy-stone shrines cowering in the gloom.

Natsuo's stomach grumbled so he took out a banana. His watch said it was already one o'clock. It had become apparent that he would definitely have to get some food the following day. With the kilometres he was walking, there was no way he would be able to go for three more days on a few pieces of fruit and handfuls of peanuts.

The experience with the man the day before still weighed heavily over Natsuo. He had read papers and treatises about people like him. He didn't want to not be able to cope with society and he truly wished he could have friends and hobbies. He was what was called a 'primary Hikikomori'; one who exhibited problems and character traits associated with psychiatrically treatable phenomena.

Obsessive-compulsive and affective disorders, severe anxiety and pervasive developmental disorders were things that could be helped by modern medicine. The problems associated with being a primary instead of secondary were more nuanced and socially constructed. There were five areas that helped either foster or describe Natsuo's primary world.

1. Episodes of defeat without a struggle.
2. An ideal self-image originating in the desires of others rather than in one's own desire.
3. Preserving the ideal image of the 'expected' self.
4. Parents' investment in the ideal self of the child.
5. Avoidant behaviour to maintain the positive opinion of others.

Mix all these factors together and what you'll have done is follow the recipe for a Hikikomori almost to the letter. Also the cruel, self-created contradiction wasn't lost on Natsuo, that in order to protect himself from the world he was, by definition of his current state, hurting himself.

When the drunk man on the beach had grabbed him and berated him, the stink of early-morning beer on his breath, none of the analysis and school of thought objectivity helped him rationalise the situation. But this, essentially, was his condition. He knew conceptually the problems he had but he couldn't do anything about it. He felt his emotions rising up from within, frustrated tears stung the corners of his eyes and were washed away as he plodded through the ever-heavier rain.

As a young boy Natsuo had spent four warm spring days walking through Tokushima on a school trip. Every day the young children would stop in at temples and pay their respects. The teachers had told them to dress in white shirts called oizuru and handed out walking sticks and conical hats called suge-kasa. At the temples they would light incense, offer coins their parents had given them, and each time different children recited the osame-fuda mantra. Then the little parade of uniformed minions waddled to the next temple on the map before spending a night in a hotel.

The Shikoku Henro pilgrimage comprised eighty-eight temples scattered across the island. This holy route was associated with an influential Buddhist monk called Kōbō Dashi, who spread his teachings around Japan at the start of the ninth century.

It was at the 37th temple, Iwamoto-ji, on the south edge of Kubokawa, that Natsuo spent his second night.

The rain was falling harder now, pounding the tarmac loud enough that he would probably have to raise his voice to converse with someone nearby. That wouldn't be a problem of course.

The temple comprised three small buildings. There was the *kondo*, or main hall, and two side temples, the daishido and nokyojo. Each building had tatami flooring, wooden walls and long, sloped black-tiled roofs that curled up and out at the base and overhung. Under these gables were primary-coloured Buddhist prayer bunting and white flags with the lotus symbol. In the little courtyard there was a small, circular and be-flagged tō pagoda. Off to one-side, by the kondo, was the enormous prayer bell, protected by its personal wooden structure and with a large log fastened to the roof by chains, a chunky rope hanging off it so it could be swung.

Natsuo, much like most Japanese people, wasn't traditionally religious as the western nations would understand it. But he also wasn't explicitly atheist. He didn't 'believe in God', but, thanks to the presence of Buddhism and Shintoism over the centuries, he shared the same gently reverent feeling when he saw a torii gate or a little temple on a backstreet. There existed traditions that even a non-believing Hikikomori observed in these places, part respect, part spiritual.

He walked through the small *sanmon* entrance gate and headed to the *chozuya*. This was a small, covered pavilion in the open air with a large basin into which a small fountain was constantly pouring water. A wooden ladle was attached to the basin, which Natsuo picked up. He first scooped up water with his right hand and poured it over his left. He then repeated the action the other way round. Finally, he scooped out water once more into a cupped hand and then swilled it in his mouth before spitting it onto the ground. Cleansed, Natsuo then darted up to the main shrine, closed his hands and bowed once.

To his right were the o-mikuji, pieces of fortune paper purchased for 100 yen, which were then tied to wooden rails and left for the gods to read and hopefully realise. Due to the rain half of these little white papers had dissolved into mush on the ground. Dreams and fortunes turned to pulp. Gods could offer no real power in the face of Mother Nature, Natsuo thought to himself.

He checked each of the temple complex buildings in the hope that one might be open so that he could shelter for the night. Due to the typhoon warnings however, they were all locked.

Natsuo decided to just set himself up under the comparative dryness of the slightly more flamboyantly-sized overhang of the daishido building. He huddled by the door at the top of the small flight of stairs and foresaw a difficult night ahead as the storm winds would only get stronger, the rain heavier and the noise more intense. He ate the last of his fruit and nuts and curled up inside his poncho.

Natsuo wasn't sleepy, just exhausted. He lay down staring out at the courtyard. The rain was still falling mostly in hard lines, which meant the cyclonic winds had yet to push everything horizontal. Natsuo was still about seventy kilometres from Tosashimizu. He whimpered to himself. A pathetic woodland sound lost to the rain.

The next few hours, he didn't know how long, passed fitfully. He drifted in and out of dreams and reality. It was dark of course, but thanks to the temple's proximity to the village, the world was gifted a slight, unreal orange glow by the electric streetlights and lamps. The rain was coming in hard now and was starting to wash over the courtyard sideways instead of falling straight. Natsuo was lucky that the storm was heading north. He was coiled up on the north-facing part of the daishido, so he wasn't hit head-on by too many of the gusts that hissed through the complex.

When he finally managed to close his eyes, he would enjoy snippets of sleep before coming to again when his face was struck by raindrops, or something was dislodged noisily by the winds. He would squint, grunt, and then try to return to some form of rest.

At some point deep in the latest part of the night and earliest part of the morning a noise stirred him once again. His gluey eyes creaked open in a natural reflex and he once again was met with gloom, darkness and ghostly swirls of rain. Then he saw something peeking out behind the small pagoda in the centre of the courtyard. Some shadowy figure that moved away the moment he glanced at it.

Maybe it was a trick of the light or a dog. He closed his eyes again. Then a new sound. Natsuo swore it was a giggle. He opened his eyes again, this time fully. Who would be out in the storm, in this temple, in the middle of the night?

The rain lightened a little, falling straight as the gusts calmed. This brief lull in the dark violence of the weather made the image clearer for him. He thought he could make out a child; a boy in a juvenile blue kimono. It looked like he was wearing clogs. He was hopping from puddle to puddle. Natsuo couldn't really make out much of a face as the boy had a red umbrella on his head. He could just about make out a whimsical little smile, pudgy cheeks and an upturned nose. Natsuo stared dumbly at the shrouded figure as it hopped whimsically, giggling to itself in the pools of water gathered in the courtyard. The boy then looked directly into Natsuo's eyes and then hid behind the pagoda again. He never reappeared.

Natsuo stared fixedly at the pagoda but nothing new appeared to him. He started to wonder if he had just made the whole thing up. Was he dreaming? He didn't remember closing his eyes, but he woke some time later to a tormented grey world.

The typhoon had arrived.

As he rubbed his vision into place he saw that there were two simple rice balls placed in front of him; dry and sat on little white handkerchiefs. It was surreal as opposed to startling. Where did they come from? He presumed some local person seeing him curled up in the temple this morning had left him some food. The thought warmed something inside of him. An act of kindness from a stranger. An act of kindness directed at him.

He picked up the onigiri and ate it slowly, savouring every bite of the sweetly vinegared rice. There was nothing inside it, but the rice was the best he had ever tasted. He found the fact that someone had bestowed this generosity on him touching. He hadn't known humanity like this since he was little and had forgotten what it could feel like. He savoured slowly, making sure he got every sticky grain off his fingers.

Natsuo managed about 20 km in the morning before the storm forced him to take shelter in the harbour village of Saga that had a little bay, a couple of beaches and an island just off the shoreline. He found a stooped, empty fisherman's house and, presuming it abandoned, set himself up in one of the three small rooms in order to wait out the worst of the passing storm. There was dust everywhere, but he wasn't about to complain. It seemed whoever had once lived here, looking out at the now churning Kashimagura Bay, was long gone.

The room he was in had a small shelving unit full of books stacked up on top of each other haphazardly. Books about fishing and boats, but also Japanese myths and fairytales.

Wedged in between one called *Fish of the Inland Sea* and a translated copy of *The Hound of the Baskervilles* was an old book full of gorgeous ink line drawings called *Magical Beasts of Japan*: *Kami, Yōkai* and *Yūrei*. Natsuo smiled grimly to himself; normally he'd sit down to read some manga no doubt based around these creatures. And here he had the original version. He flicked open the first page where the date read 1923.

Natsuo lay down on a somewhat tatty futon that was up against one side of the room and started to carefully turn through the crispy old pages. Each one had a beautiful illustration of a monster or ghost or deity accompanied by a whimsical description. He was reminded of the *Dungeons and Dragons Monster Manual* he had seen as a child when for two months an exchange student from Boston had attended his school. Some he recognised as famous beasts and characters of Japanese folklore, but the vast majority were things he had never heard of.

The book was divided by prefecture; each region of the country seeming to have its own local monsters. He idly flicked through the chapter on Shikoku and suddenly stopped when he recognised one. The name said Amefuri kozō and the picture was of a small boy with a red umbrella on his head dancing in the rain. A shiver went down his spine. That was what he was certain he had seen, or imagined, or dreamed, he couldn't remember, last night in the temple.

Natsuo was sure he had never heard of this 'rainfall priest boy', but then after a decade of reading fantastical manga and watching anime shows that would often use Japanese mythology for inspiration, he presumed he was just conflating everything together. He smiled at the coincidence and kept flicking through as the afternoon winds continued to lash at the window.

A short while later, and without intending to, he swiftly fell deeply asleep as a wave of tiredness and the oddly soothing sound of a maelstrom out of reach consumed him.

Sweet fried onions, bubbling pork broth, fragrant green onions, the warm perfume of miso, a light tang of grilled fish. These aromas, these organoleptic memories of Japan, gently invaded Natsuo's dreams. Slowly he woke up, a pleased smile playing on his lips and the now dark evening world slowly coming into focus.

In front of him, set on a plastic tray, was a bowl of simple noodles, a smaller bowl with miso soup in it, and a grilled horse mackerel. Natsuo's stomach grumbled loudly, and he instinctively reached out for the little bowl of miso soup. It was wonderfully salty and savoury with little pieces of seaweed floating about in it.

'You looked like you could use some food.' A fragile and kindly voice came from the doorway.

The man behind the voice was a small, hunched-over old man. He wore a string vest, had a thread-bare red bandana around his neck, a cigarette hanging precariously off his wrinkly mouth, and tracksuit bottoms. His face was so lined and ancient it seemed to be falling off his head, but his eyes twinkled the twinkle of decades of experience and knowledge. The house clearly wasn't abandoned, and this was clearly the owner. It could only have been his house.

Natsuo scooted himself back against the wall, curled up and covered his face, whilst apologising.

'Sumimasen...' he whispered to the room.

The old man laughed an old gurgled laugh, 'I don't bite, young man.'

Natsuo, didn't react, just hid himself.

'Not a fan of talking to people, eh?' The old man took a drag of what remained of his cigarette. 'Well, I took you for a traveller hiding from the storm and I have to admit that you probably thought this building was long since forgotten about.' He ran his fingers across the top of a small wooden cabinet and pondered his sooty hand. 'I'm old and alone so I never dust and clean really. I'm only here for the fishing season you see. The rest of the time I live inland.' The old man regarded Natsuo as one might a frightened animal in a forest. 'Well, I see we won't be having much of a chat tonight, so I'll leave you be. You can wait out the storm here.' The old man turned to leave.

Natsuo mumbled something.

'What was that boy? I'm old and can't hear well.'

'Hikikomori...'

With that one word the fisherman understood everything. He hadn't the foggiest what a young city boy Hikikomori was doing in his house during a typhoon but regardless he smiled to himself.

'Just close the door behind you when you go.'

The following morning the worst of the typhoon had passed and the world had returned to light charcoal skies and sheets of rain. Natsuo had finished the food and left the tray tidily by the door. He had also left a small note that just read 'Arigato gozaimasu.' He slipped out quietly and paused just in front of the house. He turned around and faced the little shambolic cottage and bowed.

After a couple of hours of trudging in the rain Natsuo joined an attractive path that followed parallel to the enormous and quite beautiful Irino beach.

Halfway along he paused at a wooden beach hut and decided to stop for a few moments. He planned to continue on as far as he could today, given the harshest part of the storm had moved north. Even though it had only been a few days, Natsuo felt stronger, fitter, his feet harder and his mission firmer than ever in his mind. He also thought it wouldn't be a good idea to just barge into homes anymore.

The world was still dim and the sky had a smokiness to it, as if cotton had been dragged through iron filings and then thrown into a blender. The rain persisted but the worst was over for now. As Natsuo sat and stretched out his legs, rubbing his calves in front of the seashore, he took off his heavy poncho and decided to return it to the bag.

Inside were two items that hadn't been there prior. One was a small plastic bag of food: a gummy rice ball studded with sesame seeds, an apple, a small individually wrapped chocolate muffin and a packet of dried edamame. Natsuo's cheeks glowed. A memory of a long lost parental act stung his face. Like a mother making a child a packed lunch for a school trip, that old fisherman who Natsuo had shied away from had prepared a meal for him as he slept.

The other was the book he had been reading, *Magical Beasts of Japan: Kami, Yōkai and Yūrei.* A gift? Something for him to do knowing he probably wouldn't be spending his free time talking to the locals? He ate the apple and lay back staring out to sea, wondering if more typhoons were on their way.

Natsuo at some point had dozed off as when he woke up night was falling. He felt refreshed but was annoyed at himself for losing walking time. He decided to push on further until the darkness made it a hindrance.

He managed another twenty kilometres inland, rising over a small range of forested hills, before giving up. Tosashimizu was less than twenty kilometres away but apart from a few large country homes along the road, civilisation had never truly reached this area. He would also rather arrive in Tosashimizu in the morning to give himself more time if the worst truly had come to pass.

As he plodded through the light spitting rain, he caught sight of a row of lights up ahead on the right, snaking up a small wooded hillside behind some houses. They looked like temple lantern lights, but he was surprised to see so many out here as often such a quantity — there seemed to be twenty or more forming a sort of illuminated runway — was usually to be found only around the larger temples and shrines.

He was out in the middle of nowhere and according to the map this tiny temple, Shinnenan, wasn't much more than a glorified wooden hut hiding amongst some trees. But Natsuo liked the idea of sleeping again in such a place. Less chance of being bothered by, or bothering, people.

The lights were more of a blue-green colour rather than orange, and from a distance they appeared to be real flames. Natsuo presumed it may have been for a local *matsuri* festival.

He sleepily clomped up to the little temple building and sat inside with his legs crossed looking out at the path up which he had walked. All the lights had gone out. A few minutes ago, he was following a flaming path and now it was shrouded in darkness. Natsuo was too tired to muster any interest in this occurrence and instead set to eating the food gifted to him by the old man in Saga.

The night was quiet apart from the occasional whoosh of a far-off car and the rustling of bamboo leaves. The odd chicken crowed and sometimes he heard the sounds of what he presumed were either foxes or cats mewing. Sounds of nature.

Behind his small Buddhist enclave was a slender stream that, unbelievably, was warm. Natsuo hadn't thought there were springs down this part of Shikoku island, but then what would he really know? He took out a bar of soap and, standing in the river halfway up to his knees, cleaned himself properly for the first time in almost a week; lines of filth slid off him, flowing away downstream. Natsuo felt simultaneously cleansed and disgusted.

It was a clear night, the clouds had dissipated finally and the ceiling of the world was exposed. Stars twinkled and burned light years away and a heavy stillness and almost tangible silence suffused the woods. The air smelled of wet leaves and fresh air. Now clean and enjoying this peaceful nook, Natsuo felt light and purified. Whether it was the combination of the quiet and his relaxed body, or the romance of the little temple in the trees that he now lay in, he felt closer to something unexplainable, something spiritual.

His mind drifted back to when he was a child. To a precise moment; and one of the last ones he remembered prior to shutting himself away.

Ijime, bullying, had sadly always been a common occurrence in Japanese schools. Not that it was exclusive to there; in every alpha group of children there have always been, would always be and will always be, those that prey on the lower castes. The reasons could be as varied as fingerprints: physical appearance, apparent intelligence, their accent, their clothes. However in Japan, where conformity was king, it could be as simple as stepping one inch out of the accepted circle of 'how to be' and it would begin. The tragic thing was how the authority figures joined in; teachers, parents, politicians, all extolling the mantra of sameness and maligning individuality.

One of the problems in Japan was that it may well be the top students, the paragons of virtue and academia, the brightest and best, who were the ringleaders in ostracising the weakest of the class; so nobody would believe it was them carrying out the campaign of humiliation and terror. Instead of a personal vendetta from a bully to a victim, it was more common a group would regularly and constantly gang up on one child.

Ijime was aided by the fact that schools would rather ignore and cover up problems than admit to any sort of failing or on-site bullying. So the reality would continue undetected and untreated.

For Natsuo, it was something as simple as not liking sports, in particular baseball. This attitude of not enjoying the national pastime was enough to set off another boy in the class, Toshi, who happened to be the captain of the team.

Toshi was taller, fitter, and had a blazing stare that was at once piercing and intelligent but also gleamed with an obvious cruelness that had manifested as a result of him knowing, and enjoying, that he was the top dog.

Natsuo had never enjoyed sport. It wasn't because he was unfit, but rather he lacked any coordination and found the whole concept rather dull. He never minded anyone else's interest, but it just bored him senseless. He would rather read a book or play Go. But, as is tradition in any school, you attended all the classes. You could worry about your mission in life later on, but as a teenager Maths and P.E. were as important as each other.

One day in the classroom before an English lesson and after a particularly unenthused session of baseball, where Natsuo had briefly played, awfully, and then slunk off to the sidelines not wishing to take part again, he was approached by Toshi. In front of the whole class Toshi ripped the comic Natsuo was reading from his hands and loomed over him, seething.

'What is wrong with you?'

Natsuo was in a state of shock. He didn't know what was going on or why Toshi was bearing down on him. He just gawped at him.

'Are you stupid?' Toshi continued railing. 'I said what's wrong with you?'

Some kids lined up behind Toshi, giggling under their breath; watching their heroic leader sort out this idiot.

'I don't understand.' Natsuo still didn't know what was going on, but he was in awe of the power that Toshi emanated and feared it.

'In baseball. You were terrible, looked like you didn't want to be there. You didn't help at all!'

'I don't like baseball.'

'What?'

'I don't really like baseball, or sports.'

'What is wrong with you?'

'I just find them kind of boring.'

'So you prefer being a loser and reading this?' Toshi wielded the manga at Natsuo and then threw it to the floor. The kids behind Toshi were laughing and jeering now.

Wave after wave of emotions were flooding over Natsuo, and he didn't know what they meant or why they were there. But he couldn't focus or speak.

'Err...'

'You're just useless.' He spat, clearly offended by Natsuo's comments. 'Whoever you are...'

So he didn't even know who Natsuo was despite months in the same room as him.

This was his first year of High School and he was doomed from the very beginning.

In the blissful calm of the bamboo grove Natsuo smiled darkly to himself as he recalled the seed of it all. A forgotten seed. A seed that had burst into life and branched out all through his body turning him into an automaton husk of a man.

He wondered what those harrying, cruel classmates and teachers would make of him now. If they would be proud that he finally was getting out and doing something or just be disgusted at all of it. At him.

Natsuo then realised, somewhat meekly, that tomorrow would be his thirtieth birthday.

At some point during the night a warm orange glow wiped over the inside of Natsuo's eyes and stirred him from his sleep. As his vision blurred into life, he spied a large handsome bird on a tree some twenty metres away staring at him fixedly. It looked like a cross between a chicken and a phoenix, its body flamboyant and red but with the unmistakable appearance of a turkey-sized cockerel. He rubbed his eyes and got up onto his elbows, but the bird had already disappeared.

Natsuo sighed, a shame. He would have liked to look further upon the beautiful bird.

Poor thing...

Probably an exotic pet that had got out during the storm. He noticed some more orange glows through the trees, which finally dimmed to a backdrop of deep green, and then immediately fell back to sleep.

The morning to Tosashimizu was easy and uneventful and he arrived before lunchtime. The clear skies didn't hold and the sky had reverted to slate-grey, but it hadn't rained once.

On entering the town Natsuo realised he didn't have an exact idea of where the family house was or how to get there. It had been so long since he had visited and the times he had he would have arrived by car. Kids never pay that much attention when their parents are driving.

At least he knew roughly the location: house on road by sea line of buildings between house and sea — immediately backed by a wooded hill. There were only so many areas that could be. The only thing he could remember was that the house faced eastwards over the water and that it was somewhat distanced from the main centre of the town.

After an hour of scouring the coast, a particular view triggered his memory. He reached a small man-made spit that looked out west over one of the town's two bays. On the other side of the water he could make out a building that he remembered from when he had come to Tosashimizu as a child. It was a museum dedicated to John Mung, whose real name was Nakahama Manjirō. Natsuo had visited the museum many times as a boy and had found the story of John Mung rather spellbinding.

He had been born in the town in 1827 and during his younger years was, like most men in these coastal settlements, a simple fisherman. When he was fourteen years old, he and four friends shipwrecked on the island of Torishima. They had been looking for deeper water fish but had been dashed onto the side of the small island out to sea, far south from the Japanese mainland. They were then later rescued by an American whale ship, the John Howland, and were hauled aboard at the behest of Captain William H. Whitfield.

Manjirō had, of course, never set eyes on an American before. Japan at this time was still under its self-imposed isolation from the world. A Hikikomori on an international scale. These were the waning years of the two-centuries long Tokugawa shogunate that had wanted nothing to do with the world. And yet, here was a bunch of young Shikoku fishermen being scooped off an island by a broad and towering man from Massachusetts.

Nakahama Manjirō received the nickname John Mung after being deposited by Whitfield on the island of Honolulu. Manjirō, rather enjoying this new flavour in his life called 'adventure', asked to come with Whitfield back to America. Which he did.

Manjirō wouldn't have been welcomed back with open arms to Japan anyway, as leaving the country was punishable by death.

It wouldn't be until 1853 that Commodore Perry would bring his gunboat diplomacy to Japan and gently force them to open.

As such, young John Mung would be one of the first Japanese people to see the United States of America. It was in this year that Manjirō would return to Japan and be made a hatamoto, a samurai who directly served a shogun. He would become invaluable as a translator and cultural-attaché in the following decades as Japan opened to the world and would live to the ripe old age of 71.

As a boy Natsuo always hoped he would one day have adventures on the scale of John Mung. But he did the opposite. He imposed his own period of isolation just as Japan had in the 1600s. But, he thought to himself, as Japan had been forced to open to the world, so too had he been.

The museum was on the other side of the bay, a large modern building with a sail-like roof, glass instead of walls, and views out to the water. He knew that his house was two streets behind.

Natsuo rounded the bay and found carnage. Almost all the buildings immediately lining the waterfront had been all but washed away and the other side of the road, where the Hirawa family house was, had taken a real beating. He found the home semi-collapsed, the second floor caved in having fallen down onto the left side of the ground floor. Muddy puddles and pieces of wood were strewn all about and rubbish and detritus had been blown everywhere. It was an absolute disaster.

Natsuo dropped his bag and slumped to the ground. After all his effort his worst fears had seemingly come to light.

'Okaasan...'

Innocently he had hoped he would arrive and find the house as it always had been, his mother confused but happy to see him, proud of what he had achieved, repentant for how she had been. He thought it would be the best birthday gift he could imagine. Natsuo now feared he would find his mother in another state altogether.

He entered through the crippled front door and carefully made his way inside. Pockets of light fell into the house through holes in the roof, everywhere was dripping with rainwater, droplets falling from busted ceiling beams. It felt more like a shipwreck than a home.

His downstairs bedroom, which doubled up as the guest room, was sodden. The tatami mats bled water under the weight of his footsteps. Other than the water, there was no major damage. The living room on the left of the hallway had fared far worse however; it was here that upstairs had collapsed into downstairs.

Natsuo had to step carefully through the wreck; the floor a mess of waterlogged books, broken timber, shards of glass and miscellaneous memories that had been knocked from shelves. The amado storm shutters had also been blown inwards, such was the power of the typhoon.

'Mother?' He called out to no response.

Every new room filled him with dread, to think what he might find. The blood had drained from his face. She wasn't in the kitchen or the utility room and she wasn't in the dining room either; the irori sunken hearth was now full of water and looked more like some terrible interior pleasure pool with sodden magazines and pots floating about in it.

The staircase wasn't too badly damaged, but the wooden railings had fallen down so Natsuo had to take care on his way up the narrow flight as the steps were slick with water.

At the top of the stairs his heart began to beat faster. His father's study was empty, as was the bathroom. The last room on the top floor was his parents' bedroom; a room he had rarely ventured into even as a child. He had always felt that the master bedroom of a home often emanated an aura of importance and secrecy that no other room in a house did. The door was closed.

Natsuo struggled to keep himself together. It was a lot just for him to be here. It had taken a gargantuan effort to even leave his house, let alone journey for days through storms. He had played over in his head how the meeting with his mother would be, what he would say, what she would say, what might come of it, but now he was faced with the possibility of something more terrible. He centred himself and slid the door open.

'Okaasan...?' he mewed. There was no response.

He stepped in and looked around. She was not there.

Natsuo sighed deeply and felt as if the world had just been lifted off his shoulders a little. This relief was followed swiftly by confusion. Then where was she?

A terrible thought flashed through his mind that maybe she had passed away some time ago and nobody had told him. He tried to jettison this thought for now and instead think pragmatically. He would need to talk to someone in the town and see if they knew anything.

Natsuo felt somewhat listless, but at least he knew he didn't want to stay in this house a minute longer.

On his way out he noticed that the small family shrine was completely untouched. He walked over to it and saw many photos of himself.

So I have't been completely forgotten...

He picked up one of him and his parents posing in front of the Tokyo Tower. He must have been about five and held up two fingers in a peace sign. They looked so happy. He slumped down on the sofa and started to cry.

'Hello in there!' came a call from the outside. 'Can you come outside please.'

A police officer was on the road, seemingly waiting for him. Natsuo froze and hid his face. The voice was soft and jovial.

'Please come outside.'

Natsuo wiped his eyes and gingerly made his way back to the front door, the power of authority temporarily overtaking his fear of interaction.

'Aha, so you must be Yui and Akihiro's boy.' The policeman wore a blue shirt with a navy blue tie, a large weatherproof jacket, and sported a black peaked cap. 'The last time I saw you I don't think you would have come up much past my belly. I'm Captain Tanaka.'

The warmth and familiarity in the man's voice calmed Natsuo somewhat. He was an older man, maybe in his late fifties, and had the kind eyes of someone respected and who had never really seen much hardship. Japan was a safe country and the local villages even more so. Apart from the occasional drunk fisherman or land dispute there wasn't much controversy out this far.

'I imagine you're here looking for your mother,' Tanaka said, the last syllable hinting interrogatively. 'I'm impressed you're here given your...' He trailed off out of politeness. 'She's in Osaka. We evacuated the older people in this area a while back. The whole south coast here was deemed an unsafe area so, for the time being, everyone has been taken to Osaka.

'I know it seems like a long way to go, and it is, but the government had set up some special area or other to deal with the problem in a more controlled way. Essentially, if the affected person doesn't have anywhere else to go or any family then they were temporarily carted off there.'

Tanaka noticed Natsuo shift awkwardly and realised that what that meant was his mother had chosen to go to Osaka instead of back to the home in Kochi.

'Listen, I know you want to be reunited with your mother so if you like I can get the address of the place where she is.'

'Arigato...' Natsuo said with a small bow, still not making eye contact.

Emboldened by this communication Tanaka pushed, 'Young man, how are you planning to get there?'

'On foot.'

Tanaka let out a hearty, affable laugh, 'Ah! My boy, don't you know it must be some four hundred and something kilometres to Osaka! I will ask around and see if anyone can give you a lift there and in the meantime my wife and I have a spare room you can stay in as our little girl flew the coop a while back.'

This time Natsuo finally looked into Tanaka's eyes, his own marbled with tears. 'Arigato gozaimasu.'

Chapter Three: Yōkai
妖怪

Strange apparition.

Temporary Tsunami Evacuation Buildings had been set up in the following wards: Fukushima, Konohana, Nishi, Minato, Taisho, Naniwa, Nishiyodogawa, Yodogawa, Suminoe, Nishinari, Kita, and Miyakojima. This totalled a truly vast geographical area and comprised a population of almost one and a half million people.

The evacuees from Kochi prefecture had been taken in at Nishi, in itself a 29 km^2 neighbourhood of 135,000 people. A vast, temporary shelter city had been set up in some of the large warehouses on one of the enormous manmade spits that fronded off the mainland all along Osaka's industrial coastline.

Tanaka had spoken to some friends in the Osaka Prefectural Police. They didn't at that moment know exactly where Natsuo's mother was and they were both short-staffed and worked off their feet, so wouldn't be able to help. much. They assured him though that if he showed up at one of the TEBs they would be more than able to reunite him with her.

Captain Tanaka wondered if that was what the boy's mother actually wanted...

Natsuo hadn't left his home in thirteen years. He had spent more than a decade wallowing about in a house, ordering food online, eating cup noodles, barely caring to look after himself, and doing whatever he could to not at any point have any contact with society. And yet, one day into his thirties, he was waking up in a stranger's house far from his own and preparing to travel with a different stranger to a metropolis.

The simple power of goodness was seemingly all that was necessary to start thawing him out of his frozen state. He felt like some creature emerging, albeit slowly, from a chrysalis. Though he had more or less only experienced kindness on his trip, he was nervous of everything coming crashing down. He was still wary of people but decided to put his trust in those who warranted it.

The night before he had kept the fact that it was his birthday a secret. He didn't want to risk a commotion. Initially he had kept himself in his room, accepting tea and water, until later he had felt guilty and came out to quietly sit with Tanaka and his wife Mayu at the low table.

He didn't speak to them and they didn't bother him. It was a comfortable silence, like a scene from a monastery. Natsuo was enjoying the charity and Tanaka and Mayu were enjoying the simple act of doting on someone again.

Tanaka had organised a ride to Osaka. He would be leaving that evening with a man known simply as Mr Shi. Mr Shi was a man-with-a-van who transported goods from various parts of Shikoku to the Kansai region. This often meant simply Osaka, Nara and Kyoto. He had found a niche for himself transporting high-quality produce for expensive food shops and restaurants in the cities. City folk who would pay through the roof for the best *yuzu*, *katsuo* tataki or seafood with the story of the producer attached. As far as he was concerned, he was just driving around his island picking up packages from his friends.

And now that the typhoon had passed Mr Shi had a few orders he needed to get to a couple of restaurants in the centre of Osaka as well as a high-level hotel on the shores of Lake Biwa.

As far as Mr Shi was concerned, there was no problem in giving anyone a lift. Especially, having been explained the situation by Tanaka, to a person such as Natsuo. The only thing they would have to do is spend a night at Mr Shi's home before heading to Osaka the following morning. Mr Shi wasn't prepared to waste money on a hotel in a city only a three-and-a-half-hour drive away. They would leave early and arrive in Osaka mid-morning.

Natsuo woke up late and was greeted with an empty house, both Tanaka and Mayu, who ran a local cafe, had gone out to work. There was a note on a tray with a pot of green tea.

'Good morning! There's rice in the cooker and eggs and nattō in the fridge. Help yourself and good luck on your adventure. *Ganbatte*!'

Natsuo hadn't felt that word since he was a school kid, the encouragement slung at classmates and friends, 'you can do it!', 'good luck', 'we believe in you!' Ganbatte!

Natsuo opened the lid of the plastic every-household-has-one rice cooker and scooped out a portion of sticky rice into a bowl. He took out an egg and a small pot full of fermented sticky-looking beans. Into another small bowl he emptied the soybeans, ectoplasmically held together by their own stringy gloop. He added a few drops of soy sauce and a bit of bright yellow mustard to the nattō and whisked them together with his chopsticks. This brought everything together and made the beans less stringy. He then cracked a raw egg over the top of the beans, mixed them up and poured it all over the rice. He knew from YouTube videos that foreigners had trouble with this dish, but he loved it. Umami, almost meaty soybeans, creamy eggs and a touch of tart zing over a bed of sweet rice.

The John Mung museum was unsurprisingly closed, so Natsuo, feeling energised, decided to walk south through the headland that made up the Ashizuri-Uwakai National park until he reached the cape at the very tip and where he found the 38th temple of the pilgrimage walk; the large kongōfukuji temple, with its pond and adjoining statue of Manjirō.

It had taken him about three and half hours to get there, walking almost in a daydream. Natsuo hadn't realised it was so far as thanks to the efforts of the previous week the seventeen kilometres had passed without incident. It was then he started to panic about getting back in time.

Natsuo had the lofty cliffs to himself. The wind whipped across and blew sea spray carried up from the wild surf. In the distance he saw more gloom. Down below he saw the hakusan arch, a dramatic tree-covered granite rock formation with a massive arch cutting a small headland in two. Natsuo wondered if passing through the arch would give you good fortune.

By the small, and intensely shut, tourism information centre there was a bus stop. Two bus lines would take Natsuo back to Tosashimizu, one trundling along the west side of the headland and one the right. He sat himself down on a small bench by the bus timetable and crossed his fingers.

Twenty minutes later a voice stirred him from his current pastime of staring intently across at the statued stone garden on the other side of the car park.

'Young man!' It was, Natsuo presumed, Mr Shi. 'Someone told me they saw a young man who had previously been in the possession of the local law enforcement walking dreamily down the headland. It seems I guessed right.' He popped the passenger seat door open. 'Get in, we'll pick up your things and get going.'

Natsuo felt a mixture of embarrassment, fear and relief and bowed sheepishly as he clambered into the back.

Mr Shi was a broad and stocky man, like a builder or circus strongman. He had big round brown eyes and lofty thin eyebrows, which gave his face a cheerful aspect. He was shorter than Natsuo but was more massive. The combination of his apparent workmanly power and affable countenance put Natsuo at ease almost immediately. He felt safe.

Mr Shi lived in the centre of the island, in a village called Otoyo on the banks of the Ananai River. His house was a large wood-beamed country home a few metres set back from the road a little up the hill. The veranda looked onto the quiet country road and out to the river valley beyond. They arrived around eight o'clock so the only light was that which was suffusing out from the street lamps and the small houses that dotted the roadside.

'Come on *shōnen*, we're getting some food and beer.' Despite his years, everybody referred to Natsuo as a young man. He guessed it was because of his innocence, or ignorance, and his sheltered life.

He quite liked it.

Hibari, a family-run shokudo restaurant, was only a short walk from the house and Mr Shi was greeted like a neighbour. He didn't order anything, but two beers and a small bottle of cold sake arrived. The teishoku set menu was a popular option at these little casual dining taverns.

'We'll both have the tonkatsu.'

'Hai!' came the response.

A few minutes later, for Natsuo and Mr Shi were the only diners apart from a silent old man at the bar looking into the nothingness and steadily drinking little glasses of beer, the food arrived. On a neatly packed brown tray there was a large white plate sporting the breaded pork cutlet, which was smothered with a sweet BBQ gravy, and some vinegary shredded cabbage, a steaming bowl of miso, a generous bowl of sticky rice and a small dish of crunchy multicoloured pickles. They snapped apart their chopsticks.

'Itadakimasu.' They both chanted before greedily shovelling food into their mouths.

The small restaurant smelled of broth and warm rice and the menu items hung on individually written pieces of paper above the bar. The lady behind the counter kept the beers and rice wine coming without even asking and before he knew it, and far sooner than most thirty-year-olds, Natsuo was a little drunk.

'Shi-sama...'

Mr Shi almost spat out his beer. This was the first time Natsuo had spoken to him.

'I've not had dinner with anyone for thirteen years...' Natsuo was holding his porcelain bowl, his chopsticks pincered around a small mass of rice.

Mr Shi grunted encouragingly.

'I just want to say thank you.'

He started to cry, quietly but intensely.

Mr Shi was touched but felt bad for Natsuo.

'Now now, it's no trouble. Come now, you'll ruin your rice.' Mr Shi laughed. 'And listen, from now on you should eat with people more often!'

Natsuo sniffed, smiled, and continued to eat his rice.

It was raining quite heavily when they left the restaurant. 'Storm's coming,' Mr Shi said simply.

Back at the house, Shi invited Natsuo to a glass of Duque de Veragua on the veranda.

'The Spanish have the French beat I think. I'll never turn down a cognac of course, but I'm not in the habit of paying those prices. I picked this up on a trip to Seville one year. Brandy de Jerez is the one for me. Blended from barrel to barrel over the years in those big oak solera casks. They have more kick than the French. What do you think? Don't worry about coughing, it's strong!

'I got into the habit of a night-cap around the time my son stopped coming out of his room. Hah! Got you with that one. Yes, my son was also a Hikikomori for a time, about two years it lasted. This was about... twenty years ago now; we didn't really know what to call it at the time. We gave nothing but love to him as a child, but he was badly bullied at school and we didn't see it, or maybe we chose not to see it...

'Initially we had no idea how to react. I'm sure I lost my temper. I wanted him to go to school and get a career; to move out of the village. Be better than me. And then all the hope and time and money I put into this project called "son" was locked away. At the start we played it off as illness, a phase, a rebellion; anything that made some sort of sense and gave the impression it would come to an end. But then we realised there was no end in sight.

'Although we lived out of town, news of our son, his name is Ichiro by the way, spread like wildfire. I'd hear whispers behind me when I went into town, the word "hermit" and "shut-away". I felt a deep sense of shame and embarrassment. Was it my fault? I thought I had done nothing but love the boy; but then you know how us Japanese are.

'He was a sensitive soul and was easily picked on by the stronger kids; especially those with fishermen fathers...'

Mr Shi trailed off and took a sip of his brandy. Natsuo felt a hint of jealousy or maybe inferiority when he mentioned the other parents.

'Why was he bullied?' asked Natsuo gently.

'Well, it was because Ichiro...preferred boys. And sadly, as you know, that doesn't really cut it in Japan, not back then, and not out here.

'His mother and I couldn't care less about that, and I think when he finally realised that it helped him return to the world.'

Mr Shi could sense the question dancing around Natsuo's tipsily freed up mind.

'Ichiro's mother, my wife, Megumi, passed away a few years ago from cancer. She was happy at the end, seeing our Ichiro grow up. He now runs an art gallery in Kyoto.' Mr Shi smiled widely and proudly. 'I'm going to get us some water. We need to get up early.'

Natsuo stood up and looked out at the dark rain, forming an ever-shifting veil through which he could just about make out the now pitch-black river.

In the gloom he noticed some movement down by the road. There was a woman standing at the base of one of the street-lamps. The bulb was flickering and weak, the only one like that on the road, so it was hard to make her out. She had a gaunt, depraved face and hungry eyes and she was bedraggled and sodden from head to toe. Her hair was scraggly and hung half over her face and fell far below her shoulders. Her simple white linen dress was plastered to her body, perfectly showing the outline of skeletal ribs, sagging breasts and withered legs. Natsuo took her for a homeless woman of the village.

To his surprise she started to lick her fingers and hands and then trawl her purple tongue up and down her arms as if trying to get sustenance from the rainwater. All the while she lapped at herself, she stared at Natsuo. He couldn't avert his eyes. She kept licking and licking until he thought he could hear it.

'I tell you this view is better in the day!'

Natsuo jumped and cursed.

'Hah! Sorry to scare you.' Mr Shi said, passing a glass of water.

'Shi-sama. Who's that woman?' Natsuo whispered as he pointed to the streetlight.

'Who's that now?'

The woman was gone. Natsuo was too ashamed and afraid to say anything more and just shook his head. The alcohol was making his head spin, so he made his excuses and retired to his bed. He could worry about women in the rain another time.

He was on a steep and narrow forest path that led up to a point of light. He turned around to look down the hill and only saw darkness. On both sides were tall laurel trees looming over him creating a claustrophobic dense and dark green corridor. Between the indistinguishable shadowy trunks, he saw eyes: bright red rings with dark centres. As his own adjusted he saw that the eyes belonged to handsome white foxes with multiple tails. *Kitsune*. They were all stood up on their hind legs and each one, like a repeating mirror image, was pointing with an extended paw to the point of light at the top of the path. Instinctively Natsuo took this as an order to walk. He reached the light and the trees faded away. The light evened out and Natsuo was standing in a miniature glade in front of a small waterfall that formed a perfect sheet of cascading water dropping from a sheer granite wall. The foxes had disappeared and Natsuo's attention was focused solely on the waterfall. It made only the gentlest of sounds for what should have been a hissing din. Then he noticed something strange poking right out of the middle, at shoulder height. It was a few inches long. It was a nose. Before Natsuo had time to process what on earth was happening the nose laughed and jiggled. And then a voice. An old, jovial voice tinged with urgency. 'Hurry boy. You must hurry.'

Natsuo's head was ringing when he woke up blurry eyed at around 6AM. There was a large glass of water, a pot of green tea, and two paracetamols waiting for him on the small desk by his bed.

What was with these dreams? He asked himself as he swallowed the pills and finished every last drop of the drinks in front of him.

The rain was dark and heavy outside and meant that the sun hadn't been able to brighten the world. The gloom was back.

'Another typhoon is on its way,' said Mr Shi as they loaded their bags into the van. 'There seems to be no end to it. Who knows what we've done to the planet to cause all of this.'

It would be a three-and-a-half-hour drive through the pouring rain to their destination in Osaka. They drove north, surrounded by the verdant hills of central Shikoku until they were spat out onto the main road heading east to the island's main city of Tokushima.

Natsuo sleepily lay his head against the window and looked out at the day struggling to impose itself. He felt like he was in a movie; unreality blurring past the window as lines of raindrops raced sideways over the glass, turning the lights outside into out of focus glows instead of tangible points of illumination.

Just outside of Miyoshi they pulled into a gas station.

'The old girl drinks more than I do,' laughed Mr Shi as he pulled his hood up over his head and went out to the pumps. After filling up the tank he ran inside to the tiny shop to pay, he yelled back to the car, 'I'll get us some coffees.'

Natsuo stared ahead, along another road that could be anywhere in Japan. To his right houses, businesses and a wooded hill line, to his left rice paddies and more treed hills.

There was sometimes a mesmeric power to places like this. Natsuo imagined the flatlands of Kansas or the plains of central Spain or the endless Taiga in Russia would be the same. You couldn't pinpoint where you were, but you'd know which country you were in. Landscape as an emblem.

A small open-back truck pulled up and a rather squat fat, grease-covered man got out. His trousers seemed to be fighting a constant battle against gravity. He purchased a drink and snack from the vending machine, again a constant feature of the Japanese visual tapestry, threw them into the front seat, and ran to the small toilet block on the left side of the gas station shop. Somewhat disgusted with having had to look at that man, Natsuo returned to his new pastime of gazing half-focused through the window.

A few seconds later he noticed out of the corner of his eye that a woman, in what he thought looked like a kimono, entered the toilet block. Natsuo once again was repulsed. Probably a prostitute who worked the area servicing horrid little men like this in roadside toilets and hotels or wherever they needed it to be.

A couple of minutes passed and Natsuo saw Mr Shi shuffling carefully towards the car with a plastic bag and a tray of two steaming coffees that puffed away into the air like little caffeinated fumaroles.

Natsuo accepted the coffee and nodded wordlessly. For a short while they sat there in silence just sipping coffee and quietly munching on choux cream puff pastries.

'Well, it's about three hours to the evacuation site so feel free to nod off and I can tell you when we are getting close.'

As they reversed out of the garage onto the main road Natsuo caught a glimpse of the woman drifting out of the toilet block. There was a sated look on her face like a cat that had just finished a plate of cream. She had incredibly long hair, and it seemed to Natsuo in those brief moments before they pulled away, that there were little decorative red barbs at the end of various strands. She locked eyes with Natsuo and smiled hungrily. He sank down in his chair and hid his face, embarrassed.

Natsuo fell asleep rather quickly and only woke up when Mr Shi cursed a couple of hours later crossing Awaji Island.

'Sorry to wake you, young man. The motorway is closed so to cross the other half of this blasted island we're going to have to take the local roads. We'll pop down to the coast via Sumoto. It'll add a little to our time, but that's more something for me to worry about than you. Just get back to looking out to the sea and we'll be there soon enough.'

Before Natsuo entered his social hibernation, he had only travelled out of Shikoku a couple of times. His parents weren't big travellers. Not out of any displeasure or fear, just inertia and small town thinking.

When you grow up and live somewhere small, fairly far removed from the great conurbations, your thinking grows smaller too. Distances change their meaning. For an American, in their vast country, a five-hour drive to visit a brother or sister isn't much of an expedition. From Natsuo's home to Tokyo it would be a seven-hour drive. Given the proportions of Japan, this seemed proportionally a far greater trip given the comparative amount of the country's length covered. So growing up somewhere small often meant that trips became smaller too.

Natsuo had been to Tokyo, an experience that had scared as much as fascinated him. He had never seen so many tall buildings and people, so much neon and light. He and his family one year had taken a few days and caught the ferry west to the island of Kyushu to spend some time in the smoking hot spring town of Beppu. Then there were obligatory school trips to Osaka, Nara and Kyoto; the latter two cities blending together in his memory as a blur of temples and deer. His only memory of Osaka was similar to Tokyo; lots of glowing signs, food stalls and rushing bodies.

Despite having no desire to speak to or interact with society over the years, even scuttling away from neighbours, he had always wanted to see more of his country. The curse of the modern era, the internet and television age, was that he was constantly bombarded with images of both Japan and the world. All the beautiful cities and incredible landscapes that were out of reach for him because of his own fears. The fact that he was now at least seeing and experiencing new things helped steel himself slightly. Shikoku had been quiet. Osaka would test Natsuo to his limits.

As they drove north along the coast road he could see the lights of Osaka across the bay. A line of twinkling orbs popping red, green and orange through the downpour. The rain was beating down on the water so the whole frothing surface was pockmarked with tiny droplet-craters that each only lasted a split second. It was quite beautiful.

It had been either raining or storming for nearly two solid months now and Natsuo wondered when it would end. The Japanese had a word for prolonged periods of humid summer rains and cloudy skies: tsuyu. But this was different. It felt unworldly, unnatural. Like the gods, or Mother Nature, or something had decided to keep hurling cyclones at Japan. Like they were being punished by the planet.

The usually tropical blue-coloured waters were now a churning mass of steel and gunmetal greys. Natsuo thought he could see shadows of fish, huge ones, like sharks, sliding about dark as shadows just below the surface. But there weren't fish that large out here. Still, the thought that beasts may lurk below the violent waves made the hairs on his neck prickle.

The Akashi-Kaikyo is an enormous suspension bridge spanning almost four kilometres and soaring three hundred metres above the Akashi Strait. Its central span is the longest of any suspension bridge in the world. Massive and strong. But even with that in mind Natsuo still felt a sting of nerves as they drove over in the winds.

When driving north to Osaka from Shikoku island there is a famous whirlpool just under the suspension bridge at Naruto. There are little tourist boat tours that put-put out to the gently swirling vortex. During the tides there can be a 1.5m difference in water levels of water coming in and out between the Inland Sea and the Pacific. So frequently there are picturesque whirlpools, sometimes up to twenty metres wide, dancing in the straits. They pose no threat to a boat and indeed they sidle up next to them so the tourists can take their photos.

As he peered down at the waters from the safety of the car Natsuo saw a truly horrifying sight. A few hundred metres out into the dark waters of the bay he saw a vast angry-looking maelstrom swirling in the water. It must have been half a mile wide. It looked like when one sees aerial footage of hurricanes. Frothy and white and spinning. But it was also ugly and its form kept changing. At least a whirlpool couldn't do any damage unless you went near it.

'Never seen one that big! And not over this side of the island,' said Mr Shi. Natsuo noticed that his cheerful tone was also seasoned with a flavour of fear. How could it not.

Natsuo couldn't take his eyes off the vortex. Behind the giant whirlpool there seemed to be a shadowy island. He hadn't remembered there being any such islands in the Osaka Bay, but then he had been a recluse for more than a decade.

Due to the gloom, the rain and the whipped up spray from the whirl, he couldn't make out much, but there were no lights so presumably the island was uninhabited. He could see vegetation, but it looked nothing like the woods and orchards and paddies that covered every available inch of land in the area. The island looked wet and clayish and ancient. They had almost crossed the bridge when two enormous lights seemed to come on the island, huge golden orbs that were spaced apart by probably a mile and made it look like the mysterious low island had a pair of eyes.

'Does anyone live on that island in the bay?' Natsuo asked quietly as they came off the bridge to enter the charming town of Kobe which would lead them round the continuous coastal city-sprawl to Osaka.

Mr Shi was still surprised every time Natsuo chose to initiate conversation.

'Dear boy, there's no islands in the bay.'

Natsuo chose, once again, not to push the issue.

Some 0.5% of Japan's total area is estimated to be reclaimed land, or umetachi. After WWII huge projects were undertaken amidst the country's rapid economic growth to the point where almost 90% of Japan's tidal flatlands were reclaimed. It was initially a way to house maritime and industrial factories, but over the decades has included airports, green spaces, housing, and anything else you could imagine. Creating new country from landfill. It was on one of these manmade outcrops that Natsuo would hopefully find his mother.

A temporary office had been set up in a white portacabin where the road left the mainland onto the reclaimed area. A helpful man flicked through some pages, then scrolled down on a computer screen. Natsuo stood behind Mr Shi like a shy child behind a parent.

'Yui Hirawa, Shikoku, yeah, she's here. Block 4A, just about two hundred metres down this road and on your right.'

Natsuo silently blessed the efficiency of the man and his air of bureaucracy and making sure everything was in its right place. He had silently worried he would have no chance of finding his mother but here, right away, the man in the portacabin had said her name aloud.

Various industrial hangars had been converted into centres for the people dislodged by the storms, the people either whose homes had been destroyed or who were in areas that government officials had deemed at risk. People who had nowhere else to go.

Again, Natsuo wasn't sure how to feel about the reality that his mother had chosen to be shipped off to Osaka instead of just returning home, but then Natsuo had helped create a narrative where she was no longer part of his story. He hoped that would change from today.

One, Two, and Three passed by. Then the fourth hangar arrived. It was split into two sections, A and B. At the front door was another helpful man in a blue shirt and tie. He held a clipboard.

'Can I help you?'

Natsuo remained silent.

'Err, yes. We were sent here by the young man back there. We are looking for someone. Mrs Yui Hirawa. She's from Kochi and we were told she's here.'

The man flicked through a couple of pages of his clipboard and ran his pen down the names.

'Yes, here she is. Are you family or friends?'

'We're —'

'She's my mother,' Natsuo whispered.

The man's face morphed into the archetypal shape of pity and compassion.

'Follow me.'

The room was lofty and singularly wide and empty like a huge sports hall, and it smelled of disinfectant and bleach. Dotted at even intervals were what looked like small roofless fortresses made of cardboard; the kind one might make as a child. These low-budget walls offered the people within some semblance of privacy.

As they walked past Natsuo noticed that inside was spartan; people had a couple of blue mats and pillows, perhaps a fold up chair and then whatever belongings they had arrived with.

The Japanese were stoic people and Natsuo noticed barely a hint of tragedy among the people he saw, though their eyes harboured a sadness. There would be time for emotion later. Time to dwell on the situation and stack everything up on top of each other. Only then would the Japanese burst into tears and cry. For now, it was a matter of getting on with it and getting through.

Each of the little forts had a number on a piece of white paper clipped to the top. In an instant, whole lives were reduced to numbers and letters.

'Your mother is just over there on the right. Number 21,' said the man, holding his clipboard on his chest and bowing.

Mr Shi and Natsuo returned the bow and turned towards the small cardboard cabin.

'Go on young man. You don't need me for this.'

Natsuo locked eyes with Mr Shi, thanked him and bowed deeply.

As he approached number 21, he could feel a weight in his throat. All his nerves and fear were stuck hard and he had trouble breathing. Natsuo hadn't seen his mother for a decade and questions were flashing through his mind like lightning. Would she want to see him? Would she recognise him? How would he react when he saw her?

A knot of pain and terror started to build in the pit of his stomach. Why had he done this? He could have just stayed at home, stayed in his safe place, and enjoyed the linear simple life he had been living. But no, he just had to watch the news. He would have been safer in ignorance. A state of uninformed bliss. His mother was clearly ashamed of him still. Hated him. Didn't want to see him. She could have come just up the coast to the family home but no, she had preferred to be carted off to a big city and live in a box instead of seeing him.

Natsuo clutched his head and rubbed it. He was panicking now. Surrounded by a world he had run away from, people he had for so long tried to avoid. What was he doing? He felt like running out, away, and back to Kochi.

Then a calm, soft voice cut through the anguish and confusion he was feeling and in an instant it all melted away. The stress and fear dissipated like a droplet of red ink in the sea, marbled and was consumed. One voice and one word.

'Son?'

Chapter Four: Kazoku
家族

Family.

i

'Okaasan.' Natsuo caught her gaze and then instantly looked away. It had been so many years since he had seen his mother and, in that split second, she had looked exactly as she had always looked. Her hair was greyer and she had a few more lines crevassing her face, but it was still the same one from when he was a child.

The days of Natsuo's personal bravery, his battles against that version of himself that feared the world, his journey back from the dark, were slipping away from him. The confidence he had gained from facing the world, the kindness shown by Mr Shi and Tanaka-san. This moment had blown everything to pieces, that voice, that woman. He searched inside himself for somewhere to hide.

Then he felt warm and safe. Was he back home? Had he plummeted to a safe corner of his psyche where the world was blocked off? He opened his eyes to find his mother embracing him gently. The meaning behind this small human gesture, and Natsuo's longing for it, struck right to his core and he collapsed, to his knees, in tears. He hugged his mother back and cried.

Natsuo had expected an awful, awkward exchange between an estranged mother and her thirty-year-old son. Cold and uncomfortable. But instead, he had instantly reverted to being a child. A child now experiencing the warmth he had rarely ever received when young. His mother had never been one for hugs and kisses and coddling. A lot of Japanese parents weren't. Ruffled hair and neck squeezes were about as much as he could expect.

Mr Shi arrived with two cups of hot matcha tea and placed them down on the little side table where Yui had set up her living space.

'Natsuo-chan, I'm going to have to leave you now. I'll be in the area for a couple of days if you need anything. Here's my number.' He handed over a business card with two hands. 'I wish you all the best.'

Natsuo and his mother bowed deeply before being left alone; mother and son together for the first time in a decade.

For a couple of minutes, which seemed to Natsuo an eternity, he and his mother sat quietly drinking their tea, both thinking what to say. It was Yui who broke the silence first.

'I am as proud as I am surprised to see you Natsuo-kun.' She sipped her tea. 'We thought we were broken, all of us. And that we had broken each other. We failed you and we thought you in turn had failed us. We weren't perfect parents. We knew that, but we didn't know any different. We were overcome with shame and felt you were a lost cause. And then we just left.

'When your father died, I felt that I had too. I stopped leaving the house and just started to spend my days pottering. I had become a caretaker of a house with no soul. I had essentially become a Hikikomori like you. Oh...sorry if that sounds rude. I just don't know what else to say. Don't know what the right word for anything is these days... Anyway, I had no friends to speak of really. Your father was my world. And when we...lost you, well, I gave up.

'When the storms started to hit hard I thought of you, alone in that house, and I worried, though I knew you'd be safer there than anywhere else. We were asked to evacuate to somewhere up the coast or inland, friends or relatives. I thought you must hate me, so I simply followed orders and got on the bus to here.

'I can't tell you how happy it has made me to see you. You left, you made it, and you came to see your little, terrible old mother.'

'No' was the response from Natsuo. Yui paused momentarily. 'Not terrible. It's true that I don't think you and father brought me up as well as you could have. Or should have... But then I didn't make it easy for you. We are all products of the generation before us. These storms, something in this chaos, has given me a reason to find a way out of this...'

Neither Yui nor Natsuo decided to speak more about the subject. A decade of solitary living had reached a diplomatic resolution where a few sentences held enough meaning to bring the whole chapter to a close.

As far as Natsuo was concerned, his mother was sorry and was happy to see him. And he imagined the same was true for his mother.

'*Omoshiroi, ne*?' his mother said with a twinkle in her eyes.

'What's that?'

'It's interesting that these storms brought us together? It's quite the story. Like something out of one of those comics you read.'

'Mm.' Natsuo looked off into his memories.

'What is it?'

'Oh, nothing. Well, probably nothing. But I've been having odd dreams recently. Seeing things in the rains. People. Strange people.'

'What kind of things dear?' His mother leaned in closer as if listening to some important news.

'Odd women, huge whirlpools in the bay, there was a small boy dancing in the rain in the middle of the night in a temple. At least I think I saw these things. I've been travelling and sleeping rough, so what was a dream, real or some odd warp of reality, I don't know. But —' He was cut off by his mother whispering something under her breath. 'What is it mother?'

'No, nothing.'

'Tell me, please.'

'Yōkai.'

'I'm sure there's a more rational explanation than mythical beasts and spirits! Maybe it's typhoon madness. All the darkness and rain making me loopy.'

'Other people here have said they've seen things. Strange things. Things from our own folklore.'

Natsuo laughed a little, 'Okan, you don't really think there are monsters and ghouls creeping around the streets?'

'Well, what do I know? But in all my years and all the record books, I've never heard about a summer with so many typhoons. Even the people on the television are at a loss at what to say. The scientists haven't got a clue either.' She sighed. 'Well, anyway. You're here now, so if there are bakemono walking about, we can protect each other.' She smiled and ruffled his hair.

He had missed that.

Natsuo was standing in front of an ancient temple. It was old and Buddhist and was devoid of colour. The whole scene before him seemed almost monochrome. The black temple buildings were divided into a U-formation, the base of the letter being the principal Jizodo hall. Longer halls and temples headed away forming the arms of the U. Down the centre of the U was a path that led up to the Jizodo. A path lined with grey stone lanterns. No fires burned in them, and they stood as dormant ghostly sentinels. Behind the temple rose a hill in muted green, and stretched out in front were ashy grey fields that were smoking as if the land around the temple were embers. Natsuo gazed further afield and saw that an enormous dark-looking and almost perfectly round lake filled his eye-line, which was surrounded by more gloomy de-coloured hills. He was inside a craggy volcano that seemed to be smouldering gently. Natsuo walked down the lantern-lined path towards the water. As he got closer, grey clouds started to pour down the sides of the hills circling the lake until the entire caldera was filled with a dense, milky fog. Back towards the temple he saw a red glow. He walked over to it, the only smudge of colour in a world of greys, whites and blacks. Visibility was limited; he heard the source of the colour before he saw it. A bubbling, gurgling sound. There was a statue of a monk, sitting down crossed-legged on a small plinth in the middle of a pond. It was a blood-red pool, deep scarlet, frothing and churning violently like some hellish mud pot. To Natsuo it looked like in the movies when a shark attacked a swimmer and the resulting water was a gory boiling mess. The pool then started to scream. Cries and moans and shrieks began to fly out of the water. Every bubble that popped, every splash and froth, seemed to call out as they broke the surface. And then laughter. Mad, terrifying laughter was mixed in with the screams. And a low bass grumble, a voice, a menacing presence underlying everything. Natsuo was afraid. He backed away from the pool, back into the mist. Then the noise stopped. The colour stopped. As if it had been simply turned off. His fear dissipated and he noticed a shadow in the fog. A figure about his height with the outline of a long nose. 'I'm waiting for you on Kurama-yama.' Suddenly the mist disappeared and there was a bright flash of light, a heavenly light, that shone so brightly that Natsuo had to close his eyes...

He looked at his phone: 2:42AM. What was with these dreams? He put it down to his high emotional state and tiredness, but even so they were vivid. He never remembered recurrent dreams either. The character with the long nose, the red-faced devil.

He was lying next to his mother. Natsuo had felt instantly transported back to when he was a small child. It was quite common in Japan for parents and little ones to sleep on the floor together. No big double beds, but comfortable futons and tatami mats.

He remembered watching American cartoons and was amazed that even the youngest children, toddlers, had their own rooms with painted fantastical scenes on the walls and even elaborate ceiling lights or glow-in-the-dark stickers illuminated in the darkness. He shared the simple wooden room with his mother and father, and they slept on a row of three simple mattresses. But he still felt warm and safe. That feeling came back to him now as he lay by his elderly mother. But he couldn't sleep.

He took out his torch and the book on yōkai he had been given by the old fisherman, deciding to flick through it until his eyes grew heavy.

He always loved books like this and imagined if it possibly could have ever worked having so many monsters apparently living alongside humans. Natsuo thought that also when he read books about dinosaurs and other prehistoric beasts and still marvelled that ancient man lived with the very real danger of mammoths and sabre-toothed cats.

As he lazily leafed through the book and arrived at the section on Shikoku again, a line drawing gave Natsuo pause. It was that wonderfully endearing picture of a young boy in a blue kimono dancing in the rain with an umbrella on his head. The boy he thought he saw back in the temple; or dreamt he saw.

Natsuo reasoned that his dreams were probably his active imagination mixing in with all the images he had been taking in, this book included.

The next page however pushed goosebumps up on his arms. *Ame onna*: 'rain woman'. There was a picture of a scraggly wretch of a woman, soaked from head to toe, her tongue hanging out. Each yōkai came with a description of their appearance and behaviour.

They appear as depraved, haggish women, soaked with rainwater. They lick the rain off of their hands and arms like wild animals.

Though the rains they bring might save a village in drought or bring fortune to farmers, they have a more sinister purpose— under the cover of the rain, ame onna wander the villages looking for newborn girls. If they should find a child born that night, they snatch it and carry it off into the darkness, spiriting it away to another world.

Natsuo recognised the woman as the strange lady who had been standing in the approaching storm rains outside Mr Shi's house. She too had licked her arms and hands. But Natsuo had been awake then, that was no dream. At least he didn't think it was. He had never experienced a hallucination before but that would have to have been the only explanation. No trick of the light or state of tiredness or mental exhaustion could explain seeing a crazed bedraggled woman. Also, Natsuo had no prior knowledge to create such an image.

He began to worry about his mental state. Perhaps the emotional strain his mind and soul had been put through — finding his family home smashed in with his mother nowhere to be seen, only then to be told she had been evacuated, and all the while these inputs were happening to a Hikikomori who hadn't had any contact with the world for years — was taking some toll on him. Maybe he was seeing things.

Another page. Another chill; the hairs on his neck stood up.

Hari onago; 'hook woman'.

The fearsome yōkai known as hari onago appears at night on the roads of the island of Shikoku. In the dark, they are indistinguishable from ordinary young women, unusual only for their loose, disheveled hair. Upon closer inspection, the tip of each hair is fitted with a needle-like, barbed hook – although if you are close enough to notice these hooks, it is probably already too late.

The graceful line drawing, pastelled in with colour, showed a beautiful woman, a tiny smile playing upon her lips, in a fine green kimono. Her mass of hair whipped out to the side in various glossy arms, at the end of which were bright red hooks.

Hari onago wander the streets searching for victims – usually young, single men walking alone.

It had to be the woman at the gas station. It had to be.

Natsuo tried to find something rational to hold on to. In the dim, orange glow of his torchlight his mind was racing, and his heart was beating so fast he could feel the blood pulsing through his ears. He frantically tried to cast his mind back. Had Mr Shi noticed the woman too? He couldn't be sure, but he didn't remember him making any comment about it. So perhaps he had also imagined her. But then what of the driver who had gone into the toilets? She had followed him in. She had opened that door.

But she couldn't be real. Or maybe she was. But she couldn't be this hari onago. These were characters and myths of Japanese folklore. Not real living, breathing, tangible beings.

He turned the page again, this time fearful. Two pages, under the heading of 'Marine Beasts' presented a double spread that caused Natsuo to clap a hand over his mouth to stifle a cry.

Various yōkai filled the two pages in a menagerie of aquatic horrors, but two in particular sent a cold bolt into his belly.

Kagewani, 'shadow shark', and Akaei, 'red stingray'. The former had the description of a large shadowy, predatory fish that lurked just out of sight under the surface and would snap up the shadows of fishermen should they fall upon the water. The fishermen would then vanish, their photo-negative consumed by the kagewani. Hadn't he seen gigantic fish forms in the surf as Mr Shi and he had crossed Awaji Island?

But, after all Natsuo's paranoia and worry, it was the description of the akaei that had caused his brow to sweat and his body shake from terror.

Akaei are titanic fish which live in the Pacific Ocean. Their bodies can reach 10 to 12 kilometres in length. Physically they resemble stingrays, but they are so large that they are often mistaken for islands.

Akaei spend most of their lives on the ocean floor. Every now and then they swim up to the surface and shake off the sand and rocks which have collected on their backs. This creates a maelstrom as the fish's great mass displaces huge amounts of water.

That was exactly what Natsuo had seen. And not only him, but Mr Shi too had commented on the whirlpool. He had also laughed at the idea that there were islands in Osaka Bay, but it had to have been an akaei Natsuo had seen or imagined.

Natsuo put the book down and held his head in his hands and rubbed his temples. This was almost too much information to bear, too much to process.

A week ago, he was spending yet another day sat in his own private kingdom where time had no meaning. If he wanted to eat he ate, if he wanted to sleep he slept. He would go to and from the bed whenever it pleased him, sometimes spending hours just staring at the ceiling. Other days he would lose hours to comics and games. His life had neither meaning nor a timeframe. And yet he had just walked a week through typhoons to find his mother and now felt he was either being pursued by, or was at least coming into contact with, mythical beasts. He started to whimper. This was too much, and he felt he was losing whatever marbles he still had left.

'Yōkai...'

Natsuo nearly jumped out of his skin. A low voice, a quiet voice, right above him.

'I told your mother and she agreed.'

In any other circumstance Natsuo would have hid himself, covered himself in sheets, and tried to pretend nobody was communicating with him. But her words cut straight through the core of what was going through his mind in that moment, what was causing him such stress, and he felt as if an arm had reached down and pulled him out of his personal abyss. Someone was worrying about the same things as he.

'Yes,' Natsuo whispered.

'Come with me. Don't wake your mother.'

As if under some nocturnal spell Natsuo got up and wordlessly followed the little old woman. She was very small, barely above his waist, and walked like an emperor penguin. She ushered him into her little cardboard space and motioned for him to sit on the chair. She then set herself down on the mat.

Her face was wide and lined with more wrinkles than Natsuo thought possible on a human face. The eyes were small brown dots swallowed up in withered canyons of age. Like some old mystic she seemed to suck the light into her where it caused shadows to dance and flicker. Or it could be the candle she was using for light. Either way, Natsuo felt something otherworldly about her little manmade cocoon.

'You've seen them, haven't you? Tell me which ones.' Natsuo pointed to the various monsters in his book. 'It's as I thought...'

'What is happening? You think I'm really seeing these yōkai?'

'Yes, I do. And I think others will have seen them too. But people are good at not giving in to fairytales.'

'But aren't these just monsters and stories that we've made up?' Natsuo's desire to know what was going on around him had made him chattier than he ever thought he could be with a stranger.

'Men and women have written the stories, young man, but they were as real to them as I am to you right now. But they've been hidden, lost, forgotten, and so their power and presence in this world, this realm, has dwindled. But they're back.'

'I still don't understand. I thought these were all just old folk tales. You mean to say people used to live with these things? What are they then?'

'Yōkai are as old as anything. But of course, in Japan we have a whole family of creatures and myths; yūrei, *oni*, onryō, *tengu*. Some of these are even known in the West. The first time the word was mentioned in Japan was in the Shiku Nihongi. You haven't heard of it? What do they teach you young people nowadays? It was written in the year 797 and talked about our Nara period, our first capital. It mentioned that the court had to be purified regularly because yōkai often appeared. Now, what that meant is anybody's guess. I don't think it meant your rain woman. But the word was generally used to mean some kind of strange phenomena.

'From the 8th century onwards yōkai came to be used to also refer to the supernatural, the unexplained bumps in the night. The following centuries created an abundance of literature and stories about them and slowly people started to document and draw them. What we now look back on with a rose-tinted pair of glasses thinking "such quaint drawings of monsters and ghouls" may well have been a first-hand depiction by a terrified artist. Though of course not all are evil. Some are kind, some are simply mischievous. But nonetheless a monster is a monster and thus a yōkai.

'Technology and society have a way of breaking up the old and discarding it and the same happened with the yōkai. Nowadays apart from some cartoons and comics where are they? The mascots we have to represent companies and cities and sport events? Is that what they've become?' The old lady sighed and went quiet for a moment.

'So, why now? Why are the yōkai returning?' asked Natsuo, who had been hanging off every word.

'My idea is that the status quo is upset, and something has shifted. You're young so you may not know much of the old gods. But our way of naming the deities wasn't too far off the Romans. We had gods of fertility and rice, Inari Ōkami. Yes, that's right, the foxes at the temples. Hachiman was our god of war, like Ares in Italy. And you'll know Amaterasu, our high goddess of the sun. Sort of the lady in charge of everything. I have a theory that all this comes from the rivalry with her brother Susanoo, god of the storms. I think they're squabbling. He's known to be a trickster after all. So I think he's stirring up trouble on earth to annoy his sister.'

'You think...this is all because two sibling gods are fighting?'

'Oh, I shouldn't think so. It's just a fun theory. I don't think the old gods really exist. Or maybe not anymore. Gods only seem to exist if we believe in them. But the yōkai; they seem different. More tied to us than the powers in the clouds. Linked to our fears and our daily struggles. Two things that never go away. To me it seems hard, almost silly, to believe in the kami, deities in the heavens with their own jobs and realms. But, a succubus woman who kills lonely men with her hair? Well, I can believe that and it scares me.'

Both Natsuo and the old lady fell quiet for a while. The younger of the two trying to process the enormity of what was perhaps going on and the older relishing having someone listen to her.

'My name is Mina by the way.'

'Natsuo.'

'So you and your mother were brought here from Shikoku like me? I'm from Matsuyama.'

'Kochi.'

'Ah! A southerner.' She giggled to herself. 'You are always more taciturn.'

Natsuo said nothing.

'When did you two get here? I hadn't seen you before today.'

'We didn't come together. I arrived yesterday. My mother's been here for some days now.'

'Oh.'

'She was living down the coast...'

There was a pause after Natsuo's sentence trailed off and she noticed a quiet sadness in his eyes. Mina decided not to pursue that matter. The older generation had lived through all feelings imaginable and knew when somebody was burdened with pain; as imperceptible as it may be.

'I've been having strange dreams...'

'Dreams, dear?'

'Ever since the storms. Ever since I left the house to...pick up my mother.'

Natsuo then told Mina about the strange fantastical situations that had been flooding his mind during the night. Something about her exuded an aura that acted like a safety net for Natsuo. Nothing he said would bounce back at him. The words, by his standards anyway, poured out of him.

'Well, that's quite some imagination you have there, young man. As for the red face with the long nose, that's easy. Have you heard of the tengu.'

Natsuo nodded. 'Well, I know them from manga and tv shows and... and the emoticon on my phone.'

'In ancient Japan and China they were thought to be humanoid birds, but then over the centuries took on a more human form. They say tengu were the reincarnated spirits of someone who was arrogant in life and are often mischievous and troublesome. But then, as with many yōkai some treated us kindly, were heroic, and even protected people. They say some were great swordsmen; and that one even trained the great samurai Yoshitsune. Can you believe it, hah! That may be stretching it even for me. It seems they were like people. Some good, some bad.'

'Do you know where Kurama-yama is?'

'Of course. It's a mountain about 15 km north of Kyoto. A very popular day trip. Reiki was conceived there, don't you know. Why do you ask? Thinking of going there with your mother after the storms? Remember reiki's a load of nonsense. Not helped me once in any of my seventy-eight years.'

'Well, the other long-nose tengu in my dream...he had a white face and big beard, not red...he mentioned it. The one at the waterfall and the lake. Well, he said I needed to go there to meet him. But I've never heard of this mountain so...' He noticed Mina's face change from kindly, tale-telling grandmother to one a mixture of fear and fascination. 'I mean, if I don't know this place, it's just a mountain, it's pretty crazy that a dream can tell me it.'

'Sōjōbō...'

'Is that a place?'

'Sōjōbō is a tengu of the highest rank. Think of him as the king of the tengu. The stories say he has the strength of a 1000 of his kind.'

'Well, I've never heard of him.'

'Most haven't. He was the one in the tale who taught Minamoto no Yoshitsune the art of swordsmanship.'

Natsuo grunted. Perhaps he had heard this story as a child, and it had made its way into his dream.

'The thing is, young man. The stories say he lived on Mount Kurama.'

'So...'

'So if you...if we...are choosing to believe that what is happening around us is truly happening, then perhaps Sōjōbō is calling out to you.'

Natsuo scoffed but then caught himself. After all it was he who had sworn he had seen all these things. Why choose to stop believing in his senses now.

'If this is true then why me?'

'That I cannot say.' Mina turned round and rummaged around in her handbag. She took out a piece of paper and a pencil and scribbled down an address. 'Listen, they say tomorrow evening or the next day there might be another typhoon approaching, so go here as soon as possible.'

Ask for Ichika Jinja
Bar Sakamachi
1 Chome-8 Sennichimae

'Who is this?'

'A friend in Osaka.'

'And what am I going to find when I get there?'

'Hopefully some answers.'

The following morning Mr Shi arrived to find Natsuo talking quietly with his mother. He smiled and felt a warm glow deep inside, knowing that he had formed a part of this reunion. That being said, he had been very surprised when he received a message in the middle of the night asking to take him into town. He was happy that Natsuo had made progress back into the real world but such a leap forward now? Downtown Osaka, the thumping, pulsating neon-lit, aroma-filled heart, wasn't exactly the next obvious step for a young man who still had problems meeting the gaze of strangers.

When Natsuo had told his mother he would be going into Osaka she initially felt worried for him, then he explained everything that he had talked about with Mina during the night. Japanese people, especially the older generations, were quite superstitious. Traditions and customs went hand in hand with practices that verged on the sacred. It was a country where even everyday actions and objects could take on a spiritual significance; pouring tea, the sound of wind through bamboo trees, the flavour of a piece of sushi, the visiting of the family grave. Natsuo's mother heard him out and offered to go with him. She wanted to go with him. But Natsuo said that a feeling told him this was something he had to do alone.

'Do you remember when you visited Osaka as a child with the school?'

'I only remember the canal and the Don Quijote ferris wheel, and the views from the top. All the lights.'

'This street on the paper is right by there.' She looked at Natsuo with a face of motherly concern. 'There'll be a lot of people, son.'

Natsuo grunted as he zoomed in on a map on his phone. The bar was one buried in a tight cluster of streets. To the south was an enormous multi-carriage artery road and a couple of roads parallel to the north was the canal.

The fact that Natsuo's hometown could be swallowed up hundreds of times by Osaka did send a lump of fear down his gullet, but it was the overriding worry of either his sanity slipping or the presence of genuine monsters that took primary position in his mind. He decided to use this sidelined confidence and make his way to visit Ichika Jinja.

'Natsuo my boy, I can't get any closer. The road's blocked from here; it looks like they've had a local festival. You'll have to go on foot from here on out.'

Natsuo's heart dropped. It was overwhelming enough that he was in this sprawling metropolis, but he had found comfort in the idea that he would at least be deposited at the bar. He would now have to cross Dotonbori street. Sensing his trepidation, Mr Shi placed an arm on his shoulder.

'I don't want to lie to you boy, this is going to be quite something for you. All I can say is try and let it wash over you. Dissolve into the masses. Nobody will look at you or talk to you. In the crowds you are nothing. Anonymous. Take some comfort there. By being so surrounded by humanity you'll become just another faceless number. Go in, head straight and try not to focus.'

Since the 1600s Dotonbori had been the beating heart of the city's entertainment district. Theatres, shops and restaurants are piled up on top of one another under a glowing frieze of neon. Kuidaore means "to ruin oneself by overspending on something". In Japan they say 'Ruin yourself with fashions in Kyoto, ruin yourself with meals in Osaka.'

Natsuo remembered the noise and the smells in the air. Fried *takoyaki* being whirled around in their little moulds by expert chopstick-wielding street chefs; the clouds of aromas blowing out from the stalls, ramen mist and aromatic fogs of *okonomyaki*. Then people, so many people. Couples hand in hand, families, teenagers taking photos, noise and people shouting, restaurants calling out for attention, locals standing around stuffing food in their mouths, bins full of polystyrene boxes and yakitori sticks. And above the bars, enormous robotic creations; crabs with moving arms, elaborate busts and models of octopuses and dragons.

He enjoyed it as a child, but now, as he stood at the eastern end of the street gazing upon the seething mass, it seemed the most terrifying place in Japan.

Dissolve into the masses.

He closed his eyes, breathed deeply and prepared himself to enter the corporeal maelstrom. In reality he only needed to traverse a couple of blocks and then peel off left to a parallel street.

Natsuo was swallowed up by the LED-kaleidoscope. He felt dizzy, almost drunk, as the noise and lights fuzzed in and out of focus around him. Again, those thoughts, those decade-long entrenched fears, started to take over. A normal evening would see him sat on his sofa drinking beer, watching episodes of Evangelion, yet now he was willingly strolling through a churning mass of people to go and see a woman about a monster.

What the hell am I doing?

He froze, glued to the spot. Everything seemed to spin around him; the glowing street signs, the laughing, chattering masses, the curls of food-smoke. He stood in the middle of a vortex, the points of light and focus turning into long-exposure star-lines. Natsuo covered his eyes and scrunched his face up.

He couldn't do this. He should just go back, go back to his mother. That was the reason for all this after all.

As it was all getting too much someone bumped into Natsuo, jolting him back to reality. He opened his eyes to see who it was, but he saw no-one. Just a faceless passerby who happened to collide with him and who had now melted back into the throng.

Dissolve into the masses...

This small moment and the real-world understanding of what Mr Shi meant had given Natsuo the push he needed to carry on. The irony that the more people there were the harder it was to see anyone was not lost on him. If somebody could walk into you, with nobody looking or caring, and then disappear, then Natsuo could make it another hundred metres.

Bar Sakamachi was on a street that was the classic blueprint of an Osaka back alley. Post-war three-storey buildings in a row, with lines of chaotic cables running the length and crossing over here and there. Messy, but attractive.

At floor level the street was an almost unbroken line of small bars and local shops, with signs and lanterns sporting *kanji, hiragana* and *katakana* scripts, sticking out from the storefronts. Bicycles leant, unlocked, up against the walls next to pot plants and traffic cones. Tubes and ducts crept down the sides of some of the buildings and here and there air conditioning units sat out by the front doors. And, to Natsuo's relief, barely anybody was on the street.

Inside was similarly quiet and unpopulated. In fact, apart from three salarymen semi-asleep drunk and slumped over each other, occasionally moaning and bobbing back and forth like broken metronomes, there was nobody in the bar.

It was dim and seemed almost entirely composed of faded, dark wood surfaces. Behind the bar were countless bottles of whisky, a couple of cabinets containing glasses, and a small fridge. On the bar itself were more whiskies and also bottles of sake. A cosy, low light dropped down from an old-fashioned Victorian chandelier. Every free space was busied with old advertising — Underberg, Jack Daniels, Jameson, monetary bills from different nations, stickers, movie posters. Natsuo felt he was in some dive bar in what someone imagined was the United States.

It smelled of bourbon, beer-soaked counters and barbecue sauce. Natsuo crept quietly towards the bar in an effort not to stir the drunken, suit-wearing men in the corner, looking left and right for anybody resembling a woman called Ichika.

His attempted silence was spoiled as a broad lady in a dirty black t-shirt tucked into black trousers, a headband pulling her hair back, barked out.

'*Irasshaimase*!'

Natsuo jumped. He hadn't noticed her directly in front of him behind the bar. He stared at her, frozen to the spot. She must have been in her sixties but she had a firmness and sharpness clearly honed by years managing the local lushes and businessmen.

'Spit it out then, I haven't time for this.' Natsuo looked around the vacant bar. 'Hmph...Well what'll it be? Beer? Single malt?'

'I...um...I'm looking for somebody.'

The woman raised her eyebrows in expectation. Natsuo opened up the now crumpled paper.

'Ichika Jinja...'

The woman crossed her arms and tensed up.

'Well, that would be me...' She peered at him cautiously. 'I don't know you, so what do you want?'

Natsuo started sweating. He felt like a small boy in front of a teacher knowing he'd done something wrong but unable to identify quite what.

'Um...Mina-san said I should talk to you.'

'Mina?' she said blindsided, unfolding her arms. 'Well, she's an old friend.' Ichika's tone had mellowed considerably, but still had a sting of guarded suspicion about it. 'Why did she send you here?'

Natsuo approached coyly and lent in, paranoid someone in the essentially empty bar might hear.

'Yōkai...' he whispered.

Instantly her demeanour softened. Barbed indifference quickly gave way to surprised intrigue. Ichika turned to the jumble of salarymen still attempting to converse with each other.

'If you're not ordering more I'm closing for an hour.' She called over to them eliciting some non-committal grunts. She picked a bottle of *shōchū* off the shelf, plunked it down in front of them to more pleased mumbles and then flipped the sign on the door from 'Open' to 'Closed'.

'This'll amuse them for an hour or so,' she said to Natsuo nodding towards the drunks in the corner. 'Follow me.'

She led Natsuo behind the bar through a door separated by a veil of hanging beads into a too-small and cluttered room. It seemed to be a multi-purpose space: piled up on the right were boxes of alcohol and food as well as a large refrigerator. In a corner was a coat stand where the staff presumably changed and left their things. A small desk on the right was decorated with a computer and a mess of files and papers.

Dead ahead there was a red door with a lock on it. Natsuo's sense of the thematic knew what was going to happen. Ichika took a key off a chain hanging around her neck. Dramatic, Natsuo thought. And she signalled to him to come through the door with her.

It was as if he had entered a different shop entirely. Behind the door was an even smaller low-lit room that seemed to Natsuo a pastiche of how a foreigner would describe a 'traditional Japanese room'. At the centre of the back wall, directly ahead on entering, was a shrine. There were no photos of people, so it didn't seem to be a family shrine. A table was illuminated by a collection of candles that seemed to crowd around a miniature red torii gate. Above the shrine was a long katana in a speckled mahogany sheathe. Hanging off each wall was a red Japanese lantern, the kind that hung off the sides of restaurants and of which the tourists loved to take photos.

The light suffused the room with a gentle, warm glow, adding a sense of magic to the quiet. Every other space and surface and wall was bedecked with books and papers, some of which looked genuinely ancient. On the ceiling was emblazoned a phoenix curled up into a tense aggressive ball, its multicoloured feathers circling around it, creating a cocoon of brilliance around the orange face and piercing eyes at the centre. Ichika noticed Natsuo staring up.

'Hokusai's "Phoenix Glaring in All Directions". It's painted onto the ceiling of the Gansho-in temple in my hometown Obuse. I think it helps focus me and helps protect.'

'Protect against what?'

'Well, young man, that's what we are going to find out.' She motioned to two plump cushions on the floor in front of the shrine. 'Sit.'

Ichika pulled a tea set out from under the shrine.

'So why did Mina send you to me?'

'I think I see...yōkai,' Natsuo said timidly. Ichika tutted to herself in a way that signified that this wasn't the first occurrence of this.

Once Natsuo was seated she wetted a cloth and began to gently clean each tool, the cups, the tea bowl, the wooden chasen whisk. She then took a small ancient-looking iron teapot, the kama, and filled it with water from a small tap.

As the water began to heat up Ichika picked up the chashaku bowl and added three small spoons of dry matcha. When the water was hot she added one spoonful of it. With the chasen she whisked up the water and powder into a thick creamy tea, which she then offered Natsuo to sip.

'*Dōzo*,' she said gently with a nod as she passed it, Ichika having taken on the countenance of the most professional geishas of Kyoto.

Natsuo sipped the musty and vegetal mixture. It was rich and tasted curative. Finishing his cup, he was offered a kaishi cloth to clean the bowl.

'Tell me your story.'

Natsuo started slowly and methodically from the beginning. The tea ceremony could last hours so he knew inherently not to rush. He first spoke about his life as a Hikikomori and the strange weather that had led him to leave his house in the midst of typhoon season to find his mother. He spoke about the odd things he had seen; the boy in the rain, the scraggly woman who licked herself, the enormous beast in the water. Everything.

As he talked and sipped the fluid movements of Ichika, the low light, the grassy aromas, seemed to take Natsuo away to a place outside of time, a cosy non-place where he felt safe to say anything and everything. Then his story stopped at the point where he found himself now.

Ichika then took the small tea bowl back and then made a one-to-one ratio tea to water that she poured from a height, usucha matcha, and which she then whipped to frothy with the chasen. Again 'dōzo' and Natsuo drank. Lighter, and more fragrant, this tea, though made from the same pounded green dust, was completely different. It reminded him of his grandma.

When Natsuo had finished he handed the bowl back to Ichika, who proceeded to clean everything thoroughly and carefully, as if every part of the tea set was as beloved and precious as a child. Finally, she bowed low, her hands on her thighs. Natsuo bowed.

'Now Natsuo-chan, place your hand through the torii gate.'

Natsuo got to his feet and stepped to the small altar. He hesitated a moment, but then, as if pulled along by the power of the inevitable, put his hand through the small gate.

'I have a theory,' she said calmly.

'OK...' replied Natsuo measuredly; the placid cocoon of safety that seemed to have manifested during the tea ceremony now a memory.

'You'll have to bear with me, and bear what happens. You should be in no danger, but if I am right this will terrify you.'

Natsuo fell silent. He couldn't even begin to imagine what might happen next. Ichika went round the small room with a diminutive upturned metal cone and gently extinguished all the lanterns, leaving just the candles on the shrine-table aflame.

'Don't remove your hand under any circumstances unless I tell you to. Understood?'

'I...'

'Is that understood?'

'Wakata...'

From a small cabinet in the right-hand corner of the room Ichicka took out a forest-green cauldron the size of a casserole dish. It was entirely filled with a grey, volcanic-looking sand. She placed it on the floor at Natsuo's feet and jabbed a few sticks of incense into the sand. She lit them and soon the aromatic, resinous spice aromas floated upwards to prickle Natsuo's nose.

Ichika started to hum words to herself; an incantation, a kotodama. The sacred sound, the power of language.

Yami no tori o himeshi kagi yo,
Shin no sugata o ware no mae ni shimese,
Keiyaku no moto Jinja Ichika ga meijiru.
Dekite.
Torii which hides the power of darkness,
Reveal your true form before me.
I, Ichika Jinja, command you under our contract.

Leave.

The mantra was repeated rhythmically over and over again, each time with more force and anger. The candles flickered, as if a breeze were about to blow them out, but they continued to burn, and the gloom seemed to deepen.

Torii which hides the power of darkness,

Reveal your true form before me.

I, Ichika Jinja, command you under our contract.

Leave!

Ichika had her hands together as if in prayer and her eyes closed, her head slightly bowed. At the end of every verse she would gently clap her hands together and repeat. She was waiting for something. Trying to coax something out. What it could be Natsuo had no idea, but he felt something important was happening and despite his desire to be anywhere else in Japan but here, he left his hand where it was.

Clap.

Torii which hides the power of darkness,

Reveal your true form before me.

I, Ichika Jinja, command you under our contract.

Leave!!

He started to think about his life as a Hikikomori. It was all starting to feel like a memory, though had he not left his house just over a week ago he would have been celebrating his thirtieth birthday alone on the sofa watching anime. A man with no prospects, no hopes and dreams, no future. A decade-long shut-in who didn't think he would ever see his family again, let alone travel to Japan's second largest city to take part in a ukei ritual in the backroom of a whisky bar. He was proud of himself, and his pride was mixed with a defined pang of regret, of wasted potential, of lost time.

Clap.

Torii which hides the power of darkness,

Reveal your true form before me.

I, Ichika Jinja, command you under our contract.

LEAVE.

Natsuo started to feel strange. The feeling you get when there's a bug on your neck or water trickling down your back. It felt like there was something shifting on his shoulders; a weight. More than a weight now, he could sense a presence. Something real above him. No longer was it a concept, an idea, a sixth sense. Natsuo now knew there to be a physical thing behind him, above him, on him.

Clap.

Torii which hides the power of darkness,

Reveal your true form before me.

I, Ichika Jinja, command you under our contract.

LEAVE!!

He turned his head a few degrees and saw something appear from the gloom. He was suddenly afraid; afraid of this presence, this pressure looming down on him.

Ichika's eyes opened, looked at his, then looked above and behind him, then back at Natsuo with a mixture of fear and righteous indignation. A wind seemed to blow through the room; a whistling rush that rose in volume, filling the ears and rustling the hair.

'Face it, boy!' Ichika half shouted, half hissed.

Natsuo's blood ran cold, shot down to his feet, chilling him. He turned his head just enough to spy the entity behind him. A semi-translucent figure, human and pale in a scraggly robes, hovered above him. It had long and unkempt hair that somehow left its head and went all down its back forming a sort of fur cape. Its mouth was open in a toothless, stupid grimace and its grey-blue skin shimmered like milky water. Bony arms held him by the shoulders, knobbly fingers clasped weightlessly around Natsuo's collar. But the apparition was silent, staring at him. He flicked his eyes down. There were no legs, just a tapering off of matter.

The split second was enough to fill Natsuo with enough fear to last a lifetime. A shiver trickled down his neck and he snapped his head back, staring with pleading eyes at Ichika.

'You must stare it down, boy!' Ichika shouted, the noise of the fantastical wind now moaning as it rattled the lanterns on the walls.

Natsuo turned back to the phantom. He couldn't speak but he now found his eyes locked on to the spirit's and he couldn't look away.

The eyes, its eyes, looked sad, hopeless. Pathetic even. They were the dimmed eyes that Natsuo had seen in his mirror every day for a decade. He started to feel less scared, as if this strange floating being was tragic. Like he was. Like he had been anyway. He felt an anger start to marble in with his fear. After everything he had been through, and now this. It wasn't fair.

The light of the lanterns started to intensify and the candles seemed to leap and burn more fiercely. The creature, semi-immobile, gawping at him, seemed to fade slightly. Like an old Victorian photo, the apparition looked less concentrated. The noise in the room increased, a sad howling seemed to whistle around the walls.

'All your fear, all your cowardice...' Ichika seemed to almost shout over the turbulence. 'This had been feeding off you boy. For years!' Natsuo's eyes were streaming. The force of the origin-less wind, the fear and anger. He no longer purely feared this phantasm, he hated it. 'Don't let it! It's just a parasite! Think about what you'll be without it!'

The anger Natsuo felt now warped into wrath and a huge bulging sensation of regret. Was this thing the cause of his seclusion? His years of hiding away? This spectral beast the reason he became a Hikikomori?

His neurons snap-fired questions and hypotheticals though his head; of what ifs and how-it-could-have-beens. His whole mind lit up with images of potential. Wasted due to this monster, this yōkai.

Clap.

He, Natsuo Hirawa, commands you under our contract.

LEAVE!!!

The ghostly figure started to fade out, become less realised. As its contorted, miserable face and hair-covered robes began to dissipate it emitted light, as a dying star. Energy and entropy of the hidden realm.

The brightness pulsated and intensified to a point at which both Ichika and Natsuo had to cover their eyes. A final dazzling whiteout flooded the room and was accompanied by a mournful scream and a gust of wind.

Then black.

The lanterns had gone out and the candle-wicks fallen dark.

Nothing but silence. The kind of silence that throbs in the ears, reminds you your blood is flowing.

Bit by bit the warm glow of the lanterns came back on as Ichika went around lighting them anew. Natsuo still stood by the altar; his forehead slick with sweat and his hair ruffled.

'You can remove your hand now boy. It's gone.'

'What...was that?'

'Buruburu.'

Natsuo was breathing heavily. He slowly removed his hands and looked at Ichika. She paused momentarily, catching herself for a split second, and then spoke.

'A buruburu is born when humans perform acts of cowardice. Traditionally this could have been running away from battle for example. They possess people by clinging to their shirt collars and touching the back of the neck. They are the spirits of cowardice. They feed off that as well as nervousness and shame.

'I believe that thing must have latched on at some point in your life and stayed with you. Judging by the energy it emitted it must have been a long time. I don't know if you —'

'Thirteen years,' Natsuo said under his breath.

'What's that?'

'I am...was...a Hikikomori. Before just over a week ago I hadn't left my flat in over thirteen years.'

Ichika said nothing. She just nodded with eyes full of understanding and pity. They both understood the chilling ramifications that perhaps for that long an entity had been getting fat and full on Natsuo during his years shut away. A barely moving, self-sufficient and private buffet for a parasitic yōkai.

'I think your recent adventures, which, if you'll excuse my phrasing, by your standard have been quite a tumultuous change, helped make it visible. Like a tick on a dog that you can see with your own eyes. How do you feel?'

'Like a weight has been lifted.' He paused. 'So it's all real...'

'It seems so. And now you're free.' Ichika recalled Natsuo's dreams, about the long-nosed tengu that had been calling out to him in the dreamworld. 'But it seems you have a task ahead.'

'How's that?'

Ichika went over to a bookshelf and flitted through various tomes that had been piled in and on top of each other. She pulled out one rather old, brown leather-bound book.

'There is a legend throughout many of our country's texts. A story. Something that may have happened, or will happen. A problem in hell, gods sparring, creatures from the underworld appearing on the earthly plain, a sort of holy battle. That sort of thing.'

She opened the book.

'Look at this one for example. Momotarō; you know it?'

'I don't...'

'He's a local hero of Okayama. So not too far from your island. The story goes that Momotarō was born from a giant peach, which was found floating down a river by an old woman. She and her husband brought up the child as they had none of their own. The young boy explained that he had been bestowed to them by the kami. Now, why the gods would do this isn't really explained, but anyway. When he became a teenager, he left home to fight a band of Oni that were terrifying the land. He did this by seeking them out on the island where they lived — Onigashima. On his adventure he befriended a talking dog, monkey and a pheasant and together they managed to get into the demons' fort and vanquish them with the magic hammer, the uchide no kozuchi.'

Natsuo looked at her blankly, blinking.

'What I mean to say is that Momotarō is just one example of an idea as old as stories have existed. A "chosen one" or hero figure set to defeat evil.' Ichika paused.

'Wait...you mean me? I'm a Momotarō?'

'I don't know. But if this tengu really is beckoning you in dreams, yōkai are starting to appear in number, and Japan is being blasted by suspicious storms, then I think...' She paused trying to find the words, herself not knowing where her sentence was going. 'I think you should go to that mountain. Seek out the tengu.'

Natsuo got up and bowed deeply. This woman had helped free him of a burden succubus. He would never forget that.

'And hurry boy. They say twin typhoons are going to strike the coasts of Kansai.'

Natsuo nodded with a steely confidence he'd never had before.

'Seek out Sōjōbō. And seek him swiftly.'

Chapter Five: Yama
山

Mountain.

Kyoto and Tokyo share a couple of things in common. Firstly, they share the status of being 'a capital of Japan'. And secondly their names are linked.

Kyoto means 'Imperial Capital' as for more than one thousand years this temple-filled city, nestled in a large bowl of mountains, was the capital of Japan. The emperor, the little god-man, sat plump here until the daimyos and shōgun decided one day enough was enough. Tokugawa Ieyasu dealt the final blow to the western city and moved the capital east. He created a new seat of power at Edo, a somewhat innocuous fishing village and which was later renamed Tokyo in 1868: the 'eastern imperial capital'. There the similarities stop.

Tokyo is a broiling, multifaceted megapolis, at once expansive and claustrophobic. Kyoto, though large, is more stately, more prim and refined.

Tokyo wears the many masks of what it means to be Japan under one neon-lit roof: modernity and history, the modern and the old, the new and exciting blending with the ancient. A city where Commodore Perry arrived with the Black Ships and all but forced the country to open to the world.

Kyoto is where the traditions of old live and breathe. A private city of geishas and tea houses, where lanterns, sliding doors and curtains contain a world unknowable for most people.

Kyoto still sees itself as the rightful centre of the country, the cultural heart if nothing else. Tokyo's fourteen million versus Kyoto's one and half. It was in Kyoto on a grim and rainy afternoon that Natsuo found himself, saturated to his boots.

The previous night Natsuo had explained to his mother what had happened in the bar with Ichika. Somewhat bleakly the fact that a buruburu had been living off Natsuo for more than a decade seemed to give his mother a bit more peace. A touch of absolution. But Natsuo understood and he bore no grudge. He felt more self-assured and confident. A new start.

'She's right you know.'

'Who?'

'That woman in the bar.'

'But mother, I just found you.'

'And you will again. I'm not going anywhere fast.' Yui took her son's hands in hers. 'Listen. We may have not been the best parents. We ignored problems instead of dealing with them. I don't want to say we were products of that generation and use it as an excuse, but I swear your father and I did love you. We just didn't know what to do. It's complicated. And now you're better. You're free. I would feel guilty if you stayed inside one more minute. I want you to go out, see things, experience things, have adventures. Everything you missed because of that creature, because of us, because of what we thought we had to do...'

It was in that instant Natsuo realised he maybe had never really known his parents. But then he thought to himself, do we ever? We always just see them as concepts; as mother and father. They are never fully-formed people with their own lives and pasts and secrets. He vowed to amend this on his return.

'Also,' Yui Hirawa started, touching Natsuo on the arm, 'your father he...' She seemed to lose herself trying to find the words. 'He...oh, I don't know how to say.'

'Mother, I should go. You can tell me when I'm back.' Natsuo smiled. 'It's OK.'

She hugged him, gave him some money, tousled his hair, hailed Mr Shi to take her son to Shin-Osaka station, and with that he was off to the old capital.

Mr Shi had a friend who ran a traditional ryokan in the old Gion neighbourhood and had agreed to put Natsuo up for a night or two at a generously discounted rate. The old inn was on a small, cobbled street just off the grand Kenninji temple.

Nastuo had arrived a little too early for check-in. Friend or not, the timetables were still strictly obeyed, so, to get out of the gloomy grey sheet of rain that once again forbade an approaching storm, Natsuo ducked into a small restaurant with the word "Musoshin" above the door and a glowing red lantern illuminating the smoking rain around it that read ramen. The perfect food to warm up.

He slid the door open and was welcomed by the ubiquitous calls of welcome from the bandana-wearing chefs behind the bar. Natsuo was almost the only customer apart from one ancient-looking man in a tracksuit at the far end of the bar and a young couple slurping up broth, both engrossed in their phone screens. Even though he hadn't been out since a teenager, the surroundings were instantly familiar. The blueprint for a ramen shop had been followed to a tee; the kind repeated in every town, village, movie, comic and cartoon.

Immediately as he entered Natsuo saw a large ordering point, a vending-machine-type tower of buttons with prices and scribbled words like tonkotsu, kimuchi or shio. One caught his eye: Gion black ramen. He fed in a 1000¥ note and was spat out a 50¥ coin and a receipt.

The bar was narrow. On the left side was a bank of ten chairs pulled up to a long counter upon which there were boxes of napkins, pots of complimentary matcha powder and shichimi chilli powder as well as chopsticks. Immediately in front of the seated counter area was a raised bar upon which rested some bottles of sake and where the chefs would place the bowls of noodles for the customers to take. He sat down on the third chair along and passed the small receipt to one of the chefs who bowed seriously.

'Kuro soba!' the young chef called, eliciting a grunt from the other.

A small poster by the door explained that their signature broth was made of black sesame, which was made by sesame specialists Gion Murata, whilst their seven-spice mix was produced by Hararyokaku; the latter having been in the spice trade since 1704. Natsuo thought there was a certain poetry and romance to eating a black ramen during a rainstorm and sprinkling spices from a three-hundred-year-old recipe over the top.

'Dōzo!'

An obsidian-black ceramic bowl arrived, steaming, at Natsuo's eye-line. Four slices of pork belly, some bamboo, half an egg and green onion seemed held in artistic suspension on the top of a dark grey, creamy broth, the perfection of which was only spoiled by a few drops of oil and some scattered black sesame seeds.

'*Itadakimasu*,' Natsuo said to himself, before launching into the ramen. As the smokiness of the soup whirled around his head, he opened his phone and checked on his route to the mountain. He would rest at the ryokan tonight and head up at first light. Just as Mr Shi had made him do a week before.

Natsuo opened the lid of the little matcha box in front of him. Inside was a small wooden spoon and a quicksand of forest-green powder. He tipped a couple of spoonfuls into a plastic cup and poured hot water out of a thermal jug. As the desiccated tea leaves dissolved, the garden-funk wafted up into his nostrils. He drank deeply and allowed the tea to warm him up.

As he opened his eyes, he then noticed that the old man at the far end of the counter was looking at him with a mischievous glint in his still-youthful eyes. Natsuo, feeling awkward and not knowing what to say, just smiled quietly and bowed.

'So young man. You see 'em too, eh?'

'Hmm?'

The old man finished his beer and shuffled over to Natsuo's side, leaning in.

'Yōkai...' he whispered conspiratorially.

Natsuo was stunned and for a few moments the only sound that hung in the air between the two of them was that of knives on chopping boards and the sliding doors rumbling in the wind.

'How did you...'

'You can tell who's come in contact with them. They have a different aura. Compared to someone who doesn't believe in them at all.'

'So, you've seen them too?'

'Oh yes, my boy. I've known them all my life. But never seen so many as now. It's the storms you see. Trouble upstairs,' he said, pointing upwards. 'There are yōkai that don't want to be seen, then those who need to be seen, those who are glimpsed and those who enjoy becoming an event that makes a human question his eyes.

'When someone has seen, or better to say, experienced a yōkai, that belief in their existence is set. You can then always see them. That isn't to say they are always there, all the time. It's odd. I've been for years without seeing them, and then one day, a wall will be grinning at me with its tongue out or a one-eyed umbrella will be bouncing around a courtyard on one spindly leg. It seems almost random.

'So, young man, what have you seen?'

Natsuo swallowed hard, trying to process the information.

'Many things. Though I had a...buruburu...on me for years.'

'Ah, you poor lad,' the man said thoughtfully. 'Still, I've generally found that once you know them, once you see them and believe in them, they tend to not bother with you as much. Most feed off the reactions from us poor humans. Though, better stay clear of the *Onna*; those wretched women will always try and get you somehow.'

'When did you first see a yōkai?' Natsuo asked, utterly spellbound by the old man.

'Oh, a long time ago. I must have been about ten years old. I was playing in the local forest with my family pet. A big, stupid basset hound called Kato. At some point he wandered off, so I called out his name over and over again, but he wouldn't come. I thought he may have been running about chasing fish in the fast, rocky river that ran through the woods, that maybe the silly dog couldn't hear me over the crashing water. It was a beautiful river...

'Anyway, I headed down to the river's edge but couldn't see Kato. Then I heard some shifting water to my right and, thinking maybe Kato had fallen in, crouched down to peer into the waters. Well, I can tell you boy, that noise was not from my dog.'

'A yōkai...'

'A face slowly appeared out of the water. A green, reptilian face, but also quite human. It had red eyes and a turtle-beak mouth. Then the shoulders and torso came out too. Some...warped man with dappled green frog-skin and webbed hands. On its back was a tortoise shell and, on its head, very much part of its skull, a strange dish filled with water.'

'A kappa?'

'Aye lad, it was a kappa.' The man smiled. 'It croaked at me as if it were laughing and, as it slowly stood up in the water, I screamed, naturally, and backed up on to the riverbank. Now I was a ten-year-old boy in the days before the television and these internet phones. These folk stories were ingrained in me well, you see. I knew that kappa, they said, tried not to go on land. But this one slowly crept out of the river onto the rocks with its big, webbed feet.'

'Did it attack you?'

'No, it just stared at me and slowly moved toward me. Kappa aren't usually one of the monsters you need to be worried about. Most of the time they are tricksy and can be rather smart. Indeed, there is a cunning in their crimson eyes. The stories say their favourite food is cucumbers...Though they have been known to dine on the entrails of humans. Especially anuses.'

'Ergh...'

'Haha, yes. Well. I knew a trick. Well, at least it was something the legends said. The kappa was now fully on land, stood in front of me, breathing a gurgling breath, as if its chest were filled with water. It stank of fish and was poised in a way that said "in any moment I shall lunge for you".'

'So, what was the trick?'

'I bowed.'

'You...bowed?'

'Among many things, the kappa, so went the tales, are fiercely honourable creatures. If you bow to one then they must bow back. I bowed low and so the creature felt obliged to return the same. The water in the monster's head-dish spilled out. Japanese folklore says that the water-filled depression in the head of a kappa is the source of its power and must be filled at all times or the creature will grow weak and even die.'

'Did it?'

'A-ha; no. I sensed a sort of disappointment from the yōkai. That the creature felt bested. The kappa just exhaled and slowly backed away, slipping back into the river and under the water.'

'What happened to your dog? Did the kappa get it?'

'No! The stupid mutt had run home and spent the last hour huffing and passing wind under my mother's feet as she prepared the rice for dinner!'

Natsuo laughed. It was then also he realised he hadn't laughed for so long. A real laugh with another person. It felt good.

The wind rattled the door of the ramen bar and the little electric lights illuminating the bar fluttered on and off momentarily.

'So boy, you're here for a reason no doubt.'

'I'm going to Mount Kurama.'

The old man grunted softly, as though he understood completely.

'Well, take care, for here there be dragons. Kyoto is an old place with old magic, old ghouls. Yōkai have always gathered where there are people and where there is tradition.'

Natsuo excused himself to go to the bathroom. He splashed water on his face and looked at his reflection in the mirror. There was a new strength in his dark brown eyes. Tomorrow he would go to the mountain, meet Sōjōbō, and get answers to this mad path his life had been taking.

When he came back into the restaurant the old man was nowhere to be seen, but placed next to Natsuo's bowl of ramen was a small cucumber. Natsuo smiled and finished his noodles.

Yuzuya Ryokan was owned by a very dapper man called Shinjiro Kenji. He was the epitome of Japanese hospitality and ran the traditional inn as if it were a top hotel. He and an elegant woman in a dark blue kimono welcomed Natsuo with low bows. Kenji wore a dark blue, double-breasted suit and a bright red cravat that gave him the air of a debonair British gentleman.

'Hirawa-san, welcome.'

'Arigato gozaimasu,' said Natsuo, bowing deeply and feeling a little uncomfortable with the generous formality.

'A friend of Mr Shi is a friend of ours. Dōzo.' Shinjiro signalled for Natsuo to remove his shoes, take some slippers and follow the lady. 'This is Yuki. She'll show you to your room. Anything you need, she will be there to help. Because of the strange weather, there are only a couple of other guests here tonight, so you almost have the place to yourself. At seven o'clock we will bring dinner. We hope you enjoy a peaceful stay.'

Natsuo followed Yuki down a series of wooden corridors lined with discreet sliding doors that indicated the allocation of rooms. It felt to him more like a 17th century wealthy residence rather than an upscale hotel.

After a few turns Natsuo was somewhat lost, with no real concept of which direction he was facing. Such was the nature of the labyrinthine timber buildings of old Japan. Places of whispers and hidden intrigues, not great halls and ballrooms.

'*Kochira desu*,' Yuki said quietly as she came to a halt. She slid the door open and motioned for Natsuo to enter. 'If you need anything you can use the small phone here by the door.'

The room was more expansive than Natsuo had imagined. He smiled to himself thinking that Mr Shi must have set this up to give him a good time.

There were a couple of connected spaces. A large communal area with a low table and irori tea pit in the centre, a washing room with a private *ofuro* bathtub backed by a glass window that gave an intimate view to an internal patio with reeds and bamboo, and a small sleeping room with a roll-out futon bed. The walls were reed-greens and sandalwood browns. Fine borders of wood gave the room a squared geometry and an ambience of perfect order and stillness. Nothing was out of place. It was simple and sparse, but not bare. Here and there was a painting, something clean and tasteful, a landscape or crane. When Yuki left Natsuo felt suddenly exhausted. He rolled out the futon and instantly fell asleep.

Natsuo stood atop a steaming brown-ash bluff. The air smelled of sulphur and fire; aromas carried to Natsuo by a fierce hot wind that stung his face. Similar smouldering peaks and hills dotted a dark brown hell-scape. Down in the dark, fire-pocked gloom of the valley floor he saw a wide river across which some forms could be seen fording, with others crossing a bridge, and yet others attempting to cross through what seemed like rapids. A mournful groaning and wailing clung to the air and hovered over the whole scene. Those who crossed were funnelled towards two enormous humanoid creatures that, even from his position atop the wind-swept bluff, Natsuo could make out as demons, taking the clothes from each person and hanging them on skeletal trees. Past the arriving line of souls was a dark vista of blasted rocks, gashes in the earth spewing out toxic gases, battered little huts, flocks of black birds, fireballs falling from the sky and bubbling lakes of tar. '*Meido*.' A voice came by Natsuo's ear. He spun and saw nothing. A voice carried on the wind. Behind him was a mountain; the peak of which pierced a smoky layer of clouds. Was the voice from there? 'A journey lays ahead of you.' The voice again. Suddenly the ground started to tremble. The mountain behind him was quivering, igneous chunks sliding down the sides. Suddenly it stopped and an eerie silence quieted the scene. The mountain seemed to breathe in, its slopes caving in, and then the whole thing exploded.

Natsuo awoke, sweating. Another nightmare.

No sooner had he awoken than a quiet female voice arrived with a tap on his door. It was Yuki telling him dinner would be served. He looked at his watch and saw he had been asleep for four solid hours.

'*Chotto matte, kudasai*,' Natsuo gargled, asking her to wait a moment. He was sweating all over, so went to wash his face and change into the *yukata* robe provided in the room. He returned to the main room and sat down on his knees by the low, black mahogany table in the centre. 'Hai.'

Yuki slid the door aside and appeared in a moonlight-grey kimono, sat in the hallway on her knees. She placed her hands on her lap, bowed, then stood up, taking a large tray of food in her hands, and, stooping in submission slightly, shuffled in. She placed the tray down with another bow.

Kaiseki, a multi-course symphony of dishes, aromas, textures, flavours and concepts. A ballet of sensory play and techniques; raw, grilled, fermented, boiled and pickled. A colourful playground of smells and sights where the chef combines modernity with heritage, kaiseki is one of the cornerstones of the traditional ryokan. Kyoto was the spiritual home of this food and Natsuo had never experienced it. Yuki left a menu and wished him a pleasant meal.

'Omatase itashimashta.'

Natsuo wondered if it was that obvious that he had no clue about the 15-plate edible painting before him, or if all guests received one.

When she had left, he set about deciphering the little piece of paper in front of him and tried to identify which was what on the tray.

To eat...

Sakizuke - ugni butter on homemade senbei

Hassun - tilefish topped with seaweed, ginkgo nuts, and summer roll with foraged herbs. Persimmon dressed with ground sesame and sansho.

Mukōzuke - summer sashimi: octopus, conger eel, one-year fermented aji-mackerel

Takiawase - Kansai soup; with wild ginger, aged tofu, white miso and lobster dashi

Futamono - sweetcorn porridge soup topped with blackened soy nameko and roasted nagaimo

Yakimono - Yin Yang: blade of charred A5 Kobe topped with shrimp butter/Hibachi prawn topped with beef-compote cube

Su-zakana - Matcha-yuzu citrus tablet

Suimono - light Shikoku yuzu broth

Hiyashi-bachi - grilled miso myoga and tempura goya bitter melon

Shiizakana - mini-shabu; wagyu, shiitake, napa cabbage, summer onion with udon and ponzu glaze

Gohan - steamed Arashiyama rice with marinated otoro

Kō no mono - pickled vegetables from our garden

Tome-wan - chazuke-style soup: crispy rice in wild tea-herb broth

Mizumono - mountain fruit in white miso, speckled with bee larvae and black sesame

To drink...

Osake: Nishiyama Shuzojo Junmai Daiginjo sake, Kizakura beer (on request).

Uji matcha tea

Water

Sitting there before this menagerie of little pots and plates and dishes, Natsuo had to use his phone to decipher some of the ingredients. Living off pizzas, ramen and rice variations for so long had left his gastronomic vernacular as it was when he was a teenager.

The textures, flavours, colour palette and aromas left him almost breathless. Every slow, pensive bite he took made his pulse race and his mind do somersaults. It also made him sad. He had missed out on so much. There was so much he didn't know. Not just food, but life, love, friendship. He had lost the time of his life when he should have been travelling and trying new things, forging new connections, finding out who would be the friends that would stay with him. But he had missed all that. His had been a world of comics, cartoons and isolation.

As he finished his meal, with the little wooden cup of bosky green tea, he started to cry. Quiet tears rolled down his cheeks and pitter-pattered onto the tray. A new dawn, a sunrise filled his soul, and the sadness melted into an intense enthusiasm. He realised so much joy and discovery lay ahead of him.

When Yuki had removed the empty plates Natsuo had excused himself from the ryokan, deciding to stroll the nighttime streets of Gion.

It was Kyoto's archetypal traditional neighbourhood. A cobbled, low-roofed warren of sliding doors and wooden buildings that hid tea houses and geishas. A place where around any corner you could find either a humble restaurant, a white-faced geiko in a kimono shuffling past coyly or a horde of be-camera'd Americans.

Knowing he wouldn't have much time in the coming days, Natsuo decided to brave the rain and at least try to absorb some of the atmosphere of the shining stones, warm timber beams and flapping red lanterns. Kyoto didn't stop because of bad weather.

The old entertainment district had offered amusement to both beggars with a coin and feudal lords since the 17th century with *chaya* tea houses and merchants fanning out from the Yasaka shrine and lining the Kamo river.

Visually it transported Natsuo back in time to a world of wandering warriors, greedy daimyos and ladies of the night. A city of swords, fine fabrics and ornate fans. Walking through the little alleys, past hidden-away temples and tiny homes, one couldn't escape the feeling of exploring a movie set.

As beautiful as the old town was, the rain was getting the better of Natsuo and his feet were already sodden. He quickened his pace back to the ryokan but with the fall of night and the heavy downpour darkening the already tenebrous lanes, Natsuo was soon lost.

Another problem was that he had taken the, now clearly bad, decision of leaving his phone to charge in the room. He had no idea where he was; only that somewhere in the web of streets was his hotel. If he could find somebody to point him towards the Kenninji shrine he would be fine. But where to find someone on a night like this?

After some minutes wandering aimlessly around a tight clutch of huddled alleys and houses called Hashimotocho he spied some warm orange light spilling out from a window and setting aglow the puddles on the street. He ran over to the building and saw it was a tea house; one of the few establishments that would never be lacking in clients.

To Natsuo's disappointment, despite the lights being on and a perceptible mild hubbub leaking out from within, there was a small sign hanging on the door announcing it was closed.

He walked towards one of the windows and tried to peek through the partitions. Nobody. At the second window he saw a woman lying with her back to him on a dark purple mattress in the middle of a tatami floor. On the warm cream-coloured walls hung artwork of cherry trees and mountains. The light, that orange suffusing glow that crept out into the rain to illuminate his cheeks, came from floor-lamps placed at intervals along the walls. There was a little unlit oil lamp at her back too, presumably for reading in the moments when she didn't have to entertain guests.

Natsuo didn't know what to do. This resting woman was the only person around, but he had no desire to rudely awaken her to simply ask for directions.

As he debated what to do, the lady's head started to turn.

Oh good, she's awake.

As Natsuo worded and reworded the way he planned to attract her attention, he noticed the woman's head kept turning. Her body was still but yet her head continued to turn until it was facing Natsuo's direction. A full 180 degrees.

A contortionist?

He had never seen a body twist like that. It was unsettling. The woman's eyes opened lazily as if awakening. She looked at the little oil lamp in front of her and suddenly had on her a face of hunger. She began to lap up the oil in the lamp, like some thirsty cat at the cream.

Who was this strange woman?

At this grotesque scene Natsuo started to think maybe he would brave the rain and find somebody else for directions. Someone less... odd.

The woman stopped lapping at the lamp oil and was staring right at him. Natsuo froze. She smiled vacantly, her body still motionless with her back to the window. Natsuo decided he now might as well ask, so above the rain he shouted through the thin window.

'I'm lost, can you help me?'

No response, yet the woman still stared dumbly at him.

'I said I'm lost, could you help me please?'

The woman's eyebrows arched, giving an air of playful mischievousness to her countenance, and in an instant her face was pressed up to the glass directly in front of Natsuo's. He screamed but was frozen to the spot.

How had she moved so fast?

'I'm lost...' Natsuo croaked, unable to think straight. He couldn't take his eyes off the woman's face. She was beautiful but she still didn't speak to him.

Her face started swimming about and moving like a cobra. It was then he noticed her neck extending a couple of metres back to the still immobile body. She hadn't stirred but her neck had sprung away from its home, leaving a head to freely move around at a distance from her shoulders.

At this realisation Natsuo backed away, mouth agape, and speechless still.

Yōkai...

Slowly he moved away from the room along the front of the tea-house, following the line of glowing windows. The woman's face followed him, snaking in and out of different rooms, each time meeting Natsuo at the window as he passed. At the last one before he reached the end of the building, the woman spoke.

'Boy...'

Natsuo turned and looked at her, seeing the sinuous trail of skin snaking away behind the face. As he met her gaze, transfixed into utter submission and so weirded out that he had to look, she smiled and spoke again.

'Boo!'

Natsuo stumbled back into the street, the woman's face glaring and grinning at him from the dry. He ran off into the rain trying to put as much distance between him and that cursed tea house as possible. The sound of laughter filtering through the cold rush of the downpour. He didn't care if he was lost.

He ran until he was wet through and panting hard. Ever since leaving his home in Kochi his life had been a nonstop set of challenges. He was reminded of an English expression he had once learned: 'baptism of fire'. Life was testing this new recruit. It was as if the world was saying to him, 'welcome, but you've got to earn your place'. He wondered if the yōkai were part of that plan, there to test him. He shook this thought away as self-aggrandising.

His breathing slowed and a form of internal strength returned. He had only been spooked; nothing had happened. He was still just a lost Shikoku man in the Kyoto backstreets.

He looked up and realised where he was. In front of him was a grand wooden, white-walled temple hall with a lofty and sweeping roof. There were some ornate, sculpted trees encased in rope, unlit rock lanterns and sodden pieces of prayer-paper flapping wildly in the wind. Kenninji.

Somehow, he had made it back to where he needed to be. Had his subconscious found a route through the storm? Had the yōkai played some trick? Was it sheer dumb luck? Natsuo didn't have time to care.

He arrived back at Yuzuya where he apologised to Shinjiro for his current state.

'Well, I must say I was surprised when you left in just a coat Natsuo-san.' He chuckled warmly helping Natsuo to remove his waterproof. 'I will send Yuki to you with a warmed, thick and, more importantly, dry yukata for you presently.'

'I had a strange evening so I think I shall bathe first.'

'Very well. Just ring the phone when you want.'

Natsuo felt separate from himself, as if his consciousness was floating above him. His legs throbbed pleasingly from the hot water and the warm vapours filled his head. He sat in the deep ofuro with the water up to his chin.

A part of Japanese culture he had always loved was the bath. Unlike most westerners, the Japanese liked to soak in tubs of constantly replenished hot water. You washed yourself, yes, but you also took time to drift away from the world.

In Kochi there were the public baths, the local *onsen*, and of course the family home had an ofuro, but he had only once been to an onsen out in the countryside. His memories were vague though, as he must have been very young at the time. It was in the town of Matsuyama at the Dogo Onsen.

He remembered various rooms with hot steaming pools of water, unclothed men walking around, old guys soaking like snow monkeys with flannels on their heads, doubled-up naked men washing themselves aggressively with soap and little buckets of cool water.

What Natsuo wasn't sure of was how much was real memory and how much had been romanticised. The film *Spirited Away* had used Dogo Onsen as inspiration for its chaotic, fume-filled, multi-level bathhouse. Either way, memory or warped reality, Natsuo had always loved a bath. And this ryokan one was no different. Silence, but for the trickling of hot water keeping the temperature up.

Natsuo felt the warmth bringing him back to life, but he wasn't sure he wanted to go. Here in the false safety of the water, the little fantasy land where the prickly heat tingled his body and the worries of yōkai, long-necked women, and prophesies seemed a distant memory, a joke, a non-thing, Natsuo thought about forgetting his adventure. Wouldn't it be much easier just to go back to his mother and let someone else deal with...whatever needed to be dealt with?

As his mind reconnected with his body and the placid little world he had created for himself started to recede into a blur of reality and rationality, he opened his eyes. No, for Natsuo the mountain lay ahead. He looked at his hands, his fingers pruned up and wrinkled. He couldn't just run away from this.

He got out of the ofuro, dried off in a large towel, rang the phone to call Yuki, lit the little fire in the irori and warmed up the teapot. Yuki arrived a few minutes later with a beautiful dark blue and grey yukata wrapped around a cast-metal warming iron. It had an elegant oriental dragon embossed in azure silk over the left breast. Yuki noticed Natsuo's gaze.

'Seiryū; one of the four guardians. The shijin.'

'Shijin..?'

'They are taoist. You have Genbu, the giant tortoise wrapped up in a vast serpent, who is the guardian of the north. He represents knowledge, purity and long life. Then we have Suzaku, the fiery phoenix and guardian of the south. They say it represents the virtue of propriety. Then there's my favourite Byakko, the white tiger and guardian of the west. He represents righteousness and bravery. A protector. In Kyoto we venerate Seiryū the most. The protector of the east who represents strength, ferocity, creativity and benevolence.'

Natsuo took the yukata from her, put it on and passed his hand over the smooth fabric of the dragon symbol.

'If you go to the Kiyomizu temple tomorrow you'll see a statue of the dragon at the entrance,' said Yuki with a placid smile.

'Tomorrow I'll be heading to Mount Kurama.'

The slightest hint of a quizzical expression flashed across Yuki's brow like lightning. It was there and then it was gone as if her professional training quickly asserted dominance to regain composure.

'Natsuo-san, if I may ask, why would you want to go to Kurama-yama during the typhoon? They say tomorrow evening onwards we should expect very fierce weather.'

There was a pause as Natsuo thought of what to say. Anybody who didn't already know what he was doing had yet to ask him about his plans. He couldn't say 'Oh, I'm going to meet a long-nosed, fairy-king monster who's been calling me through my dreams.' No, he couldn't say that. But then, having lived so sheltered for so long, he also had no talent for lying.

'I've got an appointment with someone there.'

'On the mountain..?'

'Yes...'

'Tomorrow?'

'Hai.'

'During a typhoon..?'

'Mm...'

Yuki's left eyebrow arched almost imperceptibly.

'Shinjiro-san said that when you arrived in the rain you told him you had had a strange night.' The eyebrow flattened out demurely, innocently. 'What happened, may I ask?'

'Oh...' Natsuo was caught off guard. 'I, well, it was raining, and I got turned around you see. Completely lost in the rain.'

'So how did you find your way back?'

'A lady at a teahouse gave me directions.'

'A lady at a teahouse?'

'Mm.'

'Which teahouse was it, do you remember?'

'No, I, as I say I was lost in the rain, so I didn't know where I was.'

Natsuo was being carried along by questions that he seemed powerless not to answer. Yuki's eyes were fixed on his, and his on hers. All the world blurred out at the edges and all he saw was Yuki's face.

'This woman, was she beautiful?'

'Yes, very.'

Her voice was calm and soothing, like a honeyed-balm coating Natsuo's mind. It wasn't that Natsuo didn't want to tell her the truth, or was trying not to, it was as if he wanted to tell her everything.

'Did she wear a fine kimono?'

'Yes.'

It felt good to get these odd thoughts off his chest, to share them with someone. Even though that person was merely a hotel-worker, it felt right to tell Yuki these happenings.

'Did she have a...' Yuki seemed to turn the last part of the question around on her tongue before gently asking, '...long neck.'

Natsuo froze, a chill spiking through his back down to his feet.

'*Rokurokubi*,' Yuki whispered. Suddenly her countenance changed. The almost hungry and beckoning eyes were replaced by a vision of motherly care and hospitality. Natsuo felt released from her gaze.

'What just happened?'

'I'm sorry, Natsuo-san. I used some hypnosis on you. It was rude and you didn't deserve it. But I wanted to be sure.'

'Sure of what?' Natsuo had no idea what was going on.

'Of what you had seen.'

'The woman?'

'Exactly.' Yuki signalled for Natsuo to sit at the irori. She joined him and poured two cups of tea.

'We haven't had many visitors to the ryokan over the last few weeks as you can probably imagine. But, despite the weather, this is still Kyoto, so we get visitors even in the worst times. A few weeks ago, we had a man here, a tired manager from the Shimadzu machine construction plant in Nishōjī. He had travelled to us from the northwest of the city just to get away for one weekend. You know what these salarymen are like, they never rest, they just work from dawn till dusk never seeing their families and never resting. We often get their type here.

'They often spend hours in the baths or spend more money than they should in the top teahouses and on personal geisha. They tell their wives and kids that it's a work trip, come here, disconnect from the world, foot the bill, and then return to their lives, coming up with excuses for the spending.'

Yuki straightened the folds and crinkles of her kimono so they were flattened to smooth.

'One night this particular man comes in bedraggled from the rain, much like you, with a face of terror and fear. I thought him drunk, but he had only had tea he said. He was crazed and clutched me and was almost weeping. I didn't say anything. My job is to attend to our guests, not to judge or interfere. After a few moments, presumably feeling safe in our inn he looked at me. "A woman...I saw a woman..." Now this isn't an uncommon thing to hear. There are stories of unscrupulous or perhaps fake *geiko* and *geigi* taking advantage of these sorry souls and their lonely purse strings. But this was different. "Her neck, it followed me. She was...was a monster." In that moment I knew what he had seen.

'Rokurokubi used to be women but were turned into creatures whose heads went wandering when the body was asleep. Usually, a curse brought on by an evil action or misdeed, often perpetrated by the father or husband. Sad really. Mostly harmless, they usually just like to scare people if anything.'

'So that's what I saw in the teahouse?' asked Natsuo.

'I guess it was the same woman, yes.'

'How do you know all this?'

'You live in Kyoto long enough you can't help but succumb to all the stories. They are everywhere; in every wall, lamplight and behind every curtain. Kyoto is drowning in magic you know.' She paused and seemed to enjoy Natsuo's bewildered expression. 'That and my mother always said we were descendants of Himiko, the shamaness-queen of Yamatai-koku. But who knows about that...'

Natsuo couldn't find any words so he just sipped his tea. Once again, he felt the gentle ease of being in the presence of someone with whom he felt he could talk about what had been happening to him.

'Do you know the name Sōjōbō?' he ventured.

'Of course. That's who you're going to meet, no?'

'Mm.'

'Look, I have something for you. If he called you that means you're probably in no direct danger. The tengu can be fierce and murderous but are rarely duplicitous. However, the darkness is drawing in and evil lurks in the storms. I don't know what else you might meet.' She reached into her kimono and brought out a small, square, embroidered amulet.

An *omamori*, Natsuo thought to himself. Little charms like this were on sale by every temple and shrine. His mother had once bought him one before his school exams as a teenager; a cheap gakyugō-jōju good luck charm with a picture of a happy winking squirrel on it.

The one Yuki handed him however was a small red, brocaded-silk buddhist design around a piece of wood within. It felt expensive and important. On that wood would be written a message, but if you took it out of its casing the spell would lose its power. That was the idea anyway.

'This is a yaku-yoke. Keep this on you at all times, it protects against evil spirits and malignant forces.' Natsuo made a face that suggested disbelief. 'This is a real one...' Yuki said, catching the opinion writ large on his face. 'Hopefully if the charm is strong enough, you'll not be harmed by any...'

'Yōkai?'

'Well, yes. You'll still see them but unless you come across something truly terrible, the most they'll do is terrorise you.'

'Fantastic...' said Natsuo bleakly.

Yuki allowed herself a little chuckle.

'Well young Natsuo-san, it sounds like you have an adventure ahead. I'll leave you to rest before your trip to the mountain tomorrow. In the morning, I shall leave breakfast for you but won't awaken you.'

'Yuki-san.'

'Mm?'

'Do you understand what's going on or why I'm being called?'

'I do not. But I believe your answer lies up in the rain-battered temples of Kurama-yama. Good night Natsuo-san.'

'Good night.'

'Oh, and remember, keep the charm with you at all times.'

The morning light failed to enter the window of Natsuo's room. There was an almost tangible darkness weighing over the world as he sat munching cold pickles and rice, checking his route to the mountain.

He would make his way to Takaragaike station and then board the local Eizan-Kurama line north to the hills. The following day a typhoon was scheduled to make landfall on the coast a hundred kilometres north at Maizuru. Given how inland Natsuo would be in his mountain enclave, he hoped it wouldn't reach him.

Whilst sipping some green tea he then remembered reading on his phone in Osaka that something called the "Brown Ocean Effect" could intensify the power of the storm with latent heat in wet soils feeding the broiling cyclone. He didn't really understand the science, but it meant potentially bad news. Either way, Natsuo planned to be back within the day. His phone alarm beeped; 6AM. Time to leave.

The world outside the Ryokan was silent but for the ever-present backdrop of fat rain droplets pelting the cobbles and the wind howling around the old wooden streets. He pulled his coat about him and ran the few minutes to the Gion-Shijo station.

It didn't take long for the little intercity train to reach Takaragaike station. Not many people were traversing the town at 6AM in the rain. There was a twenty-minute wait to connect onto his mountain-bound train so Natsuo went to the vending machine, the only thing at the tiny station, and bought a BOSS coffee. It came out of the machine hot, which brought over him a primordial wave of relief.

A little jingle, a trademark characteristic of railway stations, each one with their own little tune, heralded the arrival of his train to the mountains. Nobody boarded but Natsuo. Obviously, he thought to himself.

The timetable, plastered to a board behind the internationally ubiquitous see-through sheet plastic cover, stated that the train to Kurama station would last twenty-one minutes. And Natsuo didn't doubt the specificity of that one minute.

He recalled the news story when the Tsukuba Express line in Tokyo left twenty seconds early once and then the whole company 'deeply apologised for the severe inconvenience' even though not one member of the public complained.

The train quickly left Kyoto behind and began crawling up the narrow valley line into the trademark fuzzy-green wooded slopes.

He thought it a shame that the peaks were lost in a smoking fug of rainclouds.

It must be beautiful...

Instead, the rain-battered windows only offered a smudged vista of dark greens and browns with the occasional house breaking the watercolour.

The walk up to the Kurama head temple didn't take Natsuo long and even in the rain it was astonishingly beautiful. A magical corridor of tall green trees, a winding path lined with bright orange lanterns, bursts of colour in the drabness of the day's weather, and here and there little scarlet bridges that criss-crossed over a stream as he climbed.

He arrived at the main torii gate, where two *komainu* lion dog statues stood in frozen roars. He instinctively bowed as he passed through into the main temple complex. After washing his hands, Natsuo felt a little non-plussed.

Now what?

On the far left side, just at the edge of the principal area where various walking routes led off to more remote shrines, was a tourist-friendly map with an overly cutesy representation of Kurama-dera and its paths.

There was one main route that connected where Natsuo was west over a hill to the neighbouring valley to another famous shrine-village called Kibune. Off that main path smaller hidden tracks escaped up and down the mountains.

One shrine in particular caught Natsuo's eye: Sōjō-ga-tani. Tani meant valley and Sōjō could mean multiplication. Not helpful, of course, but the fact he was meant to meet a spirit here called Sōjōbō had to be more than a coincidence.

He headed up the path and after only about fifteen minutes of trudging uphill along a mud-covered, stepping-stone path arrived at a small pale-brown, wooden temple.

It looked like any other Japanese religious building. The ubiquitous yet attractive sloping roof, that seemed propped up by the sturdy kohaibashira columns as it loomed down low. To the right, by the path, was a large thermos tank of tea and a big bowl of hard-boiled eggs, no doubt for walkers to have a snack and rest.

At the temple itself there was a simple granite hand-washing station and a humble offering box in front of a sparse altar. It was what Natsuo saw sitting on top of the altar that gave him a surprising sense of relief, telling him he was proceeding correctly; a small wooden statuette, painted red but faded over the years, of a long nosed tengu.

He stepped up and inspected the shrine, but it was bare and stripped down. A lot of temples and shrines were adorned with zig-zag paper streamers with the name of shide and twisted lengths of rope called shimenawa, but this more bare construction had nothing else. Nothing except for a delicate kanji inscription scratched into the wood of one of the columns.

To talk to god is to know truth,
To know god is to know yourself,
To find god is to stop looking,
For god is in you and in everything,
God is the sky.

Immediately below this a slightly newer-looking line had been carved in somewhat less elegant characters as an extra sentence in the stanza.

The truth lies stepping to the heavens.

Natsuo didn't really understand what that meant so he stepped away from the small temple building back onto the path and considered what to do next. He dropped a hundred-yen coin in the pot by the thermos, poured himself a warm mug of tea and peeled an egg. The pitter patter of rain off the wooden roof intermingled with the pleasing cooked-sulphur funk of the hardboiled egg.

He could carry on along the path, hoping that something might trigger some spark of an idea. Or he could trudge back to the main temple complex and regroup. But this had to be the place. The name, the statuette of a tengu.

The thought did cross Natsuo's mind of the absurdity of the situation. The tiny voice of doubt in the recessions of his rational mind did whisper and hint at the idea of just giving up this mad adventure and heading back somewhere warm and familial. He thought about giving up looking for Sōjōbō, stopping this delirious quest filled with yōkai and premonitions and nightmares. Just stopping.

A flicker in his mind's eye stirred Natsuo from his defeatist state. A thought that had been ricocheting around his brain suddenly shone bright and almost blinded Natsuo with how obvious it was. Check behind the temple, it seemed to say. Natsuo was surprised he hadn't at least done a quick route around the back of the temple just in case there were clues there.

The temple seemed to be all but stuck to a rising bank of trees, the wall of forest, but then, as he inched through foliage to the backside of the small building, he did see a small man-sized break in the tightly packed cedars that had been cordoned off to the public. He reached the centre of the back wall of the temple, which immediately affronted an opening. A steep stone staircase rose into the gloom.

A small post with a maple-wood sign had been artfully placed on the left side of the mouth: Tengoku no michi, Heaven's Path. This must be it.

He remembered what the inscription said, the added line, 'The truth lies in stepping to the heavens.' He presumed that was a poetic way of telling him to walk up the path.

Natsuo gingerly climbed over the rope and, on entering the dark tunnel of trees, the sound of the rain all but disappeared. A hushed peace seemed to pervade the inclining corridor, darkly roofed by cedar tops.

As he climbed Natsuo soon noticed that the cobbled staircase was flanked on either side by kitsune fox statues in little bright-scarlet scarves. He was reminded of the dream he had. This put him at ease, confirming that he was on the right track.

Natsuo kept walking up and up the seemingly endless staircase. He looked back and couldn't see the bottom. There must have been a bend in the path at some point so he could no longer see the entrance. Time in this dark, leafy channel through the woods, seemed to either slow or begin to lose its meaning.

The atmosphere seemed to grow heavier and darker and Natsuo could smell fresh air after a heavy shower mixed in with the moist aromas of wet moss. But the rain couldn't have stopped so suddenly...

His internal systems, the little homeostatic clocks and bodily machinery that informed his status in the world around him seemed to sense a significant rise in altitude, that the air around him had thinned out. All he saw were dark trees and foxes, but he wondered if maybe he was nearing the summit of Mount Kurama.

Quite suddenly the kitsune statues ended and the path Natsuo had been climbing stopped at a small landing cut into the mountain. The end had come about so abruptly that it had taken him by surprise. One second it was an endless, rising staircase and the next it had immediately ceased and levelled out. Almost as if the landing had rushed to meet him; to cut the path and stop him in his tracks.

In front of him now was a dark mess of leaves, branches and bushes that formed a tight, tunnel-like vanishing point. A primal fear gripped Natsuo. He knew he had to walk into the darkness but now there were no stone fox guardians or dreamy cobblestones. Just an unfathomably dark pine-green nothing which his gut told him was the next part of his journey.

A certain grim sense of inevitability crept into Natsuo's mind, a nihilistic flavour soaked into the sentiment. He had come this far, what was the point in stopping? He felt that he couldn't stop this process even if he tried.

He then recalled what Yuki had told him back in Kyoto. 'If he called you that means you're probably in no direct danger.' Natsuo put his hand to his heart; he had placed the omamori charm in his chest pocket and hoped it would do the job it had been intended to do: protect him. He closed his eyes, breathed deep, and then walked into the darkness.

Natsuo's vision was a dark tapestry of muted hues and sylvan shapes. He couldn't really see, but he sensed where he was, he knew he wouldn't fall or collide with anything.

The absence of space offered up no structure for time to function, so he had no idea how long he had been walking. A few minutes? An hour? He couldn't tell. But at some point, which he determined to be 'up ahead', a warm light began to suffuse the tunnel, like a lamp slowly increasing in strength.

Then Natsuo began to notice the sides of the tunnel; tightly twisted vines and branches. The glow at the end became brighter as he approached it until it burned so much that he squinted and shielded his eyes. Natsuo continued to step forward.

The glow then dimmed as his eyes calibrated to this new light and he stepped out into, what his brain could only describe as, a small spherical cavern constructed entirely from moss, vines, grasses and leaves.

At the centre of the bowl was a figure sitting cross-legged on the ground. It wore a long, red robe with a starry-blue sash over its shoulder and had its eyes closed with its hands open as if in prayer. It had long white hair and a vast flowing beard that barely left space for its face. Though what there was of its face made it undeniable who Natsuo was before; it had a long, jutting Pinocchio-nose.

Sōjōbō...

Before Natsuo could get his thoughts in order, the figure spoke.

'Welcome to Sōjō-ga-tani, which means the Valley of the High Priest. That high priest would be me, Sōjōbō.' The tengu opened his eyes. 'As you can see, it's not much of a valley, and it wasn't me who named this place after myself. But here I am.' He permitted himself a little giggle. 'Seemingly, young Natsuo, you heard my call. Well done.'

Natsuo had been stuck fast to the mouth of the tunnel, paralysed by fear. But when Sōjōbō had spoken, in a whimsical and peaceful baritone, the nightmarish quality of what was happening had thawed. When the tengu had giggled and smiled it was as if Natsuo had received confirmation that everything would be fine.

He approached Sōjōbō who then signalled for him to sit. The ground was spongy and soft with moss and felt like an expensive futon. Finally, Natsuo summoned up some words and his voice cracked into life.

'Umm...what...I mean...' He searched for something clear. 'Why am I here?'

'That, young man, is the right first question,' said the tengu with a large, warm smile. 'I suspect you have a lot of questions, so, if you'll permit me, I will talk and talk and talk and hopefully answer them all. I imagine you're wondering about the storms, the yōkai and why I've been calling you? If you need clarification just interrupt me. I'm very old and I do go on.'

Natsuo simply nodded in bewilderment. He hadn't time or brainpower to stop and rationalise what was happening, it was simply another part of the inexorable flow that had been coaxing him through the last couple of weeks.

'Putting it shortly young man, there is an imbalance in the heavens and the gods are squabbling. Amaterasu, the Sun Goddess, and Queen of the Heavenly Realm, is being challenged. Heaven and Hell always work in tandem, cancelling each other out, a pact of non-intervention so that the middle-world may flourish. The benign Gods of the skies want their project to carry on and humanity to succeed, whilst Hell needs its souls. For decades in the 20th century the countries in the West had what was called a Cold War. Each side could mutually assure the destruction of the other and thus a stalemate of inaction was reached. In our demon and spirit realm it is similar. A pact of non-activity so that each side gets what it wants. But the demon realm has grown greedy.

'I don't know how much you humans of today know about the old gods, but Hell, *Jigoku*, is run by Enma Daiō, the great King of the Underworld. Were he to walk among us right now you would see a man with a furious face dressed in the robes of an ancient government official from the Chinese Tang Dynasty; his chosen garb. What would give him away is that he is about fifteen feet tall.

'In actual fact, at heart, Enma Daiō is a fairly kind and compassionate god. He's not like his western counterparts; those moustache-twirling Lucifers or hot-poker-wielding horned devils. Enma really does want to save every single soul from damnation, it is his minions who mete out demonic justice and trials to get there. That being said, he has always been jealous of the love Amaterasu received. But the balance kept everything ticking along nicely. Yin and yang, you see. First, however, a drink, for my story is long.'

Sōjōbō waved his hand over the mossy ground in front of them and a bottle of sake appeared with two glasses. He poured out the rice wine, handed over a glass, and carried on as Natsuo sipped the warm, floral alcohol.

'The gods of today are the children, grandchildren and great-great-great-great-great-grandchildren of other gods. Existence, time, matter, nothingness, everything, was created by ancient forces that are legends even to an old soul like me. Names like Amenominakanushi, Takamimusubi, Kamimusubi. Creation gods. There were five creation gods that paved the way for everything you could possibly know to come into being. They weren't born of anything, they just were. Your story begins with two deities — Izanagi and Izanami, the last of the seven generations of primordial gods and the parents of, among others, Amaterasu.

'Izanagi and his sister-wife Izanami are genesis gods. They created land and sea. The older gods gave them a heavenly bejewelled spear, the *amenonuhoko* to help with this task. They descended from the lofty celestial plain where they resided down to the floating ame-no-ukihashi bridge that would connect the heavens with the new earth. Below Izanagi and Izanami was a churning mass of creation, a swirling formless pool of concepts and misty potential. They began to mix the chaotic mass with the spear until salty beads of water began to form and drip off the tip. Instantly land began to spring up, solid ground that would be later called Japan but which they named Onogoroshima, as well as vast outspreading oceans and seas. They stepped off the bridge onto the new land of this new place and made it their home. More gods would appear and a new celestial pantheon would be created. The old gods retired and Amaterasu and the rest would take the reins, filling out all the jobs of creation.

'And so it has been ever since. Except now there is trouble in heaven. The spear, once guarded at the Grand Temple of Ise, has been stolen. According to what I have been told, the kanju and manju have also been taken. These are the Tide Jewels that were the property of Ryūjin, our dragon sea-god, which he kept hidden behind a waterfall named after him in Gifu. These jewels control the oceans, the power of the waters of the world and all the creatures within it. The spear controls earth and the jewels the seas. You see what that means young Natsuo-chan? And there are rumours these agents of darkness are now after the uchide no kozuchi sacred hammer.'

'The hammer...'

'What's that, young man?'

'I've heard of the hammer. I mean, I was told the story. The lady who removed a buruburu from me mentioned it.'

Sōjōbō giggled, 'Ah, I'm sure she mentioned the tale of Momotarō? With the peach and the ogres and such?' Natsuo nodded. 'Well, the hammer has popped up in various tales even centuries before that you know. It's even older than I am! Nobody really knows where it came from, but it seems to have entered the realm of humans', shall we say...imagination, thanks to some clumsy nether-beast having dropped it some thousand years ago. As it belongs to no-one the hammer has always been passed around, stolen, gifted, re-gifted, bequeathed and inherited over the centuries. Its power was such that everybody who owned it was too scared of it to use but an iota of its potential.'

'What does the hammer do?'

'Quite literally anything. When swung to strike the hammer will produce whatever the wielder wishes for in that moment. A mansion, animals, food, money. The only limitation is your mind. However, using such an ungodly item would, and always did, draw attention from the powers that be, the higher ups. So people, demons and gods alike either stowed it away or used it for minor wishes.'

'You said the agents of darkness are after it? Where is it and why do they need it?' Natsuo paused and Sōjōbō patiently waited, noticing Natsuo had a question dancing around his mind. 'And who is doing all this?'

'Yes. I apologise. I'm jumping ahead and there's much to tell you. But time is fleeting. Amaterasu's younger brother is Susanoo, god of storms. I have met him a few times. He is brilliant and terrible all at once. Sometimes benevolent and jolly, sometimes quick to wrath and destructive, often a trickster. In a world where yin and yang maintain equilibrium, spirits like Susanoo do create a tension in the status quo. And he has always been impetuous and jealous of his cherished older sister. However, thanks to many acts of overt heroism and bravery he has always been beloved by many and forgiven by most. It was he who slew the giant serpent Yamata no Orochi after all. But it seems both he and Enma have decided to claim the earthly realm and wrest control from Amaterasu and the light.

'You've no doubt wondered about the storms. Well, the thunder god Raijin and Fujin, god of the winds, seem to have both defected to their side. And the never-ending tempest wrought on your world is the stage being set for the take-over of the mortal plain.' Sōjōbō noticed Natsuo's blank, pale face and refilled his glass. 'In short, with the Tide Jewels, celestial hammer and spear in their possession, there would be little stopping Susanoo, Enma, and whoever else joins them, to finalise their dominion of existence.'

'You say they already have the jewels and the spear?'

'That seems to be so, yes.'

'Where is the hammer then?'

'Usually the hammer is kept safe inside the Enryaku-ji temple east of us on Mount Hiei. The temple venerates Daikokuten. He's a deity of prosperity. Great fun, loves a drink and a story. You'll see the statues of him holding the uchide no kozuchi hammer. But given the situation a decision was made to hide it away somewhere nobody would think to look. It is neither in heaven nor hell. It now exists in the hinterland between the two.'

'Earth?'

'Meido. The afterlife, or purgatory as it is known in the west. It is a terrible place; dark, windy, stinking of death and misery, full of tests and trials.'

'Why is it there?'

'Because Enma would never believe it to be there.' Sōjōbō smiled at the simplicity of it. 'And also we have a trick up our sleeves.'

'So you helped hide it?'

'If the gods need help it is to the great tengu they turn. The gods may be powerful, but they are rarely that smart or machiavellian. We are only a few who know the plan. All of the chief tengu generals, we are called daitengu, have been notified. Of the Seven Lucky Gods, of course Daikokuten knows, for he is the current guardian of the hammer. And we brought Ebisu into the fold for reasons that I will explain forthwith. Of course, I have a band of kitsune and tengu at my disposal too. Also, to help temper the storms we have been helped in a small part by Hiyoribō. He's a yōkai too and lives deep in the mountains of Ibaraki just north of your human capital, spending his days as a spirit adept in the art of warding off rains and bad weather. He's doing his best, bless him, but he's only able to really protect Tokyo.

'Ebisu is the first child of Izanagi and Izanami and always remained close to his parents. Now, Enma Daiō resides in Jigoku, the hell of Buddhism. Whereas Izanami and Izanagi sealed themselves off in a Shinto realm of the dead, a rather less fiery and more pensive and morose plain of reality, called *Yomi-no-kuni*. Well, that is where the hammer has been hidden. Ebisu convinced his old god parents to keep it.'

'Wait, there are two hells?' Natsuo interrupted.

'Aha, yes. Well, we are a complicated lot. Our two belief systems, Buddhism and Shinto, are actually two sides of the same coin. And of course, in our world, we don't label them as one or the other, they just are. But interestingly, through human belief and monikers, they have evolved into two separate entities. Almost how countries in your world have evolved into very distinct and disparate things even though you're all just humans at the end of it all.' An almost fatherly expression hung over Sōjōbō's face for a moment. 'So, to conclude, the jewels and spear are currently in the hands of Enma's side and the hammer is, for now, more or less safely with our creator gods in Yomi-no-kuni, Shinto hell if you will, the entrance to which is in Meido.' Sōjōbō exhaled proudly. 'And that's where you come in.'

Natsuo had more or less been following the tale of gods and monsters up until now as if listening to a grandfather spinning a yarn, but then he was jolted back into the reality that he was up a mountain talking to a long-nosed fairy-king.

'Me?'

'We need you, Natsuo-chan. We need you to first head to the Eiheiji temple in Fukui to pick up the *kusanagi-no-Tsurugi* sword and then head to Mount Osore, infiltrate Meido, collect the hammer from Yomi-no-kuni before meeting back up with me again here. If we can get the hammer back to Amaterasu, then hopefully balance can be restored.'

A pregnant silence lay thick on the air and in Natsuo's head. He felt drunk on the information, the weight of Sōjōbō's words muddying his thoughts.

'Wait, wait, wait,' he half shouted. 'I don't understand any of this. Temples and swords, me going to the afterlife, picking up hammers from creation gods. I don't know what any of this means. Why me?'

'Because Natsuo-chan, you're a *hafu*.'

'Mixed race? Both of my parents are Japanese.'

'Yes, young man, but they are not both human...'

'What...what are you talking about?' Natsuo's voice quivered in confusion and anger. 'My mother and father are obviously human. We lived in a small house in Kochi all our lives. They couldn't be more normal.'

'Well, your mother yes. But not your father.' A stilted silence followed. 'I see this has come as a shock to you — '

'A shock? It's nonsense is what it is. How can you say these things? You don't know anything, you can't know anything, you know nothing about my family.' Natsuo was shaking with emotions that up until recently he had never felt before.

'Actually my dear boy, I did know your father. Rather, I knew of him.'

'How?'

'He was an oni. A demon of the underworld.'

Natsuo laughed viciously, 'See, you know nothing. My father was a salaryman, a generic Japanese businessman, working dawn till dusk to pay for our family. The only demonic thing about my father was he was rarely a father to me.' The words stung at Natsuo's eyes. 'The only thing evil about my dad was that he was never there for me. Never seemed to care much about me.'

'Young man, that couldn't be further from the truth.' Sōjōbō's voice was soft and appeasing, but had a depth to it that made Natsuo yearn for an explanation. 'Your father was a feared oni in the underworld. To you he was Akihiro but to the ogres and demons of Jigoku he was Ōtakemaru. He was a *kijin*; a ten-metre-tall demon so powerful and violent he unsettled even the gods. Along with Shuten dōji and Tamamo no Mae he was one of the "Great Three Yōkai" of Japan.

'He terrorised the country for centuries and rained lightning and storms down on his enemies until the peace between heaven and hell was set in place. One day however, everything changed for him. One day he fell in love.

'There was a beautiful woman in a small town on the island of Shikoku. He couldn't explain why this particular human woman stopped him in his tracks, but he was entranced. In the centuries after the peace many oni took to disguising themselves as humans so they could still walk about the earth and get up to no good, yōkai behaviour. This woman, she was cleaning clothes in a small stream that trickled through the town and, they say, that as the summer light sparkled around her she reminded him of the goddess Suzuka Gozen, the most beautiful creature of the heavens. The evil-corrupted heart inside Ōtakemaru started to beat pure for the first time. He then courted her, spending more and more time in human form, until he finally won her over. You were conceived of their union young man. And when the judges of Jigoku found out about this it was ordered that he was to be killed.

'A plan was hatched between your father and the powerful shōgun Tamuramaro to fake his death. Ōtakemaru had been making the emperor's life misery for years so his drastic turn away from hell was perfect for the great warlord. He would be rid of a great demon, becoming the emperor's favourite, and your father would live in secret. To make the plan believable Tamuramaro built an army of 30,000 horsemen and stormed Ōtakemaru's castle. After a fierce battle Tamuramaro returned to the royal palace with a head that, after the emperor's inspection, was corroborated to be that of your father. Although, of course, it wasn't. A simple magic trick. Ōtakemaru would never again set foot in Jigoku, his home, nor continue his century's long existence, but he was happy as he could now live out the rest of his now mortal life with his true love. That woman washing her clothes, beloved of a demon, was your mother.

'So you see, Natsuo-chan, you are half oni.'

Natsuo simply stared at the floor, his mind a flurry of confused cogs trying to work in some kind of union. It was so much information. And were he told all this on any normal day he would have laughed it off as madness. But in the wake of everything that had been happening to him since he took that first step out of his house, that initial move into a new life, he couldn't help believing every word that this magical tengu told him.

And then there was that moment before he left for the mountain; his mother was going to tell him something.

My father an oni...

'Are you OK, young man?'

Still Natsuo remained silent, going over everything, struggling to understand. The more he turned everything over the more the cogs started to click into place, things started to make sense, the fog of confusion cleared and the paths of logic started to show themselves. The story, which he had to believe, would explain his father's lack of paternal affection and, by extension, and perhaps through fear of his son's safety, a contentment with the turn of events that led to Natsuo hiding himself away from the world.

'Did he know about the buruburu?'

'That I cannot say. Not necessarily. What I do know was that, in his way, he loved you, and whether or not he knew about the yōkai, he was most likely relieved you were, how do you humans call it, a Hikikomori. That yōkai sensed your weakened mental state and latched on; but who can say when? Even though you may have taken offence, that was why they moved down the coast away from you. For your own safety. It was the hardest thing your mother ever did. Abandoning you to keep you safe.' Sōjōbō sipped at his sake and arched his ancient bushy eyebrows. 'Now to the question "Did your father sense the rising evil in hell and foresee the current situation?" we can also never know the answer. But he was smart and for some important reason he decided, as painful as it was, to abandon you.'

'*Sou ka...*' Natsuo whispered. He finally looked at Sōjōbō, into his millennia-old eyes. 'What do you need me to do and why me?'

The old spirit smiled. Natsuo, accepting his lot, felt, for the first time in his life, special. Chosen. Needed. And, contrary to all logic, and in the face of the outrageous news that his father was a demon and his whole life essentially a lie, he felt heroic. All the years reading about heroes and warriors and now it was his turn. The fictional worlds on screen and page that had so inspired him were now turning out to be real.

'Being a hafu means you can enter the demon world. The portals and entryways will recognise that side of you. And, on entering, you should be able to blend in somewhat. Where needed you can be recognised as both demon and human. You can adapt where we can't. A tengu is a tengu is a tengu. You are both human and demon. But also, being neither fully, you aren't beholden to their rules. You can move around where you need to, playing the role you need to play whatever the moment calls for.

'That is not to say you can just stroll casually through the underworld. There are manifold dangers down there. You will enter into Meido and follow the longer, but safer route. We shall avoid Jigoku. The kusanagi-no-Tsurugi sword is to be your weapon should you have to protect yourself. Hopefully its mere presence will be enough to ward off any lowly denizens of the deep. Also, the charm Yuki gave you will boost your protective aura too.'

Natsuo clutched his chest, 'Yuki...'

'Charming girl. I knew her great-great-great-well, many greats-great-grandmother Himiko. Magical blood stills run through the vast family line, so the charm should hold even in purgatory,' Sōjōbō said, looking off into some distant memory.

'So, pick up a sword, head to Mount Osore and then what?'

'I shall send word to have someone meet you there. They will open the gates to Meido and your journey will begin.'

'My journey...' Natsuo laughed.

'Mmm?'

'I feel like I've already done the journey of a lifetime. I spent so long hiding, scared, from the world. And here I am with you telling me I'm going to descend into the underworld. It's...it's a lot.'

'I know, young man, but you really are the only one who we can think of to help stop the impending war.'

'Are there no other hafus in Japan?'

'Oh yes. A few. But...none of them can claim the mighty Ōtakemaru as their father.'

'Akihiro. His name was Akihiro.'

'Hirawa, don't forget the surname.'

'Excuse me?'

'He chose the name for a reason. Akihiro means bright and Hirawa means place of harmony.' The old tengu once again smiled that warm comforting smile. 'It was a good name for a good...man.'

'Ok. Right. Sword, mountain, purgatory, door to Yomi, meet the creation gods, get the hammer, give it to you, go home.'

'Not quite. I'm not permitted to wield the hammer, but I will accompany you with it.'

'And I am?'

'You are what I believe you humans call a "loophole". I will escort you to Amaterasu herself.'

'You're going to escort me...to meet Amaterasu?'

'That is correct.'

'Yeah, why not. If everything else is real, of course I'd be meeting the Goddess Queen.' Natsuo half-smiled to himself. If everything did turn out to be real he would be terrified, yes, but also would be embarking on a quest that even his imagination couldn't come up with. 'What now?'

'Go to your mother. Spend some time with her. Many trials await you Natsuo-chan and we cannot guarantee your —'

'Safety?'

'Survival...' A look of sadness shimmered across his brow. 'Also, you will need this.' Sōjōbō reached into the folds of his vast red robes and pulled out a small leather book. 'In this little tome, written by Benzaiten herself, you will find all you need to know about your voyage, the tribulations that await you, and the characters you may meet along the way. You must use cunning and guile to either involve yourself or evade. That, sadly, is down to you, young man.' For the first time

Sōjōbō reached out and touched Natsuo, laying a hand gently on his shoulder. 'But now, go to your mother. She will understand.'

Suddenly a bright light emanated from the wall of branches and leaves behind Sōjōbō. The whole cave glowed intensely and continued to brighten and burn. It stung Natsuo's eyes. He winced until he could stand it no more. He closed his eyes and heard the words "good luck" spoken distantly as if carried away on the photons.

Then, as soon as the light had risen to a level he could no longer take, it disappeared and the gloom of the forest returned.

He was sat in front of the small temple again. The vat of tea and pot of eggs were there yet the stairway behind the temple had seemingly disappeared.

Ok...Natsuo thought to himself, everything begins now.

Chapter Six: Shimeji
使命

Mission.

A ten-metre-long titanosaur stood on a rock outcrop, its long reptilian neck towering above the world, swinging back and forth with its mouth agape in what was either anger or fear. Before the monster a two-legged raptor with a mouth of daggers faced off in frozen motion against a far meeker-looking biped with a toothless, bird-like beak, the heads bobbing up and down as if sizing each other up. The two were poised in the moment of battle as the bulky sauropod looked on from a distance. The scene was set for violence, tooth and claw, ripped flesh and tendons. But the carnage would never arrive.

The animatronic dinosaurs at Fukui station were there in honour of local discoveries. Fukuititan standing over the scene of a Fukuiraptor about to charge Fukuisaurus.

Natsuo smiled and felt almost nostalgic. These long-dead animals were at least part of a real and at one time existent biodiversity. However, they only lived on in bone and memory. Yet it was all around Natsuo that the myths of old, which he thought were man-made, yōkai and demons, had shown themselves to be real and were here, now.

The hills of Katsuyama, to the east of the city, were littered with prehistory and it was towards these Cretaceous valleys that Natsuo would have to head on foot. The Eiheiji temple was a three-hour trek away along a wooded mountain path. The one local bus service wasn't running due to the inclement conditions. It was a constant and plodding route through a cleft of trees under a low-hanging spitting sky.

After his meeting with Sōjōbō Natsuo had returned and spent a few days in Osaka with his mother, waiting for the storm to pass. Almost immediately Natsuo told her what the great tengu had told him about his father. 'Well, I thought one day you might find out,' she said softly. 'And this might as well be the time.' She took his hands in hers. 'He did love you, you know. In the only way he could.'

Natsuo fought back tears, 'I want to be angry. But I can't. And in a strange way it feels like another weight has been lifted from me. The fact that I now understand, the fact that things now have a meaning to them, actually...makes me feel happier.'

'It is an odd tale. Our family isn't a normal one. I didn't know your father was an oni when I met him. Only when I had fallen in love with him did he tell me.' She smiled wistfully. 'Because who could love a demon?'

'What about him did you fall in love with?' Natsuo asked, wondering why his mother would have ever fallen for such a stoic and unemotional man.

'Your father was different at the beginning. Before you came along, before he had to escape the prying eyes of those who would do him harm. He was free to...be. We acted like all young lovers did at that time. We went on walks, went to the theatre, ate takoyaki on park benches. The usual. But there was something about him. An exuberance, a brightness, an eternal burning joy that ignited every second we were together. But when you came into the picture and started to get older he became protective, paranoid. Scared that at any moment everything he had built, his own private little human world, would come crumbling down. So when you became a Hikikomori he was, and it hurts me to say this, relieved. He always knew where you were and that you wouldn't be seen by nefarious eyes.

'One day he came home in a rage. That simmering calm anger that I'm sure you remember. He had heard that someone, some spy, thought they had spotted your father and had told the creatures of hell. That was when we left you and headed to the house in Tosashimizu. Also, your father didn't die of a heart attack as I wrote to you on that postcard.'

'How did he die?'

'He encountered the shichin misaki; a band of seven vengeful samurai ghosts. They were sent to the west coast in search of him. Spirits of the dead, powerful warlords and generals slain by your father...by Ōtakemaru. When he arrived back at the house, he was pale, and his pallor hued green. He was sick and he told me nothing could help him. He simply asked that I bring him a bottle of cold beer. The mere presence of the shichin misaki had infected him with the cloud of death. I sat in the kitchen with him, mopping his brow and refilling his glass. He died an hour later where he sat.

'I was overcome with grief and rushed to phone you, but something your father had said, more or less his last words, stopped me. "Protect our son". So I didn't call you. I maintained my distance, maintained our vigil to keep you out of whatever was happening. Later I thought that the least I could do was send you the postcard. Just so you knew. And now, it seems,' she said with a smile that twinkled with a deep sadness, 'you know everything. I'm just so sorry it all turned out like it did. Our love denied you a life.'

Natsuo hugged his mother and then told her about the journey he was about to embark on, his trip to purgatory, his rendezvous with gods and monsters. She wasn't fazed or surprised but just looked immensely sad and stroked his hair.

'And I just got you back...'

When the weather had improved slightly, Natsuo and his mother had braved the rain and headed to a yakitori restaurant where they ate grilled soy-glazed skewers of chicken skin, shiitake mushrooms and thigh meat with the smells of beer and caramelised meat-smoke soaking into their clothing.

They laughed. Natsuo was finally able to laugh with his mother. It had only taken the end of the world to do it.

The only smells lingering in Natsuo's nose now were those of wet moss and sodden earth as he trudged through the shadowy forest-route to the soundtrack of dripping leaves and distant winds.

Eiheiji, the temple of eternal peace, was founded in the 13th century by Eihei Dōgen; the legendary monk who had brought the Sōtō school of Zen Buddhism to the country. Eiheiji is a training monastery where shaved-headed monks can be seen skittering about in flowing robes, shuffling from temple to temple in slippers.

It is a large complex of about seventy different structures sometimes hiding away, creeping about behind, or blending in seamlessly with a dense and lofty forest of cedar and Japanese maples, as if the buildings themselves were hewn from the landscape.

Visitors were welcomed to the monastery but were under strict command to dress modestly and be silent. About a million people used to pass through the great sanmon entry gate every year. But not now. The rain was crashing down, bouncing off the tiled roofs in little aquatic explosions, and a sheet of droplets acted as an entry veil through which Natsuo passed into the main courtyard.

A tourist-friendly map had been placed at various points through the complex to help the visitor. A small inscription stated that it was painted by an Aichi priest and had taken him more than four and half years to finish. The thought crossed Natsuo's mind that most visitors would barely pay it a cursory glance. He scanned his finger across the pathways on the attractive map and wondered where to go. One building caught his eye; a word that he hadn't seen on any temple plan before: joyoden, Founder's Hall.

Not much of a hall, Natsuo thought to himself as he entered the clean and rather square room, punctured at various intervals by columns, as if keeping the low roof held aloft. In the centre of the wall in front of him was a large black urn. From a distance he thought it looked like a Russian samovar for heating tea, such was its large, iron-wrought appearance.

'Those are the ashes of Eihei Dōgen.'

Natsuo jumped and screamed in fright. A young monk was standing in the doorway in long dark-brown robes, silhouetted by the glinting rain behind him. Natsuo felt embarrassed shrieking in front of the man and merely grumbled a response.

'Sorry if I made you jump.'

'Is he actually in there?'

'No, not really. He's here somewhere, but we couldn't let anyone know where. Just in case.'

Natsuo smiled, reckoning that that probably was the case at most "sacred x or y location" tourist spots.

'So what brings you to our temple in weather like this?' The young monk smiled amiably. 'You're the first visitor we've had in weeks.'

'I...' Natsuo had to choose his words carefully. 'Was recommended to come here by someone who knows the place. I'm sort of searching for something.'

To Natsuo's surprise the monk didn't push the issue or seem at all intrigued, merely polite and compliant.

'Well, most who come here are searching for something in one way or another. I've been here in training since I was very young, and ever since the great disaster in Tōhōku in 2011, we've seen a constant and steady increase in people looking and searching for something. Eiheiji seems to alway provide the answer.'

'Well, I hope so. I mean, I only just arrived, and I don't really know where to look.'

'Listen, the weather isn't going to get any better. Please stay the night in the temple. There's no charge here. We have baths and beds and provide some basic food. We would be honoured to have a guest. There's a *zazen* room for meditation if you wish.'

'Arigato gozaimasu,' said Natsuo, bowing deeply.

'Just follow the signs to the kichijokaku; it is a modern building for lay people. If you have any questions or problems and need to speak to anyone, head to the sōbō living quarters or the hattō lecture hall. There'll always be somebody. My name is Kaneda-san.' The young man winked. 'Just in case you need to name drop.'

The monk bowed, opened up an old bamboo umbrella and trotted back out into the rain, quickly disappearing through a doorway into one of the multitude of similar-looking wooden buildings.

After a long soak in the *sentō* communal bathing room, which he had all to himself, Natsuo arrived back at his spartan but comfortable room and found a classic *Shojin Ryori* meal laid out on the low table pushed up to one side of the room.

In the tradition of the strictly vegetarian food eaten by Buddhists, Natsuo was faced with a selection of small seasonal dishes that included a sesame-flavoured salad of abura-age, fried soybean curd, and koya-tofu, dried tofu, konnyaku, a firm jelly made from the *konjac* plant, some simple aubergine and red pepper tempura, and sautéed garlicky wild-mountain butterbur called fuki and, of course, a steaming bowl of miso.

Everything was simple, perfectly cooked and clean tasting. What impressed Natsuo was how every element of each item of food seemed heightened. The crunchy dishes were super crunchy, the squidgy even more squidgy, the colours seemed to be brighter and everything tasting like an exaggerated version of itself. As if the saturation and volume had been turned up.

After the purity of the evening meal and soothing bath Natsuo found that he fell asleep instantly, a contented smile playing on his lips.

Something stirred Natsuo from his slumber. It wasn't sound. No, not a sound. Nor anything climatic; his room was quiet, perfectly climatized, and closed-off to breezes. But something had sucked him out of whatever placid, memory-less dream he had been having. What was it? He had no idea. But suddenly he felt the need to leave his small tatami-matted floor and return to the joyoden. He pulled a simple black yukata over himself and moved his feet into the complimentary uwabaki slippers.

The temple was shrouded in darkness, no candles or lanterns, as Natsuo, using only the milky vision provided by eyes accustomed to the dark of night, shuffled slowly through covered corridors of wooden floors and windows that looked onto dark trees and shadowy shrines.

He still felt half-asleep as he once again passed by the main temple buildings to return to the doorway beyond which the founder's ashes resided.

He couldn't tell what time it was. It was the dead of night, but he didn't feel tired or groggy from having been awoken. It was merely that his mind was swimming through the present as if in half-dream, the realness of what was happening not quite making itself known to his conscious brain. He pushed at the door to the hall, but it didn't open.

'So it is you then.' A calm youthful voice came from behind Natsuo. Natsuo turned around to see, across the small courtyard, facing the joyoden and leaning on a maple tree, the monk from earlier.

'Kaneda-san. What are you doing here?' creaked Natsuo's voice.

'Shouldn't I be asking you that?' He smiled intelligently, picking a hair off his fine white robe. The young monk seemed unperturbed both by the hour and the presence of a young man at the door of the shrine. He pushed himself off the trunk he was leaning on and strolled slowly towards Natsuo.

'I'm sorry. I shouldn't be here.'

'No?'

'I just woke up.' Natsuo pleaded. 'I woke up and I brought myself here. Something told me to come here. I know it sounds stupid. I'm sorry. I'll head back.'

'No, you won't.' The young monk smiled again. 'You're supposed to be here.'

'Why?'

'I called you here.' The young man recalibrated. 'Well, I called, and you showed up. As I thought you might.'

'I don't understand.'

As soon as the last plosive flick of the end of the word left Natsuo's mouth, the young monk's form shifted and melted in and around itself. He shrank in height to not much above Natsuo's waist, the monk's face pinched in and then outwards to a point and two long tufted ears poked up from the forehead. Natsuo was now standing in front of a white fox. And by the thick red markings that tipped the animal's extremities and the slight greying at the edges, an old one at that.

'Kitsune...' Natsuo said in awe.

'More correctly young man, a kūko.'

'Kūko?'

'The oldest and most powerful of the kitsune. Though second in command to the tenko, our younger, most active generations.' The fox smiled, and Natsuo saw the monk's smile. 'You saw a young man. That was my choice. I am, however, more than three thousand years old you know!'

'Where's your...tail...or tails?' Natsuo asked.

'When we achieve the rank of kūko we lose our tails. Don't need them. We are ultimately existing as beings of pure spirit. But I also thought it a shame, I rather liked my tails. Us kūko are also known as sky foxes, as that's usually where we are.' The kitsune pointed to the stars. 'Though I have a job to do, so I'm down here.'

'I guess you aren't called Kaneda-san then.'

'Hah!' The fox chortled. 'Only when I'm in human form, which is a lot of the time around here as you can imagine. No. My actual name is Kuzu-no-Ha.'

'And you woke me up and brought me here?'

'That's right. I wanted to double check you were who I had been expecting.' Suddenly the fox became less jolly and more perfunctory. 'Sōjōbō told me someone would be arriving any day, and I know what you are here for. Still, it is not lightly that I give up that which I have been protecting so long. So I jumped into your mind, just to check, and then called you here.'

'Well, that was nice of you...'

The fox sniggered, 'I'm sorry, young man. But I've been guarding the sword for a long time. I had to be sure.'

'Mm.' Natsuo nodded, feeling the importance of his presence.

'Follow me please.'

Kuzu produced a set of keys from somewhere deep in his robes and opened the door to the joyoden. Behind the large black urn full of the fake ashes of Dōgen was a small insert. A rhombus-shaped slot. The fox looked at Natsuo briefly and smiled, 'I always like this bit.' Another key, shaped like a small malachite crystal rod, was placed into the hold and rotated. Light shone out of the wall behind the urn and then an illuminated painting of wild blue and white crashing waves stop-motion-crept out from the light and covered the entire ceiling of the hall.

'Pretty, isn't it? A visual charm, but also an alarm if anyone but me opens it.'

The light subsided to leave a small brown door, which had to be opened by yet another key. 'Come,' said the fox.

Inside was a contained space that gave the impression of one much larger. To Natsuo it seemed he had walked into a ukiyo-e painting. A surreal Hiroshige reality. He could quite clearly see the back wall and sides of the room he was in; it couldn't have been much more than a few metres squared. But then the geometry and visual nature led to vanishing points that meant that Natsuo felt he could see into the distance.

There was a water feature, an admiral blue stream that seemed to curl away to distant hills, which was flanked by ever-shrinking trees. The whole room was white, a snow scene, and indeed snowflakes were falling, but from where Natsuo could not tell; they disappeared the moment they landed on his yukata. In the non-distance he could see a bridge crossing the river and spied a few people frozen in transit as they crossed. He knew it was art; wallpaper or something. But he could perceive the distance.

'It's my favourite painting for summer. And you're right, what you were thinking. It is Hiroshige. "Meguro Drum Bridge and Sunset Hill". In the hot season I have this one. And in winter I change it to Okumura Koichi's "Yashima in Summer". I like the pretty islands he depicts; looks almost tropical. Warms me up.'

'And for autumn and spring?' Natsuo asked, not really paying attention to his words but rather allowing the question to spill out of his still gawping mouth.

The old fox laughed quietly, knowing Natsuo was barely paying attention.

'Well in spring I like to have a representation of Kobayashi Kiyochika's "Autumn Leaves in Sangoku" and in autumn I set up the room as

Asano Takeji's "Spring at Kurama Temple".' At the mention of Kurama Natsuo was jolted back from his mindless pondering. 'And whatever the season there's always a sakura tree.'

Natsuo finally tore his eyes away from the non-distance and noticed a cherry tree in full bloom to the right hand side of the room. Its petals were bursting pink, and they all looked about to fall. The height of poetry for Japan is her relationship with this tree. The zenith of beauty just before it dies and disappears. The moment of full blossom before the leaf falls. It was the most beautiful thing he had ever seen.

'What's protected is in here.' Kuzu glided up to the tree and held both hands over the slender trunk. He closed his eyes and Natsuo noticed a gentle light emanating between the bark and the fox's paws. A vertical line appeared in the trunk, and then a small latch. 'This is what you've come here looking for. And like I said, Eiheiji always provides answers.'

The kukō pulled on the latch, opening a panel in the tree which exposed a shining scabbard nestled within.

'Take it.'

Natsuo walked slowly up to the tree, hesitating slightly, trying to understand what he was looking at. Propped up and lying back on some fine red velvet cloth, was what was clearly a sword. The scabbard was clean, but not ostentatious as Natsuo had presumed it would be. It was deep magenta in colour and the locket and chape finishings were gold. He gently placed both hands behind it and removed it from the tree.

'Well go on then. Don't look so wary.' The fox's face was eager now, expectant.

Natsuo slowly unsheathed the ancient-looking blade from its holder and held it vertical in front of him. It was light but felt strong and balanced. The grip was shaped in a way that his hand fit rather well, though the hilt had no guard. The pommel was shaped like a hammerhead and lent the whole weapon a very defined convex finish, while the blade was gnarly and chipped, covered in small gouges and scratches.

Kuzu noticed this, 'Aye. This sword has seen a lot.'

'I don't know why,' Natsuo said, 'but I expected some shiny katana or something.'

'This is a little older.' The old fox chuckled. 'It was this very blade that Susanoo used to slay the great serpent, so I'm sure it'll do you some good.' Then as if second guessing Natsuo's next thought he added, 'I'll put a charm on your bag, so it'll fit inside nicely. Can't have you walking around the human world carrying a sword now, can we? Not since you banned them in 1876!' He giggled again. 'Feels like yesterday we had samurai romping around these corridors...'

They walked back out of the painted room and left the joyoden. A natural unspoken understanding that this would be the end of their meeting hung in the night air.

'I am old and powerful. They say us kukō rival the gods. Yet as the great tengu told you, we are not looking for brute force or magical dexterity. We are looking for subtlety and an ending that can spare life. I wish you luck, young man, I truly do.'

Natsuo took the cue to leave, bowed deeply and returned with the sword in hand to his room. As he lay back and closed his eyes, he was reminded of the great trilogy of books written by Tolkien; whose smallest adventurers were the ones that brought peace to a warring land. And then the sandman took over.

In the morning he felt refreshed. It was 6AM, but he didn't feel tired at all. Indeed, were Natsuo not to believe in the reality of his mission, he may have passed off the nighttime episode as a surreal dream.

He checked his rucksack. There was the book from Sōjōbō and there, indeed, somehow denying space and time its nature, was the sword, impossibly snuggled inside the backpack. Not a dream.

After his ablutions and a simple breakfast of hard-boiled eggs, miso soup and rice, shredded vegetables tossed in sesame and rice vinegar, sweet beans and a pot of green tea, Natsuo left his room and slid the door shut behind him.

Before leaving the complex, he headed through the corridors to the sōdo meditation hall where various monks were sat on their knees in thought as a head priest chanted out sutra. The monk leading the prayer saw him, smiled gently, and nodded for him to sit if he liked.

Natsuo removed his slippers, laid his bag gently on the floor and found a free space on a tatami mat at the back. These men, both young and old, would have started their day at 3:30AM, performing zazen prayer and studying sutra. Compared to his rather spare breakfast, the monks would only have rice gruel and *tsukemono* pickles. The rest of the day was chores to clear and focus the mind; weeding, cleaning, polishing floors, shovelling snow in winter. They shaved their heads and bathed once every five days.

Natsuo could never get his head around the life of a monk. On one hand he found it inspiring. People who were able to live meagerly and find purity in mindfulness and action, striving to live a good life and to dedicate themselves to thought and the benefit of others. But on the other hand he found it almost pointless; why cut oneself off from society to eat rice gruel and chant stanzas from an old book? Who did it help?

But then every religion, in his mind, had its own methods and practices that one could deem devoid of reason. Having said that, he maintained, as long as they weren't hurting anybody...

Natsuo closed his eyes and attempted to empty his mind. For a child raised on comics and television this was almost impossible. But he followed the instructions of the lead priest. He focused on his breathing and allowed his thoughts to drift freely. He thought of his mother, alone, but safe, back in Osaka. He thought of the friends he never had, and the teenage years robbed by circumstance. He thought of his mission, and was happy, he was finally doing some good. He then thought about his father and his mind clouded; the inescapable mist of anger and resentment, of disappointment, started to curdle in with the things he had learned over the last few days. The priest kept chanting.

In the light there is darkness,
But don't take it as darkness.
In the dark there is light,

But don't see it as light.
Light and dark oppose one another
Like the front and back foot in walking.

Natsuo thought about his father and mother together. How their love, despite their differences, ignoring concepts of good and evil, triumphed and gave him life. Maybe not the life he wanted, maybe not the one he deserved, but a life nonetheless. Billions of years before Natsuo was born there was nothing of him, and when he died there would be billions more of nothing. How lucky he was to have these few moments in existence to enjoy life and make the most of it. He had lost merely a fraction of his time on the planet.

The nature of that which can be and is worshipped is empty and still.
One's own body and the body of the other are in essence not two.
May we together with all things obtain liberation,
Giving rise to the supreme intention and relying on the ultimate truth.

Natsuo had no idea how long he had been sat in the prayer hall. But, despite never having meditated before, he found himself lost in his head, his consciousness swimming through a sea of memories and potentials. The what could have beens and the what might have happeneds.

Each of the myriad things has its merit,
Expressed according to function and place.

Natsuo began to see the value in his life, the value in his parentage. For a decade-long choice taken by his father, a man who gave up everything in the pursuit of love, Natsuo now had the chance to live a life ten-fold that of one promised to the average child. Because of his parents Natsuo would now be responsible for bringing some form of order back to the world.

> **We wholeheartedly pray for the flourishing of the true dharma,**
> **Peace in the land, harmony among all nations,**
> **And that all conditions may be favourable.**

Natsuo finally opened his eyes and exhaled slowly. He would bring peace to the land.

'Natsuo-chan, wait a moment.' Natsuo was about to leave the temple complex and follow the forest route back down to Fukui. He recognised the voice of Kaneda-san. 'You won't have to walk.'

They strolled together in silence down to the little hamlet of Eiheiji, which had sprung up over the centuries to cater for pilgrims and tourists. In reality, it was a couple of streets lined with low houses and shops selling charms and trinkets.

Tamamo, Kaneda, had organised for a friend of the monastery to drive Natsuo back to Fukui. 'He runs the town Information Centre, though at the moment he's not doing much. I told him you were here and he offered to take you.'

Natsuo bowed to the jolly middle-aged man in the small box car and thanked him.

'Well, we can't have our first visitor in ages walking back in this rain now can we! Get in.'

Before entering the car Natsuo turned to Kuzu and bowed once more.

'Kuz...Kaneda-san. Arigato gozaimashita.'

The young monk placed a hand on his shoulder. He said nothing but merely smiled and nodded. For what else was there to say? "Good luck"? "Have fun in the underworld?". There were no words left, only actions.

The journey that the day before had taken Natsuo three hours, took less than half an hour in the car. The man, Itsuki-san, laughed for almost the entirety of the trip. He had a big grin with a couple of back teeth missing, which lent him a jovial, medieval air, if not one of much intelligence. Natsuo chided himself for judging him on his looks.

'Our Information Centre has been closed for weeks. In the meantime I work helping my brother at his soba restaurant. Our family has been making the local speciality — Echizen Oroshi soba they call them — for four generations! I'll drop you off there and you can grab some food on the house.'

Miyoshiya was a humble little noodle bar huddled in a crosshatch of wooden beams and orange glowing lights on the bottom floor of an old apartment block. Natsuo sat on a leather cushion, legs crossed, at a low pinewood table. The soba arrived almost instantly, steaming hot and fragrant. Thick buckwheat noodles covered in piquant grated radish lazed about in a hot dashi broth. As he levered the refreshing soba noodles into his mouth and slurped them up with the steaming broth Natsuo took his phone out to plan his next steps.

It was 10AM, which meant he must have been meditating for more than two hours. This shocked him as he thought he had only been in the room for about thirty minutes.

I guess that's meditation...

The route he'd have to take, not the fastest but the most affordable, was a series of local trains up the north-west coast of Honshu. He would pass through the old samurai and geisha town of Kanazawa, sweeping inland through the Japan Alps to connect to different trains at Nagano before heading north via the massive port of Niigata, all the way past Akita to the northern city of Aomori.

It would take a full day of travel, maybe more. So he would likely make a night-stop somewhere. Thankfully his mother had given him money for the trip. Natsuo's final thought, as he slurped up the last few drops of the umami broth: *As long I have enough money to see me to hell...*

After many hours of train travel, many hours of staring out of teardropped windows to a passing world of grey; little villages, wet temples, sodden trees and dripping roofs, Natsuo finally decided to stop. The evening had already rushed to meet him and he had no desire to carry onto another connection.

At the small city of Tsuruoka he alighted and headed towards the castle ruins at the centre of the old town. He found a cheap hostel on a street bisected by the attractive Shinuchi River canal, which was lined both sides by naked sakura trees, their cherry blossoms dotting the whipped-up waters.

For dinner he found a waterside sushi bar called Chozaburo where he ordered a *chirashi* bowl and some warm sake. This close to the coast meant the fish in the sushi bowl would be beautifully fresh and it had been a long time since Natsuo had tasted the clean taste of brightly-coloured sashimi. The rice too was perfect, seasoned with the classic mixture of sweetened vinegar. Natsuo liked to eat the fish separately with just the tiniest dot of wasabi and dip just the tip of each slice in the soy sauce. He then sprinkled more soy sauce over the rice and ate it after. That way he felt he was getting two courses in the one dish. Normally Natsuo would accompany it with a beer, but the weather was heavy and wet and for days he had felt cold and moist to the bone. The hot funk of the sake warmed him through with each sip.

Despite the never-ending cycle of awful weather: cloudy, cloudy and rainy, very rainy, stormy, typhoon, and repeat, Natsuo never got tired of looking out from somewhere cosy.

He hadn't spied a soul the whole time he was in the sushi bar until finally he saw some activity on the opposite side of the narrow canal. A palanquin, like one you'd imagine from centuries ago, came to halt outside a smart old building, which had been designed as an odd mix between English mock-Tudor and medieval Japanese. Two figures in long robes gently placed the palanquin down and the one at the head of the box trotted round to the side, opening the small door and simultaneously flicking open an umbrella. Natsuo was intrigued, though he couldn't make out much through the rain and the fact that the person inside the box exited the opposite side, thus blocking his view. Luckily the man that left the palanquin, prior to entering the building, waddled across the road to gaze down at the cherry blossoms and into the water of the canal, giving Natsuo a full glimpse of him.

It was an odd little man with an enormous gourd-shaped head and the shrivelled and wizened features of someone very old. Natsuo was reminded of the head of a catfish. His face seemed benign and even kindly and there was barely any hair left on his wrinkled skull. In his small mouth he smoked a long, fine pipe and in his hand was a knobbly old cane. He wore a beautiful royal blue silk kimono that looked to Natsuo like it was worth a lot of money. All in all, he looked like a refined gentleman, though somewhat misshapen and stunted, who had maybe come from a rich and long family line. He was clearly important and as soon as he had decided the time was right, he was ushered into the fancy building and the palanquin taken away.

'*Sumimasen*,' Natsuo said, calling out to the barman in the empty sushi bar. 'Did you see that old man getting out of the palanquin?'

The barman, cleaning his knives, seemed not to hear Natsuo.

'Sumi —'

'Hai. I saw him,' came the curt, yet not rude response.

'What is that building he went into?'

'That is the villa of the Honma family.'

'A rich family?'

'Mm, and old. A famous family round these parts; they travelled the world and were some of the earliest visitors to Europe. And they designed that beautiful residence, combining eastern and western styles.'

'So, is that man part of the Honma family then?'

'No...' The man seemed guarded. 'Not exactly.'

Natsuo crunched down on a piece of salmon and relished the tingle of the wasabi in his nostrils. 'Biru, kudasai,' he said to the barman who nodded tightly.

When the cold beer arrived, having had his fill of sake, Natsuo pushed again.

'So, if you don't mind me asking, who was that man if not part of Honma family? Are the Honma still there?'

'Oh they're there, but so is he. He...' The barman scratched the back of his head as if he shouldn't be talking about this, but also seemed that there was something he wanted to get off his chest. 'Nurarihyon is his name.'

'Strange name...'

'This town is haunted, you know. Or, at least, has been for the last few months. But Nurarihyon, he has always come and gone.'

'Haunted?' said Natsuo swallowing a large gulp of beer. 'There are yōkai here then?'

The barman relaxed and seemed almost relieved. He pulled up a chair and sat next to Natsuo.

'Yes,' he said eagerly. 'More and more. They're everywhere. The town is terrified. And I think it's all to do with him.'

'One moment.' Natsuo opened his bag and pulled out the old fisherman's book. Sure enough, flicking through to "N" in the index, he found there was a small section on Nurarihyon.

The short, comical, elderly Nurarihyon is actually the most powerful and elite of all the yōkai.

Nurarihyon is known as kaibutsu no oyadama – the supreme commander of all monsters.

Every yōkai listens to his words and pays him respect, treating him as the elder and leader in all meetings.

He arrives at homes unexpectedly in his splendid palanquin and slips into the house unnoticed by anyone. He acts as if he owns the residence, helping himself to luxuries. His power is so great that even the real owners of the house can do nothing to stop him.

In fact, even after they finally notice his presence, the owners believe the Nurarihyon to be the actual owner of the house.

As to origins, little is known and there is only speculation. Nurari means "to slip away" and "hyon" an onomatopoeic word for floating upwards. Little is known about Nurarihyon given his slippery evasiveness.

'What a strange monster...' Natsuo said quietly.

'You see. He's been coming and going from the finest establishments for years.'

'Doesn't sound particularly dangerous though. Though it says here he's the "commander of all monsters".' Natsuo prodded at the line in the book. 'Seems to me more like a freeloader with a skill for not getting noticed.'

'Every time he comes to this town, I notice more yōkai. People think I'm crazy. And recently there have been more and more. I only leave my house during the day. And of course now...' The barman looked at his watch. 'It's ōmagatoki, the hour of evil spirits.'

Sure enough in his book it explained that the ōmagatoki was the twilight hour between when the sun sets and the sky goes dark. Neither day nor night. The line between *sekai* — the world — and *ikai* — the spirit world — starts to blur. The mind starts to play tricks. Or are they tricks? This is when the yōkai and other evil spirits stir and cross over.

Natsuo decided to tell the barman his story. On the one hand the young sushi chef was somewhat appeased by the fact that what he had been experiencing was indeed real, but then panicked a little when he understood the impending and overarching danger shrouding the whole situation.

When Natsuo asked for the bill, the barman just shook his head, 'You don't pay.'

The rain wasn't as heavy as it had been, though a cold wind was blowing and there was a faint smell of fish on the air. Natsuo decided to stroll back slowly on the other side of the river, hoping to snoop a look through the window of the Honma villa. He couldn't see any sign of life inside, though the lights were on. He pressed on south along the attractive canal path.

Suddenly a building caught his eye, a bone-white Catholic church with a bright red spire top. It was set just off the main road and had a small grassy area in front of it.

In all of Japan there weren't even half a million Catholics, under 0.5% of the total population, so Natsuo was somewhat surprised to find a clean and white-wood slatted church here in Tsuruoka. The design made it look like something you'd find out in the cornfields of America, not in a small Yamagata city.

At school he remembered learning about the Hidden Christians and had found it fascinating. After Tokugawa Ieyasu had united Japan together and implemented a strict policy of national isolationism he continued Hideyoshi's ideas that Christianity should be severely repressed. Foreign missionaries were exiled or killed. People were tortured or converted. The Kakure Kirishitan were those who continued to practise Christianity in the shadows. Many had secret rooms in their houses or transformed figures of the Virgin Mary to look like a Buddha.

There were a couple of Catholic churches in Kochi, though Natsuo had only been in one; the Nakajimacho Church, which was, in his opinion, a horrible-looking concrete turret stained by years of rain. Most of the famous and historic ones were out in and around the western city of Nagasaki; that great port which was the entry point for Spanish and Portuguese traders, and, by extension, missionaries.

The church was sadly locked when Natsuo tried the door, but he was able at least to peer through the window and see the lofty white arches leading to the criss-cross design on the ceiling. Apart from the large wooden organ fixture and inserts like lecterns and cupboards, the whole nave was pristine albino. Even though this kind of building must be so average and mundane to much of the world it was, to Natsuo, rather exotic.

To the right of the church, just off the pavement, was a little stand selling mochi. Natsuo had never been the biggest fan of the pounded gummy rice balls, though after all the sushi and sake he thought at least something sweet would be welcome.

He approached the little kiosk. The man behind the counter, with his back turned to Natsuo, was busying himself by pounding out the large glutinous mass used to make the little sweets. He wore a blue *happi*, a sort of robe cut short into a shirt, and the ubiquitous dishcloth-like headband that all chefs and cooks wore, tied around the forehead.

'Good evening. Do you have any red bean mochi?' Natsuo asked.

'And *konbanwa* to you, young man,' answered a rich and playful voice, clearly having worked long enough to identify all the necessary information just from the customer's voice. '*Mochiron*!'

'I'll take two please.'

'Coming right up,' answered the mochi seller, his back still turned to Natsuo. He slid open a box and brought out two small blobs, one green and one cream-coloured, and placed them in a small paper bag. 'Here you go.' The man said simultaneously as he turned round.

Natsuo stumbled back and screamed. The man had no face, the seller's face was a blank orb with no mouth, eyes, nose or features at all. Despite this lack of mouth, the mochi vendor began to cackle maniacally.

'What the hell!' screeched Natsuo.

The seller leant over the counter and loomed over Natsuo. 'Did I scare you?' he cackled. 'Boo!' He shouted and shot out his hands, dropping the sesame-dusted mochi balls into a puddle.

Natsuo began to run as quickly as he could away from the kiosk. 'Yōkai...' he hissed through his teeth.

He ran past the church back to the canal path and followed it back to his hostel. He came up on the Honma Villa and as he careened past it he glimpsed the old man, Nurarihyon, smiling at him from the doorway, waving jovially at him with his pipe. 'God damn monsters...' Natsuo seethed again.

A couple of minutes of sprinting later and he arrived back at his hostel. The front door was unlocked, and he crashed through it slamming it shut behind him. He leant back on the door and for a few moments just caught his breath, trying to slow his heart rate.

When he opened his eyes, he noticed how quiet the hostel was. Nobody was behind the reception desk. He took his shoes off, swapping them for some slippers provided at the entrance, and went to his room two floors up. He needed to bathe, rest and forget about this haunted town. On the second floor he came to a halt. At the top of the stairs on the landing was a smudge of red on the pine floorboards. His eyes followed the stain. It wasn't a smudge, it was a trail. A trail of dark crimson leading down the hall left towards a room. The corridor stank of iron and rust. Blood.

He heard a moan, a sort of tired groan.

Pain? Had someone been attacked?

'Hello? Is someone hurt in there? Do you need help?'

Again the groan, now with a flavour of fear about it.

What the hell?

He slowly came up fully onto the landing and made his way towards the room at the end of the corridor three doors down.

Why am I moving towards the danger?

Every logical synapse was firing at him to go the other way, to leave the building, to call someone. But something else was pulling him towards that room. Something righteous? Something salvational? Maybe he just wanted to see if somebody needed help.

It could be anything, right?

He inched closer and was just passing the first room when the floorboard creaked loudly. He paused. He didn't know why he paused, but it felt like he was living out a scene from a film, and in films and in situations like this, people stopped. A new sound appeared. An animalistic, gurgling screech. Some tortured and angry growl. Then he heard scraping and pitter patter sounds. Something was in the room.

A dog, maybe?

He instinctively took the sword out of his bag and held it out in front of him with two trembling hands.

'Hello?' Sliding his feet closer.

Suddenly something shot out into the hallway in a brown blur of fur and splattering blood. In an instant it skidded to a halt and stared at Natsuo. It was the most grotesque thing he had ever seen. It looked like some shrunken hairy ape on all fours with hair sprouting messily out of its head. The creature was covered in blood and amniotic fluid and trailed an umbilical cord behind it. It hissed at Natsuo, who was frozen to the spot, exposing small fangs and two tongues, one red and one white.

'Kuso!'

It emitted an ungodly noise again, a gargled squeal, and scrabbled along the floorboards towards him. Natsuo spun on his heels and ran the other way down the corridor towards his room. Looking over his shoulder he saw the odd simian monster turn and run off down the stairs, but Natsuo didn't stop until he had entered his room. Closing the door behind him he stood, breathing heavily and sweating from fear, holding the sword in front of him facing the sliding door, which was locked only by a simple latch. He had never been so scared in all his life. He wretched and then crumpled to his knees.

'You can put the sword down, young man,' came a sharp voice from the windowsill.

Natsuo screamed again and swung around, taking a moment to locate the voice, the sword in one hand, drying tears away with the other. For a moment he saw nothing and then two birds appeared through the teary blur.

'Crows?' he sniffled.

'I am no crow,' chirped a bright and haughty response from the window. 'I am a yogen no tori. A celestial prophetic messenger bird.' It was then Natsuo saw it was just one black bird with two heads, one of which was white. 'With that charm of yours, and me here, you are safe.'

Natsuo dropped the sword and slumped down onto his futon bed. The little bird hopped off the windowsill down onto the side table. 'I was sent by Sōjōbō with a message, but I see now I arrived at an opportune time indeed.' Every new sentence was said by one or other of the heads, though the voice never changed.

'What...was that thing?'

'A kekkai. Nasty little creatures. Childbirth monsters. When they emerge from their mothers as the twisted little hell beasts they are, they scurry away and escape. Later they return to kill the mother, often burrowing up through the floorboards, tearing her apart. Horrible business.'

'Is the mother...?'

'She is alive, but that thing will be back. But leave her, and it, to me.'

'And there was a creature without a face selling sweets...' Natsuo was thinking out loud.

'A nopperabō, yes. They exist only to spook and scare.'

'And the old man...'

'Nurarihyon. We know. Listen young man you have to focus, important days are ahead.' Natsuo took a moment to collect himself. So much had happened in the space of so little time and now he was being pulled together by a strict, two-headed crow. 'Boy!'

'Mmm, yes. Sorry. I just...' Natsuo rubbed his eyes. 'Never mind. You have a message?'

'Indeed. Tomorrow you are to make your way to Mount Osore and you will meet an *itako* who will open a connection with Meido for you to enter.'

'Itako?'

'They are shamanistic mediums.'

'And what do I do when I get there?'

The bird, slightly testily, but not without understanding, simply responded 'You'll find out everything you need to know at Mount Osore.' Natsuo nodded, taking the hint. 'Now please, rest and gather yourself. You will soon start to view what happened tonight as a mere triviality. Rest, and I shall see to these troublesome beasts.' The bird took to the air. As the heavy flutter of the wings passed out into the night, the last thing Natsuo heard was 'Rest...' before succumbing to a deep and dreamless sleep.

The itako are dwindling in number. Fewer than two dozen remain in all of Japan. The usually blind old women enter training when they are young girls before their first menstruation. They then spend years learning chants, prayers and fortune telling before completing a ritual known as kamitsuke, in which they go into a trance, and it is believed they form a holy marriage, shinkon, with a spirit. Thus, an independently practising itako is born to go out into the country and help people who are anxious to communicate with the dead. Their dead.

Every summer at Mount Osore many itako gather around Lake Usori and the temples there while hundreds of people make pilgrimages there in order to speak to the blind shamanesses. The itako speak in the voices of the dead, an activity called kuchiyose, and transmit messages from loved ones lost. They are said to be able to communicate with the kami too, having a direct line to the gods.

Over the decades many have shrugged off the itako as charlatans or merely tools of extracting money from naive believers. But they have persisted, just.

Once again Natsuo suffered through almost a full day's travel to get close to Osore. First two trains to Aomori, changing at Akita, which took him about five hours, and then another two trains in order to get to the fishing town of Mutsu, huddled in the clenched fist of the Shimokita Peninsula. This was about as far north as you could get on Japan's main island of Honshu. North was the vast mountainous and scarcely-populated beauty of Hokkaido, the nation's frozen Wild West Island.

He took out the book given to him by Sōjōbō. It was cream-coloured paper from front to back and the bare front cover simply had the word Meido written in kanji.

Meido; the dark way.

> **To enter the underworld the soul must find and cross the Sanju River, the River of Three Crossings. The boundary between the world of the dead and that of the living.**

After death, three oni will escort the soul on a seven-day journey to Meido. The path is dark and accompanied by a constant raging wind. The corruption of the living world is embodied by swords that pierce the body of the dead, spilling blood that turns the land red.

After a few days hell birds will tear at the traveller's flesh and pluck out their eyes, taunting them. They will then arrive at an enormous thorn-covered mountain. "The mountain is made of your greed" shout the oni as they hit the slow climbers with their clubs.

After seven days the souls reach the Sanzu River and face the first trial from the judge King Shinkō. He will judge how much killing has been committed, down to the ants and fish of the world. Those deemed truly wicked are sent straight to Jigoku. Others may cross, though a fee of 6 mon must be paid.

There are three points to cross: a great bridge, a shallow fordable part, and then the wild deep of the river. Those souls with the most good deeds to their name will cross the bridge. Those with a mixture of good and bad can wade across. And those lacking a good life must swim across the snake-infested rapids.

After the crossing the souls will encounter Keneō and Datsueba. These oni will take the traveller's clothes and hang them up on a tree. The more the branches bend under the weight, the more sin was committed in their lives. If the soul arrives with no clothes, Datsueba will flay off the skin and hang that instead.

After 14 days King Shokō will perform another trial and judge how much they have stolen.

Before the third trial the soul must pass through a fortified gate guarded by a fierce oni. He will decide which parts to chop off the bodies of the travellers. If any part aided a sin it will be removed. The souls then cross a boiling bay whose aromas cling to the nose.

After 21 days King Sōtei will perform the third trial. He will judge the sins of lust and lasciviousness by using a snake and a cat. The cat will bite the sex organs of the men. The extent of the injury will determine the extent of the sin. The snake will go inside the women and the depth it can enter will determine the depth of her sin.

After 28 days the fourth trial is performed by King Gokan. He will judge how many lies the soul has told in the previous life, by weighing them against a large rock. The number of stones needed to balance the scales will determine the extent of their lies.

As at every stage, heavy sinners are sent straight to hell, whereas those more virtuous will carry on to be judged.

The dead then cross an unending barren and punctured landscape, constantly beaten by balls of hot iron that rain down from the sky, burning the souls and their bodies.

After 35 days, the fifth trial is performed by King Enma himself, ruler of the underworld. He will show each soul a mirror that reflects back the life of the dead, with all their sins visible. This is the last place of appeal, through prayers and memorials given by the living. Enma will decide into which realm the soul will be reborn: heaven, humans, beasts, asura, gaki or hell.

After 42 days the souls meet King Henjō. He will decide the location of the rebirth based on the information relayed by King Enma and King Gokan.

The souls must once again cross a dark and ominous land of bizarre creatures whose cries pierce the darkness, horrible birds that attack them with fire and beaks, and suffer weariness from their weeks of trials.

On the 49th day the dead arrive at King Taizan. This is the final point to avoid entering hell. He will weigh up everything and finalise the new path for the traveller.

Upon completion the souls pass through a road with six unmarked torii gates, each representing a realm. After travelling along a vast frozen river the soul will avoid Jigoku and leave Meido for the next world, whichever it may be.

At any point, and depending on the sin of the soul, the dead may enter Jigoku, either to the great hells, the cold hells, the lesser hells or any other of the thousands of hellscapes depending on their crimes.

Natsuo closed the book and rubbed his eyes. It was the first time he'd thought to read about what was awaiting him. The first time in a while he'd had a moment to himself to prepare his mind for what he was about to go through. But he didn't expect that. Kings and trials, flayed skin and demonic birds pecking out his eyes. Thankfully he wasn't a soul undergoing trials. Though, he still had no idea what parts of the dead's nearly two month-long ordeal he would have to encounter, or witness.

Despite coming all this way and undertaking such an important task, Natsuo still knew fairly little about what he was going to have to actually do.

On the last leg, as the little Ominato line two-car train crawled around the vast and almost enclosed Mutsu Bay, Natsuo crunched down into a shiny, cherry-coloured apple, the local Aomori speciality, and thought about how far he had come. Not only in terms of distance — his phone telling him he was over 1500 km from his home — but also, and he hated to think of the hackneyed expression, how far he'd come as a person.

Hikikomori were almost like a social caste; a part of society either shunned or ignored. Natsuo had grown accustomed to his isolation and fully expected, up until a few weeks ago, to spend of the rest of his life bumbling around his house interacting with the world only via the Internet or the television, yet he was now on a train to enter the underworld with a magical sword in his bag. If Natsuo was honest with himself, he still didn't fully believe the reality he was living.

Despite it being a cardinal sin, he was proud of himself. Of having gotten out. Of having undertaken this mission. He was proud of himself for experiencing new things, new emotions, and taking them in his stride. He was proud of himself for having reconnected with his mother. This pride and excitement at all the newness was helping assuage the abject terror he should have been feeling.

His thoughts then turned to other people like him, other Hikikomori. He wondered if after all this, when life went back to whatever normal people called normal, if he could do something to help. Yes, he thought to himself, he wanted to help.

He remembered the old man at the support centre who offered them oranges. Would that be Natsuo when this was finished? Would he be telling young men about how he got out and vanquished evil to restore peace to the world? Would he hand out oranges too?

'Next station: MUTSU-OMINATO. End of line. Thank you for choosing Japan Rail,' pinged the tinny voice from the tannoy. Natsuo got off the train with two other people, a couple in their seventies, who politely nodded to him as he headed away from the little platform and went off in search of a room for the night. It was 7PM and tomorrow he would make his way to the mountain.

Natsuo headed to an unattractive block of a hotel which was astonishingly cheap but at least offered views out over the small city and the nearby peaks. He had headed to an izakaya nearby with a wonky sign showing the name Takedaya and, because he wasn't very hungry, simply ordered some small plates: spicy maguro tuna, Some fried tofu with *katsuoboshi*, a sliced tomato, tamago omelette and a bottle of Sapporo beer.

As he headed back to his hotel Natsuo remarked on the clarity of the sky. It wasn't raining. It was the first time in quite a while that the sky hadn't seemed concentrated and angry. He could make out the soft tendrils of early summer evenings, wispy clouds dancing off the tops of the mountains, and the water in the bay glassy and calm. Natsuo took this as a good omen. Perhaps, he joked macabrely to himself as he got ready to sleep, everything will turn out fine.

Mount Doom was the English translation of Osore-zan. It was, in reality, part of a range of eight somma volcanoes forming, when viewed from above, a towering half-ring around the southwestern part of the Usori caldera lake. The acidic waters of the lake were dead and forbidding and the area's fumaroles, emitting sulphurous gases and steam, added a hellish haze to the lifeless lands around the temple buildings.

This is the place from my dream...

Luckily for Natsuo the owner of the hotel had a friend willing to take him the short twenty-minute drive up the hill to the Bodai-ji temple. To his surprise there were actually a few pilgrims who had made the trip to the lake. They were mourning at the Jizō statues down near the water.

Jizō is regarded as the bodhisattva guardian of children and patron deity of deceased children and their souls. The pilgrims were families and they were leaving toys, bibs and items of clothing by the statues. Lost children.

The ground was dry and dead, a grey and chalky film of volcanic ash covered everything and Natsuo's shoes were quickly dirtied. He had no idea where he was supposed to go to meet the itako and so just wandered around the temple buildings hoping for some form of inspiration. East of the main temple complex Natsuo saw a rising line of smoke. He found a monk sweeping ash and dust off the steps of one of the shrines.

'Sumimasen. Could you tell me what that is over there?' Natsuo pointed to the smoking area some five hundred metres away.

'Sanzunokawa,' smiled the old robed priest. 'We like to say that that misty brook, the real name is Shozu by the way, is the Sanzu River, the waters over which the deceased souls must cross to make their way to the afterlife.' He gave a little laugh and went back to his sweeping. 'Well, that's what we like to say, anyway.'

Natsuo followed the lake's edge round to a small stream that entered the caldera waters under a pretty red, arched bridge. Natsuo couldn't work out where the steam was coming from.

'Don't touch the water...' came a voice upriver through the smoke, though he saw no-one.

A few metres upstream on the left bank he spied a small house, white-walled with a simple red roof. A guard rail separated the driveway from the main path and, staring at the little abode through the milky air, it all looked rather overgrown, as if it were huddling, abandoned, amongst bushes. 'The water will burn you...' The voice was definitely coming from that house, though the sound and volume made it feel as if it were speaking directly next to his ears. He thought of the expression 'a voice carried upon the wind.'

Natsuo climbed over the metal barrier and slowly approached. A small wooden sign hung on the door.

Akari
Naganohara
Itako
Please knock.

Well this must be it...

'Come in, Natsuo,' the voice said.

Yes, this is definitely it...

Natsuo removed his shoes and put on some slippers before heading to the main room. The interior was a lot cosier and more welcoming than it had seemed from outside.

Beautiful woodblock paintings of trees and birds hung on the wood-panelled walls and under them were small tables covered with candles, images and statuettes of Buddha and Jizō. Off the ceiling draped shimenawa rope and white *shide* zig-zag papers as well as royal blue flags bearing the lotus symbol. In the middle of the room sat an old lady in a simple white robe and loose black trousers.

She was old but still sported short brown hair, giving her an air of youth. Her forehead was heavily lined, but her cheeks were still smooth and touched with rosiness. She had kind, bright eyes, however from the way her head searched, but her eyes did not, her blindness was evident.

'Mrs Naganohara.' He kneeled down in front of her and bowed.

'Are you enjoying the nice weather here?' She giggled to herself.

'Um, yes.' Natsuo was slightly taken aback by the question and the old lady's temperament. He expected someone far more serious.

The old itako smiled, as if she had understood what he was thinking. 'We are in a sort of no man's land here. Mt Osore is the entrance to the underworld, a crossing point, and so isn't really in the hands of either side. Therefore, all the noise they are making doesn't affect us here.'

'The noise.'

'Oh you know, all the yōkai, the storms. Not here. It wouldn't be good for them to make a ruckus on their own doorstep now, would it?'

'I guess not.'

'Tea?'

'Um, yes please.'

With movements as flawless as someone with perfect vision she pulled out two china cups and a piping hot kettle and poured out two servings of fragrant green tea, stopping her pour just before reaching the top of each cup.

'I've been blind a long time.' She smiled, once again guessing what Natsuo was thinking. 'If I still couldn't pour tea, I wouldn't be very good, would I?'

'I guess not.'

'Many people think us itako are charlatans, fakes. And believe you me, over the years there have been many who have taken advantage of the sad and lost to make a few yen. But there are still many of us with the *reikan*.'

'Reikan?'

'Mm, the sight, the spirit vision. We have a link to the underworld. We can talk to and see ghosts.' She took a sip of tea and gently put the little mug back on the saucer. 'We can offer closure to people. They want to know the souls of their loved ones are ok, or sometimes they want to relay a message or hope for an answer.'

'What if the souls are...not ok?'

'Therein lies our duty and our curse. We can either give them the truth or we lie.'

'You lie to people?'

'Sometimes to help someone, causing them more pain isn't the right path. But, thankfully, most people in the grand eyes of the gods, are good.'

'I think I understand.'

'Anyway. I'm told I need to send you down to Meido,' she said, quite casually.

'That's right.'

'Well, I suppose there's no time to delay.'

'Wait...'

'Mmm?'

'Before I...go...I had a couple of questions.' Natsuo had been so caught up in the forward movement of his mission that he hadn't had time to think of the small things. Another saying came to him 'the devil is in the details'; and for Natsuo this could actually be the case. 'How long will I be down there? What do I eat and drink? Where do I sleep?'

She smiled, 'I see they haven't filled you in.' The old lady chuckled to herself and poured some more tea. 'You are entering a demon realm. It is not connected to this plane of existence directly. Time that passes down there does not pass the same as here. You could spend a month in Meido or Jigoku and only a few days might pass here. But you will feel the passing of time yourself. It's like the gravity of space. For example, if a space traveller were on a planet close to a black hole with far denser gravity, time would elapse faster there than in normal space. If that traveller went to the planet near the black hole they could spend an hour there, and it would be an hour for them. Then, returning to their ship in normal space, away from the heightened gravity, they could find that the rest of the crew there had experienced many, many years of time. And it would have been, relatively, many years for them.'

'Ok...'

'Hah! I bet you didn't think an old crone like me would know things like that!' She cackled, enjoying Natsuo's surprise. 'Anyway, your other questions. Given you aren't on a normal plane of existence, you also won't be a slave to things like human thirst or hunger. As your body won't be existing, by definition, in your own existence, it also will not register as needing to exist. By that I mean to say, your body will almost be on standby mode. But thanks in part to your demon blood, you won't get tired as the humans would. So lucky for you, you can just get on with the job in hand. You may still have the desire to sleep though, and that, sadly, will be up to you to manage.' She finished her tea. 'And, young man, you'll be down there as long as it takes. So better not dilly-dally.'

'I had one more question.'

'What's that dear?'

'My father?'

'Your father?'

'Yes.' Natsuo searched for a moment. 'Is he...there? Can you speak to him?'

'This isn't really —'

'Please,' Natsuo implored. 'Everyone seems to know him more than I did. In fact, I didn't know him at all. If you could even just send him a message?'

Akari Naganohara's eyes dropped and she sighed deeply. 'Given you are about to embark on a perilous quest and my life as an itako is one devoted to this very task I feel it would be cruel of me not to try. Though the souls of one like your father are not to be found in the same places as those wandering the human path.'

After Natsuo passed her the message she closed her eyes tightly until all that was left were whorls of wrinkles and began to chant. It sounded like gibberish to Natsuo, but he had read that the itako used a private and ancient Aomori dialect when conducting their seances.

After maybe a minute she went completely silent except for the occasional mumble. What Natsuo hoped to come of this particular surreal moment in his life he did not know. Many people would liken it to closure he supposed. Just knowing that his father knew everything was enough for him.

A gasp of air startled Natsuo as the old lady's eyes un-whorled again, as if she had been a dormant creature jolted into life.

'Did you see him?'

'I'm afraid not, my boy. But I managed to pass it on to a *namahage* demon down there who owes me a favour. Maybe if he's not too busy scaring naughty children into being good he can root around for you.'

'A favour?'

'Mm?'

'You know what, never mind.' Natsuo decided he already had enough information to process. 'So. Where do I need to go?'

'Sit right where you are; no need to go anywhere.' Mrs. Naganohara smiled as she moved aside the tea set. 'Just try to empty your mind. We'll get you down there in no time at all.'

Natsuo had often seen scenes in films where characters 'emptied their minds' and he always thought it an impossible task. To him the sheer act of thinking about nothing was thinking about something. And he was currently sat in front of a blind shamanness who had a debt to be paid by a demon before heading to purgatory.

Clear his mind! How was he going to clear his mind? The mind is a sparking, bubbling mass of thoughts. In his mind the only way a mind could be completely cleared was if there wasn't much to clear in the first place.

He had never been one to value his own intelligence; in fact, his years spent as a Hikikomori evidently showed how little he thought he was worth. But even Natsuo didn't think he would be able to empty his mind. And if he couldn't do that, how was he going to make it into Meido? And if he didn't get there, how would he help save the world? And would he ever find out if his father got his message? He just had to not think about not thinking and then maybe he might be able to start not thinking about clearing his mind.

'We are here young man,' came Akari Naganohara's voice. 'Welcome to the underworld.'

Chapter Seven: Meido
冥土

Dark way, the Underworld.

'What do you mean we are here?'

Natsuo looked around. He was still in the small room, sat on his knees in front of the old itako.

'Outside that door is Meido.' She smiled. 'I've shifted us onto another plane of existence. As soon as you walk out that door you will be on your dark way and you won't be able to come back in. Once you are out there you cannot return until you are done. I hope you understand this, as right now, sat here with me, this is the last chance you have to return to your old life. Are you ready?'

Natsuo took a moment to process. This was the first moment on his journey since leaving his home that he wouldn't be able to just put his fingers in his ears and pretend he couldn't hear what the people were saying he had to do.

In reality he had always had the choice to throw in the towel and head back to his insular life in Kochi. He could ignore everything and return to his mother. Why should he risk everything, his newly acquired freedom, to help a world he didn't even know? But then he thought, there may be no freedom, no world, to enjoy if he didn't carry on.

'I'm ready.'

The world outside the house was alien and terrible but also vividly familiar. It was like what he had seen in that dream. Was he witnessing what he had already seen? Or was this new? Behind him was the lofty mountain, the peak scratching at some dark shards of cloud.

That must be the mountain of thorns...he thought to himself, remembering what he had read in the book.

He turned back and found his view unobstructed. The itako's house had vanished. Natsuo found himself once again on the outcrop looking out to the cratered fiery hellscape and again, just like in that dream, down in the valley he spied a river. The river...

The pieces were falling into place, and he understood what he had to do. Cross the Sanzu River. There was no other option.

Natsu descended off the outcrop down towards the craggy valley floor. He slipped and slid more than walked; the ground was black cinder and every footstep sank him halfway to his knees. It took him a while to regulate his breath and get accustomed to the hot roasted air that clogged his throat and left a savoury taste in his mouth. The air was thick with rotten fish and cooked meat.

The ground here was brown and cracked. It at once looked desiccated and alive, as if something terrible were bubbling just under the surface. Here and there fumaroles steamed out odorous clouds and everything looked dead. There were trees, but they were now only blackened trunks and crooked lifeless branches.

Natsuo soon arrived at the procession of dead souls. Sullen-faced individuals who were scratched and covered in grime. They looked tired and weathered. Natsuo remembered the seven days of toiling they had to have gone through just to arrive at the river of judgement. He felt himself lucky and slipped in behind a large man with brightly coloured chest tattoos visible under a torn white shirt. A tie hung loosely around his neck and, judging from his trousers, he usually wore a black suit.

Yakuza...

King Shinkō came into view. One of the nine Kings of Hell sat at a towering desk teeming with papers and scrolls and feather pens. He must have been at least ten metres tall and wore fine white robes lined with coral blue finishes and a red belt. On his enormous head Shinkō sported a velour crown with elegant dragons embroidered on the front. His face finished in a clean black goatee flourish and bore an expression of passive aloofness; as if he had seen it all before. At his feet the moaning hordes received their judgement and split into three lines: one to cross the bridge, the other to wade, and the third to take its chances with the snakes.

Little winged devils flew about the great king and swooped over the procession whilst large, muscular, red-skinned oni shepherded people towards their fate.

Behind the king was the great river, the other side of which was lost in mist. The great Sanzu bridge, as wide as ten city buses, rose from the banks into the unknown like two red arms carrying the souls onward. Down in the water Natsuo could just about make out people wading across, using their arms to balance against the current. He heard the screams and the crashing of rapids further down the river and was thankful he couldn't see those poor souls attacked by serpents.

It was then Natsuo remembered he wasn't supposed to be there. And by 'there' he meant the line of dead people seeking salvation. If he arrived for judgement at King Shinkō what would he say? No. To cross the bridge he had to carry himself as one of the underworld. This was easier said than done given he was dressed in outdoor gear and had a backpack with a sword in it. He would have to cross the bridge, that was a sure thing, there were no other options, he would have to just head up and over as if he belonged there. But how to do it?

It was then Natsuo remembered a line from a film he had once seen. He had always loved American movies about con artists and there was one he particularly enjoyed called *Confidence*. The plot twisted left and right so many times you didn't know where it would end and who would come out the good guy with the money and who would be the double-crossing villain. But it was that line. That line had stuck with him.

"Confidence. It's just confidence."

As if you could get away with anything as long as you had that.

Arriving near the looming figure of King Shinkō, mechanically and impassively scribbling, and stamping, and passing on messages to his minions, oblivious to the humans below, Natsuo stepped out of line and continued on towards the bridge without stopping.

Confidence. It's just confidence...

'Hey you!' came a voice. 'Would you look at this one?' came another. 'Back in line!' barked a third. Sharp, creaking voices from above and around. He knew they were for him, but he didn't stop. Natsuo kept walking to the bridge. After a few more metres a brown, goblin-like creature holding a curved knife swooped in and touched down in front of him.

'Didn't you 'ear, human? We said get back in line.'

Confidence. It's just confidence...

'Haha! I didn't realise you were talking to me!' Natsuo felt outside of his body. Fronting in front of a demon. 'I'm not one of them! You can check.'

There was a pause as the creature gave him a once over, sniffing the air around him. It seemed to relax.

'Then why do you look like one of 'em then?' its strangled voice gurgled, still tinged with suspicion.

It's just confidence...

'It's the form I've chosen. I like them to see me as one of them, then see me pass through unscathed, unblemished, carefree. How it crushes their spirits. It's the easiest form of taunting them, of utterly defeating them. To see the soul of a dead soul die again. It's art.'

Natsuo thought the last words were too much. Too theatrical.

The creature gurgled with laughter, 'That really is evil! Even for down 'ere. I just prod 'em see.' It waved its knife about and then launched itself into the air still cackling to itself.

Natsuo exhaled and panted and almost fell to his knees.

Confidence...

He collected himself and continued to the bridge.

How long had he been walking for? He didn't feel tired, had no need to drink water or stop and rest. But then everyone else looked beaten and exhausted. Natsuo felt a little guilty, presuming his demon blood was the reason for not suffering.

'Seven days,' came a weak voice to his right. It was a girl with dyed pink hair, fake-tanned skin, white eye makeup and long fake lashes. She wore high boots, a schoolgirl miniskirt and a cravat. Kogal fashion. Natsuo had seen girls like her in his comics. Though now all her clothing was torn and soiled.

'I'm sorry?'

'They say it takes about seven days for us to cross this bridge.' She smiled darkly as a tear rolled down her cheek. 'Almost there then.'

'Almost?'

'This is the seventh day starting.'

So they had already walked six days. Natsuo hadn't even noticed the passing of time as he plodded along wordlessly, shoulder to shoulder with these doomed souls. Natsuo didn't know why, but before he had a chance to stop his mouth, the words poured out as an awkward question to fill the silence.

'So, how did you end up here?'

What an idiot...

'Car crash at Shibuya crossing,' she said matter-of-factly. 'Me and my boyfriend jumped a red light and then had to swerve to avoid the dozens of tourists already running into the road to take their photo. We span off the road into a lamppost.'

'So your boyfriend surv —'

'We both died in that car. But he...' she paused and looked right. 'He's crossing the river. I don't know if they gave him the snakes or not.'

'Oh, I'm so sorry,' said Natsuo, trying, probably in vain given their present circumstances, to offer her some sort of comfort.

'Apparently when he was younger, he ran around taking photos up girls' skirts. A hentai. A pervert. Well, that's not the guy I knew, but they said he had to take the river.' She looked out again and fell silent.

'Well, I hope you find him on the other side,' Natsuo offered limply, to no response.

The water hissed below them and there was a constant buzzing noise of moans and far-off screams. White noise. Black noise.

After what was, by some indistinct, muddied definition, the rest of a day's walk, the river fog thinned out and the opposite side of the bridge was visible. It was here the true horrors began.

Two 25-foot-tall ogreish creatures awaited the long line of new souls. They were oni, but they looked elderly and bitter. The female was grey-blue-skinned and wore nothing but a loin cloth around her waist. Her chest ribs were visible as her long breasts sagged sadly down to her stomach. Despite her looking old there was a ferocious glint in her red eyes. She clearly relished the job she had been given.

Datsueba would accept the 6 mon toll of the dead. This was why the Japanese placed coins in the coffin at a funeral. She was stripping the clothes off the backs of each person who arrived and was handing them over to the horned, pointy-eared and red-skinned giant next to her: Keneō. Natsuo could see him hanging the clothes onto an enormous dead tree behind him.

Natsuo had no desire to reattempt talking his way out of a potentially lethal situation with these two sadists.

He never thought he would think to himself 'I wish I looked a bit more like a demon.'

He also wondered why he hadn't seen anyone run, anyone try and escape their fate. On this side of the bridge, it was only Datsueba and Keneō. It was nothing like the other side with its flying devils, buzzing like so many evil gnats or its bulky and officious oni. Here were just two elderly monsters and a wasteland.

Then, looking around the sullen masses, Natsuo realised bleakly why. These poor people had already toiled a week even before reaching the bridge, and then had been made to trudge another seven days; some by crossing the river through the water itself. They wouldn't have the energy or desire to run even if they wanted. They were already beat. Well not him.

Towards the end of the bridge, he shuffled and shimmied through the crowds towards the left side and vaulted over, landing in the shallows of the riverbank. Not one person bothered to look or notice. About 10,000 people die every year in Japan. With a population so large Natsuo understood that there might be a lot of people. He then wondered if the dead of other countries had to go to Meido. Who was right in the end?

No time to think...

Natsuo's plan was a simple one. Hop from scraggly dead bush to gnarly petrified tree and make his way behind the backs of Keneō and Datsueba as they went about their grisly tasks, and then rejoin the path further on. Simple, he thought to himself. Just don't get spotted by the demons...

To his surprise the two old demons were utterly focused on their work. The only moments Natsuo had to really take care was when Keneō turned around to hang the clothes on the tree branches, watching how much they bowed under the weight. Every now and then Natsuo would hear a chilling whelp or scream as Datseuba, perhaps out of boredom, snapped a finger or two on somebody's hand.

Suddenly, Keneō laughed proudly, as if catching someone out. Natsuo froze behind a small, stunted tree trunk. Had he been caught? He peeked out and saw Keneō pick up a naked man.

'No clothes, eh?' He barked, spittle flying from his sharp-toothed jaws that had opened into a gratified smile. 'Well, I must weigh something.' Keneō trilled like a giant from a children's book.

Datsueba then took the screaming man, holding him stretched out aloft, his arms in one of her hands, his legs in the other. Keneō picked up a rusty, blood-stained yanagiba willow knife and wiped it on his loincloth. The man's eyes were bulging with fear, bloodshot with terror, and he screamed for mercy. 'And to fink you lot use this for fish,' Keneō snorted as he placed the knife on the nape of the man's neck.

The sound that came next would never leave Natsuo. Curdled in with the guttural and primal screams was a sound like that of cellophane or Velcro being pulled away. With a smooth action, and a hot swooshing sound, Keneō had sliced and peeled away all the skin from the man's back. 'Turn 'im.' The man's cries were now feeble and limp. With a hungry grin on his face the huge red ogre sliced away the skin on the man's chest too. Datsueba, oddly gently, placed the man back on the ground as Keneō collected the two wet haunches of torso and laid them on the tree branches, leaving the man to limp away in line looking the same but now his whole back and chest a weeping red anatomical presentation of musculature.

No sooner had they skinned the man than they were back to taking clothing off the new arrivals; business as usual. Natsuo fought the urge to vomit and carried on creeping through the scorched scrubland eventually making his way back to the path.

Darkness and horror. This is all that filled the pages of the miserable guidebook given to him by Sōjōbō. All he had to look forward to was misery.

Flicking through the pages he was given a sneak peak to the hell that lay before the dead. He would soon arrive, along with the groaning line of humanity, at the great wall on the other side of which lurked a maniacal oni ready to hack at their bodies. After that he would have the joy of pungent boiling lakes, snakes and cats that attacked your genitals, barren wastelands blasted by meteors and more.

There had to be a way through, a quicker route. He was half-demon after all. A shimmer of guilt at that thought, while so many here had to bear the hardships.

Another thought that had been niggling at him since he had left the great tengu's forest lair was where exactly he was supposed to find the doorway to Yomi. When he had asked Sōjōbō the response he received didn't exactly fill him with certitude and was the mystic equivalent of 'you'll know it when you see it'. And so, he trudged on through Meido, silently joining the ranks of snake-bitten, bleeding and weary people as they continued their march of judgement.

The stone wall was so tall Natsuo could barely make out the top, yet there was only one door; a huge arched gate by which two blue hobgoblins stood holding tooth-topped staffs ushering people through.

On the other side was a twisted Hieronymus vision: the background of the painting was a vast lagoon simmering like a bowl of fetid stew in a basin between two steep mountain sides. Natsuo was reminded of the Norwegian fjords, though this was craggy brown and baked earth where Scandinavia was all Nordic forests and green glades.

He could smell it already as the surf washed in with the fumes; rotten fish guts, the iron-funk of blood and stale broth all greeted them as they passed through the wall.

The foreground of the painting was more horrific still. There was an enormous mould-green oni, a little taller than Keneō, but muscular and massive with huge fangs and wild hair. He was grabbing each passing soul, eyeing them and then, after dumping them on a wooden table, hacking at them seemingly randomly. Blood and matter spattered his grimy peach-coloured happi as the giant tossed away flesh and body parts, which were snatched by denizens lurking in the shadows.

'That foot looks like it helped you sin! Let me take it for you!' He would laugh, bringing down the machete.

The brown dirt that made up the barren land was darkened even more by the blood. Natsuo thought he was again going to be sick and had to look away to stop himself from retching. The hot and putrid meaty smells combined with the screaming and the violence were too much. Or so he thought.

A sardonic thought crossed his mind: that playing too many violent games and having watched more than his fair share of hyper-violent films and anime might have actually prepared him well for such a moment.

If Natsuo had been keen not to have to try and talk his way out of a situation with the last two oni, he had even less inclination to try and reason with this mad titan. He needed to get out of the line.

There must be a way to avoid the lake...

The beasts and demons must have a way through.

In the way of small mercies, there were a lot of people still ahead of him in line waiting to be mauled, so he had a few bleak moments to look around. To his left was the gore-splattered butchering area and up ahead was the gaseous lake. About fifty metres over to the right, where the wall met the mountain, was a small cave-like opening through which goblins and other sōshin, or lower-class monsters, were occasionally coming and going. *Must be a route out of here...*

He waited until his immediacy was clear, for there was still the occasional flying guard to worry about, and slinked off out of the line.

Nothing but scabrous and scorched open land was between him and the mountainside, so he made sure he walked with confidence. The worst thing about being somewhere you weren't supposed to be was looking like somebody who wasn't supposed to be there. He stayed close to the stone wall. It was ancient-looking and Natsuo thought it seemed like it could have been carved out of the mountain itself; exposed like a sculpture. Wet black moss grew in the cracks and here and there a putrid dark brown goo seemed to be leaking down the side.

To Natsuo's genuine surprise, this only happens to characters in movies, he made it to the hole in the wall without being seen and encountered no-one when he arrived. As he slipped inside, he could still hear the crazed green butcher laughing away and uttering, 'And I'll remove you of your hand now!'

He was in a tunnel lit by torches. It was, mercifully, a lot cooler than out in the wastes. Presuming, or hoping, that the tunnel would take him somewhere useful, Natsuo pressed on.

'Oi! What're you doin' ere?'

Natsuo had no idea of how long he had been walking. In eternity time had no meaning. He could have been in the tunnels through the mountains hours or days. But sound was still sound and sight was still sight. A pug-faced little creature with dark oily skin and warts all over its neck was standing right behind him. Natsuo jumped a little, but he had expected to encounter someone...or something at some point.

'What do you mean what am I doing here?'

'How did you sneak away from the butcher?'

'You idiot, I'm one of you lot!'

Again, the creature sniffed around Natsuo and untensed.

'Sorry. Don't get many dressing up as humans down here. Gets confusing see.'

'My fault, I'm not usually posted across the bridge. Not so used to this side of things.'

'Ah...Where you headed then?'

Natsuo quickly tried to remember the upcoming days in the little guidebook he had.

'Ermm...Enma. I have a message for King Enma. It's about the mirror.'

'Sounds important that does,' grunted the pug-faced beast, almost impressed. 'You'll find your way quite easily. First left you come to'll bring you out at the gonads — that's what we call King Sōtei's area. He knows we do. Hates it he does. Says his station is the most pure. But come on, it's snakes biting cocks.' The monster actually rolled its eyes. 'Then, next right you've got the rock-weighing area, after that the blasted plain and then the next left you've got Enma.'

Natsuo simply nodded.

'Another thing. Take this.' The creature tossed Natsuo a brooch made of twisted brass with a green eye at the centre. 'This is from my guild. If you insist on walking around looking like one of 'em this'll at least tell the rest of us you're on our side.'

Natsuo made a mental note of everything the creature had said and carried on down the fetid tunnels.

He didn't know how long he spent there trudging through the dimness. He only remembered passing one turn and was having trouble recalling what that awful little creature had said.

The seemingly endless worming lanes through the mountain were devoid of any real definition. A never-ending brown channel only broken up here and there by the monstrous and ungodly creatures Natsuo had the non-pleasure of passing. Each time he would point to the brooch, they would grunt, and he would carry on. Much like when he crossed the Sanzu bridge time was flowing in an unmeaning way. The natural passage of things didn't happen here. He started to forget details. If somebody gave you a piece of casual information how long would it be before you forgot it?

Walking ceaselessly through this stony, mud-coloured, tubular world he was struggling to organise the muddied memories. His rational mind told him it hadn't been very long since he entered the tunnels and talked to the goblin, but when he searched the swimming thoughts in his head for the actual memory of that moment the image was fuzzy, as if weeks had passed.

Natsuo arrived at another turn, a path heading off right. Was this the one he should take? It was the second of such turns he had encountered. Or was it? Natsuo rubbed his temple and tried to remember what the pug-faced monster had told him. How many rights, or lefts, and which one to take? He couldn't remember. How many days or months had he been down in this warren? Should he take this turn or wait for the next one?

'Out the way!' A gruff voice came from the darkness, breaking Natsuo's dazed inertia. Behind him a short, nasty-looking green devil with a long nose, toothy mouth and a dagger slung off a leather-sash over his bare chest. It was pushing a wheelbarrow full of manuscript paper; no doubt for some kingly judgement.

'Sumimasen.' Natsuo apologised, bowing involuntarily.

The creature pushed the barrow past Natsuo a way and then slowly stopped, its pointed-eared head cocked to one side.

'Sumimasen?' the creature said to itself before letting down the wheelbarrow and turning to Natsuo. 'Manners?' It spat. 'Nobody apologises down 'ere?'

Natsuo froze and made sure the monster could see his brooch. 'I must have picked up some bad habits from the...humans.'

'That right? Never met anyone "picked up habits" in all my centuries 'ere.' It slowly crept towards Natsuo, spying the pin on his jacket. 'What guild's that then?'

The blood shot down to Natsuo's feet and sent a flurry of butterflies to his stomach. The name...what was the name? Had he been given a name? He didn't remember a name. Had to make one up.

Make something up...

'Meido Hellbeasts...' he said cautiously.

The creature's mouth curled into a wide, feline smile and its sharp yellow teeth gleamed hungrily. 'No, it ain't.' The words slithered out. 'There ain't no guild with that name. And that little thing you got on you is of the Bone-suckers. You don't look like no Bone-sucker.' Its fingers quivered as the hand moved towards the blade. It sniffed the fetid air, confused at the creature in front of it, but decided. 'Which all makes me think you're a dirty human who's got away from the pack.'

Before Natsuo had a chance to think, instinct kicked in and he swung off his bag and took out the kusanagi-no-Tsurugi. The heavenly sword shone brightly causing the creature to squawk angrily. It felt perfectly weighted, light but powerful. Natsuo felt strong. Safe.

'What?' The demon shouted, a glint of fear in his eyes. 'Human scum!' There was fear in its eyes as the power of the blade rippled out in the tunnel. But duty came first. The monster made for Natsuo, brandishing its weapon over its head.

Unthinkingly, and without truly understanding what he was doing, Natsuo shouted and swung, eyes closed.

Then silence.

Only silence.

And breathing. But only one sound. His own breathing. He opened his eyes and gasped. On the floor were four separate shapes. Two slender serrated metallic oblongs — two parts of a sword, a pair of legs tapering off into a steaming mess of guts, and then a chest that was topped off by a death-face and lifeless eyes. He'd cloven both the creature and the sword in two. But he hadn't felt a thing, thinking he'd missed and fully expecting some burning pain that would signal his own death. But no. He wiped the blood off the sword and put it back in the bag.

Can't stay here...

He decided to take the side tunnel, wherever it may lead, and get out of the maze. It wasn't safe to stay there.

Nowhere's safe...

Life is a sequence of choices. Fate and karma aren't real. Every person, every day, makes decisions. And that decision, like some cosmic domino, falls and affects the next part of that individual's life. That individual's choice then will affect what others around him or her will do. And so, the choices ripple outwards until a butterfly causes a hurricane. Newton's third law.

Natsuo had made his choice; perhaps his only choice, but a choice nonetheless. He had killed a demon and ran off down a tunnel at the end of which lay some fresh hell.

Hot wind blasted his face as he came out into the open. How long had he been running down that tunnel? He didn't know. Now he realised, after the time-melting route he had been on, he couldn't know. The other remarkable thing was the lack of other beings. He had met no-one as he sprinted as fast as he could away from the spliced-up cadaver. As he exited the tunnel into the brimstone-coloured underworld again, he understood why.

Ahead lay a blasted plain of smashed-up monoliths, stone towers and craters. It was desolate and unending. The horizon seemed to stretch left and right to the infinite, even if that horizon was just darkness, and way across the plain, impossibly distant, was another mountain range.

He walked gingerly out onto the flat valley floor, the ground of which reminded him of those photos of Mars taken by the Perseverance rover; though Mars seemed more hospitable. The sky looked like it was raining, or hailing. Natsuo remembered the book: they were balls of red-hot iron. Tiny hellish meteors designed to torment and burn the souls and blister their feet as they made their way to King Enma.

Natsuo looked left and right and saw the mountain he had just exited stretching off as a jagged granitic wall as far as the eye could see. It was either turn back to the tunnels or head over the plain.

In the distance, a few hundred metres or so away, Natsuo spied a line of tiny beings trudging along, never deviating from their course, occasionally collapsing and getting back up again. He surmised these were the souls who had made it past King Sōtei and his sexual torture and King Gokan's soul-weighing boulder-scale. He did not envy them and decided to follow at a distance along what he hoped was the comparative safety of the mountainside.

Every so often little red-hot pellets would whip through the air and ping into the rock walls to his left or fizz into the baked meseta on his right. After not too long Natsuo's jacket was scattered by little melt-warts where he had been struck. He had also garnered a nice cut on his forehead. It seemed the worst of it landed out in the plains as if, despite the seemingly random nature of their descent, the fireballs knew where to strike. Out there they fell harder, more often and were larger.

On and on Natsuo mirrored the procession of people. All he knew was that the next stop for them was a meeting with King Enma himself. Natsuo had no intention of coming face to face with one of the architects of the very plan he was tasked with helping stop. But with no map, no direction, no knowledge of how or when or where he was supposed to find the doorway to Yomi, he couldn't do anything else but follow the torturous route through Meido.

He didn't hear anything, but he felt it. A hot punch on the side of the head. For a moment he looked around in a daze wondering who had hit him. But there was nobody there. His eyelids suddenly took on a weight that made them difficult to keep open. A throbbing then started to pulse in his temple. He brought up his hand instinctively to the pain and winced. His vision shone and sparkled. Suddenly the deathly brown-black plain shimmered. His fingers were coated with a glimmering red liquid. Then the world went dark.

What was that? It was familiar...

Someone's grandfather's house? No. But almost. Something that was in that house. A restaurant maybe? Yes, closer. It was sweet. But not too sweet. And funky. Like warm flowers. A garden? No. No, not a garden. Closer was the restaurant.

The hairs in his nose flowed against the smell. The familiar smell.

Malt? No, not quite. But something cooked.

Rice.

Fermenting rice.

He knew that smell; every Japanese person would.

Nihonshu.

Natsuo's eyes opened groggily and then quickly darted around: he was lying down in a dingy room, all wooden beams and hewn rock furniture. The air had a pleasing warm pungency of fermentation. A sake *kura*? It couldn't be. What would he be doing in a sake brewery? He was in Meido. But the smells were undeniable and the more his eyes got accustomed to his surroundings the more the primary thought was confirmed.

Rice kernels were dotted about the floor here and there, an attractively designed giant white barrel, a taru, with some flowery unintelligible kanji sat in one corner, and empty serving jugs, katakuchi and tokkuri were hanging haphazardly off the walls.

'Drink?'

Two bulbous eyelashless eyes were looming over at him. Under the eyes was a long nose that ended in a frozen smile. Although were they eyes? They seemed to be connected to two pendulous bags. No, not bags. Breasts. The eyes blinked and Natsuo cried out. Then came laughter. Natsuo sat up with a start. This twisted, comical non-face covered the belly and chest of whatever creature was lolling and swaying in front of him. Its face was, to his surprise, oddly jolly and inoffensive. It was a pale face, like that of a powdered geisha, with black high-flying eyebrows, whose mouth ended in something more akin to a fleshy beak instead of lips. It was smiling and its tongue was hanging out. It looked like a character from some twisted children's movie. The creature wore a light grey, open shirt and a red skirt and its feet were pronged and reptilian. The monster was an odd cocktail of grotesque and amusing.

'You're safe here,' it belched out before giggling. Natsuo simply gawked, still somewhat taken aback by the appearance of the creature, let alone the news that he was apparently safe. 'I'm a *haradashi*.'

'Haradashi...'

'Go on. I know you want to look in that little book of yours.'

'How did you..'

'You've been here knocked out cold for quite some time. In your human timeframe I guess it would be something like five or six hours.'

'What?!'

'You took a fireball to the head; it's a wonder it's still connected!' The creature laughed and its body jiggled like jelly, causing its eye-breasts to sway. It took a swig of sake out of a bottle it was holding casually. 'Don't worry though. We haradashi are quite fond of humans.

We generally like to appear to you lot when you are drunk or drunk and sad and join in the fun or try and cheer you up. Sadly, with the advance of modern technology up there it's tricky for us to join in without someone trying to capture an image of us. So most of us have had to slink back down here. But we don't really get on with the rest of them. So we've found our own little nooks and crannies here in Meido and Jigoku, where we won't be bothered and bullied by the others. And here you are little human, in my humble nook. My little sake kura. Nobody knows I'm here, not even the kings! Well, they know my sake, but they'll never find me.'

The goofy-looking creature instantly endeared itself to Natsuo. How much of that was due to the fact that up until this moment everything else had been so beastly, he didn't know. But he did feel safe here. Hidden.

'So you make sake down here?'

'Oh yes!' said the haradashi, even more animated. 'Do you like it?'

'I only know the little cans and jars I get from the local supermarket.'

'That muck?!' The creature feigned dramatic disgust. 'That's not sake.'

'I don't suppose you have any water?' Natsuo asked even though he wasn't actually thirsty, he still felt he wanted to drink something.

'Hah! No, just this stuff. But I have some lighter styles which will do the trick!' The jolly monster-penguin walked over to a box and brought out a large blue jug. 'This is a so-shu style of *Junmai*. I managed to polish the rice down to almost a *ginjo*.'

Natsuo had no idea what any of that meant and cautiously took a sip when offered a glass. It was somehow cool and crisp and smelled of apples and white flowers. Over his tongue an almost sweet, rice flavour intermingled with some notes of melon.

'Gosh, that's delicious,' he said, genuinely impressed.

The haradashi chuckled contentedly. 'Well, I learned from the best,' it said, nodding towards Natsuo in a way that seemed to intimate he meant "from humans".

'So why are you here?' came another voice, more gruff and echoey.

Natsuo looked to his left and saw an old, beaten-up sake jug with holes and cracks in the ceramic forming hollow eyes and a mouth. Two long turkey-like legs shot out of the bottom and the battered tokkuri stood up. Natsuo found, somewhat amusingly, that a talking sake jug had almost no effect on him.

Seems about right...

After a quick internal debate about whether it was truly a good idea to share his plans, he decided to tell the haradashi and the talking sake jug, a *kameosa* — as it presented itself with a bow — all about his mission.

They listened on enraptured; a whimsical blend of childlike interest and drunken focus, slow blinking and nodding. Natsuo didn't know how long he had been talking but he spared no detail and the bizarre creatures in front of him never interrupted.

'Well...' concluded the haradashi, 'that's quite a thing for a human! Passing through Meido searching for a magic hammer in Yomi-no-Kuni! Wouldn't you say?'

'Mmm.' The kameosa agreed.

'It's not fair that they left everything up to you,' the haradashi said, the words bubbling out of a sake-moistened mouth. 'I think I know someone who can help.' It turned to the sake jug. 'Get a message to Danzaburou-danuki. See if he can send someone to help this poor lad.' The jug bowed and bounced away out of the room.

'Who is that?' Natsuo was getting tired of having to ask for clarification all the time. Moving through a new life, a new hell, in complete innocence and ignorance. But he had no other option than to be constantly explained everything by gods and monsters.

'He's one of the three famous *tanuki*. You know the tanuki? Those trickster, shape-shifting racoon-dogs. Well, fortunately for me they love my sake so I get on rather well with them!'

'I know them.' Natsuo was glad there was finally something he was familiar with.

The tanuki; a popular symbol of Japanese folklore, was a stalwart of toys, ceramic decorations for garden and home, and amusing cheeky characters in anime and manga. Usually depicted as a merry, potbellied animal in a straw hat, standing upright on its hind legs, a gourd of sake in one hand, a promissory note in the other, and an enormous scrotum hanging down to the ground between their legs.

'Danzaburou-danuki helped build the wall around my brewery to protect me from any prying eyes. If you are lucky, he might be able to give you a hand; he owes me after all. I sent my finest Junmai to him for a party and he's yet to pay me back!'

Natsuo winced as feeling started to come back to him.

'You should probably wait a little longer. Also, it might be a while before we get word from above. I don't think you should rush to head back out there.'

'Hai.' Natsuo nodded, rubbing his temple.

'In the meantime, we can have a proper drink! I have mostly *nama* styles, though I do have a koshu I'm experimenting with, and I think I have some of the ginjo that Danzaburou didn't get his little paws on. They're all Junmai; it's a bit complicated to make a *Honjozo* down here. I don't have all the equipment.'

'Sorry, Mr...haradashi...' Natsuo interrupted, at a loss. 'I don't really know anything about sake I'm afraid.'

'Well, if you like I can teach you!'

Natsuo thought for a moment.

Well, there's nothing else to do...

'That would be fine, yes.'

'Follow me.'

'Young man, if wine is like an opera with lots of big, larger-than-life, distinct characters and emotions, then sake is more like a poem. It's a drink of quiet corners and aromatic nuances.'

'OK.'

'I read that in a book; good isn't it?!' said the haradashi bursting into laughter, then turning suddenly faux-serious, 'But it's true, eh!' He signalled for Natsuo to follow him.

They entered a much larger room that felt humid and had the aroma of cooked grain.

'In this room I prepare the rice. Now, of course, there's not many useful ingredients down here as you can probably expect. I have a friend in Niigata and he's able to bring me Gohyakumangoku rice. I then have to polish it to remove the outer layer. You see, every little grain of sake rice has a yummy, starchy centre called the shinpaku. This is the part that'll be broken down into sugar by the *koji* mould and then fermented into alcohol. Of course, I have no machines so I have to instead mill everything by hand!'

'That sounds like a lot of work. Why bother?'

'Well, around the shinpaku is an outer layer of fats and proteins and stuff which can give unwanted flavours. The more I take off the finer and more elegant my sake. I recently, after ages with my pestle and mortar, managed to remove about 40% of the rice leaving me a polishing rate that would be considered a ginjo style. If I could get another 10% off, I could call it a daiginjo! I'm almost there, but I don't think I'll be able to it very often; also that would mean a lot of rice for not a lot of booze! Anyway. When I've finished all that polishing, I wash the rice to remove the bran, soak it all and then steam it in that big thing over there.'

Over to one side of the room was a large wooden tank fuming away and spilling out steam through the cracks.

'That's my *koshiki*; built it myself,' the haradashi said proudly. 'When the rice is cooked, I take about a fifth of it and add the koji spores. This little mould infects the rice and will break down those starches into sugar. I then add a small load of that rice and a bunch of yeast to this bucket here and leave it alone a while. This super yeasty mix is called the shubo and is what'll help us really kickstart the fermentation.'

'It sounds a bit like beer.'

'Hah! Good observation young man! Parts of the process are similar, yes! Though, beer doesn't use koji.'

'So the shubo turns into sake?'

'More or less. Over the course of a few days I add more rice, more koji-rice and more water to the shubo and build up a big full tank which I'll leave for about a month to bubble away and turn into sake!'

'That seems ever so complicated!'

'It is! But it's a hobby of mine. Keeps me busy down here!' The haradashi laughed, its eye-breasts wobbling with abandon. Natsuo still couldn't work out whether it was a female or a male, or indeed if gender even existed here. 'Then I like to tinker away creating new styles. I usually don't bring the alcohol down when it's finished, so I let the sake stay as what's called a genshu. Sometimes I don't bother to pasteurise them either. These are called namasakes. Problem is, with the heat down here, they can go off quite easily. And I'm experimenting with an aged sake called *koshu*! Smells like dried fruit and nuts and caramelised onions and tastes sweet! Also, I don't have any fancy filtering technology, so all my sakes are what they call muroka.'

Natsuo's head was swimming with all the information, the percentages and the niche vocabulary, and, if he was honest with himself, he only really understood about half of it. But the creature's enthusiasm was infectious and for the first time since he entered Meido he found himself in a good mood, finally distracted by something completely unrelated. The haradashi seemed to sense this so relented a little in his barrage of information.

'Well, anyway...' it said, busying itself with bottles in a cupboard. 'A toast!' It held a bottle in its hand. 'I want you to try my Junmai ginjo.'

'But isn't that your fancy one? You don't have to!'

'Young man, it's not every day I get a visitor from up there. Even less someone half human! We should celebrate!'

'Yashima no Hage-tanuki is here!' came a surprised and elated ceramic squawk from the sake jug, bounding in on its turkey legs.

'My my, aren't you lucky Natsuo-chan!'

'Who's Yashima no Hage-tanuki?'

'I'll tell you myself.' A voice came from the doorway.

Standing about four and half feet tall, perhaps coming up to Natsuo's chest, was a fairly dapper-looking tanuki, far removed from the flabby, mischief-loving ones of lore. He wore a dark blue jacket, like that of a buccaneer, a sword around his hip, and was naked from the waist down. He sat back proudly on his enormous scrotum and crossed his arms. The raccoon-dog had a swagger about him and exuded a surprising charisma for such a small and, if Natsuo were honest with himself, cute animal.

'So you must be Sōjōbō's hafu. I hear he's left you in a bit of a jam. My name is Yashima no Hage-tanuki, one of the three great tanuki. Pleased to make your acquaintance.' He nodded. 'Danzaburou told me you might need a spot of help.'

Natsuo nodded as the tanuki took a swig from an open bottle of sake he found lying on the ground.

'This is good stuff Hozaki,' Hage said, wiping his whiskery lips.

So that was the haradashi's name. Natsuo felt something flirting with shame that up until now he had only seen the creature as another Yokai. But he supposed they were, in their own twisted ways, all individuals.

'Have you heard of Yashima-ji young man?'

'Afraid not.'

'Well, well, you should!' boomed the laughing tanuki, 'It's on Shikoku! It's my temple. I was told you were from that island.'

Natsuo felt a bit embarrassed that he didn't know the place.

'I haven't really been...that is to say...I don't really know...'

'It's alright Natsuo-chan; I know all about your previous life as a Hikikomori. Shut away from society and all that. Bit weird, odd choice, but I suppose we all have our kinks.' Natsuo was somewhat rebuffed by the brightly dismissive opinion concerning his yōkai-curse sentence as a solitary shut away. But he found it refreshingly amusing.

Why would a mythical creature care anyway?

'Yet, at your service you have me.' Hage's eyes glistened darkly and softly as he said these words, so charged with meaning.

The little dapper racoon-dog had an air of unbending confidence mixed with a sage disposition that impressed Natsuo greatly

'Sōjōbō informed me of the plan, so I was somewhat ready to leap into action if needs be. And the needs seem to be being!' He winked. 'When that old tengu was teaching Minamoto no Yoshitsune swordsmanship, I was dazzling him with phantom magic.'

'Phantom magic?' Natsuo inserted dumbly to the void left by the end of Hage's sentence.

'Means I can produce ethereal beings which can act and do as I say in the real world. Very handy in a battle!' The tanuki bellowed and rocked back and forth on his testicles. 'So when I found out you and I were from the same place I thought I couldn't not help! I know you're looking for the entrance to Yomi-no-kuni where Izanami and her brother are and I know you, poor chap, haven't a clue where it is.' Natsuo nodded blankly. 'Well I do...' Hage spun around on his enormous scrotum as if it were a space hopper. 'This should be fun, dear boy!'

'Have you ever heard of the expression "hiding in plain sight"?' asked Hage. Natsuo and he were sat on an outcrop above the sake brewery, backed by a high wall of jagged dark mountain, looking out over the hellish, meteor-blasted plain towards the distant shadowy range of hills on the other side. 'It's an old military tactic, but also a favourite of human detective writers and filmmakers. The idea that the last place you'd think to look for something, or someone, is right there in front of you, as that would seem too obvious, or too stupid.'

'Uhuh...'

'See that peak over there on the left side of the hills. The other side of the plain?'

'Yeah.'

'On the other side of that is King Enma with his sin-showing mirror trick.' The tanuki smiled intelligently. 'Near the top of that peak is the doorway to Yomi.'

'There?!'

'The last place they'd think to look for the uchide no kozuchi hammer is just above where their great plotting leader is working!' He started laughing. 'Brilliant, really.'

'But how am I to get there?'

'Well young Natsuo m'lad. That's where I, and this,' he patted his enormous scrotum, 'come in.'

'Ah...'

Images of tanuki and their portrayal in popular culture were widespread over the centuries. Paintings and woodblock prints of them flying through the air using their genitals as gliding devices were commonplace.

'We can't all fly you know. But there's a reason I'm one of the greats!' He winked and giggled. 'Whenever you're ready, and remember young boy, there's no rush, we'll go. The flight won't take long and when we arrive, I'll use some of my talents to distract any prying eyes, but I'm afraid you'll have to go up and in yourself. I'm not supposed to be down here so if I get too close there's a risk that Enma or any of his coterie may sense something's amiss.' He slapped Natsuo on the back. 'But with that wonderful demon blood of yours you'll have no problem!'

Natsuo wasn't tired. Tired wasn't a concept that existed where he currently was. But he felt he needed to ready himself. He excused himself from the weird menagerie of new friends and went and lay down. He just felt he needed, even though it wasn't one, a rest. Just a few moments, whatever moments amounted to down here, of peace.

Since entering Meido he had witnessed a continuous torrent of horrors, slain a monster, been struck by a fireball, and generally allowed himself to be carried along without stopping to process anything. Right now he just wanted a bit of time to stop, to let it all sink in.

He thought about his mother, up there in Osaka, in his world, waiting for him. He worried for her more than himself. She had lost her husband years ago and, after reuniting with her son, now risked losing him too. This wasn't lost on Natsuo, and it made him feel a little selfish leaving her alone. Then he looked around at the sake kura of a monster with a face on its belly and a talking tokkuri sidekick and thought how small the problems of the 'real' world were.

He wished he could go back to his teenage self, to that young boy bullied at school, to that little kid burrowing in on himself, grab him by the shoulders and shake him. Don't give in. This is nothing. It stops. Life moves on. You'll forget this. There are greater things at play in heaven and hell than whether the teachers and classmates like you. He would slap himself across his vacant face and then hug himself tightly. It'll be OK. He would stop himself becoming a Hikikomori.

But this was the great fallacy. He probably wouldn't be where he was, doing what he was, if he hadn't followed that course. The grandfather paradox. It was a trope used in many of the movies and shows he watched. The present is the present because of every little step taken in the past. However much you wish that you had done something different in the past the outcome may not give you the future you desire. Every second changes the next one to produce a unique now.

And Natsuo's 'now' was flying across a fiery altiplano on the back of a legendary tanuki and then entering Shinto heaven to retrieve a magic hammer. He smiled.

No.

He'd not go back in time.

He'd leave everything as it was.

Chapter Eight: Yomi-no-kuni
黄泉

World of Darkness.

His face was hot and his eyes were watering, though he was at least thankful for the ceasefire in the nasal attack of burning flesh, rancid meat and sulphurous rot that had permeated his clothing, his olfactory system and every corner of Meido up until this point. Natsuo figured that most Hikikomori, after adopting, for whatever reason, a life resigned to one room or one house, would never imagine that at the end of their sentence they would be flying through purgatory on the thermals of hell clinging to a magical racoon-dog held aloft purely by the immutability of physics and the sheer grandeur of a scrotum.

But here he was.

They would circle like vultures up the invisible thermal columns and then Hage would twist almost imperceptibly causing them to shoot off and glide a while before dipping into another upshoot of warm air. Natsuo had no idea how, but the pilot seemed to instinctively know where the fireballs would be coming from and how to swoop out of their way.

'We are going to fly...through that?' Natsuo had whined before they set off, pointing to the molten rain falling over the flats.

'Dear boy,' barked the tanuki, patting Natsuo on the back. 'Do you think I would be who I am and where I am and doing what I am doing if I couldn't negotiate some inclement weather?'

Once again, this bravura paid off and Natsuo had found himself gripping onto the two sides of the tanuki's leathery scrotum without much complaint. He was positioned in front of Hage so that when they were in the air it looked a little like a World War II soldier holding onto a rudimentary parachute topped by a woodland animal.

From the lofty heights Natsuo looked down at the bleak and blasted wastes and was reminded of photos of Nagasaki and Hiroshima after the bombs came down.

Natsuo's family, on his mother's side of course, had died during the August 9th attack. Everyone knew the story, although the west seemed to focus more on Hiroshima. After a full year of air attacks, the

Americans sent the Bockscar B-29 Superfortress plane to bomb the castle town of Kokura but, due to the simple fact of cloudy weather, Nagasaki was chosen. His grandparents didn't stand a chance.

At 11:02am the Fat Man bomb exploded its plutonium load over the north of the city. Natsuo's grandfather worked at the Mitsubishi Munitions plant, one of the primary targets. 7,500 employees worked there. 6,200 died.

The black and white photos of those cities showed mountains and rivers surrounded by a 2D outline of what used to be thriving neighbourhoods and industrial areas. He had never visited Nagasaki and so, while clinging onto Yashima-no-Hagetanuki, he made the decision that if he ever got out of this he would visit and pay his respects.

Humanity's hubris and the wars of the previous century seemed to him now even more stupid and pointless in the face of this current, more perilous celestial situation. The knowledge of what was at stake made Natsuo even more resolute.

Suddenly there was an uncharacteristic wobble, like when an airplane hits an air pocket. They banked left and then right. Natsuo didn't feel stable at all.

'Is everything OK?' He shouted up to Hage. There was no response. 'I said is everything OK?'

They flopped side to side again forcing Natsuo to hold on tighter to the folds in Hage's billowy scrotum.

Shit... he cursed to himself. 'Hage-sama is everything' — It was then, craning his neck up, that Natsuo saw his tanuki pilot had his eyes closed, a fine line of blood dribbling generously from his forehead.

Shit, shit, shit, what do I do?

Natsuo couldn't judge the distance remaining to the mountainside but it wasn't far. If he could just keep gliding in a straight line, he should be able to simply meet the mountain head-on.

Every so often he would hit an air pocket and fall some metres, which made the blood in his head shoot down his body into his feet, while his stomach did the best it could to jump out of his throat. Then he would be buffeted on updrafts that threatened to turn him over. He held on tightly and did as best he could to avoid tumbling over left or right, keeping steady.

The details of the mountainside slowly revealed themselves as he closed in, as a photo coming into focus or the world after rubbing morning eyes.

'*Ie, ie, ie…*' He seethed, shaking his head.

Whether they had dropped too much altitude or simply that the course was off from the moment Hage had been knocked unconscious, Natsuo didn't know, but what was once a distant brown mass had now begun to transmogrify into a craggy cliff-face, not a landing strip on the gentle open arms of a mountain-slope.

One thing was clear: following the current trajectory — and Natsuo had been secretly proud that, despite the fear synapsing through him, he had kept the course — he would soon crash straight into the rocks. The vague concept of a sierra was now an imminent, looming wall that he would soon be dashed over.

Closer and closer the cliffs came. Natsuo didn't know what to do.

Closer.

In seconds he would smash into stone. Everything he had achieved up till that point would be for naught. His life as a Hikikomori a pointless prelude to a meaningless death in Meido.

With only a few metres between him and the mountainside, Natsuo pulled down hard with his left hand. They dropped out of the sky, performing a hard left turn, just barely missing the wall of rock. Then, as soon as they had plummeted maybe thirty feet, a thermal blooming vertically up against the side of the mountain punched them upwards and above the rim of the cliffside. They were then sucked downwards right towards solid ground where they slammed hard into the dried ruddy earth and rolled some metres to a stop.

Pain shimmered through Natsuo as he groaned himself up onto his elbows. He was sat a good few yards from Hage, who was completely encased in his scrotum like a cat curled up in its tail. Natsuo on the other hand was bleeding from a long cut on his left arm and, having got to his feet, found himself limping a little from an injury to his right leg. He shuffled over to the tanuki and shook him gently.

'Hey...' A muffled murmur came from within the ball. 'Hey, come on. Get up.'

Natsuo looked uphill towards the smoking peak of the mountain and saw dark, twisted figures and shadows. The path was not clear.

Slowly the racoon-sphere unfurled and Hage-tanuki appeared.

'Seems it has a mind of its own.' He grunted, nodding towards his own testicles. 'Thankfully...' He massaged his temple and then looked at Natsuo. 'Oh, my boy. Are you OK?'

'Yes. More or less.' Natsuo had lived a sheltered life and hadn't really felt any form of physical pain since his years of bullying. And nothing like this. 'We are close, right?'

'Look up there.' Hage pointed to the peak.

'Yes, you told me the entrance to Yomi was up near the top.'

'No. It is the top.' The tanuki smiled, though this time the bravura was cocktailed with tiredness and pain. 'That smouldering crater at the top is a lie, a facade we created, a fiery fake. An illusion. That's where the entrance is.'

'It seems we aren't alone up here.' Natsuo guessed that they were a couple of thousand metres up on the mountain from the valley floor, but were no more than a couple of kilometres from the peak itself. However there remained the issue of the creatures of darkness between their cliffside location and the mouth of the crater. 'More yokai...'

'Not yokai. Those are the husks of a darkness more ancient and tragic than my people and the rest of the yokai. They are concepts of evil. No, not evil. Before evil, for evil entails thought. Just chaotic malice. A violence that is part of this underworld but is even too grubby and untameable for the Kings. Enma lets them be, to wander these lofty hinterlands of Meido. In the belly of the many hells of Jigoku you can find them, but Meido is supposed to have some control. Checks and balances. But up here, away from where new souls would ever be, you'll find them.'

Natsuo squinted. Far off as they were, he could still make out different shapes. Some slithered, some clomped along like malformed giants, some were insect-like, some hovered just above the ground. Aimlessly they plodded about. They were all black and fuzzy, as if their resolution had been turned down.

'There's no intelligence there, but I'll have to distract them while you head into the crater. I won't see you after this moment, young man. When I give the signal, you go. You don't look back and you don't stop. Nothing will be gained from doing so.'

Natsuo bowed.

They walked together in tense silence until about halfway to the summit. Hage-tanuki nodded, peeling off left further onto the mountain away from the cliffs. Natsuo carried on alone.

The pain in his leg was lessening as he walked it off, but the slash on his arm, now that the adrenaline of their crash landing was wearing off, had begun to throb. He was sweating profusely as hyperhidrosis set in from the shock to his unprepared body. He thought he wasn't supposed to experience the physical trappings of humanity down in Meido, yet he felt tired and beaten. Maybe his mind was playing tricks. Regardless he kept walking, doggedly focusing on the fuming top of the mountain.

Suddenly a brilliant blue light stung the far left corner of his peripheral vision. He turned and saw Hage-tanuki standing out in the open, arms outstretched, his elegant coat flapping around him, emitting a brilliant, pulsating bubble of ultramarine energy. Forms billowed out of the aura around him: more tanuki, Muromachi-era samurai, modern soldiers, ninja, tengu, vikings, centurions, and all manner of different warriors from history, all with a shimmering blue outline.

A low moan-cry sounded from up the hill and Natsuo saw the darklings and malice-beasts herd together and make their way downhill in a lumpen stampede.

The glowing blue army met the shadowy hordes and an azure-charcoal skirmish broke out. Yashima no Hage-tanuki took to the sky, the blue light increasing in intensity. He hovered above the violence below, floating over the mountaintop battle, and then locked eyes with Natsuo and nodded. The blue light increased until a fierce neon fluorescence burned so brightly that Natsuo could no longer make out any details. That was the signal. He turned back to the smoking crater and ran as best he could.

As he ran, pain cascaded up and down Natsuo's body in waves. He stumbled a few times, his feet rolling awkwardly off rocks, and he was getting light-headed.

Come on...almost there...

He could still hear the sounds of battle ringing in his ears. Human war cries curdled with the monstrous screeches and gurgled caws of the hell beasts. Natsuo fought the temptation to look back, remembering he had been told not to.

Not much further.

Just a couple of hundred metres to where the smoke was coming from.

The hairs on Natsuo arms and neck prickled and he felt a sort of static energy fizzing in the air. He stopped running. It was then his vision adjusted and he was aware of a black figure, a dark presence, maybe eighty metres to his left. The figure was stationary and, if it had eyes, Natsuo thought it seemed to be staring at him. If it had lungs, Natsuo would have said it was breathing in and out steadily and deeply. It was maybe three metres tall, bulky and boxy, with what seemed to be three legs and four arms. Though they weren't exactly what traditional limbs looked like. It didn't move; but Natsuo had to.

Fear gripped him, but the excitement of being so close to his destination, the maw of the volcano almost within reach, made him route around in his bag for the sword. He couldn't fail now. He was literally going to hell and back and if he was going to die it would be in his own world, not atop a smoking mountain in the underworld, snuffed out by some walking black hole.

As soon as he removed the sword and started walking forward the obsidian hulk twitched, shifted, its dark outline fuzzing like a radio-wave, and immediately began to gallop towards Natsuo.

Without knowing if he had time to make it to the crater opening, Natsuo started to sprint automatically, the blood draining from his head to reach every fibre and tendon and every bone and muscle in his body. It was hard to pick up the absence of light in peripheral vision, but he felt the static buzz getting stronger.

He was now maybe within twenty metres of the volcanic pit where the entrance to Yomi was hiding. When the electrical discharge verged on the point of blinding and confusing pain, he knew he wouldn't make it.

In a split second everything happened at once; time softening into a marshmallowy melted slow-frame.

Natsuo, sensing the inevitable, swung his head round left, his vision instantly picking up on the vast atramentous mass that looked to cover him like a wave. There were eyes that weren't eyes. Scratchy spheres of perfect un-light. A mouth. Was it a mouth? A murky opening, with stygian teeth that glinted even though they didn't. He was about to be consumed. But then there was the rest of his movement in that momentary reaction as he faced certain death. When his head decided to spin left, so had his body, and it had brought that heavenly blade with it. The kusanagi-no-Tsurugi flashed golden light as it sliced through the air quicker than Natsuo's own perceptions had time to react, as if it had a life of its own. Natsuo was cocooned in blackness for the shortest fraction of time before the sword exploded the hell-beast in an ethereal outburst of light and power.

Go. Go now...

Don't look back. Do not look back. Get to the crater. Go now...

Natsuo ran to where the smoke was boiling out of the ground in an opaque column of magmatic effuse.

I don't know what to do...

Natsuo remembered the words of Yashima no Hage-tanuki — 'It's a fake'. He approached the crater and felt no heat emanating whatsoever. At the lip of the crater, he decided to do the only thing he could think of. Without looking back, without seeing if his tanuki companion was still alive or if there was some bloodthirsty black being on his tail, Natsuo jumped into the crater, into the smoke, and hoped for the best.

The body's relationship with the mind has amused and bemused scientists and thinkers since the dawn of independent thought. Especially the study of pain: the results of complex brain processes that are nudged and shifted by various physical — nociceptive and neuropathic — factors combined with psychological and environmental ones. Touch a flame, it hurts and your brain screams and tells you to take your hand away.

Another interesting side of pain and discomfort is the body and mind's shrugging willingness to just deal with it. And following that route the euphoric alleviation felt when it abates. A mild example would be if someone suffers a cold or flu for days or even weeks. Initial bodily perturbations caused by several blocked noses, painful throats and scratchy coughs, give way to a new normal. You start to live with it. You don't think about it. Your nose just is blocked now. And that's that. Your brain switches off the instant responses to being unable to pass air through the nasal canal and just clicks into the unconscious mode. You now breathe through your mouth.

And then one day you wake up and you're clear. You're breathing through your nose, there's no guck in your throat and your head feels lighter. The absence of the pain and discomfort is now more noticeable in its not being there. Like having your blocked ears suddenly cleared. The world is crisper and more in focus.

It was the absence of pain that Natsuo felt when he opened his eyes. And silence. No crying hell-sounds or screams. No fireballs smashing craters into the earth. Silence. Well, almost silence. The sound of water. Trickling water.

He was lying down in grass. Natsuo got up on his elbows and looked around. It was sunny, but there was no actual sun to speak of. It was just brighter than where he had been in Meido. Then he sensed the grass wasn't really grass. An assimilation of grass. Something green flowing away from him in wavy fields.

Natsuo got to his feet, feeling energised. The cut on his arm was gone and there was no longer any pain in his leg. He blinked a few times and drank in the surroundings.

It was a pastoral Japanese idyll. Fuzzy green hills with the saturation turned up, a fast-flowing river — the rivers in Japan always flowed fast — and rising staircases of limpid rice paddies and pools climbing up the slopes. Here and there little timbered temples and shrines dotted the view, but there were no people though. In fact, as beautiful as it seemed, the whole vision seemed oddly devoid of any actual life. Like a 3D painting or some highly rendered animation.

Natsuo walked to the river where a little arched, wooden bridge jumped over and put his hand in the water. He felt nothing. The water, or at least what he supposed looked like water, curled around his palms and found its course, but he couldn't feel anything. No cold, no wetness. The sound too, unchanging. Like a soundtrack being played over the top of an image, not reacting to the surroundings.

'Do you like it?' asked a soothing voice, startling Natsuo.

He turned around and saw two enormous and graceful figures in robes; a man and a woman. They seemed quite far off towards the edge of the idyllic view but they filled the skies. They were giants but as they walked towards him they quickly shrank. The opposite of perspective. Then, as soon as they had walked just a few paces, they were before him.

'Anoo...hai...kirei desu...' Natsuo nodded in answer to their question. 'Are you..?'

'I am Izanami,' said the beautiful woman, who was dressed in a long, resplendent white kimono lined with crimson velvet finishes and golden filigree. 'And this is my brother Izanagi.' She motioned to a rather more stoic-looking figure with wild black hair, a large beard, serious eyes, who was modestly dressed in a caramel-brown tunic and pale trousers. 'Welcome to Yomi-no-kuni.' She smiled.

'Sit, please,' came the low baritone rumbling out of the chest of Izanagi.

A chair that hadn't been there before was now behind Natsuo. He took a seat and then, on turning back, noticed that Izanami and Izanagi were now also both seated. The three of them, sat in the middle of the non-countryside, by a river that ran with fake water. It was all rather surreal.

'Do you know what Yomi is, young man?' Izanami asked in a mellifluous purr.

'As far as I have understood it is the Shinto version of Meido.'

'That's more or less right,' replied Izanagi. He crossed his legs and continued. 'It has many names here. Ne-no-kuni, the land of roots; Soko-no-kuni, the deep land; and Yomi-no-kuni. It is usually translated as "world of darkness", but Izanami and I prefer its ancient meaning of "underground spring".' He nodded in the direction of the river. 'You've probably already noticed that that isn't water.' He smiled for the first time, revealing a warmth Natsuo hadn't noticed until now. 'It's the life-force of Shinto and it runs through here keeping everything in Yomi ticking over.'

'You must have seen the horrors of Meido?' Izanami continued. Natsuo nodded. 'That is a world of pain and misery. That's not so much the case here. There are, of course, darker areas in Yomi – you wouldn't want to meet the hisa-me female spirits of death or the Ika-zuchi-no-kami, seven shinto demons, but ours is generally a more contemplative space. The truly bad get judged but we do not needlessly torture the innocent. Buddhism's more doctrinal presence on Earth means that we have a lot less...what's a word you humans use...traffic.' She smiled sadly. 'As a result, we are often forgotten about somewhat, thus leaving a quieter place to hide things.' At this her eyes twinkled at Natsuo, almost suggesting a wink.

'The uchide no kozuchi...'

They both nodded.

'Because why would a pair of old creator gods be hiding a magic hammer?' Izanagi explained. 'And yet we have; successfully.'

'For weeks, maybe months now, I don't know how much time has passed, I have avoided goblins and oni, I have killed and almost been killed, I left home for the first time in years and now I really, really miss my mother.' Natsuo spooned a tear out of the corner of his eye with his left index finger. 'I would very much like to rest a while if possible. For this place is truly beautiful. I'm not tired, but, you know, I just need to stop for a moment.'

'Where we are now is a small bubble world that we created inside Yomi in order to stow away the hammer.' Izanagi stood up and pointed to one of the hills on the far side of the river. 'You see that somewhat unassuming stone torii gate hiding halfway up those old stone stairs?' Natsuo glanced over and, true enough, spied a rather pedestrian-looking gate, just two rock pillars linked by a *shimenawa* rope; the kind you find unloved in thousands of roadside villages and towns around the country. 'Well, that door leads you, young man, back to your world. It is the only human link with Yomi. It'll release you out in Izumo province. Until you need to leave you may stay as long as you please. But, at the risk of asking too much of you, the swifter we can get the uchide no kozuchi to Amaterasu, the sooner we can bring this troubling episode to a close.'

Natsuo nodded, remembering the weight of his responsibility that had been lost in a haze of flying demons and magical battles. He had almost forgotten why he was doing what he was doing, simply being carried along by a seemingly never-ending and never-tiring procession of mad moments.

'I haven't forgotten.' Natsuo sighed, bowing to the creator gods.

He decided to just wander around this picture-perfect Constable painting of a landscape and try and think of anything else other than imminent dread and supernatural goings on.

The invented reality of the place did feel like the gods had created, by accident, a walkthrough oil painting. A fake breeze ruffled his hair and the non-river kept trickling. Everything before him was the brainchild of the very beings who had created Japan. This was what they hoped the nation would aspire and continue to look like. Natsuo thought it was the most beautiful place he had ever seen.

Izanagi had told him where the uchide no kozuchi was kept, but declined to come with him.

'It's yours to take when you are ready to return.'

Natsuo had expected the hammer to be kept in a grand Shinto shrine but in fact, presumably for the sake of seeming inconspicuous, he was told to follow a cobbled path behind the back of a plain wooden building — the honden main hall, which was rather small and simple-looking — just off the banks of the river and make his way into the tree-line. There he would follow the path up the treed hillside to a small hokora standing by a stone incense burner. These small shrines took their name from the word hokura; a kami repository. They were said to often be used to house objects called yorishiro; things capable of attracting gods and spirits.

When he opened the box in the centre of the cupboard-like shrine, he was surprised; it was like no hammer he had ever seen. The word "hammer" conjures images of a hand tool with a metal, weighted head perfect from striking nails. The uchide no kozuchi had little in common with the tool you found in every shed, garage and toolbox across the world.

The shape of the hammer head itself was rotund, like a small wine barrel. The handle was stubby, barely a fist and a half long. It seemed the handle continued through the head of the hammer as it had what looked like a crest poking out of the top. It was colourful and ornate. On the striking sides were painted moons and stars and on the main body there were multicoloured swirling flower patterns, bonsai trees, a cat design on one side and a white crane on the other, symbols of fortune. Two red, hemp cords trailed off the end of the handle, finishing with frilled loose ends. The whole object was shiny, as if recently polished, and all in all it appeared decorative and expensive.

Natsuo thought it looked more like something a rich person would have bought to display in their home, rather than a tool that gods would fight over. He closed the little doors of the hokora and continued up the path.

The forest opened up as he arrived at the ridge. The view was contained; the only vistas were of the little, green canyonette in which he had awoken. Natsuo surmised it was only a few kilometres long.

Beyond that the world lost focus, smudging as if the still-wet painting at the edge of a watercolour had been pawed at.

Bubble world...

Natsuo sat down on the non-grass and crossed his legs. He looked down below at the little river and its miniature bridge. It reminded him of Ochiai Village back on Shikoku. A lot of the local tourist offices emblazoned photos of the small, terraced settlement onto posters with the hope of drumming up some visitors. Natsuo mused bittersweetly about how many villages like that were fighting for survival, lost as they were in the depths of mountain valleys, themselves in the depths of isolated island reaches.

On television they called them genkai shūraku, marginal villages. Tiny towns, villages and hamlets with no industry, ageing populations and which were losing their residents to the cities. Abandoned houses called akiya still gave a visual illusion of cohesion, until you realised no-one was home. In recent years local town councils had been trying to rent them or sell at knockdown rates.

Interestingly as the Japanese left for jobs in the big towns and cities, foreigners were sometimes moving in; drawn to the villages by the peace and quiet, fresh air and beautiful surroundings.

Perhaps the only time in his years as a shut-in that Natsuo had felt the momentary flutter of desire to leave was when an American man opened a brew pub in the Nakatsu Gorge area. It was only about an hour's drive from his home. He had seen it on a NHK report about the rejuvenation of regional areas, and as soon as he saw the images of the American pouring out locally-made ales for villagers, smiling and laughing with tourists, and finally standing, arms crossed, outside the Blue Brew bar whilst the Niyodo River rushed past the front door, Natsuo was tempted to leave. But, of course, he didn't.

He did, however, add it to his every growing list of "Things to do after I've finished saving the world from total destruction."

Shattering the peace and serenity was a great scream. No, not a scream. A word: No, frothing up from some guttural depths within.

Izanami was down by the river on her knees, her head in her hands, screaming, her throat rasping. At the blurring edges of the little bubble-valley electric sparks and what looked like blue and yellow lightning bolts were appearing in the faded edge of the private universe.

Natsuo had no idea what was going on. Izanagi turned immediately to look up and lock eyes with Natsuo, knowing exactly where he was. The voice was in his ears, as if the creator god was standing next to him.

'Take the hammer. Go. Back to your realm. Hurry!'

Natsuo still had no clue what was happening. He had been peacefully day-dreaming and enjoying the view and now there was screaming and chaos.

He followed Izanagi's orders and ran back down the stone steps towards the small hokora. As he descended the path the sky started to darken, attracting his attention to the now burning bright electrical storm that seemed to be emerging through the blurred walls that had been sealing off the valley from the rest of Yomi. Natsuo couldn't help but stop and watch. He needed to understand.

There was Izanagi, on his knees now, holding his wife as she screamed and sobbed. She was pushing him away, as if telling him to flee. He kept shaking his head. She stopped screaming and was looking in his eyes, nodding, and now smiling as the tears glinted with the light bouncing off the river water. She stood up and walked off, alone, towards the now seething, static mass bulging through the sky like a tumour. It looked like an inky black cloud with lightning bolting through it, glowing areas here and there that menacingly spoke silently of the violence within.

Izanami then stopped, removed her clothes and lay down flat on her back, her arms and palms upwards, her eyes closed. Suddenly various shapes flew out from the broiling electrical aberration in the sky, and started darting about; dark, nebulous shapes, fizzing and cracking with electric energy. Then, with a speed that the eye couldn't catch, they descended upon Izanami's naked body, settling on her. Izanagi then took his sword out of its sheath, holding it up straight with two hands. The sky grew gloomier still, the only light coming from whatever it was that was pulsating its way through the invisible wall, and, on the now dark valley floor, those beings of charged light that now illuminated the porcelain-white flesh of Izanami, creating some macabre beacon.

'Where is it Izanagi?!' A voice boomed, reverberating through the sky and thumping the walls of Natsuo's ear canal. 'You are making history repeat itself.' It boomed again. 'Your poor sister. Your poor wife.' Natsuo thought he could make out something moving in the simmering, black sparking mass in the sky.

A face? A hand?

'The uchide no kozuchi. Where is it? I know it is here.'

The intensity of the light increased, with Izanami now invisible under the aura of electrical fire around her.

Izanagi remained stoic, standing with his sword out, between the hill Natsuo was on and his wife.

'You know I won't tell you that, son of mine.'

Son?

'Susanoo...' Natsuo said under his breath.

Izanagi turned his head slightly, the corner of his right eye somehow, even at this distance, piercing Natsuo's gaze through the trees.

'I said go!' The voice hissed urgently in his ears.

The lighting ball seemed to notice Natsuo's whisper too. A wind blew out from the sky and rolled along the valley, whipping up Izanagi's mane of hair, and then ruffled through the grass and branches until it blew Natsuo back off his feet and onto the ground. The shock stirred him.

Get up...

He instinctively got onto his feet, opened the shrine, removed the hammer and started to run along the path, making his way down to the torii gate.

Shadows started to coat the spaces between the trees as he ran. Something was searching, hunting, but Natsuo remained hidden for the moment. Flashes zipped and pinged above him and he felt a pressure in the air. At the bottom of the path where the cobble staircase in the woods gave way to the open grassy banks of the river, he stopped. He was breathing heavily, and sweat was streaming down his forehead. The humidity, like when a dense summer storm is above, was suffocating.

The torii gate, with its innocuous string lolling clumsily between the two stone pillars, must only be a short run away, maybe no more than thirty metres. His thoughts instantly turned back to the volcano down in Meido. Once again, he was running for his life, for everyone's lives, to enter a portal.

This time felt different.

The danger was colossal and godly. But it would only take him seconds. He would be completely visible, however. Natsuo grunted to himself.

As if I have any other option.

He slowed his breathing and clutched the hammer tightly. He decided against putting it in his bag, as if holding it made it, him, safer and more secure.

The second Natsuo left the line of cedar trees he felt the air bubble up around him and intensify in heat. The sky cracked and the sound of thunder and lightning pealed out around him. The valley was aflame with bolts of energy and the sound of tofu squeaking in a hot pan.

Just a few more metres...

Whatever was chasing him couldn't know that the plain-looking gate would lead him back to the human realm so, in a moment of quick thinking, Natsuo changed his course immediately back into the trees, running parallel to the river, just inside the copse.

Booming laughter, a haughty, imperial laughter, rang out through the glade. Natsuo felt an inevitability about the situation, like whatever it was, if it was indeed Susanoo, was toying with him.

'Screw this,' Natsuo hissed to himself.

When he was all but level with the gate, he darted back out of the trees, making a break for it.

The air fizzed again and, for the first time, Natsuo, looking left back from where he had come, had the shortest of glimpses of what was pursuing him. A swirling mass of black-crimson clouds was looming out over the valley, and in the middle of the aerial maelstrom, was a face. The electrical charges and undulations in the clouds had formed a sort of angry, imperious mask with bright searching eyes.

'Boy!' The cloud boomed the moment it met Natsuo's gaze.

Just a couple of metres...

A sonic boom cracked in the heavens and bolts of lightning-smoke helices punched out along the river towards him. Fear overcame Natsuo as he swung the hammer in front of him; a last ditch involuntary attempt at defence.

'Leave me alone!' Natsuo screamed as the world exploded into a shattered window of spectral rainbow light and white noise.

Then silence and darkness.

And nothing else.

Chapter Nine: Hyakki Yagyō
黄泉

Night parade of one hundred demons.

Trees are important in Japan. A festival or public holiday is called matsuri, which is born out of the word for pine tree: matsu. Trees find their way into different fields and spheres of society. For example the Japanese usher in the new year with bamboo and pine decorations, whilst sugi cedar is highly prized around the world by designers and carpenters alike.

And arguably the most famous symbol of both the country and its art is the sakura cherry tree; its falling petals inspiring centuries of poets and artists to comment on the very nature of what it means to be alive, as well as giving joy to the populace as they celebrate under the pink in *hanami* blossom-viewing parties.

People treat trees like the living beings they are, caring for shrunken bonsai more attentively than they do sometimes their own homes. In temples and shrines trees are both decoratively important and sacred. And hope was given to a bomb-blasted Hiroshima as little green shoots began appearing out of the blackened and shattered remains of the city and out of the charred branches and stumps of what used to be parks and woods. Hibaku jumoku; survivor trees.

Humans believed that trees were conduits for the kami and so often built their temples among them, wrapping the shimenawa ropes around the trunks to warn others not to tamper with the sacred plants. Anyone who chopped them down would have to deal with an angry spirit. The humans were partly right.

Chinju no mori are the sacred, often ancient, shrine forests. A place where these old, wooden sentinels have stood watching over the world for hundreds and sometimes thousands of years. On the island of Yakushima, flung off the south coast of Kyushu, there is a gnarly old cedar tree whose xylem and phloem, bark and roots, have been slowly breathing for seven millennia.

Trees can talk to each other. The mycorrhizal networks, sending root filaments out underground, can be vast. Limitless connections created by fungi, joining every tree and providing a direct link for defence or growth.

This tree, having remained isolated on its island for so long, unknowingly bore silent witness to the first artistically productive cultures of Japan, the mysterious Jōmon, the birth of rice production by the Yayoi, the rise and fall of the shogun and great clans, the shift towards democracy and finally the nuclear hellfire of the twentieth century.

At every stage this old Mother Tree received the news, even on the island. And now the tree was glowing. In the dark heart of the claustrophobic and overgrown mossy forests of Yakushima, an algae-green light was slowly pulsing. Sending a message.

A cooling sensation suffused with an otherworldly light stirred Natsuo into consciousness. It was dusk and it was raining.

Rain…

His mind instantly focused, he felt awake.

'*Ame da*?' he said to himself.

Rain meant the real world. Rain meant clouds, meant the hydrologic cycle, meant…he was back.

Natsuo was lying in sodden grass in the open air on his back in front of the torii gate, as the droplets fell down on his face.

So he had got through.

He bunched up his hand, nothing. Looking to his right he saw the uchide no kozuchi a few feet away, shining with fallen water. So he had made it back with the hammer.

Turning his head left he saw the cause of the light. Some jade-green, glowing orbs were hovering a couple of metres from him by a little thicket of trees. Specifically, they were floating around an old-looking pine tree with a shinto rope around its broad base. Natsuo felt calm.

Kodama…

Natsuo had no need to read the old fisherman's bestiary for this. Everyone in Japan knew about kodama; there was even a Shinkansen high-speed train line named after them. Tree spirits, holy guardians of the sacred trees, kodama had appeared in art almost as much as oni and tengu. And, unless you were planning to chop said tree down, they were benign yōkai. It made sense there would be something waiting for him on the other side.

He looked up at the sky again, enjoying the feeling of being cold, like when you welcome the first chilly tendrils after a long summer, and revelled in the abundance of water that he had so missed down in the barren belly of the underworld.

Somewhat glumly he reminded himself that the rain meant storms. The whole heavenly plot of his new life flooded back. He got up, retrieved the hammer, stowed it in his bag, and approached the kodama.

'It is said that when a tree reaches the age of one hundred, it has a kami that will show its form.'

A bodiless, breathy voice.

'Hello?' Natsuo ventured.

Out of a large, crooked branch halfway up the tree something akin to smoke was fissuring out of the wood. That line of smoke collected on the ground in front of Natsuo, curling and pooling as though it had weight and intention. As the smoke cleared there was a small and very old man in a kimono. He was faint though, somewhat transparent, like a faded photograph.

'We have been awaiting your return.'

'Well...that's good I suppose.'

The tree-spirit smiled and nodded. 'It is.'

'Izanagi told me I am in Izumo province...'

'This is Yomotsu Hirasaka. Where the human realm connects with that of the gods.'

'So what do I do now?'

'The hammer must go to Amaterasu.'

'I know that,' said Natsuo a touch curtly.

'The Mother Tree has notified Sōjōbō. At some point he will reach out to you. More I don't know, young man.'

'So...I just wait his call, is that it?'

The tree-spirit didn't respond. Riddles and missions and mystical objects, demons and goblins, gods and monsters. Natsuo was slowly approaching the end of whatever tether he had managed to hold on to. However, he decided against starting an argument or getting testy with a kodama who looked like everyone's favourite grandfather.

He exhaled.

'So, I guess I'm miles from anywhere in the middle of a mountain range or something?'

'On the contrary Natsuo-san. The main road is a five-minute walk down that path and the town of Matsue is a short bus ride away.'

'Finally, some luck!' Sardonic seemed to be part of his personality nowadays.

'Take care Natsuo...' the spirit said, dissipating in a similar way to how it had appeared, seemingly being sucked up back into the branch.

'Wait! Tell me about...' But it was too late. The spectral man had gone, and the glowing orbs had disappeared with him. It was as if a light show had been turned off.

A quietness returned to sit solidly under the old soundtrack of tinkling raindrops. He had wanted to ask if the spirit had any news of Hage-tanuki. Natsuo feared the worst.

The three-hour trip back to Osaka was odd. After however long he had been down in the bowels of the underworld he had forgotten the simple pleasures of the real world. The little jingles at the stations and the hiss of the train doors at each stop. The gentle forces that pull your body to one side as the train brakes, leading to an inexorable tug throughout your whole body and then the tiny jolt in the other direction as you came to a stop. The quiet hubbub of the Japanese people in and out of these metal snakes going to who knows where. The smells of platform ramen bars, oily pork broth and soy sauce. The bright colours and buttons of the vending machines and the taste of a cold 140 yen bottle of Calpis. The bowing. So much bowing. Platform attendants, polite commuters, ticket office officials handing you over the change into small dishes instead of hand to hand. Little maneki cats in the windows of shops and bars, their arms rocking up and down.

Then the neon of Japan's second city. How you'd missed the neon. The way it bounced off the walls and off the faces of gawping, phone-wielding walkers. How it reminded everyone of *Blade Runner*. You wanted to hug people, to touch everything. This was real. This was human. The guilt once again of having missed out on years of this! How stupid you had been! This was everything. It was perfect, down to every exposed cable, rain-stained wall and seedy back alley.

The Eight Thunder Spirits. Ōikazuchi, Grown Thunder, attached itself to her head. Honoikazuchi, Blazing Thunder, and Sakuikazuchi, Splitting Thunder, crawled upon her breasts and privates. Kuroikazuchi, Darkening Thunder, instead busied itself by falling upon her stomach. Then the extremities. Wakaikazuchi, Young Thunder, took the left hand, while the right hand was suffocated by Tsuchiikazuchi, Earthen Thunder. The left foot succumbed to Nariikazuchi, Booming Thunder, and finally her right foot's freedom was sapped away by Fusuikazuchi, Bowing Thunder.

So that was what had attacked Izanami. On the inner-city from Shin-Osaka station Natsuo, finally having charged his mobile phone, frantically searched for information about what had happened to him in Yomi. His yōkai book didn't quite stretch to those depths, but the internet was an endless source of information, some academic, some just sites compiled by interested parties.

At some point in the lost beginnings of the world Izanami had died in Yomi, her corpse then swamped by the thunder spirits. Izanagi had later struck an imposing pose, sword held aloft, which was enough to send the spirits back to whence they came. Though according to another historical text, he instead scattered the thunder sprites by hurling peaches at them. Natsuo knew which he had seen with his own two eyes.

So was this a repeat of the past?

He hadn't known the creator gods long enough to really feel anything for them. He hoped they were OK of course; seemingly they were on his side in all this. But, more than anything, Natsuo was confused. A moment in Yomi, another purgatory, and then chaos again. And now, he was out of the demon realm, back on the very human train network and making his way to see his mother.

His time trudging through Meido, meeting, befriending and even slaying monsters, and then the thunder-ruined, pastoral heaven-scape of Yomi, seemed both immediate in his mind but also like a surreal dream. Conjuring up images of human-hacking oni butchers, stinking bubbling lakes, magical flying tanuki and sake-swilling monsters with faces on their bellies seemed almost ludicrous as he peered out at the rain pelting down across the blocky cityscape. More important was his mother.

He opened the calendar on his phone again; he had been away just a few days, but after everything he had been through it felt like a lifetime had passed.

'Is it over?'

'Not yet,' Natsuo said. 'Not quite yet.'

He wanted his mother's embrace to last forever. She could never know what he had been through, what he had seen. No one could.

When Natsuo had walked back into the temporary shelter, everyone still hiding out away from the never-ending storms, his mother had flung herself at him and wept. She had been sitting with old lady Mina playing *shogi* on a little table. When Mina saw Natsuo all the tension had dropped out of her face and a relieved smile spread out. She gently placed a hand on that of Natsuo's mother, who had been slowly pushing a pentagonal ceramic tile across a checkered board and nodded in his direction.

They sat on little chairs and Natsuo recounted his adventure, sparing them the more gruesome aspects. A mixture of fear, awe and incomprehension wiped over the various faces who had gathered to listen to him. Mr Shi arrived and brought some tea. It felt ancient, like some Viking gathering to hear tales told in the time before science and books. Though instead of Scandinavian rains pitter-pattering off atmospheric timber longhouses, it was Japanese summer yōkai-storms colliding with corrugated iron and concrete.

'We've seen them,' Mr Shi stated, his hands round a steaming cup of green tea. 'We've all seen them now. I saw *bakeneko* cats tormenting some drunks outside a yakitori bar two days ago. Standing up on their hind legs they were, scratching at their shins and elbows and taunting them in perfect Japanese.'

'Only last night my granddaughter was approached by the kuchi-sake-onna,' Mina said, carrying on the hushed campfire tone. The other old ladies hissed and gasped. 'I know. She said a young woman approached her and her friends as they were walking home from school. This stylishly dressed young woman wearing a white surgical mask stops the girls and asks "Am I pretty?" My granddaughter, being the well brought up young girl she is, says "Yes, you're pretty." The monster then takes off her mask revealing a hideous mouth-slit, ear-to-ear, dark and full of stunted little teeth. "Even like this?" The kuchi-sake-onna says. Well of course, my granddaughter ran home in tears and came in shaking.'

'Well this morning,' started another woman about Natsuo's mother's age, 'all the old kitchen utensils and bits and bobs in the attic came to life! They opened the door, jumped down onto the landing, danced around me laughing, and then headed out the front door!'

'Tsukumogami...' Natsuo said to himself, recognising the famous idea of old, discarded household objects getting a life of their own.

'Whatever happened to you down there Natsuo-kun,' said Natsuo's mother, resting a hand on his cheek, 'it seems to have stirred the pot.'

Yomi-no-kuni...

'If the yōkai are being this bold, this present, something big is happening,' added Mina forebodingly. 'What happens now I wonder?'

A pregnant silence lingered in the air as everyone's attention slowly turned back to Natsuo. Suddenly the cosy relief of being back among familiar company began to wither under the real-world weight and pressure of these expectant faces. They weren't looking at him as Yui

Hirawa's thirty-year-old Hikikomori son. He was now tainted; tainted with expectation and potential. Some awkward saviour.

He toyed with the idea of explaining about the hammer and the small detail of having to hand it over to the top goddess of Japanese mythology; details he had also decided to omit. Instead, he simply summoned a weak smile, bow, and it'll-be-fine sentiment.

'*Daijoubu*, desu.'

Natsuo couldn't sleep. He just stared at the lofty ceiling of the hangar and listened to his mother's gently rhythmic breaths. He had no idea what would come next. Every single mythical creature, powerful beast and magic being had simply pushed him along a little more each time. It was as if he had been offered the Cliff Notes of his own story with the final chapters missing and had been asked to reproduce them in full.

Well, if that was how the gods and spirits wanted to play then so be it. He would continue to be their divine hockey puck, their mixed-blood secret weapon. And in the meantime, he would wait, like a good soldier, for the next directive.

The ceiling that he had been staring dumbly at for who knows how long started to look different. The enshrouded, pale gloom of the bare-white panelling was warping, rippling. And then a sound. A slurping sound; like that of a cat's tongue lapping at a can of tuna. The rippling turned inwards, the undulations centring in on themselves to form more of a simmering mass on the ceiling. The mass lengthened and grew limbs. A body. A head. And an old man's chest and bony knees. Then a long tongue seemed to probe out of what was now a grotesque demonic face. Strips of what looked like paper flags, matoi, covered its body, forming a skirt, forming claws, forming a beard and eyebrows.

Tenjōname, Natsuo thought to himself. He had seen this creature in his book. The ceiling licker. So esoteric and single-minded, he couldn't forget it. This odd humanoid yōkai, crawling in the rafters, licking and tonguing the walls and plaster. It was obscure and disgusting.

He then noticed eyes. Eyes blinking at him from the walls; little bright, palpating orbs in the gloom. Just eyes. They sent a chill down Natsuo's spine as he felt the walls literally watching him. The ceiling-licking creature was making its way down the wall at the far end of the hangar room, licking the scummy plaster, licking the strange walleyes, which seemed to enjoy being licked, and tonguing the door handles and locks. The sound was disgusting.

Then Natsuo's ears locked onto another noise; rattling and light banging. Creaking and echoed shuffling. Over the far left-side of the airy room he saw small men, no, not men, little shrunken oni-like goblins scratching and hammering at the corners and poles and beams and columns of the building.

'The eyes are mokumokuren and those little trouble-makers are yanari,' came a sleepy voice to Natsuo's right. 'The yōkai that fill the gap where you humans struggle to find a tangible force.'

A surreal Dali-esque creature, a hodgepodge of animals Natsuo had seen before; a bear's body, an ox tail, elephant's nose and tusks, the small dark eyes of...a rhino, and the strong legs of a tiger, stood looking past him at the goings on in the room. Overall, it resembled a tapir drawn by someone given only the crudest of descriptions, like when medieval artists created images of creatures they'd never seen.

'They're coming close now.' The tapir-creature yawned. 'The night parade is upon us. Well. Upon you.' It smiled. 'Don't worry though. For right now, I've got you.'

Natsuo was paralysed with fear.

Suddenly a dark, bipedal cat-creature, the size of a human and covered in cracking orange fire appeared at Natsuo's feet and leapt, claws out, towards him with a hiss.

Natsuo sat up with a start, breathing heavily and with sweat blossoming through his t-shirt.

Nightmare.

Again with the dreams...

His mother was still soundly asleep, breathing in, breathing out.

2:30am.

Need some air.

He quietly got to his feet, put on a hoodie, instinctively looked to the ceiling just in case, and then made his way past all the little temporary booth-rooms to the door.

Outside it was raining heavily, but the winds weren't too strong. Natsuo closed the door behind him and just stood there enjoying the cold, wet, very human air. He held his arms around him, rubbing them to get the blood flowing.

The docklands skyline was throwing glimmerballs onto the bouncing waters, while fat raindrops shone and danced in the lamp lights in front of him. There was always a hush during those hours of the day when humanity had decided that no matter your colour or creed, religion or salary, you were supposed to be asleep in a bed somewhere.

'Trouble sleeping?'

'*Kuso*!' Natsuo jumped at the voice in the rain.

'Sorry to scare you,' replied a tall man in a dark purple coat, a gold-lined collar turned up against the cold. He had a thin cigarette burning demurely in his mouth as he spoke. It seemed to be attached to his bottom lip and never left its position except relinquishing its buoyancy when he took it out between two long fingers to exhale. He wore curt, circular sunglasses despite it being nighttime. They reflected like obsidian against the streetlights so you couldn't see his eyes.

'That was a baku by the way.' The man said, turning to Natsuo slightly, leant back on the wall of the building as he was. 'It's an ancient creature that has the ability to eat nightmares. If you suffer from headaches, you can sleep easy if you have something protecting your head bearing an image of one.' The slender cigarette was close to burning out as it bounced off his lips and surrendered ash to the night air. 'Did you know its urine can melt iron and turn it into water?'

'Er...no,' Natsuo said. 'Sorry, who are you?'

The man in the deep burgundy coat flicked away the butt a second before the fire touched his skin, reached into a deep pocket and brought out a box of cigarettes and a business card. The former he patted against his arm, pushing out one lone cigarette which he mouthed out of the pack and lit with a match, and the latter which he handed to Natsuo.

Abe no Seimei
Onmyōji
BUREAU OF DIVINATION

'*Hajimemashite, yoroshiku onegaishimasu*,' said the man, offering his hand.

'Anoo...nice to meet you too,' Natsuo replied with a handshake, still utterly bewildered.

'Follow me.' Abe no Seimei lowered his glasses down his nose slightly, revealing deep green eyes. 'Because if the yōkai don't get you, the cold will.'

It looked like any normal izakaya; though why it was open at such an hour Natsuo had no idea. Plumes of broth smoke and the sound of a sizzling grill emanated from the shoebox kitchen at the centre of the back wall, which opened up into a small space in the middle of a u-shaped line of seating counters.

'This is a midnight diner,' said Abe, sliding over a glass of shōchū, which Natsuo clasped but didn't drink. 'The izakaya as you know them have been around since the Edo period. Under the Tokugawa bunch liquor stores sold alcohol by weight so people would often go, stand around, and order loose amounts of sake or plum wine or whatever was going. Later came the barrels as makeshift seating, and after that the sakana, little snacks like edamame, tsukemono, and, depending on where you were, sashimi or grilled meat. That being said, I had been drinking in taverns for hundreds of years before that. A couple of centuries before I was born, I think it was the year 700 and something, King Ashihara got drunk and was murdered in one. Can you imagine that happening in your time, Natsuo?'

'You know my name?'

'Of course. I wouldn't be very good at my job if I didn't.'

'Sorry,' Natsuo interjected, his sleepy brain finally catching up with the reality of the moment, 'who are you?'

The elegantly-dressed man smiled foxily and downed the rest of the distilled liquid in his ceramic cup. 'I'm in charge of the Bureau of Divination.'

'Divination...'

'Yin and yang masters, wizards, sorcerers and the like. Divining through the centuries. Though most of us were just bureaucrats in the end, going door to door warding off spirits and selling charms, interpreting dreams, and performing purification ceremonies. Then, with the passage of modernity, the world stopped wanting us.'

'Hang on, hang on. You said centuries?'

'I was born in the year 921 in Nara.'

'Abe...' The name triggered something.

'The metro station?'

'That's right!' Natsuo had passed the Abeno station in Osaka to reunite with his mother.

'For magical pencil-pushers, it seems we're quite well known. Anime, manga, computer games. But really just the name Onmyōji. Our bureau is split up into four different departments: divination, calendar, astronomy and meteorology, and time measurement and scheduling. It's not all mystical of course. It was us who used to simply keep the gong ringing every hour so the people knew what time it was! But everything is connected. I was always mostly on the divination side of things, what with the powers and all.' He twirled his hand in front of Natsuo and a small glowing, feathery dodecahedron appeared in his palm. 'Everything comes together, all four bureaus, whenever needed, to predict the when and the where of the *hyakki yagyō*, the night parade of one hundred demons.'

'What is that?'

'It is a night when all the spirits, yōkai, oni, ghosts and tsukumogami leave their homes and hideouts, leave the woods and hills, and come together during a pandemoniac festival of chaos, singing, dancing, and mayhem.' Abe poured himself another glass of shōchū, having noted Natsuo wasn't drinking. 'It is our job to know when and where so we can avoid humans coming into contact with it as best we can.'

'How come I've never heard of this?'

Abe no Seimei smiled. 'Again, I wouldn't be very good at my job if you had.'

'So why are you telling me this now?' Natsuo asked, still trying to work out what this millennia-old wizard wanted with him.

'It just so happens that one such auspicious night is approaching, in three days time in fact. It just so happens that it shall be occurring in Nara. And it just so happens,' he said, enjoying stringing out the word "just", 'that a certain Shuten dōji will be in attendance.'

Natsuo was tiring of being strung along, being reduced to a mere vessel asking "who's that?" and "what is that?" and "what do I do?".

'Just tell me who the hell he is and what the hell you want from me.'

Abe no Seimei smiled again, before a hint of sadness tinted his brow.

'I apologise.' He put down his glass. 'You must be lost and confused and sick of this. Part of me is sorry Sōjōbō got you involved at all. But, with your father and all.'

'My father?'

'Well, that's where I enter the picture.' Abe took off his sunglasses and carefully folded them closed, placing them in his breast pocket. 'I knew him. Well. I knew the later him. The him that you more or less knew.'

'You knew my father?'

'Considering his fame, his infamy, his history, most of the spirit realm knew a version of him. I knew the version that would later fall in love with your mother. Shuten dōji is the link. You see, among my divination powers I have always been able to divine the location of even the most hidden oni if they are powerful enough. And Shuten dōji, like your father Ōtakemaru, is really rather powerful. One of the "Big Three" we called them in the Bureau. Since the peacetime Shuten dōji has resided in his iron palace atop Mount Ōe out of reach and out of touch. Your father, as you sadly know Natsuo, passed away. The whereabouts of the other of the three, a lustful nine-tailed fox called Tamamo no Mae, who often took the image of a beautiful woman, we don't know. Some say her plotting and conniving are responsible for half the world's wars. I don't know about that, but every time I get a lock on her somewhere she disappears.

'Anyway, I'm tangentalising. Shuten dōji will be entering the human realm during the hyakki yagyō. He will most likely just enjoy watching the revelry, drinking heavily whilst the minor monsters terrorise and cavort. He's a terrible drunk you see; hence his name. Shuten dōji — "little drunkard". He used to be the proud king of the oni; now he's a lazy, alcoholic ogre. Not that I'm complaining. He used to run rampant through Kyoto, snatching away young virgins to drink their blood and eat their flesh raw. He and his band of oni were much feared. Now he sits in his castle hosting monstrous banquets and drinking the demon plane dry.'

The smell of soy sauce bloomed into the space between them. The salty aroma then mixed with the ricey perfume of *mirin* followed by a sugary sweetness. Teriyaki. A rice cooker pinged to a stop. The cook was pushing some beaten eggs round a smoking hot pan as little flakes of katsuobushi danced in the yolk.

The only sensory elements in the room came from the tiny kitchen. Everything else was hushed and shadowy. Faceless drinkers mumbling to themselves in the wee hours of the morning.

'Now this is where you come in.' Abe paused. 'You're going to want to drink that.'

Natsuo felt that last sentence charged with foreboding. He took the little ceramic cup to his mouth and drank the slightly sweet, slightly musty distil, then nodded expectantly. 'You have to kill Shuten dōji.'

Natsuo didn't say a word, just reached for the bottle of shōchū and poured himself another serving, which he again downed. After a third pour he asked the only inevitable question.

'Why?'

'The Tide Jewels. He has them on him at all times. If you can get the jewels off him we can at least stop the storms, stop the rains and waves. Bring some meteorological order to the world again. Then, after you deliver the hammer to Amaterasu, the rest should be fairly straightforward. With her in possession of the jewels, the hammer and the sword you currently have on your person, she'll just need to demand the spear and then...order restored.'

'I suppose you need me because of the connection to my father?' Natsuo said grimly. 'My demon blood.'

'*Sou desu*...' Abe affirmed sadly. 'On the night in question I will accompany you to the Night Parade and get you as close as possible to Shuten's location. The rest, as I'm certain you're sick of hearing, is up to you.'

'Mm.'

'All I can say is whatever you end up doing, do it quietly. There's not much I can do against a baying horde of yōkai.'

'And I'm a spy to boot...'

'Pardon?'

'Nothing,' Natsuo said darkly.

Something sizzled in a pan, raw food hitting boiling oil. Then bubbling and the soft glug and purring fizz of beer spilling from bottle to glass.

'Can I ask you something Seimei-san?'

'Of course.'

'My father. You said you knew him?'

'Mm.'

'I always hated him. No, not hated him. Disliked. It's hard to truly hate your parents as you don't see them as people do you? They're just Mum and Dad. But even when I was little, I never got anything from him you know? The most loving emotion was something that seemed like he was thinking "that is acceptable". Not that he never really treated me badly; not until I turned more into a teenager and became a Hikikomori.'

'He talked of you a lot,' Abe said, inserting himself gently into Natsuo's monologue. 'He worried constantly; was paranoid. I feel sadly you saw the wrong Ōtakemaru, sorry, Akihiro, but for the right reasons. You were doomed not to have the father you deserved from the day you were born. It's all terribly sad.' He placed a hand on Natsuo's back, his debonair mystery slipping to simple empathy. '"The goodness of the father reaches higher than a mountain; that of the mother goes deeper than the ocean." I think that's rather nice. So take heart Natsuo, your father went from being the most feared oni in the under-realms to a father so protective of his child that he left everything behind and hid from the Kings of Hell. Absent he may have been, but his love for you wasn't.'

'Arigato...'

'Come, let us return to your mother. You'll sleep easy tonight. I'll come for you in three days.'

In Japan's Broadcasting Act from 1950, Article 108 states the following:

In conducting the domestic basic broadcasting, etc., if a windstorm, heavy rain, flood, earthquake, large-scale fire or other disaster occurs or is likely to occur, the basic broadcaster shall transmit broadcasting which will serve to prevent such occurrence or mitigate such damage thereto.

This relates and refers directly to the country's principal public broadcaster NHK — the Nippon Hōsō Kyōkai or Japan Broadcasting Company. They have a national network of seismometers and other pieces of equipment that are shared with the Japan Meteorological Agency so they are able to provide warnings within seconds of detection.

They are obliged to broadcast early warning emergency reporting should the country experience emergencies such as tsunamis, earthquakes and imminent attacks during potential wartime. Or now, as was the case as Natsuo sat in a small cafe with his mother drinking screaming hot black coffee, the appearance of certain yōkai.

A man in Gifu complaining that there were human-faced cows in his farmlands; a bent-over old man with an evil glint in eyes, washing his azuki beans in the river and smiling creepily at kids, sending them crying to their mothers; furry, wild, red-haired creatures that looked like pink-skinned children in grass-skirts were running rampant in the woods, trapping people in hollow trees, and which the Okinawans interviewed were calling Kijimuna; and now a shaky phone video of what looked like weasels with scythe hands whirling around in a wind vortex above some confused farmers in a Niigata rice field.

'Everything seems to be spilling over,' Natsuo surmised, blowing gently the top of his coffee, sending little ripples out to the other side of the mug.

'This is exactly what your father was trying to protect you from. And now look, my son, the son I thought I had lost, is now journeying through hell and trying to save the world.'

'I'm more of an errand boy really.' Natsuo smiled bleakly.

His mother signalled to the waitress to bring a slice of cheesecake and a strawberry mochi.

'I know I haven't asked, but you haven't told me what you have to do next.'

'Mm.'

'I think I'm ready to know now. At first, I wasn't. I didn't want to imagine any of it. But now, now I see you, how capable you are, I want to know.'

'I have to go to Nara, where there's going to be a lot of yōkai, some Night Parade they call it. Anyway, I'm supposed to...meet this Shuten Dōji character and collect something we need to help end all of this. Then I take that, this damn hammer I have, and, get this, deliver them to Amaterasu.'

A quietness hung over the table. Natsuo's mother slowly took a bite of the fluffy cheesecake, her mind clearly jumping about, working things out.

'Shuten...' she said.

Natsuo had expected his mother to be more shocked that he was going to meet a deity, than 'another' oni.

'So you've heard of him too?' he asked. 'Let me guess, Dad?'

'He used to talk about him. I never met him. Never met any of that world. But they used to be friends way back. I get the image that this Shuten is truly terrible, but not without reason. Generous at times, bloodthirsty the next. I always imagined him like some old English king or Shogun. Fickle and with a need to be pleased, but not mindless. That's what made him so dangerous your father said. An intelligent monster. Though when the time came for balance and the warring stopped it seems he turned to drink as your father turned to exile and parenthood.' She took a butter knife and cut the pale pink mochi in half revealing a perfect red strawberry within. 'I'll just say take care.'

Natsuo was glad he hadn't revealed the true nature of his meeting with Shuten and, after his mother's words, began wondering if what Abe no Seimei had in mind was indeed the only course of action.

Yui Hirawa put her mug down, smiled, and changed the topic.

'So, Natsuo, what do you want to do when all this is over?'

For the rest of the morning mother and son only spoke of the future, of trips around Japan, of tending the plants in the garden, of rebuilding the house in Tosashimizu, and teaching Natsuo how to cook dishes other than instant noodles and toast. No monsters, no end of the world, just a mum and her boy nattering in a little cafe during the rains.

The deer were all bowing. Despite the torrential and constant downpour, the little sika deer were crowding around, sniffing at his hands and pockets. Some were babies mimicking the movements of the adults; bowing their heads like visitors to a shrine. Polite begging. Leathery lips hunting for the crunchy senbei sold at little stalls along the paths around the parks and temples.

'Sorry, little ones.'

Natsuo gently pushed his way past them and headed for the grand Tōdai-ji temple where Abe no Sembei had said to meet, punctually, at 15:09, inside by the giant Daibutsu statue of Buddha Vairocana.

Despite having once visited on a school trip, Nara felt completely new. This was always the case. Holidays and moments of one's youth were compartmentalised into a different box within the mind. A place of innocence and experience where rational thought was left aside. Most of it wouldn't be remembered; photos in the mind.

A child isn't in control of its life, it's carried along in the flow of adults, and usually experiences everything in the wake of their parents. This is why friendships are so strong at this time; it is usually one of the few moments the child is in control of what happens. It's only when teenage years bleed into adulthood where memories get placed into the other box. The adult is usually the one in control and the one creating the memories.

This is exactly why the Tōdai-ji temple took Natsuo's breath away as if it had been the first time he had seen it.

Clipped green lawns of the temple area led up to a vast wooden structure, for most of human history the largest in the world: the fifty-metre tall, fifty-metre wide Great Buddha Hall, a centuries-old, dark-brown, two-tiered behemoth that loomed over the surroundings. The dark veil of rain gave Natsuo a sensation of a slumbering, shrouded giant sitting with its knees up to its chest.

Inside was almost more awe-inspiring. Lofty, rust-red, interconnected hinoki cypress columns held up a chequered roof; gilded statues of buddhas and yōkai, huge bells and gongs and cauldrons with incense sticks poking out of them, tried their best to fill some of the enormous space.

And there, immediately on entering, the fifty foot Daibutsu, was sat on his bronze plinth, one palm raised up while half-closed eyes gave him a dreamy and peaceful countenance. Something that Natsuo could only describe as dust seemed to be hanging in the air, catching the light and adding to the somewhat hushed magic of the interior.

'Impressive, isn't it?'

Abe no Seimei, once again in his circular sunglasses and long indigo coat, was lighting some incense sticks in front of the great Buddha. He held two between closed palms in front of his face, bowed slightly, and then placed them in the small sand pit. He bowed again more deeply, palms closed again, and then wafted some smoke over himself.

'This probably won't be as helpful as I hope, but it's always worth covering all the bases.' He winked. 'Just in case.'

Aromas of sweet, burning, resinous wood, spices and flowers wafted towards Natsuo. He had always found the smell of incense enchanting.

'In precisely two hours the hyakki yagyō will begin. At ōmagatoki, which today is at 18:09, just as the sun sets, the spirits will arrive en masse to start their debauchery in the streets of Nara. In precisely three hours the parade should pass along Zoshicho streets, just up beyond here on the hill. They'll set off fireworks and kites and tumble down the slopes. This is the where and when you need to be. I have information that Shuten dōji will commandeer the Matsunoya *ryokan*, so as to have a view to the party. How you get in and what you do next is up to you. I'm still human after all, so I can only get you this far.'

'Why me?'

'Hmm?'

'Genuinely. I've seen magical tanuki reigning energy balls down on demons, I've met all-powerful tengu and even creator gods. Why is everything left to me? Where's the logic there?'

Abe no Seimei smiled.

'You know, you're right. There isn't much logic on the face of it.' He removed his sunglasses revealing those cool, emerald eyes. 'Look, I can't pretend to second guess the movements of the gods, but you're being used for a reason. I know it must seem like it's all being left to chance. But think about it. Your half-blood gives access enough for you to be useful in both worlds. Then there's the power of deception. No, not deception. Bamboozlement and the beauty of the left-field choice. That is to say, no one would suspect you or even see you coming.'

'Okay. I think I've understood that up to this point.' Natsuo sighed. 'It's just been a lot. And now...now you're sending me, up until recently a Hikikomori, off to kill an oni. You can see why I might be a little wary about placing that much faith in the plan. In me...'

'If I live on longer, shall I again, I wonder, yearn for these days? The world that I once saw as bitter, now, is dear to me?'

'That's a waka poem.'

'Correct. From the "Ogura Hyakunin Isshu". A hundred poems by a hundred poets. This one I think is apt for tonight. It's about nostalgia. Fujiwara no Kiyosuke wrote it in 1161 and I thought it was so good I made him send it off to be considered for the anthology. Anyway, I digress. The poem speaks of how bitter things soften and sweeten with time. And that things will get better. In the west they speak of time healing all wounds. In Japan it's all melting snow, dreams and falling cherry blossom.'

'I don't get your meaning.'

'The power of nostalgia, Natsuo. That's your other weapon. You are the son of his once friend. Your secret weapon. It's also why the yōkai are intruding more into the human realm. They thrive on being believed. Nostalgia is their power too. They remind people of a bygone age, folkloric fear. Do you know the word furusato? It literally means "old village", but might be more similar to "home" or "native place". It's one of those words tied to our close links to the land, the landscapes, the villages, the fuzzy mountains and raging rivers, the cereal waves of a rice field. An ideal memory of Japan. The people of Galicia talk of *morriña* for their land when they are away. The English say "homesickness", which I feel is a little blunt for such a nation of poets. Nostalgia is everything when yōkai are concerned. And your name Natsuo, doesn't it remind you of something?'

'I guess it relates to natsu, summer.'

'Did you ever stop to look at the kanji?'

'I suppose I never did. At school we wrote in Katakana.' He shrugged. 'When I closed myself away from the world, my name became meaningless. Just a collection of vowels and consonants.'

Abe no Seimei took an unlit incense stick and began to deftly draw lines and swirls in the prayer cauldron sand.

'And how would you translate this kanji?'

'Feelings?'

'Or yearning, to miss somebody or be attached to them. Natsukashii, a poetic yearning nostalgia. You were named after it. So tap into it.'

He took out a delicately-lined gold pocket watch and then tutted. 'Tick tock.'

'Come in out of the rain, young man, you'll catch a death!'

A tiny old lady was peeking out of a half-slid-open door to a little sweet shop stuck on the side of a cutlery store called Kikuichi. Fortuitous as it was next door to the ryokan where Shuten dōji would be appearing in an hour's time.

Natsuo had hurried through a cluster of ancient-looking temples along some muddy paths that, in any normal summer, would be full of families, couples and tourists strolling about and taking photos of deer.

There was an enormous solitary cedar tree standing alone over everything, with a small name tag saying "Ryobengi". The tree reminded him of the Hikikomori. There, but not engaging with the world. Locked in its own personal immobility. He also thought the tree had a better life than him. A name with meaning and fans and visitors.

'Arigato,' Natsuo said, hurrying into the little confectioner. He removed his wet shoes and sat on a bench next to a machine that smelled of caramelised pancake batter. A constantly rotating and gyrating selection of waffle-irons smoked around, receiving a dollop of mixture, a gloop of custard cream, then snapping together with another batter-splashed hot plate, clipping together before shortly depositing out a hot little griddled cake in the shape of a deer.

'You like my kanoko machine?' asked the old lady, laying down a steaming glass of fluorescent green tea by Natsuo.

'Amazing, really,' Natsuo cooed, enthralled by the metallic ballet, spinning round and smoking sweetly.

'My own design,' she beamed. 'Reworked it from a man who made *taiyaki* in a van up on Mount Yoshino.'

'Can I buy a couple please?'

Natsuo sat nibbling the spongy little waffles, staring out at the rain; grey lines falling like a wet barcode. One hour to go.

The rhythm of the rain plink plonking off the tarmac, pebbling the puddles and whooshing through the leaves, began to push the first warm fingers of sleep through Natsuo's body. Before he had a chance to realise he was getting sleepy he had nodded off, leaning gently on the doorframe.

Natsuo had been lulled by the calm before the storm, his brain waves exhibiting alpha activity. Quiet wakefulness they call it. Not asleep but disconnected from the active perception of the moment. Then comes the theta-band activity. Hovering just below the surface, not quite swimming the slumber lands of REM, but instead teetering on the limbo knife-edge between awake and dreams.

KA-TA-SHI-YA

Cleaning our brains of junk information, strengthening memories, restoring our bodies, conserving energy, even hiding from predators. We still don't know why we sleep; but there are theories. But then almost every animal sleeps. Are otters strengthening memories? And why would a monitor lizard need to sift through the filing cabinets of their brains?

E-KA-SE-NI-KU-RI-NI

They say the perfect nap is around half an hour. You awake feeling refreshed and reenergised. Don't sleep though. REM drags you in and keeps you coddled until morning. Breaking that stranglehold leaves you groggy.

TA-ME-RU-SA-KE

It's easy to wake from a nap. Those forty winks can be interrupted by a delicate noise, the tweet of a sparrow, a change in temperature, perhaps a breeze caressing the back of the neck, or the brain simply regaining control and firing on all cylinders again; reminding the body to run properly.

TE-E-HI

Natsuo opened his eyes slowly and refocused. He hadn't moved; still perched against the doorframe, sat with half a kanoko in his hand. The tea had gone cold, the waffle irons shut off, and there was a musical sound in the room. A frail, wobbling chorus.

A-SHI-E-HI

The little old lady was chanting to herself. The curtains had been drawn and she clutched onenju rosary beads.

WA-RE-SHI-KO-NI-KE-RI

'It has begun,' she said simply as Natsuo stirred.

'How long was I asleep?'

'Not too long dear; I didn't want to wake you.'

Natsuo looked at his phone: 18:43. So the hyakki yagyō had already started.

'I'm glad you did. Your...chanting woke me,' he said, trying to add some warmth to a smile.

'This is not the first night parade I've experienced.'

'No?'

'It was 1945. I was a young girl and remember hearing on the radio Emperor Hirohito give his address. It was the 15th of August when the Gyokuon-hōsō surrender broadcast crackled through the radio. I also remember how unclear it was. My father kept shouting "Why the hell doesn't he just say the word surrender?". Instead, it spoke of accepting a joint declaration with the USA, UK and China and the USSR. It was the radio announcer afterwards who had to essentially confirm to us all that we had, in fact, lost the war. Everyone burrowed themselves away in their homes that night to digest what this all meant. Four years of war was over. That was a lot to take in back then...

'That night was when the yōkai paraded through the streets. Why, I don't know. Were they celebrating the end of a human war? Were they there to add more misery to an already dejected people at their lowest point? Was it just a coincidence? Who knows. My grandmother was terribly afraid as she felt what was coming. "*Obaachan*," I said to her, "are we going to be OK?"; only this time I was talking about monsters not Allied bombs. She told me to draw the curtains, lock the doors and chant the spell. If we did that the yōkai wouldn't bother us. My father thought it all preposterous, but my mother simply nodded. Despite his scepticism, when the time came, he joined us. Tradition and myth are powerful tools in Japan. We never saw them, we heard it, but didn't dare open the curtains to look. But something did come in, because when it was over all of the kanoko had been eaten. Listen.'

Natsuo did what she asked and sure enough he could hear jovial music and laughter outside.

'Don't you think it just sounds like a matsuri?' she said, still turning the beads over in her old hands.

'Mm.' Natsuo nodded as he stood up. 'I must go now. How much for the cakes?'

The old lady simply smiled, shook her head, and made her way further into the building, chanting as she went.

Natsuo took a moment for himself, checked the bag with the hammer and sword in situ, and finished the last drops of the cold tea. He had been through purgatory and survived an encounter with gods. Now he was on his home turf. This should be the easy part. And yet the idea of actively taking a life still made his blood run cold. There had to be another way.

He zipped up his jacket tight and pulled the hood over, so as to show off as little of his humanity as possible. He knew it was absurd, but at least it made him feel more hidden. He slowly slid open the door to the shop and prepared to make the dash next door.

Outside was a grotesque Tokiyama Sekien picture scroll of hideous yōkai dancing, eating, drinking, and falling over each other laughing.

A beautiful, pale woman in long white robes, stood elegantly as snow, appearing from seemingly nowhere, fell down onto her, whilst gangly sinewy, bipedal yōkai with crazy eyes and long dangling tongues cooed around her. A long-necked rokurokubi was conversing with a similarly long-necked man in a kimono that Natsuo recognised as a mikoshi-nyūdō; a popular character in folklore. He saw tanuki and kitsune up on the hillside setting off fireworks and banging drums, and little boys in wide hats running around with trays of tofu, their tongues lolling out dumbly. Some lightning strikes crackled through the rain and Natsuo glimpsed dark, wolf-like shapes with long claws appearing as electrically-discharged shadows with every flash. Young teenager-looking beings in robes were running around pinching the backsides of other yōkai; they were cyclops with no noses. A gaggle of googly-eyed house ornaments, umbrellas and boxes on chicken legs hopped about, tumbling into heaps here and there.

There was chaos all around, but it followed a general flow uphill, left to right, along the road. There were kappa, floating multicoloured fireballs, spectral ghostly visages of women, naked and furry monkey-men, cats walking on their hind legs, and a rotten humanoid slab of flesh moving like a slug that Natsuo recalled from his book as a nuppeppō. It was a twisted carnival that inspired awe instead of fear in Natsuo.

Nobody, if that was the right word, not one yōkai paid him any attention as he exited the shop. Arriving at the ryokan next-door Natsuo slid open the shoji and was immediately greeted by a dark burnt-orange oni, stooping under the doorframe to growl at him. He held his nerve.

Just remember, this is your world...

'I'm here to see Shuten dōji.'

'Oh are ya now?!' The words left its throat like a spluttering exhaust pipe. Its nostrils flared, scanning Natsuo. 'And what makes you think he'll talk to you?'

'I bring a gift.'

The eight-foot-tall oni snorted.

'And what could a weird thing like you bring to our great lord?'

Natsuo took off his bag and thrust his hand in. The oni's hand moved to a particularly unsavoury axe slung off its loincloth. Then, on seeing that what came out of Natsuo's bag wasn't particularly sharp, pointy or serrated — somewhat the basis for an average oni's deductive powers — it relented.

'I think he'll be very glad you let me through,' Natsuo said triumphantly.

'Wait 'ere.' He was brought into a large open foyer, all wooden beams, shoji doors and glowing lanterns. A typical traditional inn. The oni stomped off to a staircase and clicked his fingers at a creature standing silently nearby. 'Watch 'im!'

After a small bow, what looked like a Buddhist priest shuffled over. Though dressed as a monk, it wasn't human, but did look more or less like a man in his seventies. Its skin was green, wrinkled, and its toes, poking out of sandals, and fingers, peeping out of long green robes, ended in long, sharp nails. It bore an expression that seemed to Natsuo to be one of passive boredom, as if not really interacting fully with the world around it. It held a collection bowl and reminded him of the takuhatsu monks that begged for alms at temples.

'Konbanwa,' Natsuo said, bowing out of tradition more than anything.

'Do you have any millet?'

'Excuse me?'

'Do you have any millet, so say I?'

'Umm...no,' Natsuo replied, at the same time trying to recall what exactly millet was.

'Damned kosamebō; I said watch 'im, not talk to 'im!' The oni was back. 'Right you, follow me.' As he followed the demon he heard it muttering to itself, like a bureaucrat complaining about his lot in life.

The upstairs opened up into a large dining area facing the street, views to the fiesta. The street-facing wall was one of wide, sliding windows that had been opened fully to provide a full, open-air view of the parade. At the centre of the wall sat a vast, rather portly, red oni, with its right arm on the windowsill, gazing lazily out with a turkey leg in its left hand.

The room smelled a compelling mix of roasted meat, fermented alcohol and sweat, and there was a light mist of tobacco smoke hanging just below the ceiling. The red oni had tattoos all over its back and gave it an air of a yakuza boss.

Irezumi, traditional ink, applied by hand using wooden handles and metallic needles connected with silk thread, were often painted on criminals during the Edo period. The location of the tattoo was determined by the nature of the crime; the shape denoted by where the crime occurred. Thus, the tattoo became associated with the world of the criminals, even being outlawed during the start of the Meiji period.

'I hear you have a gift for me,' asked a bubbling, deep voice from the oni, still looking out of the window.

Natsuo took an object out of his bag and the bruised, tangerine-coloured oni took it over.

'Oh my, oh my.' Shuten laughed. 'This is quite the surprise.'

Finally, he turned to face Natsuo, a bottle of Hozaki's Meido junmai daiginjo in his hand.

The haradashi had gifted Natsuo the bottle of sake before he had left with the flying tanuki. Natsuo had planned to drink it with his mother when everything was over, but on hearing about Shuten dōji's predilection for alcohol, he had thought maybe this was an easier way to get close, in lieu of charging in with a magical sword.

'I had heard that clever *tōji* had finally cracked it; but I hadn't yet got my hands on a bottle. My thanks.' He caught Natsuo staring at the tattoo, which had crept over his back and descended to cover the whole right side of his chest. 'Yakuza. As well as their booze, I always found those slightly honourable criminals to be one of the more interesting aspects of the human realm. I run my life like an *oyabun* runs his family. That there,' he said, nodding to the oni who had let Natsuo in, 'is my *kobun*. He, my adopted child, like everyone here, owes his allegiance to me. More specifically he is my first lieutenant; my wakagashira. Isn't that fascinating? It's so much more organised up here than in Jigoku. I respect them for that. So for him to lead you to me, meant it must be something I'd want.' Shuten smiled greedily. 'Low and behold,' he added waving the bottle. 'And I see you too are somewhat taken by the humans; even taking their form!' He laughed and took a bite of moist turkey meat.

'Not quite.'

'What was that?' He waved Natsuo to come closer and then opened the bottle, passing it to his lieutenant who then poured him a serving into a porcelain cup.

'I'm actually half human...' Natsuo felt the tone shift. Not silence but a shift away from the previous bonhomie, a prickle on the skin denoting a step towards danger. The possibility of fighting and flighting. The shoulders of the red Yakuza-demon, haunched up and tensed a little. 'You knew my father.'

'Oh did I?' came the response, syrupy with suspicion.

'I believe you knew him as Ōtakemaru.' Natsuo knew that this could be a risky move. Other than the fact they knew each other he had no way of knowing their relationship. The big red bulk placed the turkey leg down on a greasy platter, wiped his enormous hands on a towel, and brought over another cup. Silently, almost reverently, he poured out some of Meido's finest sake and offered Natsuo to approach, sit and drink. Which he did.

'So you're the boy.' He smiled. 'The one that made my old friend leave the underworld. Kampai.'

Natsuo nodded and then accepted the drink with a small bow. 'I only found out recently. So I wanted to find out more about him. I knew there was a parade today, and I knew you'd be here. I wanted to see if you could tell me more about my father, the real father. The one I never met.'

Talking, get him talking. Find the jewels.

'I'd like to tell you a story. Turkey?'

'No thanks.'

'It's about my childhood and involves your father. I think you will find it most interesting indeed.'

'Please. Anything you can tell me will be greatly appreciated.'

The crimson-beast, with his upturned fangs, wild mane of dark brown hair, and piercing, intelligent tiger-eyes, shifted in his chair and lent back like a sated king. Instead of a crown, gnarly old demon horns.

'I was born more than a thousand years ago in Shiga, which so you know, means I'm fairly youthful.' A spluttering drainpipe laugh. 'My father was the great dragon Yamata-no-Orochi.' Natsuo almost felt the sword in his bag calling out. 'And my mother, like your mother, was human. And when I was young I looked and lived like a human. I was a good little apprentice priest on Mt Hiei in Kyoto. Compared to the other boys I was strong, very strong, and intelligent. I found it all so boring, and those priests a bunch of pious blowhards. At that time, I didn't know I had the blood of the great serpent coursing through my veins. So I slacked off and drank; which those Buddhists forbid. See...boring lot!

'I got into fights and riled up the other boys into drinking contests, which obviously I won, and which obviously the priests weren't too happy about. That's why everyone started calling me Shuten dōji. But I rather liked the nickname "little drunkard".

'Anyway, one night there was a big matsuri and I showed up completely drunk. I had had enough of these pretentious robes, so I put on an oni mask and went around scaring people, jumping out from behind bushes, making kids cry and ladies squeal. Just a bit of fun. Well, the elders were not impressed; they publicly admonished me. "We'll make an example of you yet!" They bleated. Well, what happened? The damn mask wouldn't come off! I tried to remove it but it wouldn't budge. It had fused to my face. Fused to me! I explained this, but the priests and festival-goers simply jeered more, calling me a useless drunk. So, ashamed and angry, I ran into the mountains. Where I never really left.' A small pause of reminiscence.

Then a glint. A sparkle of light. And there, the jewels. A gauze bag attached to the back of the scarlet hulk's hip. Two plum-sized orbs; the colour of oil in a puddle, refracting and reflecting all the colours. And a whirl, a bright blue spiral on each.

Shit.

'I started to hate people. Humans. I lived for years stealing food and drink from the villagers and, of course, drank a lot of alcohol. I started a gang of misfits, mastered strange magics and dark arts, and, in turn, taught that to my followers. Over time I turned into an oni. We all did. The one that let you in and brought you here is Ibaraki.' Shuten gestured to the orange oni. 'I met him first. Another demon-child. He's been my chief servant ever since then.

'Your father was already well-known by that point. You could say I was a fan. Anyway, he helped foil a bounty on my head hundreds of years ago. Minamoto no Yorimitsu, some upstart Fujiwara samurai, came to kill me, bringing us tainted sake, making light of our hospitality with the hope of getting us drunk on poisoned booze. Ōtakemaru saw through it and scuppered their plans. We never touched the sake, sending them on their way instead of killing them. You know, peace and all that. We were reasonable. Yet the humans, as is their way, twisted and turned the truth and made a legend; saying he cut off my head.' Shuten dōji theatrically palmed his neck. 'But as you can see...' He took a large swig of the Meido sake. 'After that I was indebted to you father, and then we became friends. And then, after meeting your mother, he left. I was sad for a long time, but not angry like the rest. How could I hold a grudge against the one who saved my life?'

'What was he like back then?'

'Ah kid, he was a sight to behold.' Shuten picked at his teeth with a claw on his little finger, dislodging some hidden, left-behind morsel which was chewed and swallowed thoughtfully. 'Terrible. Truly terrible. I was in awe. He once summoned a great storm, blanketing a mountain in black clouds, confusing a human army that had been pursuing him. A whole battalion. He brought lighting and wind and rain down upon them. They searched for him for seven years. Seven years! Nothing for us, but these stupid human soldiers wasted seven of their years looking for him. Then he killed them. All of them. Over a thousand souls. Ripping them limb from limb, drinking their blood and guzzling their innards as he laughed in the lightning-fire. It was truly beautiful. Inspiring for us. This was before the peace, of course. I was still young at that time; reckless and easily impressed. I never reached your father's level of greatness.' At that Shuten waved a bottle of sake as if to offer up the reason for his failure.

How to get the damn jewels?

'Did you ever meet my mother?'

'I did not. But having one myself I was also sympathetic to your father. It was a shame how it ended, how we exiled him. But, sadly, at the end of the day. I am who I am and I can't be seen to be weak. I'm an oni king and have a bloodthirsty legend behind me,' he said somewhat regretfully. 'So I stayed put and let your father disappear. And now you're here.' Shuten smiled.

A delicate pause settled over the moment like dust falling in a living room.

No other choice...

'Sorry for asking. But what are those?'

"Go for broke" was an English-language phrase that Natsuo knew well. Originally a Hawaiian Pidgin expression, it was used in dice games like craps. Wager everything. If you lost, bankrupt. If you won, all the glory.

It was also the motto of the Japanese-American military unit of the 442nd Infantry Regiment during World War II. In 1951 a film with that name was made following the exploits of this unit, and was important as few movies at that time had shown Asian Americans in a good light. Natsuo had seen it and quite liked it. Especially the part where the white American learns the meaning of the constantly uttered 'Baka tare'; stupid idiot, which the nisei — second generation Japanese-Americans — used as a password. Ever since then, Natsuo had rather liked the expression "Go for broke".

'Those things in the bag...'

The hunched over, tattooed slab of carmine shifted uncomfortably; seemingly irked that a reference had been made to the pouch on his hip. Natsuo offered up his most innocent expression as he watched the muscles ripple under hairy shoulders.

For a moment bloodshot eyes searched and bore into Natsuo's. Then came a grunt that seemed to signify that this small half-demon was no threat. He spun the leather belt round his rather prominent waist and, surprisingly delicately, undid the cord that closed the bag, and tipped the two prismatic orbs onto an enormous pie-hand.

'These are...' Shuten dōji clearly still meant to choose his words carefully. 'My magic jewels. A gift from a friend. I always carry them with me.'

'They're beautiful.'

'That they are.'

The noise of the parade in the street was increasing as the night began to draw in and the revelry ever more suffused with sake and songs. Up on the hill multicoloured fireworks were fizzing about and popping into the black; starburst colours that illuminated a rogue's gallery of folklore. Natsuo could see the tops of bannered poles floating past the upstairs window. Sashimono, identifying flags for samurai during battles, danced along.

Were these the groups and guilds of hell?

'Can I see?'

Go for broke...

'I don't think that's —'

'Please.' More puppy-dog eyes. If this monster had heart strings Natsuo would try his best to pull them. 'I never knew my father the way you all did. It would mean a lot. Anything you can show me of his world, your world. Well, our world.'

Shuten dōji looked about the room as if searching for someone to say something. Stop him. Ibaraki, the gruntish, orange oni, just shrugged with a mixture of indifference and cluelessness. Another concessive grumble from Shuten. He lent forward and placed them on the table, adding an elegant sparkle to a space hitherto populated with meat fat, bones, squished fruit and empty bottles of alcohol.

Natsuo picked up one of the jewels, which filled his whole palm. It was dense, like an objet d'art bought from a high-end shop. One of those things that just feels expensive and comes with an intangible sensation telling the holder "don't drop it". At the same time, it felt soft, smooth, and quite light. As if on picking it up it had adapted to his hand, to the ligaments and tendons and muscles working away like so many corporeal cogs and pulleys under skin, so that the result was, how could he describe it, the perfect weight.

When he turned it around, back and forth, it caught the lantern light, split apart the multicoloured flashes from the night sky, the colours melting and shimmering like the iridescent liquid nacre of a pearl in its shell. The whole ocean was thrown back at Natsuo in each fluid surface. It was transfixing.

'Kirei...'

'Sou desu. So beautiful that I have spent hours just staring at them,' Shuten dōji said proudly.

Natsuo picked up the other one in his free hand and held them aloft in front of his eyes, submitting his whole world view to these oceanic spheres. For some moments Natsuo tuned out forgetting where he was, forgetting who he was sitting in front of, forgetting what he had to do. That the very objects he had in his hands were exactly what he came here for.

Ibaraki, who had apparently left the room at some point, entered again and bowed like every apologetic salaryman does when entering his manager's office.

'*Shitsurei shimasu*...Nurarihiyon is here, sir.'

Natsuo's seafaring dream state ended as the blood plummeted from his temple, crash-landed around his toes and his throat shut up like an Asari clam. Nurarihiyon...The gourd-headed, old man from Tsuruoka. The elite head of the yōkai meeting an oni king.

Shuten dōji got up, walked past Natsuo and greeted the elderly creature. Natsuo pointedly did not turn around.

'Good tidings Shuten, I trust all is well, that the larder has been stocked sufficiently to your liking, the sake ever-flowing and that the view is to your taste.' The words slithered out of a mouth that spoke confidently but placatingly. The language was formal and showed a nuance that although Nurarihiyon was important, and knew it, there was a vein of hierarchical deferral bleeding through his tone.

'Yes, yes, very good indeed.'

As the two monsters shared formalities and nattered over details behind him, Natsuo, his fear still clinging to his ribcage, realised that he still had the jewels in his hands. The sudden appearance of this important guest had thrown Shuten dōji's attention. He would have to act fast.

Natsuo's presence seemed to have been temporarily forgotten by the other creatures in the room, the gruff Ibaraki included, as Shuten's retinue flitted and fussed about Nurarihiyon.

He quietly slid the zip open on the front pocket of his backpack and placed the pearly globes inside. Natsuo was now hoping his lack of importance would be to his favour. He gently picked up his bag and in one motion slung it over his shoulder and twisted up to his feet.

Natsuo was aware, out of the corner of his eye, that Nurarihiyon was gesticulating to Shuten dōji as a person would proudly point out the accoutrements of their new apartment, and had made their way, aware from the entrance to the right side of the room. The evil little bulb of a yōkai was purring demurely to the oni about some painting or vase or other.

Natsuo, avoiding eye contact, slowly made his way round the sofa and to the door that led downstairs. Ibarakai stood there.

Of course he's there…

'I see Shuten dōji has a guest; so I'm going to excuse myself for the moment.'

The massive, sunset-coloured oni nodded and made to open the door to escort him out. Natsuo was elated and proud of himself. He had managed to do everything asked of him and had done it his own way.

The perversity of the universe has been essayed, written about and pondered for as long as things have gone wrong for mankind. The Americans came up with a phrase called Murphy's Law, widespread around the world, with the idea that anything that can go wrong will go wrong. It was originally popularised by John Stapp, a U.S. Air Force Colonel and Flight Surgeon who had coined it, making an upbeat reference to the fickleness of technology. He had been reacting to the comments made by an aerospace engineer called Edward Murphy, who was pensively miffed that his devices were failing during tests.

The British often say Sod's Law instead, a slightly broader and more pessimistic version. Not only will something go wrong, but also the thing happening will be the worst possible version of that scenario.

There is another law, one that never seemed to attain quite the same levels of vernacular embedding of the previous two, that seemed to perfectly encapsulate this precise moment in Natsuo's life. The American science-fiction writer John W. Campbell Jr. authored it around the same sort of time as Go For Broke! was released: Finagle's law, anything that can go wrong, will — at the worst possible moment.

'Young man, are you leaving us?'

Shuten dōji's voice slid through the air like a serpent through sand.

Kuso...

Natsuo had barely begun to grace the doorframe with his presence, before that voice stopped him in his tracks. He instantly discarded the idea of running. Where to? How to escape a den of thieves and murderers. He rotated on the spot, bowing as he did.

'*Hai.* I see you have company, so I thought it rude of me to stay, no, overstay.' Natsuo employed his most formal Japanese; bent double like a quivering, besuited zero in front of the boss.

'Nonsense, nonsense!' Shuten dōji nudged Nurarihiyon gamely. 'Can you believe that odd little human-looking thing over there is Ōtakemaru's boy.'

Natsuo felt searching eyes, flittering intelligent eyes, prickling over him from the other side of the room. He started to sweat and felt hot and uncomfortable as if there were bugs itching under his shirt. He remained bent over at ninety degrees, terrified to look at the unwanted guest. Had Nurarihiyon seen him that time? He didn't know. Could he just run for it? Doubtful.

'That boy?' came a concerned, staccato voice from the bulbous-headed yōkai. A thick tofu silence filled the room, squishing its way into all the cracks and crevices. For Natsuo, time melted and the clock-hands quivered frozen.

'Yes; looking for information about his father I believe. Somewhat green in our world. Seemed harmless enough.'

'Seize him.' Nurarihiyon seethed. Natsuo stole a glance and their eyes met. He instantly realised that he was seen, found out. 'Seize him!' The yōkai leader's eyes were arched thin like those of an eagle and from across the room he prodded his cane in the air. 'Don't let him leave!' Natsuo slowly straightened himself out and looked at Ibaraki with a face of feigned incomprehension.

To Natsuo's surprise Shuten dōji came to his defence, 'Now, now, what's all this? I said he was Ōtakemaru's boy. He's alright. One of us so he is.'

'No, you foolish ogre.' Nurarihiyon's tone had changed completely from pandering host to that of an imperious bureaucrat. 'That's the one Sōjōbō has been using behind our backs!'

'What?'

'He'll be after the jewels.'

Shuten dōji turned to Natsuo with an expression that was a chaotic mixture of anger, confusion and disappointment. He then glanced at the table in the middle of the room. At noticing the distinct lack of the jewels, he groaned and covered his face with his palms. Natsuo instinctively plunged his hand into his backpack.

'How dare you!' Shuten growled, spittle gutter-piping out of his mouth. Any goodwill gained from their amicable conversation had now fizzed and evaporated off like water on a griddle.

Ibaraki, slow on the uptake, finally turned on Natsuo but was met with the sharp end of the Kusanagi-no-Tsurugi pointed directly at his eyes. Sensing the inherent power of the blade he backed off slightly and looked to Shuten.

'And he has that fucking sword!' The irate red giant spat again. 'Back away, that thing'll cleave you in two even if it is being held by that little snake.'

Natsuo had his back to the doorway and had no idea who, if anybody, was downstairs apart from the odd monk creature from before. He dared not take his eyes off the room. Ibaraki took some paces back towards his boss, his oyabun. A lieutenant returning to his general's side.

'You see fit to use my old friend's memory against me?' The upstairs room seemed to dim, and Shuten dōji to grow in stature. The sounds of the parade outside were dulled and muted, the fireworks popping as if underwater. Natsuo was frozen to the spot, clutching the sword so hard that his knuckles were pale. 'I don't care if you are his son. I'm going to rip you limb from limb, sucking your bones and eating the marrow as I do.' The once welcoming, if not monstrous, face had turned arched and inward, like some crazed scarlet Grinch. The teeth seemed longer and sharper than before, his back larger and hairier, the talons and claws more gnarled and yellow. Shuten dōji's muscles rippled and tensed and his whole body seemed to curl in on itself like a panther about to pounce.

Natsuo, sensing his own imminent obliteration at the hands of this apoplectic ogre, immediately ran through the doorway and headed for the stairs. He didn't see Shuten dōji coming as much as sense the utter destruction that was spiralling out behind him. The foundations shook as the smashed-up beams, wood chips and window-glass filled every inch of space the split-second he had passed through it. Energy, pure coiled-up furious energy, was annihilating everything behind. The carnage was accompanied by a snarling oversized Rottweiler sound. Animal. Beastly, in the purest sense of the word.

Barely halfway down the one-floor staircase, which was long and wide and made for gliding down demurely in a kimono, the ground under Natsuo's feet gave way.

A couple of seconds of silence lingered, bowing under the weight of their collective potential energy as they crashed to the floor. Natsuo got to his feet as quickly as the shock of the impact cleared out of his mind, as fast as the fear reset itself within.

A maddened growl seeped out through the crack in a heaped pile of lumber and wallpaper just behind Natsuo. The growl crescendoed and built into an enraged scream.

'Flea!'

The loosely-jumbled mess of pieces of wood, smashed up furniture and what had once been an attractive entrance hall suddenly billowed into life and all the household particulates, the splintered memories of what used to be a beautiful inn, changed colour and were displaced by angry red flesh. The face of an oni dissolved into view, increasing in size as it rushed toward Natsuo.

Natsuo yelped, spun left, closed his eyes and swung the sword out in front of him. Shuten dōji's giant tiger eyes lost focus and the gravity seemed to drop out of his cheeks and jaw. He landed with a thud and the enormous horned head slowly peeled away from the torso accompanied by a puckering wet sound, as blood-slick meat separated from itself. It lolled away and came to a stop by the front door of the inn, the eyelids at half mast and the vast fleshy tongue falling out between smilodon fangs.

Natsuo, breathing heavily, heart pounding, brow dripping, quickly made for the door to leave. As he tried to shift the massive bodiless head the eyelids flashed up and it began chomping at him, some wind-up chattering teeth, muscle memory. Gnashing wildly and throwing phlegm and blood everywhere.

Natsuo, in a rare moment of clarity and assuredness, didn't back away, and instantly flipped the sword round and brought it down, sliding through the middle of the forehead as if killing a lobster. It was as if a switch had been turned off in the head as it instantly fell still.

'Oyabun!'

Ibaraki screamed from the top floor, observing the disaster below and seeing his once master and friend, skewered like some hellish yakitori.

Shit, shit, shit.

'I suggest you leave.' Natsuo looked round and saw the odd kosamebō monk creature, still standing dutifully, unruffled, with its prayer beads and begging bowl, by an open door at the end of the corridor on the other side of the entrance hall. A placid smile played upon withered old lips. 'I fancy your chances.'

Sparing not the slightest moment of thought, Natsuo bolted down the hall further into the ryokan and made for the open door. It led outside into the gardens behind the row of connected buildings. He didn't look back, didn't stop. A small sign said "Chayama-enchi Park; Please treat the gardens with respect." The furious roar emanating behind him could only mean Ibaraki had decided to pursue him. Ignoring the sign he beelined through some orange flower-arranged plots and startled a herd of sleeping deer that flocked away en masse.

Natsuo had no idea where he should go or what his destination was now. The never-ending procession of life-threatening situations that, on one hand were out of his control, yet on the other seemed to be utterly contingent on his actions, wasn't letting up. He briefly wondered what Toshi, the school bully who had helped send Natsuo into his Hikikomori spiral, would make of all this. If he made it out of this, he wanted to let him know.

Natsuo wouldn't be able to evade a berserk demon for long, he'd have to hide. On the other side of the little park Natsuo turned onto a small street lined with low houses and which was peppered with shrines.

He could hear roars and insults ringing off into the night air behind. Before Ibaraki had time to catch up to the turn, Natsuo slid down a small alley between two bungalows, hopped the wall at the end and found himself in a small temple complex. He immediately tucked himself away in one of the halls, closing the sliding door behind him.

The thing about being chased by a nine-foot-tall oni is that the pursuer is not one exactly graced with the characteristic of subtlety. Natsuo heard Ibaraki stomping about, slowing to a walk as he searched around the streets. It was clear that the demon had twigged that his prey was no longer running. Natsuo held his breath as best he could, trying to quieten his thumping heart.

He was reminded of a famous English children's book called *The BFG*; a story about giants and dreams. He had once seen an animated version from the end of the 1980s and had found the initial scenes rather unsettling. A towering, cloaked figure, who later would be unmasked as the big friendly giant, was galloping around the streets of London collecting children's dreams in glass bottles. One girl, Sophie, cannot sleep and then spies the giant careening along her street. He spies her, grabs her, and takes her.

Those initial moments of a massive, hooded spectre running through the city instilled a real chill in Natsuo as a young boy. That same powerless feeling flowed through him now; a human being chased by a giant.

'Come out boy.' A grumble came from the soul of something truly malicious. 'I need to talk to you.' A pause. 'And when I say talk to you, I mean to say I intend to pluck you apart and gorge on your lymph and your blood. You will pay for killing my oyabun. That I can assure you.'

Natsuo tried to make a mental picture of where Ibaraki was. He was somewhere in the side streets encircling the small temple but he reckoned it would only be a matter of time before he thought to check the shrines themselves.

'There you are,' came a demure purring voice flavoured slightly with haughty exasperation.

Natsuo almost screamed aloud at the voice as the sliding door opened without him realising. The only thing that stopped him was the presence of a two-tailed cat standing on its hind legs and looking distinctly unimpressed. The cat entered the small room and gently closed the door behind him. Each tail was tipped with a blue flame that emitted light but no heat or sound.

Nekomata, Natsuo thought to himself.

'Correct,' said the cat aloud, as if reading his thoughts.

Here was another yōkai well known to Natsuo; a very smart, very malicious breed of bakeneko shape-shifting feline. They were often said, in the stories at any rate, to be violent and contemptuous towards humans. If Natsuo remembered rightly, Homo sapiens could also be part of the menu. However, between a bloodthirsty oni and a bipedal cat, he'd take his chances against the latter.

He searched the ground for the gore-covered blade.

'Oh, don't bother with that for heaven's sake.' Natsuo could sense the eye-roll dripping off every word. 'I was supposed to find you and take you to Sōjōbō. Hage-tanuki is still recovering from your battle on the volcano so, given this is my town, they sent me in his place.'

'Hage-tanuki is alive?'

'Yes yes, of course. Takes more than what you two went through to take him out of the equation. Although you did your best.' A smarmy laugh. The nekomata seemingly couldn't hide its distaste for having to deal with a human. 'Anyway, that old wizard Seimei told me that you and I need to make it to the ittan-momen awaiting us back at the Tōdai-ji temple. That flying cotton sheet will get us back to Sōjōbō in Kyoto.' Natsuo just blinked dumbly. 'Then perhaps you can go back to your fascinating little human life.'

Natsuo was tempted to ask the creature's name but then, given it seemed not the least bit interested in offering its own introduction, he relented. Instead, he just nodded.

'Now, fortunately your mad dash has brought you within spitting distance of the Todai-ji. We are in the Shingonin temple. Just behind here is a small copse of trees covering a graveyard and then just behind that is the entrance to the main temple. We'll head through the graveyard. Hopefully the big oaf you brought with you won't see us.'

'Should we really be running through a cemetery on a night like this?'

'Do you think that matters now after everything you've been doing?' The cat laughed distastefully. 'Anyway, I can call the dead. We are going to need something to keep that orange brute busy. And lucky for you, I'm rather good at it. Didn't you know that the more us cats are mistreated and abused in our previous domestic lives, the more powerful we become later?'

Natsuo felt a sting at the meaning behind the words and started to understand why this bizarre, fork-tailed cat seemed to take no pleasure in apparently saving his life.

'We can't wait around. We are leaving now.'

The cat made for the door, paused, signalled for Natsuo to stay put, and then slowly crept out sliding the shoji closed behind it. Dust motes hung in the air and sparkled as moonlight and the distant glow of fireworks bounced off them. The small room smelled of old incense sticks, dusty wood and intentional neglect.

Natsuo could still hear, still sense, Ibaraki stomping around the streets, an oni furious at his master's death. Natsuo knew that Ibaraki wouldn't stop until he was dead. An injustice had occurred. If the oyabun of one family was murdered, the only option is honourable revenge and even all-out gang war. These were demons not yakuza, but it was all the same. His only method was escape. The shoji door slid open again causing Natsuo's heart to miss various beats at once.

'Come. Now.'

Natsuo scrabbled to his feet and followed the beckoning paws of the bipedal cat. They crept quietly behind the small hall they had been sheltering in and vaulted the low wall into the graveyard beyond.

Natsuo could see the towering haunches of the Tōdai-ji temple in the firework-crackled darkness. It seemed at once close and impossibly far away. Like a space between two rocks that looks far more deadly and uncrossable when you know there is a death-ensuring drop below.

The nekomata stooped and gestured for Natsuo to do the same. 'On my order you run. You run and you do not stop, you do not look back. You keep running.'

They started to creep through the graveyard between polished black stone columns with family names inscribed on them. There were fresh flowers laid out at the bases, and food items, glasses of sake, photos of smiling ancestors. Some had little wooden planks, sotoba, resting against them, engraved with prayers and dates.

The non-stop summer storms had left the cemetery ground moist and spongy, which made their progress near silent. That being said, like some twisted and obvious horror movie set up, Natsuo managed to make the only sound to be made; a branch catching on his jacket that, after being forward-snapped back, struck a commemorative flower vase that crashed to the ground. The pregnant pause that followed was accompanied by a simultaneous wincing and eye-roll from the nekomata and a great smashing sound from the temple. Ibaraki blasted through the low perimeter walls in a burst of rubble and rock.

'Ike. Run!'

As he bolted across the cemetery between the lonely sentinel stones and their offerings, Natsuo was aware of other noises. Scratching, earthy sounds, of roots ripping out of the ground, of tumultuous turned over terrain. He permitted himself the briefest moment to see what was happening. It was human nature. 'Don't look down.' And of course you look down. 'Something is chasing you. Don't stop.' And of course you have to look. It was rarely curiosity that the cat killed.

It was a scene straight from the Sam Raimi movies Natsuo loved to watch. Corpses with skin like fibrous ripped-up shirts, earth-covered skeletons and fresh apple-bruised bodies, all scrabbling through the soil, grabbed onto the beserking oni and slowed him down. The flame-coloured beast roared in annoyance and picked them off or swatted them away like so many necrotic wasps. The nekomata stood, arms aloft, seemingly calling them, as it steadily walked backwards with its eyes closed.

So many dead. Generations of entire families mindlessly clawing through the turf to clamber onto a raging demon.

I thought we cremated our dead?

It wasn't working. And as Ibaraki continued his, albeit slower, rampage, the nekomata seemed to sense this and bunched its left fist into a ball and brought it down with a flourish.

'I said go!' It screamed without even looking at Natsuo as small fireballs fizzed into life seemingly out of nowhere and began to rain down on the oni.

It was hard to take his eyes off such an apocalyptic vista; a twisted pyramid of grabbing and moaning cadavers in various stages of decay leading to the snarled-up face of an oni, who, with one hand, was slapping away the baying claws of the dead whilst, with the other, shielding his eyes from the burn and impact of the golfball-sized fireballs.

'Fucking cats!' Ibaraki screamed. He spun around, whirling on the spot, dislodging most of the animate corpses, and then leapt forward with a speed afforded to flight, fight or fury.

The nekomata didn't even have time to open its eyes before the taught-leather palm was clasped around its throat. The cat then found itself hoisted up into the air by the jugular, choking its breath out in bursts. While it was still conscious, it sensed the other hand closing around its slender feline legs. Its inner gyroscope, still just about working, told its brain that it had been turned horizontal. Then a pain, a sharp tearing pain. The elastic bands of the body had reached their stress point.

Natsuo had never seen a creature ripped in half before, but the sound of the magical cat splitting in two at the waist, its hot guts spilling to the floor with a wet slap, reminded him of both moist fruit being torn to shreds and wet laundry falling out of a machine. And the sight...the sight was enough to make him run.

In the courtyard in front of the gargantuan temple floated a long, narrow sheet of cloth; as if some spectral mummy had lost its bandages. It snaked around in the air and one end pricked up to reveal two bight-yellow Jack O'Lantern eyes. All it took were a pair of eyes to add some animal sentience to an object.

Noticing that its charge, a beleaguered and out of breath man with a backpack, was being pursued by a demon from hell, the ittan momen shot out to meet him.

Reaching Natsuo before Ibaraki, one end of the flying cloth wrapped around him whilst the other whipped round and struck the oni across the face stunning it and drawing a weeping line of red that leaked out across its cheek.

No sooner had Ibaraki come to his senses than Natsuo was hoisted up into the air, vertical like a bottle-rocket take off, and was lifted away from the fury below.

The immediate sense of relief washed over Natsuo in such a cascade as to override the more rational fear of floating through the air in the embrace of an airborne cotton yōkai. But he wasn't scared. He felt strangely safe, swaddled tight as he was like a newborn. If he needed to move, to scratch his face or stretch a muscle, the fabric flowed around him, constantly recalibrating to ensure he was held completely.

Beneath them, the popping candy flashes of the matsuri were still blasting in the air, though this time multicolour-mushrooming far, far below. The lights of the houses burned and glowed like fireflies and the procession, now from a distance, seemed less like a hellish grotesquery marching forward, but rather a line of ants falling in step.

As the ittan momen carried on away from Nara west to Osaka, human civilisation was briefly reduced to sparkling puddles in the antimatter darkness of the nighttime countryside, like a mirror image of space.

They then flew towards a dark, inky line cutting the lights north to south, a ridge of forested hills, the iridescent smudge of Osaka appearing on the horizon behind. The cloth banked northwards instead of continuing towards the vast neon metropolis and headed, as if beckoned by all the weight of its history, inexorably towards Kyoto.

Natsuo began to give in to sleep. This was the first moment in many days that he felt genuinely safe, removed from danger and the expectations that the world had deemed fit to place on him.

They descended, hugging the right side of the city limits, hemmed in as Kyoto was by mountains, and slid through the air like a spectral silverfish. Over the mausoleum of Emperor Meiji they soared, over the thousands of orange Fushimi Inari torii gates, past the imperial tomb of Prince Akira and the Eagle's Nest lookout of the grand Kiyomizu-dera temple, and all the other hundreds of hillside shrines that sat quietly twinkling in the woods.

The northern fronds of Kyoto, those last houses and bars where a town finally gives up and relinquishes its control to the countryside, finally arrived, Mount Kurama rising into view. Soaring as a dark tip in a folding ripple of peaks.

Natsuo felt a squeeze on his arm, muscle-like cotton-tendons pin-pointing to awaken the dozing human within. He was once again in the branch-cave of that long-nosed almighty tengu. The ittan momen placed him down gently on his feet and whip-whirled off him elegantly, before flying away somewhere. Natsuo watched it go and thought it a shame he hadn't time to say thank you.

Then a voice. An old familiar voice.

'Welcome back, young man. You have been busy.'

Sōjōbō.

Chapter Ten: Sensō
戦争

War.

Although its scent still lingers on
The form of a flower has scattered away
For whom will the glory
Of this world remain unchanged?
Arriving today at the younger side
Of the deep mountains of evanescent existence
We shall never allow ourselves to drift away
Intoxicated, in the world of shallow dreams.

'Do you know this poem, Natsuo-chan?'

'I'm afraid not. I was never really into poetry to be honest...'

'The Iroha is a classic piece of human poetic history. It's over a thousand years old and is a perfect pangram.'

'A pan what?'

'A sentence, or in this case an entire poem, using every letter of a given alphabet. Here each consonant-vowel syllable of your alphabet is used exactly once.'

'Ok...' Natsuo was tired of the riddles. 'So what deep meaning am I supposed to extract from this poem? Scattered flowers...the fleeting nature of life or something like that?'

'No, no. The importance of this poem is not the meaning. That is the least important thing of all. The key is the sound.'

'The syllables?'

'That's right. Every part, every phoneme, can only be exactly where it is. If anything is misplaced or moved around it cannot work. The poem fails and everything loses its meaning. What I mean to say is that Natsuo, even though we are now to journey to Amaterasu to hand her over the holy artefacts and leave the rest of the fight to the gods, I cannot, will not, underestimate your role in this. You might not think it, but you are a phoneme, you are a letter in the poem. Without you none of this would have been possible. I've seen some truly impressive things in my long life, but not usually from a human. So before anything else I just want to thank you, young man.'

Natsuo's cheeks flushed with pride and he bowed. He thought it all a tad over-dramatic, but praise, he thought, was something he could get used to.

'I guess now you magic up some tea and tell me about the next part of the plan.'

Sōjōbō seemed pleased with Natsuo's cheekiness.

'Exactly.'

Contrary to what Natsuo had come to expect from past interactions with all of these otherworldly characters, there was no convoluted mission, no unholy exorcisms, no peril-filled quests.

'You'll come with me to Amaterasu and then hand her the jewels and the hammer. They may well have the spear but we have Susanoo's sword too. Then I'll take you back to your mother.'

'That's it?'

'That's it. With those objects in her possession Susanoo and King Enma won't dare do anything. Peace restored.' The old tengu clapped his hands together as if drawing an end to a very simple plan. A full stop.

'And Amaterasu, I presume, resides in the opposite of Jigoku.'

'That's right. We'll be going to Takamagahara, the High Plain of Heaven.'

'Is it safe?'

'Yes, quite safe.'

'After what happened in Yomi how can I trust you when you say that?'

'You're right to be wary Natsuo, but the kings of the underworld can't enter Takamagahara, in the same way Amaterasu can't enter Jigoku. Two planes sealed off by the Ame-no-Ukihashi bridge. If you're not on the right side, the bridge doesn't appear. Luckily for us, I've always been in her good books.' He winked at Natsuo.

He was used to things moving at a breakneck pace. The constant flow of madness that had been Natsuo's life since shuffling off his Hikikomori coil had become the new gear. How he would fare when it was over he didn't know. He found himself imagining a turtle with a jet engine tied to it one day having it snatched away and being expected to return to its plodding existence.

He had to admit it; despite the fear and danger, monsters and chases, life-threatening situations and physical pain, he was almost enjoying himself. He had become the hero of his own story. Hell, you could pencil-line and ink this into an award-winning manga comic series. Why not add a few more frames to the story with a visit to the Almighty?

'Normally we would have to journey to Takaharu, an ancient capital, on Kyushu island. As you can see, they really put a lot of work into that name. Over the eons this has been the only way for humans to enter the upper realms. Our spies have told me however that the town is swarming with yōkai. And some particularly nasty ones have descended from the heights of Mt. Takachiho; some kasha, vicious flaming cats, have been snatching corpses and raiding kitchens. So, safe to say, we'll take a different route. Fortunately, thanks to your father, I can call the bridge at certain points for the mystical, which you were unwittingly made a part of.

'Ancient British cultures knew of these points of power and linked them up with paths, ley lines they called them; in ancient Peru, theses points were marked out with monuments called huaca; and more modern human scientists have noticed electric energy flows, telluric currents, caused by natural and, perhaps, unnatural activity. Your own ancient country has myriad points. Mandala, maps representing deities, kami, shrines and paradises, exist in your museums, but of course the modern world pays them no heed. Just curios devised by the minds of the imaginative, the ignorant and the mad. But no, they saw the truth.

'And it just so happens that my humble mountain is such a place. So, you'll be happy to know, young man, that for once in all these long weeks you have been toiling, I need not send you off anywhere.'

Sōjōbō smiled his twinkling Old Saint Nick smile and behind him the vines and branches began to creak and rustle and unfurl. Rays of warm, honey-coloured light spilled in through the opening and exposed the beginning of a bridge. A red, arched bridge that reminded Natsuo of the one he had traversed down in Meido, shuffling shoulder to shoulder with the thousands of dead.

'You're right of course; we aren't very creative with our designs,' laughed Sōjōbō as if reading his mind.

Clouds billowed about beneath the bridge as if ordered by some celestial directive to make the scene look as heavenly as possible. It was so obvious looking that the sense of awe was lost on Natsuo; especially after everything he had hitherto seen.

To Natsuo's surprise they were across the other side in a few minutes. He was inching towards disappointment until the woolly clouds parted and the most beautiful scene came into view.

An undulating patchwork of velvety green pastures and rice paddies rippled away to shamrock pine peaks that reminded Natsuo more of images of the Scottish Highlands he had seen rather than Japan. In the cyan-blue sky rocks and mountainous lumps of land floated, held in dreamy status, while vast ropes connected to torii gates dangled off the edges like frayed white cotton on old jeans. It was as if due to a shortage of space, whole hillsides had been hoisted into the air and left there creating the impression, as they walked down into the glades, of a roof above them.

They were making their way down a twee, cobbled path that snaked away towards a limpid blue lake in the middle of which was a house. It was an odd house that, though clearly Japanese, almost had a Swiss look to it. Indeed, if this was what heaven was really like, then Natsuo was somewhat taken aback by the slightly European flavour to everything.

A small, ferry-like platform took them to the islet in the lake. The water was strangely both intensely blue-coloured but also so clear you could see the bottom. It wasn't deep, perhaps a few metres, and the lakebed sparkled as if covered with sequins.

The platform came to a graceful stop as it sidled up to a wooden quay lined with unlit stone lanterns. Apart from an elegant corridor of cherry trees, the tiny island had no other features other than the house.

On approaching the abode Natsuo realised what was off with the house; the roof. The roof was thatched; something he had only seen in photos of the historically protected village of Shirakawa-go. The interlocking reeds and rushes forming the upper part of the dwelling lent the building a Nordic air. Yet the rest was all timber frames, white walls, sliding shoji doors and overhanging gables, as if the builder couldn't make their mind up. But it worked. There was a beauty, a harmony, in the mismatched nature.

Yin and yang probably...

The door slid open and out swept the most wonderful smells. Somebody was cooking. They took their shoes off, placed their feet in the two pairs of slippers that were there, and announced their presence.

Following the narrow corridor through they turned right and entered a large open room. Wide windows on each wall informed them that this was the only room in the house. In the centre was a young woman in a simple white kimono tending a large pot gently bubbling on the *irori* sunken hearth.

They approached her slowly as she delicately moved pieces of food around in the broth with two long chopsticks. She had yet to acknowledge them. In the pot chunks of daikon, some boiled eggs, konjac, fishcakes and strands of tofu were bobbing around in what smelled like a soy sauce dashi.

Oden...

'Yes, that's right,' she said out of nowhere. 'Would you like some Natsuo?'

'I...uh...'

'He would love some Amaterasu-sama,' Sōjōbō said, coming to the rescue.

Suddenly there were chairs where previously there were none.

Spontaneous seating seems to be a popular trick in the heavens...

They sat themselves down as the high goddess of Japan pulled her sleeves up and slowly ladled out some of the steaming stew into three humble wooden bowls.

'Itadakimasu,' she said, bowing over her bowl. Her face was at once strikingly beautiful and pure, and at the same time utterly plain and devoid of anything remarkable.

For a while they sat in silence, quietly slurping the mild and savoury soup and picking out the individual items with chopsticks, savouring each morsel in turn.

'The beauty of oden is you focus on the individual amongst the mass.' She smiled and sipped at her bowl with her eyes closed. 'And the beauty of these...' She twirled the chopsticks in front of her as if they were some obscure foreign object. '... Is that you must take your time and contemplate what you are eating.'

Natsuo was somewhat lost. He had been taken to meet the all high, all powerful, queen of the gods and here she was, serving him oden and talking about chopsticks.

'You know human society first invented the knife and fork and the spoon. Implements for prodding, slicing, shovelling. No grace, but utterly and perfectly designed. No culture has improved on the efficiency of these three; though I have heard that one nation fused some of them together. Did you know in a country called France they even have a specific fork just for eating snails?' She made a little laugh, one placid and aloof, and again sipped her soup.

They're mad, all of them...

'Other nations don't even bother. In India many will use their hands and flatbreads instead of worrying about dirtying cutlery. Some nations may look down on this as primitive, and perhaps it is, but there's a simplicity and base intelligence to the method if you think about it. Much of the rest of Asia uses chopsticks. Ancient China invented them three thousand years ago. But then they also probably came up with the fork. So isn't it interesting that first came the fork and then two sticks, maybe from the same nation.

'One idea is that peace-loving Confucians were happy to eschew a vulgar knife at the table in lieu of the more elegant chopsticks. "The honourable and upright man keeps well away from both slaughterhouse and the kitchen. And he allows no knives on his table". They didn't come to Japan until around a couple of millennia ago and were mostly used in religious ceremonies, which is when I first noticed them.

'Shrines and prayers in my name, offerings to me, often done with chopsticks. We gods don't really need to eat but I enjoy the quiet process of using chopsticks. And every time I do, I am reminded of all the humans down there, every utterance to me, every shrine and sermon. For me, these uninteresting pieces of whittled wood represent Japan.'

Natsuo side-eyed Sōjōbō who, arching an eyebrow, also seemed to want to move the conversation with the Almighty on to more pressing issues.

'My lady, we have brought the items. Well, this young man has.'

'Let us first finish our broth.'

There was a gentle weight to the sentence that seemed to say 'in silence'. And so they did, quietly pushing stock-boiled vegetables into their mouths and slurping the umami soup.

Natsuo thought back to the first time he had eaten oden. A vision of his mother and father, one that had fallen down the cracks of his memory and found itself lost and covered in cerebral dust. They were stood around the kitchen stove watching a simmering pot, observing mutely how the heat bubbles punched up through the liquid and gently nudged the vegetable flotilla around. Everything, including the stock itself, had a somewhat beige colour, but in that small spectrum of colour variation lay shades and nuances that made Natsuo salivate. Natsuo, maybe a couple of years shy of ten, was up on his tip toes.

'Smells great mum!' His mother smiled and squeezed his shoulders. 'Don't you think so, Dad?'

'Well of course Natsuo-kun; your mother is the best chef in the world!' A big smile wiped across his father's face. 'In all the heavens and all the hells, there's nobody like your mother.'

He had forgotten that. Little Natsuo didn't understand the depth of that comment; he just grinned as a contented child does and continued watching the slices of daikon and tofu bob around the soup.

A bird, a crow, landed on the windowsill outside. It was barely able to divert Natsuo's attention for more than a second, fixated as he was on the upcoming dinner simmering in front of him. But, now as he looked back through the spyglass of his memory, his father's smile fell away from his face. The warm glow of that family scene, the three of them huddled around a giant saucepan, dissipated in that instant.

Natsuo was too innocent, too naive, to notice it, but had he had the perspicuity of adulthood he would have seen his father notice the bird and in that moment lose any joy that there had been in his face. He would have seen how his father's contented red cheeks lost their colour, how his brow had furrowed and his shoulders had slumped. As an adult versed in the paranoid micro expressions that ruled society, he may have clocked his mother's face flash with confusion and defeat as she herself saw her husband's face fall.

He may also, were he not so childishly and youthfully concerned with his stomach, oblivious as he was in the family embrace, have noticed that the bird had two heads.

That memory, Natsuo realised now, having lost it to the cognitive annals of history, was the last time he had seen his father happy. That was when the darkness came in, the stern father figure appeared, the first seeds were planted in Natsuo that would later grow into the character of a Hikikomori.

The bird must have notified his father of something, something that put him on edge and made him keep his distance, something that made him content for his son to become a shut away a few years later.

In the warm light of the heaven in which he found himself, sharing a stew with the high goddess herself, Natsuo cried. Fully. Tears clogged his eyes and fell into his bowl. Nobody helped him, nor did he want them to. This was animal and necessary. Something his body and mind needed. He cried with pity for himself, he cried for his poor mother and father whose love had put them in a situation where they were doomed if they did and doomed if they didn't. He cried for all of it. The wasted years cruelly snatched by machinations far beyond anyone's control. And all because of love. If love couldn't prevail, Natsuo thought, as he dried his face with his sleeve, what was the point in any of it?

He blew his nose, wiped his eyes, and looked at Amaterasu, who had just finished her bowl of oden and placed it gently in front of her.

'I have the objects for you, so we can finish this.'

Amaterasu nodded and as soon as the decision was made, and Natsuo had blinked, the objects were laid out in front of them; the sunken-in hearth and bubbling oden pot having seemingly disappeared.

The fist-sized jewels sat gleaming like two oversized tie-dye cherries, the sword lay flat and glinting with that almost elemental power it had, whilst the cartoonish hammer looked awkward, being so bulbously-shaped as to not seem comfortable on its side.

'It is a shame we do not have my father's amenonuhoko spear that controls the land, but at least we have the jewels so the seas are ours. And thanks to you Natsuo,' she looked up, 'we have my brother's sword. Though I do not wield it like him, without it he'll not be as powerful if he stands against us. But hopefully it won't come to that...' She stroked the hammer and looked sad. No, not sad, disappointed.

'Families are complicated, aren't they?' The words came out of Natsuo's mouth without him thinking.

She nodded and cast her eyes down.

'Sorry, I didn't mean —'

'No, no. You are quite correct. And if anyone would understand the tribulations of the family it would be the poor young child of a beautiful human and a reformed demon.'

In any other mouth the words might have tripped out as sarcasm or madness, but Amaterasu said them with a calm, matter-of-factness and the smallest hint of pity.

'Belief is an interesting thing. And we gods are here and have any and such power because of it. As old gods of Nippon our abject power has waned at the same time other nations and their piety have increased. What the humans call the Americas, Africa and the Middle East are pregnant with religiosity though, erroneously, it isn't directed towards us. Indeed, maybe thanks to the meddling of shoguns who kept this country closed during the time of expansion, our truth hasn't travelled around the world. Gods have almost left Europe. And here we are left, in Japan, where the people only half-believe. We are a tradition instead of a presence. But we are happy for that. Indeed, my parents created everything not to rule it, but to allow humanity to flourish. And it did. But now Enma and my brother are threatening to ruin the peace, seeking to rule instead of observe.

'A German philosopher called Friedrich Nietzsche once said: "A casual stroll through the lunatic asylum shows that faith doesn't prove anything". This is not the same as belief. Many Japanese people may harbour some faith in us; the farmer leaves an offering at a shrine hoping, as he was taught to do so by his father, for a good harvest. Humans celebrate the dead during *Obon*, they bow and clap their hands at shrines and temples. But do they believe? Perhaps not. But it's enough for us.

'As far as Enma is concerned the era of men is over, time the Gods wrested control of the world back from the humans, turning them into puppets and playthings. And my tempestuous brother has been convinced of the merit behind this idea. There is no need for us to do this. The message will get to him, and to my meddling brother, that we are in possession of these artefacts, and, with a little hope, that will quell any further revolt.'

'I have a question, if that's alright?' Something had been tinkering in the back of Natsuo's mind since this whole debacle started; since the talks of yōkai and gods and their feeding off belief. Amaterasu smiled and nodded. 'Why not just show yourselves to us? Why leave your power up to chance? You could just appear and then we would believe in you.'

'Free will, Natsuo. We chose a path not to scare humanity into believing in us. We hoped, had faith you might say, that they would make their own quiet and personal way to us. You may see it as a missed opportunity, but we would rather remain in the shadows as relics and figments rather than force them into it. Human writers have grappled with this for centuries. "God moves in mysterious ways".

'Or people like Pascal, he was a French philosopher, adopted the mathematical reasoning that "you might as well believe, just in case they do exist". The simple fact is that we just decided that was the course of action and have stuck to it. The idea of letting humanity find its way one way or another was beautiful, regardless of what it meant for us.'

'But...' Natsuo tried to choose his words. 'Don't you think things would be better for us if you had shown yourselves? Especially today. All the wars and the different books that cause people to fight and to kill. You could just come down and end it all. Tell everyone the right answer.'

Amaterasu looked out of the window. The postcard-perfect fantasy world of floating mountains and cerulean skies.

No rain...

It was almost as if he had forgotten what the world had been like before the rains and storms. Like the absence of pain after suffering, the return of silence after noise, the sight of a calm and clear day was shocking. Only here in the peaceful moment with the goddess of the sun did he finally have a chance to really see.

'Do you think that would really change things? In this modern world of your invention, technology, the internet, fake news, visual effects, digital consumption, we could come down in a blaze of glory in Tokyo and the world would still shrug it off as a publicity stunt or a scene from one of those moving pictures you create. No. We have missed that time. A time when humanity was more basic, more innocent, more natural. We wouldn't last five minutes as gods these days unless we resorted to more...drastic tactics.' Natsuo noticed Amasterasu's golden eyes drop and the light fade a little.

'Enma and Susanoo...'

'Exactly,' she said softly, gently touching the hilt of the sword. 'I want to maintain the status quo. I want the yōkai to return to their fairytales and I need the Kings of the Underworld to return to their lands without ignominy.' Amaterasu said these words barbed with an old strength that belied her dainty and almost elven appearance. 'And then I can return to my oden and you, young Natsuo, can return to your mother.'

The serenity of the little house and the perfect temperate day outside its walls, the waters around the little island that rippled gently, bodies of rock that silently slid through the air, and calmness that reigned. Heaven wasn't about ostentatiousness. Heaven was peace and quiet.

Much like typhoons and yokai becoming the new normal, so had his life as part of this celestial adventure. He had evolved. Natsuo was no longer a shut-in, a social reject. No; his life as a Hikikomori was gone, a past him, a different him. He felt the vestigial limb of his former life dissolve within, the last motes and fragments of Natsuo the Hikikomori had gone, flown up to join the granite icebergs in the sky.

Natsuo breathed deeply with his eyes closed. He felt the burden slink off his shoulders and melt off his bones. His duty fulfilled, he could start anew. The sheltered Japanese man turned phoenix from the flames.

Looking out of the window of the small house Natsuo saw the large floating islands, the mountains in the sky, careening weightlessly through the air. A noiseless dance. He then saw as one of the alpine behemoths crashed into another. As light beats sound, it seemed like an odd silent movie until a thunderous boom exploded in their ears and a shockwave blew through the grass, smashing in the sliding doors and nearly toppling Natsuo.

Amaterasu's eyes glinted and her hair glowed bright gold and seemed to emanate a static energy. Her hand moved to the hilt of the sword.

A further gargantuan impact was felt as the mountains, like two planes at their vertical limits finding their engines cut, slowly toppled and hurtled to the ground. When they landed all of heaven shook and the roof of the small house fell in. A huge blast-wave could be seen on the horizon, hurtling out in all directions like an elemental nuclear explosion.

Amaterasu leapt out of what was left of the front door, cracked and buckled as it was, and ran over the water like she weighed nothing.

The impact-wave arrived mere seconds later. She held the sword in front of her upright, one hand braced behind the flat of the blade, and sent out a blossoming pulse of pure white energy. The shockwave spilled around them like iron filings round a magnet, blowing down all the trees and flattening the fields, and then a second later everything went quiet again.

'They wouldn't dare...' Natsuo heard a now stern-sounding Amaterasu say to herself.

'My lady?'

'I can feel him. It's my brother. Just him. A stupid move.' She paused. 'Unless...'

'Enma heads to the human world at the same time...' Natsuo said. All the comics he had read, all the films and anime he had seen. It seemed so obvious. A coordinated attack.

'Sōjōbō. Take Natsuo and return to the human realm. Take the jewels and the hammer and go!' Her hair began to glow again as if white-hot and stood up on its ends like a lion's mane. 'Now!'

The heavenly bridge was broken and in ruins, the shockwave having smashed in the long arches and beams, leaving a vast rubbled space between the land and where the bridge now stopped. Unusable.

Sōjōbō knelt down and closed his eyes, placing his hands, palms flat, on the ground. The dust and rubble began to vibrate around him and an old power seemed to ripple out, a noiseless noise pulsating in Natsuo's ears, ever-building.

'Natsuo, you will put your arms around my neck!' He shouted without shouting.

This was the first time Natsuo had felt the magnitude of the ancient tengu's strength. The very ground beneath them was disappearing, as an object becomes dust against a circular saw. Sōjōbō was literally punching a hole out of heaven.

Another dull pounding boom exploded in the distance followed by a sound reminiscent of fine fabric being torn in two.

'Sister!' came a furious cry.

As Natsuo and Sōjōbō seemed to be swallowed up by the ground, which was dissipating and powdering into a fine sparkling dust, there was just time for Natsuo to see a man with a flowing wild beard and mane of hair falling, no, flying down through a nebula-tinted hole in the sky towards Amaterasu.

Red and white robes fluttered around him, and he sported a terrible face like some enraged shogun lord from a painting. As bright light almost fully surrounded Natsuo the last thing he saw, or he thought he saw, were Susanoo's eyes locking on his. To Natsuo it felt like those eyes were smiling, a righteous intelligence saying, "everything is going exactly to plan".

Abject fear turned to worry as Sōjōbō materialised in the human world, somewhere in the sky above Osaka. Natsuo clung tight around the old tengu as they descended through what looked like some Blitz chaos, fire-cracks and explosions popping in the dusk-dark; the orange glow of burning buildings mixed with the pillowing grey of smoke clouds. They descended lower towards the docks.

'I shall leave you with your mother, Natsuo-kun!' Sōjōbō shouted over the whipping wind. 'For war is upon us.'

'It was the least I could do,' Abe no Seimei said coolly, though Natsuo could sense his unease. The hangar where his mother resided was under protection of the Bureau but had already been raided once by some fire-spitting mermaids. 'The akugyo can't come on land, but there are some other yōkai which have been making some more audacious moves around here. The time of secrecy and hiding in the shadows, the time of that chill down the back of the neck or the creaking floorboards is over. It is now war.'

Sōjōbō recounted what had happened with Amaterasu.

'So...' Abe stroked his chin theatrically. 'Her brother keeps our Ladyship at bay whilst Enma and his cronies bring their particular brand of chaos to the humans.' There was a persistent humming noise punctured occasionally by dull booms and reverberations. 'The human armies, their cannons and tanks, will do the job against most of the lower castes, but not the King of the Underworld. And once they take Japan they'll carry on, until all the lands of man are burned and scarred.'

'What can be done?' asked Natsuo, who had not even had time to check on his mother.

'First of all, I'll settle the waters,' Sōjōbō said, prompting Natsuo to open his bag and pass him the two tide jewels. 'At least then we can calm things down our side.'

'And then we'll need that hammer young man.' Abe smiled. 'As a deterrent. By now Enma will know we don't have the sword, but with the jewels in our possession and the uchide no kozuchi by our side, it might be enough to make him think twice, or perhaps delay enough for Amaterasu to reach us.'

Sōjōbō bowed, patted Natsuo on the back, and headed out of the hangar towards the bay waters. Natsuo then took the bulbous hammer out of his bag and offered it to Abe, who subtly recoiled.

'I'm afraid I can't take that, Natsuo.'

'But you said we'd need it.'

'That is true. We might. But I cannot wield such a thing. The temptation at the near limitless power to grant my every whim would be destructive. You must hold onto it.'

Of course. Of course I do. I'm like Frodo fucking Baggins...

Abe then placed a gentle hand on his shoulder. 'But let us hope it can just stay in your bag, eh?'

'Mm.'

'I shall get your mother.'

It had been so long since he had been home that this ugly, functional hangar by the water, had started to feel like one. A space of rest and return, a building he now associated with his mother. Natsuo had no desire to return to that house in Kochi. A block of timber and brick that only stood for one thing: a life wasted to an identity his country had named Hikikomori. Maybe after this his mother and he could rebuild the house in Tosashimizu and start anew there.

'My boy.' Natsuo turned around.

His mother looked tired and stressed. Natsuo couldn't help feeling pity. What this poor old lady, and indeed thousands of other people around the country, had been through. Her grey hair sat wispy and thin on a face of wrinkles, but her eyes, her eyes were pools of sadness that now glimmered with relief. She had lost so much, the love of her life, her husband, her house and each time Natsuo was swept up into this madness, she stood to lose her son too.

'I'm still here.' Natsuo smiled wearily, hugging his mother tight.

They talked for a while, huddled over each over on a couple of low stools, a clutch of murmurs and intimate whispers. All around the hangar there was a hushed worry clinging to the conversations and the people looked cold and frightened. Confused.

For years the yōkai were figments of the imagination, fun stories passed down through generations, or the outbursts of the drunk or delusional. But now they were tormenting and even attacking people. Real people. The myths and fantasies had become non-fiction.

Some wept, some clutched their heads, unable to fathom their new reality. But this was Japan; there was no screaming or flailing, this was abject fear beneath a blanket of understatement.

Why do we have fairytales and stories? Storytelling was born out of the primordial soup of early human interactions. Before televisions and computers, before books and script, there were words and images; images born of vowels and consonants. They brought communities together, bolstered the family and friendship links at the dawn of mankind's imagination. Stories of everyday real life mixed in with the fantasies that put names and faces to the unexplained. Some of these stories became religions and some of them became fables and tales. The genetics were the same.

These fables and tales were then injected into drops of ink that found their home frozen still on parchment and papyrus. The tales stuck, proof, unedited, of thoughts and ideas, until one day they would be copied en masse and change the world. The most pernicious and powerful tool that humanity had: the written word. The mighty pen versus the withered sword.

Finally, humanity would surge ahead, exploding into the following centuries at a rate and advancement that threatened these old stories. But they found a new life captured by light and flickering celluloid, by electronic super-brains that allowed the listener-turned-viewer to even partake in the fairytale and control it. They could become the heroes of the stories their distant forefathers would have only been able to listen to.

And so many stories.

Humanity of old, dispersed as they were throughout the continents, had their own tales. Isolated, uniquely flavoured, legends and epics and parables, that would help define their own cultures moving forward.

From pixies and goblins, Osiris, forest huts on chicken legs, small wooden boys that came to life, to fire-spitting samurai heads. The breadth of the human mind gave the world a multitudinous spread of villains and heroes, monsters and angels, tapping into the base ideas of good and evil, tales of loss and love, of heroism and fear. The world, through man's attempt to understand it and control it, gave birth to folklore and legends.

But they were never meant to be real.

Or perhaps they always were.

Now everything was muddy and confused and the beasts were at the door. Literally.

The main hangar doors buckled and squeaked like gas popping through a crack, until a wall of water burst through in a tidal surge that hurtled towards the people huddled inside and threatened to drown them in an instant.

However, almost as soon as the mass of liquid had crashed through it stopped, suspended in a watery status over them like some poised cobra about to strike. But it didn't. Screams subsided into terrified and confused murmurs as the frozen wave defied gravity and sparkled in the refracted ceiling light.

Ominously the water retreated back through the room like a school bully refusing to hit you but still staring into your eyes. And then Sōjōbō came into view outside, a glowing tide jewel in each hand. He moved his hands and the water followed. Turning away from the hangar and towards the bay he made a motion with both arms as if throwing a net; the water mimicking his movements and leapt back into the squally waters.

'Abe-san!' The old tengu bellowed. 'The akaei is on the move. I could use your help here.'

Leaving his mother, Natsuo stepped outside and sure enough, a dark island out in the bay seemed to be approaching.

The monster I saw from the road...

Natsuo suddenly felt small, like he was being swallowed up. This was worse than Meido. The Underworld was the underworld. But this was his home. This was Japan. The threat of death, the threat of everything ending now felt more real. The sky was filling with flying goblins and the cities and villages of his homeland were going to be overrun with demons and monsters.

Abe no Seimei brought out a wand and began to launch pulses of bright blue energy across the waters. As they hurtled over the waves and struck the huge beast, the little illumination-impacts gave the impression of minuscule, coloured paint-drops hitting and disappearing onto a black canvas. A low loud rumble rippled towards the shore.

'This is good. Keep at it. It's clearly not happy.'

Three black vans pulled up and out of their sliding doors emerged men and women in long cloaks.

The Bureau...

Like a military firing squad, the newcomers lined up alongside Abe no Seimei and produced wands. Synchronised tracer fire of all different colours fizzed away from the wharf and slammed into the island-sized water beast. Another angry groan from the distance arrived, now flecked with a tone of pain.

The waters were calm, and the rain was seemingly stopping. Sōjōbō's wielding of the tide jewels seemed to be quelling the storm front at Osaka. The waters were still thrashing with yōkai however; and that was to say nothing of the chaos no doubt raging in the city streets further inland.

'This calm will spread, but I can't be constantly interrupted by these blasted denizens of the deep. We need more firepower!'

As if directly answering the ancient tengu's call, a large globe of light seared down through the sky like a meteor and slammed hard into the massive eye of the akaei. Natsuo looked up and was elated to see a small raccoon with a bandage around its head gliding towards them, a massive scrotal sack buffeting on the wind, a sword in one hand and light in the other.

Hage-no-Tanuki screamed a battle-cry, and another pulse of energy leapt out of his hand, careening towards the leviathan. The combined firepower of the mighty tanuki, the agents of the Bureau, Abe-no-Seimei and Sōjōbō having robbed the water of its energy, caused the massive creature to pause, moan mournfully, and slowly submerge and disappear beneath the surface. The other marine yōkai that had been pestering the coastline soon gave up and quickly made their exit too. All of a sudden, a quiet fell.

'Better late than never, eh?!' Hage-no-Tanuki strolled over and, despite looking tired and beaten up, still maintained the foppish rapscallion confidence that had enamoured him to Natsuo back in the old sake brewery. 'I'm glad you're OK, young lad.'

'This will buy us some time, but Enma will come,' Sōjōbō interjected. 'With Amaterasu engaged, we are on our own. And having repelled this first assault at Osaka we must be ready for the next. If we can hold them off until She comes, we should stand a chance.'

Screams could be heard from inside the hangar. Fearing it might be an attack they all ran inside bearing wands and blades. They were greeted with people covering their mouths and crowding around their phones.

...we repeat, these aerial images that you are witnessing are live from the capital.

Tokyo Tower has collapsed and a five block area around it has...

...been swallowed up by the ground. We still have no information about how many lives may have been lost. But it could be in the hundreds.

Please stay tuned for more updates.

The footage, shot from the skies, showed a vast chasm in the Minato district where the orange and white Eiffel-esque tower used to stand a thousand-feet in the air. Columns of green light, a fluorescent artificial Halloween green, began to shoot up out of the crater. The news helicopter got closer, and along with exclamations from the man behind the camera, creatures could be seen exiting from within. Suddenly there was another blast of shocked lime green and what looked like the long body of a red dragon appeared. Then a face, the face of an old hate-filled giant, not the face of a dragon, filled the screen. A pilot screamed, the camera shook, and the feed went dead.

'Tokyo is in chaos. The walls have been burst open. Abe, you will be with me.' Abe nodded at Sōjōbō. 'Natsuo, you will stay here, stay safe, and stay hidden.'

This was not a movie, not a manga comic or great book. Natsuo was no confident hero. He knew when to do as he was told.

'Mm,' he assented.

And so, it was the following day, that in a cafe near a hangar by a now quiet Osaka Bay, Natsuo found himself sat with his mother, no mythical characters of folkloric myths around. Just a son, a parent, and a pot of green tea again. Mustered smiles and platitudes. Trying to force normality into a moment of frozen madness.

'A small measure of peace,' said Natsuo's mother.

'What's that?'

'Oh, just a piece of music. I know it's not over,' she said, sipping gently at the tea. 'But we at least, for a while, can enjoy this. Leave it to them to bring this all to a close.'

'Do you think they will?'

'Hah, well...' She giggled. 'You know them better than I.' Her eyes twinkled rakishly.

Natsuo smiled and looked out of the window. There was smoke over Osaka. A city still reeling was coming back out of their homes to assess the damage. The fug of assault lingering in the air.

'When I met your father, I didn't know...I mean, I just met a man. I was falling in love with Akihiro Hirawa. He did show me once, you know. The real him. And it didn't scare me. It made me love him more. What he was, what he had been; what he was pushing down deep inside so he could be something else. I thought it brave and romantic. And it's easy the lies we tell ourselves to deal with the reality of the now. But I saw a man, not a demon. That other side of him seemed remote, false, a story.

'Though none of this seems fair. It's not fair what happened to me and your father, it's not fair what's happening and what's happened to you, and it's not fair what's happening to the world now. None of it is our fault. We are victims of malignancy and greed. Just so happens that those perpetrating all this are gods and monsters. And we are the little people. Everyone who came before had no problem. But us, we are the ones chosen by fate to lose. It's just not fair.' Yui Hirawa took out a tissue, dabbed her eyes, and blew her nose.

Natsuo moved round the table and placed an arm over her shoulder.

'Yes, it's unfair. But we are not going to lose. They won't let that happen. I won't.'

Yui sniffled and smiled, nuzzling her head into the space between Natsuo's head and shoulder, 'When did my son become this brave warrior?'

The waitress came over with a plate of skewered chicken skins and livers and another with some salty fried fish fins. Then she brought over two beers.

'My first drink with my son!' Yui giggled. 'I saw your first steps, heard your first words, but, when you shut yourself away, we missed the man.'

They brought the glasses together and Yui, in the way of an old lady, slowly, clasping the glass with both hands, took a dainty sip, while Natsuo, one-handed, took three large gulps.

'Isn't it funny how quickly things get back to normal in this country. Yōkai are invading our capital and here we are, hours after having our second city attacked, eating yakitori and drinking beer as if it were a normal Friday lunch. I mean we almost died!'

'Mm.'

'It's the only good way to deal with a crisis. You have to be strong through normality. Don't forget what is happening, but don't give in to ruin. It's something us Japanese have in common with the British. They call it a "stiff upper lip" — I always liked that. But if you give in too much to your emotions in times of crisis you can lose yourself. Also, it sends a message of strength. So you see my boy, us, here and now, sipping tea and beer and eating grilled skewers, shows we are ready, that they can throw what they like at us, but we'll not bow.'

'When did my mum become such a badass?'

Yui chuckled and picked up her beer.

'Shall we get another?'

'Yes m'am!'

[High up in the sky two balls of light, trailing like sentient comets, smash into each other again and again. Like celestial pinballs they wheel and arc in the air and come together with crashing radiance. If you were there, if you were close, you would hear battle cries and the sound of steel on steel, you would see the two faces full of sadness and anger. Power unimaginable on a plane almost unattainable.]

{From a large dark maw of soil, bodies emerge; twisted wretches, hell beasts and the bestiary of legend. Spear-bearing toads with rainbow breath, green-skinned hairy creatures with horns and claws, the walking flaming corpses of old monks, pudgy and naked little humanoids with greasy hair and mocking faces, red demons with multiple arms and faces wielding blades, long-nosed devils in kimono walking on all fours, elegant women with bird-eyes all over their arms, various evil-looking old ladies, some wearing straw hats and with burning torches in their mouths or dripping blood from their serrated teeth, some with snakes crawling over their haggard and wiry bodies.}

(A young boy sits with his mother and for the first time in a long time feels at peace. A small bar pretends life is normal despite the battle in the east. It was like the old times, villagers going about their days, drinking sake and sowing rice and fishing and courtesaning and acting and cooking, as shoguns and warlords fought for Edo. Ignorance is hard in the face of phones and computers, but the hush after the calming of the waters is at least in effect here within the walls of the izakaya.)

[The sword-wielding meteors continue to collide again and again in a blur of robes and long hair and power. Faces of fury are bloodied and bruised. A sad result of siblings at odds. One shouts "Brother, stop this at once. The Zōkasanshin did not come into existence for you to ruin it. Existence wasn't wrenched from primeval chaos by the first gods so that my sibling, in a fit of jealousy, could destabilise everything!" Though the battle is loud and fierce, fuelled by millennia of emotions, they speak to each other as one would to a neighbour on a bench. "Sister. The three creators don't know the meaning of existence. They have drifted into concept." "Brother, you forget the others, who with the Zōkasanshin make up the great five; the Kotoamatsukami." "I do not forget, dear sister." "Then you remember Umashi'ashikabihikoji is the god of energy. And you trifle with that, dear brother..." And the swords clash again.]

{Names from the old days filing out of the underworld. Shokuin. Ōgama. Hinoenma. Ubume. Monikers penned by people and fairies to name the creepies and the crawlies, the bumps in the night, the chills down the neck. Jikininki. Ubagabi. Dodomeki. Denizens of the deep crawling and clawing and flying and floating their way up to the human world following the call of King Enma to do his cruel bidding. Bekatarō. Apposhha. Kawahime. Tenome. A world thought to be only found on page and parchment bleeding into one of people and jobs and restaurants and mobile phones. Order losing its grip.}

(The mother and child. Mother and man now, but a mother always sees a little boy, the mother and child walk along the waterfront. It is not beautiful. Cargo ships, prows rusted from years at sea, bob in the hemmed-in waters of the docks. Hangars, rubbish piles, cranes, car parks, salt-faded cafe signs, shipping containers, sad-looking men smoking cigarettes darkly in packs, tired faces working jobs nobody wanted, people rebuilding and repairing, hoping it's all over. It wasn't beautiful, but the boy, no, the man smiles and puts his arm around his mother as they stroll along. It was human at least. And sometimes that was enough.)

["And then what?" The sister asks, breathing heavily, spitting out dark blood, "You and Enma then rule over everything? Why?" "Sea, storms, the harvest...is that all I am?" He responds through gritted teeth, wiping red off his chin with his sleeve. "I slayed the great serpent, and yet am I loved?" "There are those who love you brother." "These humans. Unless I act as pious and banal as you, I am demonised. A god! And our moon-brother Tsukuyomi, who you yourself ignore as day to his night, is loved by them, romanticised by them. But me? I want justice sister." "Then the answer lies with you Susanoo, not them. Can't you see that? Has Enma twisted and blinded you with the tricks of Jigoku?" "Enough!" The brother roars, clenching his mighty ten-span totsuka blade.]

{The tide of yōkai, demons and gremlins filing out of the underworld into Tokyo is met by the protectors of the earthly realm and other yōkai and powers sympathetic to Amaterasu and order. Around the rim of the crater they stand their ground; or try to. A long-nosed tengu with a katana fast as lightning cleaves the incomers in twain; besuited magic-users cast violent spells sending blasts of coloured fluorescence into the crowds; a battalion of red-faced tengu flying around, attacking a giant red serpent with the head of an angry old man. No sign of the gods. Hachiman, the god of war, where is he? Raijin is there somewhere, casting his bolts, and Fūjin's winds are blowing. The old tengu smiles grimly to himself. "What good are gods of poetry and wisdom and fortune when storms, lightning, wind, and the great king of hell are against us? Luck and enlightenment are no use when staring down claws and blades."}

(The mother and her son arrive back at the shelter but stop just before entering. The atmosphere feels static, effervescent, charged. The air turns gusty and mean and the sky darkens. The man turns around to look at the sky over the bay; it is gloomy and angry, the clouds pillowing and churning. "What now?" he says in an exasperated whisper. Sheet lightning zig-zags and flashes through the cumulus, while ribbons of electricity fork and spider down to the water. Waterspouts and vortices whip over the waves forming a vast black wall of weather approaching the land. Then they show themselves; two vast, furious-looking sky giants. One scarlet-coloured, like some enormous horned oni, beating a drum on a flying cloud wrapped in coils of lightning. The other, similar, but more wizardly with a white beard and algal green skin, flying through the clouds holding a windbag in both hands like an ancient parachutist. Each is the size of a ten-story building, each muscle the size of a bus, each horn and tooth a telephone box. They are such the embodiment of elemental power and strength that fear leaves the equation and is replaced by awe and a sense of immense inconsequentialness. Gods. "Raijin and Fūjin..." But there is another that appears.)

[Amaterasu feels something shifting. Something is wrong, and it isn't the fight with her brother. Something is falling through. Something is moving in Takamagahara. The once idyllic heaven-scape is now a sad scene of razed fields, broken mountains and scorched earth. The calm bliss of her upper realm is in ruins. But again, that is not what is ailing her. She takes refuge a moment behind a small floating hill; one of the few that has yet to be blasted to pieces by the battle with her brother. She needs time to think. "Oh sister! You hide? But you can't hide here." He taunts, swinging his sword, loosening his muscles. Then she sees it; an aura, purple? A blurring. The reality of her heaven fusing with something else, like a double exposure. Then she hears shouts and screams. The sounds of war. The blurring spreads and the marbled lines between worlds curdle like oil in water. She sees men and mages fighting yōkai, sees her general Sōjōbō fighting back the great wurm Shokuin. Even her brother forgets his quarrel and looks down confused. A confused god is something not witnessed much during the course of existence. "You see brother! Your meddling has broken the walls between our planes." At this even the great Susanoo seems to pause.]

{The forces seeking to keep balance intact are managing to keep the creatures of the dark at bay. Amidst the rubble of Shōwa-era apartments, now a blanket of cracked and dimmed neon signs, and a sea of scattered kanji, the fight to keep the underworld out of the human plane continues. Then light. But not light from some bright day, but as if the world's luminosity has been turned up, someone moving the slider. The stormy sky above is fading into another image, like a ruined piece of film. The ancient tengu sees, as if through water, the sight of Amaterasu and, it seemed after a violent confrontation, Susanoo, at opposite ends of the sky, staring down, befuddled, at the conflict on earth. "What?" is the only word Sōjōbō can muster. He knows the gravity of what is happening, though he cannot begin to understand the forces and magic that have contrived to cause such a situation. Chaos seems to be the only explanation. The status quo lost.}

(The two gods hover in the sky some leagues out at sea. They breathe heavily, barely moving, chests heaving, fixating on Natsuo, like silverbacks staring at intruders. Poised but inert. A great noise rumbles into the world; low foghorns mixed with bass guitars and an elephantine hum. Like some cheap magician's trick or movie effect a swirling cloud-column the size of a tower block curls up from the surface of the water and then dissipates to reveal a giant man dressed in ancient Chinese governmental robes, clutching the amenonuhoko spear in one hand, the other draped lazily over a scabbard at the hip. Enma Daiō. Eyes aflame with fury and disdain bear into Natsuo's. "There you are. The nuisance. The little human, well, half-human as I have been informed, who walked my lands under my nose. I am almost impressed." Natsuo does nothing, says nothing, fear gripping him as he stands, in front of his mother, before two elemental gods and the demon king. "You have something I want." Enma speaks in the old fashion, polite, haughty. "I would deem it smart of you to bequeath it unto me now lest you invite ruin unto yourself and your...human mother." "You stay the fuck away from my mother!" Natsuo shouts, the words leaving his chest before his mind has a chance to stop them. King Enma is momentarily taken aback by the tiny life-form answering back, fury flashing across his features. Then his brow relaxes and a smile slides over his whole face. "If you won't give it to me willingly, I shall take it. Or at least, for sport, hold you to ransom." In a flash two figures, in the robes of Tang party officials, appear behind Natsuo and grab on to his mother. As soon as they arrive, they dissolve back into the air and reemerge next to Enma, standing, like their king, on cloud-discs above the Osaka Bay. "As you can see little creature, my secretaries Shiroku and Shimyō have now graced me with the presence of this one so dear to you." Yui Hirawa cries out for her son, her eyes like some terrified confused animal. She doesn't struggle, instead she goes limp. "What do you say half-breed, a trade? A hammer for a mother?")

[{The realms are fusing, the borders that separate the waking human world and the dreamworld of the higher gods are melding into the same. No precedent. As the lord of storms and tempests and the great high goddess descend, unwillingly, into the human realm — a place not visited since time immemorial — a calm spreads over the skirmishes and bloodshed and chaos in the centre of Tokyo. Neither side, neither yōkai nor mage, neither goblin nor tengu, seems confident what to do. An impasse forged in the fires of uncertainty. Forces of light and dark waiting for instruction. An accidental ceasefire takes hold and stops both beast and man in their tracks.}]

'Do you know what it means to be a god?' Natsuo was silent, still trying to process what to do next in his head, his mother moaning quietly in the arms of Enma's aides. Enma hoped to get his hands on the uchide no kozuchi without having to waste any energy. Violence he left to Susanoo, a brilliant blunt object full of rage and pride. Enma was a thinker not a fighter, so if he were able to simply get the human to give it him, then that would be fortuitous. 'No, of course you don't.'

'Let my mother go!'

'Ah, it has a voice after all.' The giant king purred. '"Men must be governed by God or they will be ruled by tyrants." The finest quote I'm sure you'd agree.' He paused as he noticed Natsuo's blank face. 'Your incomprehension shows your ignorance young man. William Penn? No, nothing? Regardless, he once said "Men must be governed by God or they will be ruled by tyrants." And he was right. So again, give me the hammer and I shall return your mother. And then, be on your way. This is no place for you.'

Natsuo was frozen, an inconsolable rage was simmering under his skin, mixing together with fear. Fear of the terrible beings before him. Fear that he would lose his mother. Fear at not knowing what he should do.

'Release yourself of this burden and of your father's legacy. I won't harm your mother.'

He looked at the bulbous, golden hammer in his hand, looking as it did both innocuous and childish. He could just give this to Enma, end it all, get his mother back safe, go home and forget everything.

But what home would he be going back to? What world? Wouldn't he just be delaying the inevitable? And after everything he had been through, to just give in, give up...

Natsuo looked at his mother and tears sprung up to sting the corners of his eyes. She looked so helpless, so pathetic. Like two guards were carrying away an old lady for dissenting at a protest. He couldn't lose her; he'd rather lose the world.

Would Enma even keep his promise? Of course he couldn't be trusted, that much was obvious, just look at what he was doing. But in this one instance, did he maybe mean it? Perhaps his mother was insignificant enough that he would just return her. Or perhaps he would crush her instantly. He didn't know what to do.

'Boy! Stop this dallying. Hand me the hammer and do it now. I shall not indulge more of this time wasting.'

'First, let my mother go. Then you can have the hammer.' Natsuo called out across the waters. Years in solitude, in isolation, reading mangas, watching anime and movies. The countless scenes of the standoff. Who goes first. As long as he could get his mother back, or get her free of his adversary's grip, he could at least try to formulate a plan.

'Enough of this; I tire. Kill the woman.' Enma called to his two secretaries, one of which unsheathed a long, curved blade. As he made to run her through, Natsuo screamed and brought the hammer down on the ground.

'What? What is this place? What have you done?'

In the momentary confusion, the same as when you wake up somewhere you don't remember even falling asleep in, Natsuo wondered the same thing. He had simply swung the hammer. A tiny fraction of a thought also hid behind the main narrative sloshing around his head: he rather liked the voice of a Hell King confused.

'I told you boy, you shouldn't trifle with that thing.'

As the fog of befuddlement drifted away, one thing became immediately clear to both parties and another thing only revealed itself to Natsuo.

First of all, his mother had disappeared, as had the thunder and wind gods and Enma's aides. It was now just Natsuo and the King of Hell.

The second was their surroundings: it was his house in Tosashimizu. But instead of the battered, caved-in corpse of a home he had found after his days toiling on foot to find his mother, instead it now looked brand new, the brown wood beams shining. Stranger still was the fact that the house stood alone. All the other buildings of the town hadn't disappeared, they simply weren't there. Nothing. No boats in the water, no flats and homes, no cars. Just land, pure and untended, and his house.

This clearly isn't real then...

'This is my home.'

'This is no home, boy, this is a dream, a memory, an idealised hope of what you want to see. You are meddling clumsily with a power that you are not prepared to deal with. Hand me the hammer before you cause irrevocable damage!'

'Damage? You talk of damage?' Natsuo, since they had taken his mother, had felt anger bubbling under the surface, ready to erupt, and now King Enma, on top of kidnapping his only remaining parent, had the hypocrisy to lecture him on the correct course of action. 'You've caused storms and destruction, killed I don't know how many. You've destroyed my house. And you accuse me of maybe causing damage. That house you're seeing, that building there, is what it looked like before you.'

Natsuo glanced over at the house and fancied he saw people inside; forms really, shaped to look like...him? Was that his mother and father? It was as if the dreamworld he seemed to be in only had enough information to make the house; the people left as ghostly half-baked ideas. But the hammer had taken him where he felt he wanted to be...

'Where is my mother? Is she alive?' Natsuo was suddenly frantic. 'Tell me!'

'I cannot possibly know.' King Enma half-chuckled. 'You brought me here, remember.'

'Liar!'

'I tire of this. I tire of you; you maggot, you nothingness. You puny human. I've spent millennia judging your souls fairly, helping you on your way to the places where they shall remain, but as you overpopulate you get stupider. You know yourselves less. You know us less also. I am hated. A boogey man. A baddie. Why? No reason. Whilst the gods, most of them anyway, are loved, prayed to, exalted, what of the great Enma Daiō? A grumpy and unfair Chinese official. Well, not anymore. I don't need love. I'll take it.'

In an instant the giant had unsheathed the blade at his side and rushed towards Natsuo bearing both spear and sword, his luxurious robes blurring from the speed.

For a being of such size to move so fast surprised Natsuo in the purest sense of the word; his attention diverted by the non-understanding of his surroundings. The blade itself was three times the size of Natsuo, and it came down fast; he had time enough only to bring the hammer up in a knee-jerk reaction of defence.

Everything around them was smouldered earth and ruin. A vast urban landscape opened up in all directions leading off to some low fuzzy hills that seemed to be a natural stopping point for the settlement. Every building had been blasted down to its bones; foundations and broken half doorways. Square outlines showed where families and coworkers had once been. Smoke, the smoke of destruction, particles of civilisation, hung in the air. Trees had been stripped back to blackened skeletons, gnarled fingers that were sad and ravaged, reminding Natsuo of Meido.

Was this purgatory again?

A dirty river to his right was shepherding bodies and lumber downstream. The grass was brown and singed. One building still stood, defiant against the cataclysm. A blockish, russet-brick and cement building, all facades, crowned with a latticed metallic dome-shaped frame.

Hiroshima...

'You're moving in time child. You must relinquish the hammer.'

Natsuo remained silent. There was no sound here. Just a fidgety, live and in-colour photograph of a memory burned into the heart of every Japanese person.

'This is why I am doing what I'm doing.' The purring, influencing voice of the official returned. 'Look what you did to yourselves.' Natsuo knew he meant humanity, not nationality. The concept was probably lost on a hell king. 'Have you ever heard of the expression "benevolent dictatorship"? Absolute power to rule but with regard for the benefit of the population as a whole. Do you all still not understand? I seek not to kill you all, but to rule you with love.'

'And how many have said that throughout history?'

'Human history,' Enma retorted with venom. 'And I do not intend to look to any of you for approval. I shall take what is owed to me. With Susanoo removing his oh-so-high-and-mighty sister from the equation, it should be a fairly simple procedure. But you continue in the role of thorn rather persistently.'

Through all of King Enma's self-aggrandising Natsuo couldn't stop thinking about his mother. He feared her dead, but he couldn't know. He needed to get back, to get away from this time-shift, alternate reality hopping and away from Enma.

The atmosphere became denser; Natsuo felt pressure on his arms as if the very air he was breathing was thickening. The same feeling when a storm is brewing, one of those dark thunder-filled tempests that rip through the world in hot summers. The light fell as if a dimmer had been turned down.

Enma...

The lightness and brightness was folding in on itself and concentrating on him. A black hole in the shape of a man. The spear was the only shining thing in the ever-increasing point of blackness. The officiously dressed man with the finely-cut black beard and high-arched eyebrows had morphed into a suction point of light; a consuming vacuum with the outline of a person. As if it were charging up.

The colour began to leak away from the world, the burned-out ruins of Hiroshima, the green hills, the burnt umber of what were once trees and the red bricks and white walls now all faded to black and white until Natsuo felt like he was standing in an old photo; a greyscale corpse of a city.

'This is it boy. This is the end of you. You think you really stood a chance against me?' A voice, fuzzed with the sound of air being consumed, boomed out. 'Enma Daiō, Yama, King Yan-lo, Karalupa, Son of Heaven, King of Hell? I am a dharmapala; a wrathful god, and some human with the uchide no kozuchi will not stop me.'

Shit, shit, shit...

The dark mass with the shape of a building-sized man again launched itself with the speed of a shadow at Natsuo. The spear sending jagged darts and shards of spiked-earth towards him in the same moment. Virgin land as a weapon. All Natsuo could do was swing the hammer.

It was his fifth birthday. He was hugging his mother while his father took the smoking candles out of a small sponge cake with strawberries on top of the white icing. Wrapping paper was abandoned on the floor and an action figure of Ultraman stood on the table. Everyone was smiling. Then Happy Birthday was sung, in heavily accented English, followed by clapping and the slicing of cake. A memory. Then darkness and evil, the lights of the house went out. He swung again.

Everyone was gathered around him laughing at his jokes. The girls in their black skirts, white tops, and red and blue ties draped around their necks, and the boys in black buttoned-up military-style shirts making them all look like sailors and officers. Natsuo was recounting some story and his classmates were enthralled. The popular boy, beloved by friends and staff. The teacher was there, wiping a tear from his mirthful eye. Toshi was there. But in this world, he was at the back of the class alone, long mangled hair, pencilling in some doodles in his workbook. A dream. Tendrils of black crept into the classroom through the windows and door followed by an angry growl. He swung.

A volcano erupts around him, bursting as a boil, but instead of molten rock spilling out, magma turning to lava, instead sprays a shower of comics. Manga of all kinds blow up around him, picking him up as a wave would a paper boat. Batman, Sandman, Jonah Hex, The Authority; Western characters swirled throughout like flotsam and jetsam in a sea of familiar Asian faces. The flow of pages and heroes and villains buffeted Natsuo and the magmatic parchment flow carried him along making him feel safe. He knew it was a metaphor; the hammer extracting that part of his cocooned life as a Hikikomori. It was warm like a drug. The pages then erupted into flames and Natsuo felt the real heat snapping at his skin. Bursting through a wave of graphic novels came the surging dark shadow of Enma. 'Just stop, please!' Natsuo cried. He swung.

'Well, this is interesting,' came the voice from the dark shadow, which slowly de-intensified and after a few moments seeped away, once again becoming a stern giant in Chinese robes.

'What is this place?' Nastuo asked. To his right was a copse of trees and to his left was a channel of water that curled off right up ahead. On the other side of the water was a line of buildings and streetlights and roads. He had the feeling, something deep in his bones, that he was on an island and this was a moat. The same feeling when you enter a castle.

'Well this is the Daisenryo Kofun tomb.' Enma's ever-changing voice now seemed playful.

Natsuo did know of the place. The Mozu tombs were a selection of megalithic burial sites in the Sakai neighbourhood of Osaka, just over ten kilometres from where his mother had been sheltering. So he was close.

Mausoleums from the 5th century, often keyhole-shaped, and separated from civilisation by water. They were as mysterious and guarded as the Great Pyramids.

The Daisenryo Kofun, the largest tomb in the world, was the resting place of Emperor Nintoku, reputedly famed for his goodness and generosity, and who protected the people against famine, built canals and public structures, reigned for 86 years and lived until the age of 142. Not even the Emperor of Japan can enter the inner islet. And yet here they were. But why here? Natsuo had no link to this place.

'And that...' exhaled Enma, his face flushed with a small shade of confusion, 'would be your father.'

Natsuo spun round to see not the stern face of Akihiro Hirawa but instead a fifteen-foot red oni, slender but with every muscle strained and bulging as if every possible gram of fat had been eschewed in favour of tight musculature. Two large horns pointed skywards from its forehead and the creature's underbite was a line of fang and tooth. A long mane of dark brown hair met an equally full beard. The monster was naked except for a loin cloth and was contemplating its massive, taloned hands when it noticed the young man and the King of Hell.

The beast got to its feet, no monstrous anger or terror in its face, just confusion.

'Father..?' The oni looked at the young man in front of it. 'Natsuo?'

'Ōtakemaru. How delightful of you to join us. Though I must admit, I don't quite know how you are here. You were in my realm after all. However, as you can see here, your son has been a thorn in my side for a while now. A real baragaki. I'm certain your presence here is down to him. He has been fooling around with the uchide no kozuchi. Perhaps one of our finest ever generals might like to talk some sense into him?' Every word was clipped, uppity and staccato.

Before the great oni had a chance to respond, let alone comprehend what was happening, he found himself being embraced by the young man. Natsuo barely made it up to his waist but as he looked down into the tear-filled eyes he knew it was him. Of course, he had last known his son as a boy and now, before him, stood a man, dirtied and bloodied and a world apart from the shut-in he once knew.

'Natsuo-kun...' The incredulous whisper came, slinking out between kitchen-knife teeth. 'What...what is happening?'

Natsuo wiped his nose and eyes. 'Enma is in league with Susanoo, and they intend to oust Amaterasu to rule the various planes of existence as active overlords and not the gods they are.' He sniffed. 'Also, this thing brought you back.' He waved the hammer.

'I must say, that was rather succinct, boy,' said King Enma, his calculating eyes trying to work out how this new situation would play out.

Despite his power, Enma was no great fighter. His plan was to leave the heavy duty activity to his tempestuous partner, while he politicked his way to victory.

Ōtakemaru was no god, but the beast of old would have perhaps been able to tussle and dispatch many of the higher ups one-on-one without much trouble. He was, however, all brute strength and wrath, and the oni before him seemed beaten and tired; ground down by his memories and his sentence in the underworld. He had died on earth; but in Jigoku he had been imprisoned. Enma now had to be careful, play to his strengths and keep the great demon calm.

'Old friend, what we did to you was terrible. I can see that now. You must understand that as the leader of hell I had no choice, no choice, but to put a stop to your earthly activities. The Underworld was beginning to smell of mutiny and rebellion. Questions and doubts. If the great Ōtakemaru could gallivant in human form around the earth, why couldn't we? I erroneously believed the best course of action was to put a stop to it by putting a stop to you. I understand that I was wrong.' He poured more honey into his voice. 'Don't you see what I am doing now will be the reality you had, the life you had, the love you had, for all and every creature of our realm. I am trying to bring utopia to all peoples. But your son...your son is meddling and can't see the whole picture.'

'Lies!' Natsuo turned to his father, to the great red kijin. 'He was going to kill mother. In fact, she may already be...'

'Your mother...'

'Yes.' Natsuo smiled and tears once again began to pinch his eyes and his mouth wobbled. 'I left home, Dad. I got over it, my life as a Hikikomori, and I made my way back to Mum. Through storms and battles, fairy kingdoms and hell itself, I got back to Mum. And this... colossal fuck wants to take her from me, from us, take everything. They mean to rule us with total authority. Humanity enslaved.'

'Yui...' Akihiro Hirawa had spent his time in Jigoku thinking of nothing else except the wife and son he had left behind. In the same way months in Meido could feel like only days on the human plane, so could years on the human plane, should the choice be made, feel like centuries in Hell. The bright spark of the love he had for his family had been the sole light in the darkness, the unbreakable diamond at the heart of the abyss.

'Ōtakemaru...'

'My wife...you would kill my wife.'

'She is unharmed. That I can promise you.' Enma's balancing act. 'We just meant to force your boy's hand.'

'Bullshit! You were about to run her through with a blade!'

'Prove it,' snarled the great demon general. 'Prove to us she is alive.'

'Ōtak – '

'My name is Akihiro Hirawa, and you will bring me my wife!'

There was a pause as Enma Daiō hesitated, then smiled, and then nodded at Natsuo and the hammer. 'Your son can do that.'

Natsuo didn't know what he was doing when he brought the hammer down. During his defence against the great King Enma he was merely defending himself, holding up the hammer as a shield as his emotions and his memories guided the magic. This time he found himself actively trying to get to his mother. It didn't work.

Before he swung there had been an odd colour in the sky, a blurring, a lightening. The once gloomy, dark clouded sky that had accompanied Raijin and Fūjin was changing, as if a grand painter were smudging oils over it, trying to replace the darkness with a bright blue clear day. Monet's last-minute change of heart.

Natsuo, his father and the Hell King materialised, if that was the right word, in the midst of a frozen war zone. Natsuo had hoped, had winced down hard in his mind, to be back in the hangar with his mother. But instead, they were standing in front of a scene from a big budget movie.

In the film *Spartacus* Stanley Kubrick employed 8,800 soldiers. At that time, and not since, had anybody witnessed so many people in one place at war, albeit a fake one on film. But nothing is as affecting as seeing actual mortals clashing into one another. The eye knows.

They were surrounded by a still-life battle scene. A clashed together bloodied frenzy of fantastical beasts, beleaguered human fighters, monsters and men, all stopped, dazed and confused, and just staring at the appearance of the King of Hell as well as their ex-oni general and a small human wielding a magic hammer.

Neither side, neither hell-beast nor wizard or artilleryman, quite knew what to do. Like cars arriving at a small junction, no-one knew what to do next, everyone waiting for a signal.

The light intensified in the sky. The gloomy battlefield now became a saturated, ugly view accompanied by shrieks and pained sounds. It was Amaterasu shining above it all, Susanoo in the sky away from her looking on. A brief sibling ceasefire at the presence of Enma Daio.

The crawling, creeping denizens of the underworld scuttled away under the rubble of broken buildings or slithered and clawed their way back down through the hole to the dark safety of their world.

'Enma!' Her voice crashed through the air, strong and powerful and full of anger. It made Natsuo's eardrums hum and the ground shake, and for the briefest of moments he noticed a glimmer of an emotion cross over Enma Daiō's face, the twinge in the brow and the waxing of the eyes: fear.

She descended, gliding as a beacon, down towards them, pursued slowly at a distance by a now wary Susanoo, like a jackal behind a lioness.

'Your majesty.' Enma cooed, clearly summoning as much bile-loaded sarcasm as possible whilst subtly moving his hand towards the hilt of his sword and gently shifting the weight of the spear.

She settled gracefully in front of the still standing but heavily singed Zojoji temple, an island of old opposite the now toppled Tokyo tower.

Despite her being some way away, almost a kilometre, her spoken voice could be heard clearly. As if the gods had a direct line into your ear canals. Natsuo was stood in the bricks and mortar and upturned foundations of what used to be a multi-storey office building. At his feet was a flickering Lawson convenience store sign, its royal blue neon blinking like a dying firefly, reflecting in the puddles that had pooled in the holes created by the carnage.

'This ends now Enma. Do you see the damage you've wreaked?'

'The damage I've caused?' spat Enma, like a prissy teenager. 'You are the one who has caused this. Sullied your station and mine and that of all the gods. Vague concepts and vestiges of an older time. And what of me?'

'We have our ordained roles great King, you know this. You can't change. It is the will of the makers. It would be like a bird angry it was destined to flight or a fish unappeased by its life underwater. It is what it is.'

'It is what it is...' Enma echoed. 'Well, I choose it not to be as it is.'

'You cannot simply choose not to be who you are designed to be.'

'But I can, and I am, and I will.'

'I won't allow it, Enma.'

'I am not asking for your permission.'

At that Amaterasu's hair glowed; Enma noted her annoyance at his cocky insubordination with something akin to pride.

'Do not mistake my proclamations. When I say I won't allow it, I shall not only be delivering a verbal warning. If needs be — '

'Great Queen, for all your might, I fear you may not win this bout. Here I stand alongside your brother.' He brandished his terraforming spear and battle-worn sword. 'A two-on-one if you will. And in the realm of the gods I have sympathisers. Do you not see the lighting and the winds? You think it ends with Raijin and Fujin? Junshi, Daimyojin and Takeminakata are with me.'

'The god of provocation and the god of the hunt...' Amaterasu thought aloud. 'Well, they would bow in front of Hachiman before they knelt to me. And Hachiman is...with us.'

'The god of war? Hachiman has been a lazy oaf ever since the old times. You know he has hundreds more shrines than you. That old warrior is content to watch things pass by.'

Amaterasu paused. It was true that Hachiman had remained somewhat passive in all these goings on. One could argue it was a win-win for him. Should Enma and Susanoo's mutiny turn out victorious, well then, he reigned as a powerful god. Should things return to the way they were, then the love and fascination of the innately violence-loving humans would keep him fat and comfortable.

Only Inari, the great fox-kami of fertility, rice, sake, industry, the list went on, had more shrines; a third of all of those in Japan.

'I imagine you're thinking of the fox?' Enma purred. 'Her, his, its, whatever form arrives, power is deep that is true. But I think we both know My Lady, we are talking about a creator, a provider, not a destroyer.'

'Takemikazuchi also rallies behind us. I feel the great sword god might prove troublesome to you and your blowing winds. How will lightning stop a blade through the heart?' Amaterasu countered.

'I'm sure Takeminakata would relish the chance for a rematch with Takemikazuchi. But there is no time for tests of strength.' Enma chuckled. 'There is one left, although he is yet to join us, taxing as it is to locate him in kakuriyo.'

'Ōkuninushi...'

Enma smiled, appearing to grow in stature and strength as Amaterasu's crestfallen face accompanied a dimming in her luminescence.

Natsuo had been watching the verbal tennis match, or chess match, he couldn't decide, barely able to keep up with the names of the gods being traded like some sports team roster. But Ōkuninushi he had heard of.

A very old god and not without his shrines. He was the original ruler of the terrestrial world, the one humanity now inhabited. Though he had taken on this rule himself, proclaiming himself lord of the land, quite literally. When Amaterasu and the other heavenly gods saw he would not relinquish his hold over that realm, they descended from

Takamagahara and forced his hand. Not only that, Ōkuninushi was banished forevermore to the unseen world. Kakuriyo. He would no doubt be an angry god if he returned.

The celestial bartering and cajoling and haggling aside, Natsuo just wanted to talk to his father. Arm around him, the giant red oni seemed tense, poised. Natsuo felt protected.

'Father,' Natsuo hissed. As if remembering he was there, the great fang-toothed head bore down on him and the sharp eyes softened. In an instant all the scarlet features, the mane-like hair and full beard, the wild feline eyes, and the immense muscular bulk, withered and discoloured until Natsuo was face-to-face with a slender, square-shouldered man of the same height sporting nothing but a baggy loincloth. 'Dad,' Natsuo said again, embracing the man.

With the backdrop of the Lord of Hell and the High Goddess squabbling back and forth about who had the mightier army, in some prideful effort to perhaps avoid conflict, father and son finally had a moment to talk.

'You've grown. You've really grown into a man.'

His father's face was full of so much emotion, a Shakespearian palate of sadness, anger, regret, depression, pride, and happiness, all bunched up in the brows, the eyes and the smile. He clasped Natsuo by both shoulders, nodded deferentially, and hugged him again. Under his breath a mantra-like apology. 'I'm sorry...I'm so sorry.' Pleading for forgiveness and mercy: '*Yurushite...kanben...yurushite.*'

'I know everything father. I know it all. I get it. *Wakarimasu.*' Suddenly Natsuo saw the change. Akihiro Hirawa, the great warrior-general of the oni who had become a stern salaryman, was now simply an old man defeated by his choices in life and the weight of those consequences. Despite being the same height, Natsuo thought in that moment his father looked crumpled and fragile.

It was a strange time to have a reunion and heart-to-heart — whilst the gods of the heavens and hell were bickering — but Natsuo felt like he was in a vacuum. As if he had become accustomed to chaos, he only saw his father.

They both then seemed to notice the absence of his mother. The tired and beaten-down countenance of his father changed as a kabuki actor changing his visage by passing his hand over his face. Rage bubbled up into his cheeks and his mouth, red flushed up from his neck and his jaw grew into a spiked maw. In a second his father was gone and the multi-storey demon was once again before him.

'Enma!' The roar, like that of some infernal Bodmin beast, tore through the air. Amaterasu, Susanoo and Enma all paused, turned, and regarded them as if they were parents interrupted by children at a soiree. 'My wife...'.

'Oh, Ōtakemaru my old friend, would you give it a rest?' Imperious as ever. 'Can't you see the adults are talking. This is hardly the time or place. The fate of the world, our world, our future, your future, is being decided. Your little human whore can wait.'

'You would do well to watch your words when talking about her.'

'Oh please, you were my greatest deputy, feared across the hellscape and the human realm. Even that pompous lot up on high would mostly tremble before your wrath. But look at you. You're pathetic. Whining and bemoaning some brief fling you had with a mortal woman, some tawdry little tale you came up for yourself during your fall from grace. You disgust me. No. You disappoint me.'

Natsuo thought he noted on the face of Amaterasu, and perhaps even Susanoo, an apprehension at Enma's verbal attack. As if he was needlessly prodding a wasp's nest.

'Where are our shrines, Ōtakemaru? There are none. We have none. Eternally relegated to the dark pages of tales and tomes. Are you happy about that?'

'I won't repeat myself again oh great king.' Akihiro snarled, blood flushing through his body, expanding the muscles, tendons tightening. Everything felt as if it was about to explode.

'I care not for your repetition. I care for your understanding. I can give you a second chance. You can be my right hand. I will build shrines to us all and we can reign.'

'You have a shrine.'

The voice was small and light, barely audible through the crackling bravura and tense masculinity soaking into the surroundings. As if they had forgotten the existence of the human with the magic hammer, the giants all looked at Natsuo.

'Oh, it's you. The half-blood.'

Nastuo stomached the insult and didn't react. 'I said you have a shrine.'

'What?'

'Enno-ji temple.' An emotionless face from the King of Hell. 'Thirteenth century, in Kamakura. You have a shrine. There's even a statue of you. Has the same ugly, angry face you have here today. So you see, you aren't forgotten.' Natsuo hoped the knowledge may assuage Enma, perhaps make him see things differently. But of course, Natsuo was naive.

'Nice try boy. I know about Unkei's little statue. People go to see it, to gawk at it, to gawk at me. To mock. Not to venerate.' A deep sigh. 'This is why I hate humans.'

Suddenly, to the shock of all parties present, Susanoo, who had been prowling in the background getting steadily angrier, flew towards Amaterasu from behind, the tip of his blade leading the movement. The great queen of the heavens didn't have time to fully dodge her brother's attack and screamed when, despite her attempted evasion, the metal plunged through her left arm spraying bright ruby blood.

In an instant Natsuo's father had left his side, on instinct, and hurtled towards Susanoo. He was met mid-leap by Enma whose blade he only just managed to avoid through some acrobatic contortions. He slid to a stop on all fours, poised like a wild dog, snarling teeth.

So this is it then...

The father he had only just reunited with against the King of Hell, whilst the high goddess stood injured and bleeding, her light fading before the bloodlust-face of her mad brother.

This is the end...

A throb. A hum. A weight.

The hammer in his hand, reminding him of its presence.

Use me. Swing me. Strike me.

With Akihiro off to the side and ready, Enma immediately turned his attention to the now-wounded Amaterasu, deciding to make the most of this window to gain the upper hand.

Between his power and the might of Susanoo this was the best chance he had to rid himself of his main obstacle. Amaterasu, still bleeding heavily out of her arm, was now to be seen fending off the attacks of both Enma and Susanoo.

As if it were a sign to the generals and monsters of the underworld, the dark forces and twisted beings slid back out from where they had been hiding, waiting to see how the battle would go. War resumed. Natsuo's father leapt to Amaterasu's defence, creating a four-way melee of swords, spears, claws and fangs.

Natsuo had recently regained his mother, though he recognised she may be gone. Some cruel twist of fate had replaced his mother with his father. But that father with whom he had embraced for the first time in well over a decade, was now at risk of being taken from him too. And if he lost his father, what would he have left?

Again, the hammer throbbed in his hand, power waiting to be unleashed. Wanting to act.

The image of his father, an enormous, muscular, crimson-skinned barbarian wrestling with the god of the tempests, trying to put himself to use against the now dimmed brilliance of the high goddess, as she parried blows from the ruler of Jigoku. They looked, at least in Natsuo's eyes, like they were losing that fight.

The battle sensed it too. The rebelling yōkai, the goblins and the demons, smelled the change in the air. They knew they just had to hold out a little longer, to throw their grotesque bodies at the light beams, blades and energy pulses just long enough until the head of Amaterasu was held aloft for all to see.

Kill the leader, take the win.

The vibrations were rippling out of the hammer through Natsuo's hand, tingling his fingers and shaking his bones.

Emotion.

It needed emotion.

Don't think.

Don't attack or defend.

Just feel.

'Stop this!' Waves of energy, sound at its most tangible, washed away from Natsuo. The men and the monsters, the gods and the devils, all stopped and clutched their heads as if in great pain. Some fell to their knees. It passed in an instant but the clarion call from the young man was enough to halt everything. 'Just stop.'

They did stop. The gods observed Natsuo with a mixture of surprise, disgust and a hint of trepidation. The power required to do what Natsuo just did was not one that should be in the hands of a mortal.

'Natsuo-kun,' said Amaterasu, clutching her arm and breathing heavily.

'No!' he fired back.

Enma cooed. 'Listen here boy, just —'

'No! Shut up. Just shut up!' Natsuo was seething with anger. 'I'm sick of all this. I'm sick of you; all of you.'

'Son.'

'No, Dad. I'm sorry; but no.' Natsuo's shoulders sagged a little and he exhaled deeply. 'We don't need you. Any of you. And you can't seem to see that.'

Everything had been bottling up inside Natsuo these last few weeks. Years of living alone had turned into the greatest adventure of his life. For a time, he had enjoyed it. He had felt like finally he was living. A thirty-year old man discovering what it was to be alive. Then he had reunited with his mother, and then, against all odds, his father, summoned as he had been from the depths of hell.

But everything had soured. Fear and pain had set in. They had taken his mother from him and now his father was at risk too. The thrill had turned into threat. Too much had been placed on his shoulders. And now the sad truth of the gods, quarrelling with each other as they were, in-fighting and backstabbing in front of him, power their only goal, was utterly apparent.

'You need us...'

'You dare talk to the gods in this way?' Susanoo's rage frothed up, affronted as he was by the disrespect.

'Hah! See? I hate humans...' The words slithering out of Enma's mouth.

'Half-human,' Natsuo said proudly, looking at his father, who approached his son and stood behind him. 'If only people knew what you were like, they'd despise you. Not love you. This is not the way to get people's belief or respect. Brute force. No-one ever really loves a dictator. They just say they do out of fear. It's always easy to hail the leader when the alternative is death. And dictators don't last.'

'Dear boy.' Amaterasu.

'No, I'm sorry. Look at you two. You're fighting your brother. He's worse, but are you any better? What did you do that it has all come down to this? Family against family. My father fell in love with a human woman, and I was born. That's love. That's belief. Yours is a charade. "Do you or do you not believe?" Well fine. Great. But to what end? What's the point? Gods yeah, sure, but you're a family.' The word family made Natsuo pause momentarily. 'A sad, pathetic, putrid family full of deceit. Well good for you. But that's not our fault. Why do we have to be involved?'

'Power, Natsuo,' Enma replied, suddenly serious. 'Power.'

'Strangely, great king, I understand you the most. In reality you are a sad little man. Us humans have seen your like before. All over history angry men have overcome their puniness through conquest and murder. You even have the facial hair to fit the profile.' Natsuo was content to let all these feelings out. The fear had withered away. He felt righteous and calm. With the hammer in his grasp and his father at his side he was unbeatable.

'The great king of the netherworld being swayed by a human child.' Susanoo said, his face full of snark.

'Again, not human,' said Natsuo, turning to Susanoo.

'A corruption...' The god of the tempest looked upon Natsuo's father. The great oni. The terrible violence. The general of hell itself, standing behind this little halfling, his great right hand resting protectively on his son's shoulder. It was an image that quelled him slightly. A connection between the realms not based on power or rule. A father and his son. He huffed angrily and turned away.

'It is not the first time brother and it shall not be the last.' Amaterasu's light strengthened and she smiled at Natsuo. 'Love always conquers everything. You should know this. Do you not remember the whole reason you wielded this very sword to slay the Yamata no Orochi serpent?' Amaterasu turned to Natsuo and his father, though it was clear her words were for her brother. 'To save the beautiful Kushinadahime. A wife, a mother, a beloved.' Susanoo deflated and drifted away, his anger simmered and then seemingly gave up. As if the whole moment, the whole plan, was a momentary lapse in judgement, a brief angry flash in the pan idea that he was now seemingly done with.

Natsuo marvelled at the fickleness. Just some moments ago he had tried to point blank murder his sister, and now, as if it had meant nothing, he had moved on.

Gods...

Enma seemed to be getting bored, restless and angry. He was pouting and the grip he had round the hilt of his sword was tight, his massive knuckles white.

'Love,' the goddess queen continued. 'A concept you know nothing about great king of Jigoku.'

'I will take what is owed to me.' Enma, it seemed, was not done. He spun round the spear and, turned away from the baiting Amaterasu, instead leapt towards Natsuo, blade aloft. In the same instant Natsuo's father, quick as lightning, moved to put himself in harm's way. He pushed Natsuo out of the way, but not before receiving a deep cut to his chest as the spear slid across his torso.

He landed, clutching at the gash and wincing as dark purple ooze appeared from a weeping ravine in his skin. A vast mound of earth slammed into the ground behind him as the amenonuhoko spear flung new land into existence.

The great oni regrouped, growled and bore his claws, leaping at Enma. He managed to parry the great king's sword and was even able to shred and tear at his robes. But he had been slowed by the injury.

'Natsuo...you must flee.'

Enma saw fear in the oni's eye. A fear not for his own life, but the fear a parent shows when their pup is at risk. This seemed to fuel him; Enma seemed to be delighting in the situation.

Avoiding the slashing talons of Ōtakemaru, Enma ducked, swirled and swept his sword and spear around him as he spun. He passed under swiping arms and, carrying the trailing blade low, slid sharpened metal across the ankle-tendons of Ōtakemaru's left foot. Natsuo's father fell to his knees in a heap of muscles and blood and screams.

Natsuo was still on the ground. He had been frozen in place, unbelievingly looking on as his demon-form father fought and seemingly lost against the king of the underworld.

Enma went behind Ōtakemaru, stuck the spear into the ground and took a bunch of his hair tightly in his free hand. He then brought his sword up in a killing, downward position. An execution.

'You shall meddle no more, boy!' Enma seemed to be refining the position of the sword, pinpointing exactly where he intended to drive it down into the nape of the fallen oni. 'Give me the hammer, or your father will be the last of your family to go.'

NO, NO, NO...

'Your last chance.'

Catch 22. Rock and a hard place. Paradox. Tied hands and no right answers. He can only lose. Lose his father, lose his reality. He was stuck. He couldn't think. His brain was a mess of broken synapses all trying to make some form clarity in this muddied chaos before him. Where were Sōjōbō and Hage-tanuki? Fighting somewhere. Where was his mother? Why him? Why did everything boil down to him? His father. He'd just been reunited with his father...

'Your time's up, child.'

No, no, no...

Natsuo closed his eyes, felt the be-rubbled ground under his feet and clenched the hammer tight.

Chapter Eleven: Mono no aware
物の哀れ

The pathos of things.

The walls, the now familiar walls. The little groups, the makeshift cubicles, and the air of disaster. The hangar.

'Darling?'

As with every time he entered the building, Natsuo's little mother was there, wide-eyed and happy to see him. He embraced her.

'You're OK.' He was out of breath. 'What happened?'

'I was going to ask you that question. Ask if it was over.' She held him by the arms. 'One minute I was being held by those men in robes and then next minute I was here. Then on the radio, the TV went down you see, it spoke of giants fighting in Tokyo. And then, a while later, well now, you appeared. And...' Yui's voice trailed off as her gaze headed behind Natsuo. A man stood there in rags, cuts over his body and face, looking bashful and frozen.

'It can't be? Koibito...' She began breathing heavily. 'How can it...I don't believe...I don't understand.'

'It is.' Natsuo beamed. 'It's Dad.'

Yui Hirawa let out a cry, as if all the pain and sadness and loneliness of the last decade was flowing out of her and she grabbed Natsuo, slipping to the floor. Akihiro, weeping, limped over and held his wife. Natsuo, Yui Hirawa, and his father, clutching each other with the intensity that all families experience after a disaster. But this had the added element of love lost and found. Natsuo had his father back and his mother her husband.

The Japanese aren't a nation that wear their emotions on their sleeves. Natsuo as a young man always looked upon Italians and Americans with a mixture of curiosity and jealousy. At the drop of a hat, they would be crying, shouting, screaming, laughing, kissing. Whereas in Japan they were trained to keep their emotions to themselves.

He remembered reading about rui-katsu, tear-seekers, a practice where people are paid to help others, predominantly women, cry and let out their emotions. They called them Ikemeso Takkyubin, tear couriers.

Natsuo tried to think if he had ever really cried before he had stopped being a Hikikomori. However, when it rains it pours, and when the Japanese really need to cry, it puts other more casual everyday displays of grief to shame. A profound, deep offering of tears.

Here was a family that had collectively gone through so much.

A mother who, her hands tied by the love story she had created, had to witness her only son hide away from the world and then lose her husband to dark forces, ultimately finding herself alone, rattling around a big house that stank of family.

A father who, against his nature, against his roots and against all of hell, gave in to love and had it conquer him, forced his only child, a product of mixed breeding, into hiding and was then killed because of it, losing his son and forcing his wife into solitude.

And a son who, through no fault of his own, was brought into a world, into a situation of intoxicated ignorance and love-blind innocence, where he would be at threat, and was pushed into a wasted life by parents who he thought hated him, where a yōkai took hold of him like a parasite and fed off his misery and fear for years, and who would then spend weeks duelling with death itself before regaining everything and getting a second chance.

A second chance...

'Fine work, lad!' Hage-tanuki bounced in through the hangar door on his enormous testicles. His raccoon-face was bright, proud and victorious, though Natsuo could see the tiredness and war-stress in his eyes.

'My boy!' Sōjōbō followed, majestically dirtied and bloodied, his gleaming katana slung lazily over his shoulders like a Viking overlord after a great battle. So different from the ancient, wise old tengu of before. 'I don't know what you did, but it seems to have worked.' He nodded towards the hammer in Natsuo's hands. 'I don't want to cut this beautiful reunion short,' Sōjōbō bowed to Natsuo's parents, 'but if I may steal your son away just one last time we must go to Amaterasu and finish this.'

'Is Enma?'

'The Enma situation is dealt with. You dealt with it. We just need to hand over the tide jewels,' he patted the little bag around his hip, 'and that hammer you've got there, and we can all finally slumber quietly in our beds tonight.'

Natsuo paused a moment, seeing his parents in each other's arms and looking a mixture of proud confusion and sadness.

'Don't worry, Natsuo-kun. Hage-tanuki will stay here, the Bureau are around, and don't forget, despite his injuries, your father still is Ōtakemaru. Nothing will happen I can assure you. Come, Amaterasu will explain everything, such is her right as High Queen.'

There was no grandeur in the handing over of the sacred objects. Instead of a god, Natsuo merely saw a beaten-up and tired-looking yet still beautiful woman. Almost like some fairy queen, pure, but tainted by violence. He felt sorry for her noticing the face of someone wondering what the point of any of this was. Such a waste of time, of energy, of lives. But also, the countenance of somebody done. Finished. Aware that what needed to be done had been done.

'How you did it we don't really know,' she started after closing all objects in a large wooden chest, which sealed itself with beams of light and promptly disappeared; something which a year ago would have given Natsuo a panic-attack and now seemed utterly logical. 'Enma has been banished. You sent the great Enma Daiō to be locked away in Meido. A power that, despite the hammer's wish-granting capabilities, shouldn't have been possible.' She paused and smiled. 'Humans...love really does conquer.' A glow returned to her cheeks and Natsuo finally felt like he was in front of the elegant oden-cooking lady once again.

'My brother conceded. He is tempestuous and angry at times. But his rage is as quick to disappear as his love and passion is to appear. He had been whipped up into a sustained furore by Enma, who worked out how to manage his temperament to stop him exploding early on.'

'He tried to kill you.' The comment slipped out of Natsuo's mouth without him meaning to.

Once again a smile, 'This is but a scratch. We've always fought. This time was one of the worst, it's true. But as eternal beings we shall forget it and move on. He is my brother after all. He is not evil. He is wild, but he has the capacity for such good. It is just necessary to keep him on the side of the light. And with Susanoo calmed, Raijin and Fujin and the others returned to their posts with their tails between their legs. I love that expression.' A tiny chuckle. 'Ōkuninushi never made it out of his prison realm so that is one other piece of good news.

'That there is order, more or less, in the heavens however is one thing. Your human realm has changed forever. Well, maybe.' A pause like a doctor giving a stark diagnosis. 'The yōkai attacking have relented but that does not change the reality of what happened, what humans have seen, and what will be out in the ether. This is the first age, the technological age, where people have proof of yōkai that aren't just tall tales and whispers and paintings. You will have to live with the very present knowledge that these beings are among you, live alongside them. It is a new world order, so to speak.'

Natsuo hadn't had time to think ahead like that. He'd been living in the moment every day since he'd taken that first step out of his house in Kochi. Taking it every minute at a time. Every terrifying second. Now he was being offered a vision of the future that hadn't even crossed his mind.

'Or perhaps, given the element of surprise has gone, the magic gone, the yōkai may decide to return to their myths. Because what are they to humanity if they become commonplace features of your reality? Maybe what your world has just experienced will, after some generations, also be thought of as a fairytale, some absurd legend written, filmed, talked about, to amuse others in your tribe. Or perhaps everything has changed forever. Intrinsically. Folklore has finally made its long journey into reality, cancelling itself out. Nullifying the word.' She looked off to nowhere in particular. 'Only time, your time, will tell.'

'So it's not over...'

Sōjōbō looked at Natsuo, who seemed a little deflated, disappointed even.

'You expected a heroic end, like all the stories you've read?'

'Not with a bang, but with a whimper,' Natsuo said.

'What's that?'

'At school we had to read wartime poetry. A man called Eliot wrote that line. It just came into my head.'

A paternal timbre coated Sōjōbō's words, 'Through that blasted hammer you have saved everybody, do not forget that.'

'It's like those "she-woke-up-and-it-was-all-a-dream" stories. A cop out.' Natsuo was unfulfilled. 'I just swung with a feeling, not even a thought. And then it stopped. I guess I felt there should have been something grander, something more.'

'Natsuo,' Amaterasu interjected. 'Susanoo, the gods, the beings you've met along the way, even Enma himself, should thank you for that. You chose love, not fury. You could have got rid of them all. Got rid of us all. But some part of you wanted to keep the fairytales.'

'So what happens now?' Natsuo asked the tengu.

'Well. The good news is you can finally go back to your mother knowing that no adventure will wrench you away from her again. Mission accomplished, as they say.' Sōjōbō's forehead prickled up into lines indicating that the words he had to say next weren't quite so pleasing.

'I guess that means there's some bad news?'

'I shall be blunt and direct Natsuo-chan, as you deserve that much.' A sad smile widened through the bushy beard of the ancient creature. 'Your father can't stay. Not even if he wanted, or you desired it.'

Natsuo's mind started racing, his thoughts stumbling over the hurdles put up by that simple phrasing.

Can't stay...

'But the hammer?'

'The power you somehow unleashed to bring your father back into the human plane is beyond even my understanding. It shouldn't have been possible. The fact of the matter Natsuo is that order has to be restored. He wasn't just in hell. He was officially dead. And that can't be messed about with.' He sighed. 'There are laws Natsuo, a status quo that has to be maintained. You already saw Susanoo's meddling almost fused heaven and earth. That in itself could have spelled the unbalancing and end of all things. But we just can't bring back people from the dead.'

'But I did...'

'You did. But it can't be permanent. The gravity of hell will pull him back eventually regardless. Molecule by molecule. Over the next few days, as reality settles and the ordained order returns to its place, he will be taken back strip by strip. It would be far less painful to just say goodbye and allow him to return at once.' Sōjōbō's shoulders sagged. 'I am so very sorry.'

The fight had gone out of Natsuo. Deep down he felt he knew it. Happy endings didn't really exist in the real world. In the same way every bad situation had a silver lining, so did every happy moment have a vein of bittersweet running through it. Nothing was ever black or white.

Yin and yang...

Despite the news, Natsuo felt he knew what he needed to do.

'How long do I have?'

'Until the pain hits him, a couple of days at the most,' Amaterasu answered, her voice a mille-feuille of compassion and aloofness.

'Take me back now, please.'

After some surprisingly emotional goodbyes, during which Hage-tanuki cried immensely while rocking back and forth on his giant testicles, Abe no Seimei shook his hand so hard it hurt, and Sōjōbō smiled like Father Christmas, Natsuo had broken the news to his parents. They had taken it matter of factly. Perhaps the older you get the better you are able to deal with bad news, Natsuo thought to himself.

Taking public transport to the family home in Tosashimizu would have taken the better part of ten hours. Fortunately the ever-generous Mr Shi had overheard Natsuo and his parents planning their next steps and, after embracing everybody with over-the-top bear hugs, immediately offered to drive them. 'I'll get you there in less than six!'

Mr Shi would probably never understand how much his generosity really meant to the tired-looking men and little old lady in front of him. Three more hours with his father. Three more hours as a family.

Many people believe morality comes from a sacred book. This was, as far as Natsuo was concerned, absolute nonsense. He always thought that if you really needed a book written by some people centuries ago to tell you not to kill, not to steal and not to be cruel, then you probably weren't a very good person to begin with. And having met the gods, it had confirmed to him that they were certainly not the source of human values.

Through co-evolution with each other, the need for disparate communities to get along more often than destroy each other, a human altruism became the base model. Mr Shi didn't have to do what he was doing, but he believed it to be good. Scientists said morality and altruism were subconsciously selfish. Your genes knew that to help rather than hinder might, in the long run, turn out dividends for you further down the line.

Natsuo's idea was to do something he hadn't done since he was a teenager, a time when living in the moment was all he did, and everything was taken for granted: a family dinner. To be more precise, a final dinner.

They had driven fast on still rather empty roads, stopping only once in Aizumi to go to Wanwanken, a ramen restaurant that Mr Shi assured his passengers was the best place to have lunch en route.

He ordered Tokushima ramen for everyone: a thick brown gravy filled with noodles, bamboo, spring onions, bean sprouts and masses of folded pork. A raw egg was the added flourish, which half-poached in the heat of the broth. It tasted glorious.

After their lunch Yui and Akihiro passed out asleep in the back of the car, each head cradling the other, snoozing gently.

He felt it in his bones and his marrow as soon as he had arrived back in the hangar after the battle. He knew it was there. The family home, that old timber and beam stalwart whose typhoon-battered form had been enough to tear Natsuo from his solitude, was there, pristine as the day it had been built.

His mother had been ushered away during the storm evacuations of the summer and his father had died there as it was, so neither were to know the disaster that awaited that house; blasted as it was by the storms. Natsuo nudged his mother awake and nodded to the outside world. She smiled sleepily.

'When I came looking for you the building was a wreck. But look.'

Yui just grunted approvingly as if it were just another thing, and then tapped on Akihiro's leg to wake him. Natsuo's father looked upon the house, the small empty driveway, the bicycles leaning on the walls unlocked, through doe-eyed watery eyes.

Natsuo, now a man himself, saw his parents as small, old. Indeed, the last time he had been with them both he had been a scrawny teenager. He thought they looked like nostalgic characters that Miyazaki would draw, a late-night cigarette hanging off his bottom lip, ash falling onto the pencil lines.

Depositing his parents in the old house Natsuo headed off to the conbini to buy food for dinner. Now that he was no longer terrified to be outside, Natsuo noticed some of the smaller details of the neighbourhood. Things he'd ignored as a child that now he thought quite beautiful: the postcard-perfect entrance to the forest-shrouded Sugishima shrine — a torii gate with pristine rope, red paintwork and komainu each side; the cables that snaked their way along the walls and spidered over from building to building through the air, forming picturesque latticeworks and webs; the vending machines selling energy drinks, water, and cans of coffee that come out hot; air conditioning units standing freely on the road outside of buildings; the cars and vans, so shrunken and toy-looking compared to those of the rest of the world; hoses, buckets, potted plants, gas canisters, stuffed postboxes, all clinging to the sides of homes without a care in the world; little children, cute as buttons, clucking along in pairs, without adults, their square backpacks bobbing about just above their long socks; crusted, salt-washed walls making everything look weathered and hardy; a quietness to the clean roads, the only sound the mournful cry of the gulls, the hum of the vehicles and the ping of the supermarket doors and the welcoming call Irasshaimase!.

By the time Natsuo had returned to the house the sun was a fat, warm, jellied sphere melting into bruised clouds, bringing the slow summer night with it. Fronds of fire-red and mulberry were smudging around its descent as the moon began to wait its turn on the other side of the sky.

Perfect...

The low table was set with chopsticks, small ceramic plates and beer glasses when Natsuo entered, shuffling into slippers and calling out 'Tadaima', the call and response 'Okaeri'. He smiled, instantly transported back to his youth.

They were all playing their parts; performers on the stage. The play: a final dinner scene between the actors with their roles as dependable father, doting mother and perfect son. They were all quietly pretending it was just a normal meal though the veneer was thin and the truth lay heavy behind every move and glance.

The symbology was plain as day.

Natsuo poured sake out into his parents' small ochoko glasses from a large 1.8L bottle with a Chinese tiger on the front label. All three knew, though the words weren't stated, that the bottle would be empty by the end of the evening. The food Natsuo had bought was premium sushi: nigiri of fatty tuna belly, crystalline horse mackerel, deep orange salmon; sashimi of bluefin maguro, yellowtail and shrimp, served with freshly grated wasabi; a circular bamboo box packed tight with rice under a layer of soy-glazed *unagi*; and a small pot of pickled ginger to cleanse the palate.

It was funeral food.

Sat on their knees around the low table they ate quietly, delicately lifting the nigiri up, tilting them and touching just a part of the fish in the little saucer of soy sauce, enough so the umami would enhance the flavour of the flesh but not soak up into the rice. Then a sip of rice wine, bringing the cup up to the lips with both hands before someone took the initiative to take the bottle and fill up their neighbours and then finally themselves.

The conversation wouldn't flow. What was there to talk about?

How was the almost end of the world for you?

Isn't it nice that father is a demon back from the dead but now must return to the darkness?

Wasn't life easier when I was just a loner in my room?

Instead, it was sad polite smiles, grunts of appreciation at the quality of the food, *umai*, *oishii*, and nods at being poured more sake. What would words serve?

Natsuo's cheeks felt hot and his eyes prickled. Tears were knocking on the doors of his vision, threatening to come out in waves. He placed his chopsticks flat down in front of him, got slowly to his feet, walked over to his father, and simply put his arms around him. He felt the small frame of his father loosen in his embrace. Akihiro then wept, quietly and dignified. He finally had gotten to properly hug his son.

By the end of the dinner Yui was snoozing peacefully, laid out on a futon enjoying the effects of the sake. Natsuo was drunk and he knew it. A nice, cozy drunk, like a warm blanket. Emotions felt stronger and his mind was a little slow to catch up with his vision. His mother had done what she could, but his father and he had polished off the rest of the sake, and they were down to the last glass.

Outside the cicadas, that had been silenced by the constant rains and typhoons of the summer, were now creaking out their scratchy, rhythmic sonic pulse in the garden trees. The heat had returned with a vengeance, prickling the skin and teasing out sweat from every pour. It was a little cooler on the Shikoku coast, but after weeks of storms it felt like somebody had flipped a climatic switch.

Natsuo's father let out a hissing noise of assent, rubbing the nape of his neck with a brown cloth and nodding whilst staring, unfocused, at the gently snoring Yui.

'Thank you for this, my boy. I spent an age staring at dark brown walls, listening to the sounds of my home, sounds I had come to hate. Screams and chains and ironwork. Of my once compatriots, even friends, murdering and killing and laughing.' He paused as his gaze slowly drifted up to meet his son's. 'I had come to love the sounds of birdsong, your mother humming to herself, even the buzz of passing cars. Everything here seemed so much calmer. And I thought of you, the son I bore, the son I pushed away.' He sipped his sake. 'Centuries. I lived for centuries and did so many bad things. Your mother was the first time I'd known true happiness, and you were the one good thing I did. The first time I made something instead of ripping it apart. I want you to know that. I may have ruined it, may have broken your life, but you were the best of it. And every time you ignored us, every time you crept out around the house thinking we couldn't hear you, it broke whatever was left of my heart. And now, look at you. Just look at you.' He wiped his eyes with his free arm. 'You turned from sweet little boy to unwitting Hikikomori to saviour of the damn world.' His tears blubbed into a proud laugh. 'All thanks to me.'

Natsuo, whose face was now shining, also laughed.

'You know otousan, I secretly think, in some strange way, those thirteen years shut away in the house, somehow got distilled, bottled up, and became a kind of potion, a social potion, which when I took it, helped me find my new way. All those manga and anime, all those adventures I was digesting and collecting. They primed me. As if I was the only person who could have done it and that our family's story was the only way it could have gone.'

They clinked their glasses together and finished the sake.

'Come. Let's sit in the garden. Go on, I'll follow you out.'

Natsuo headed into their little back yard and unfolded two wooden deck chairs. The night was warm, and the sky was a crystal-clear explosion of stars and moonlight. His father followed him out with two glasses and a bottle.

'More booze?'

'Hah,' exhaled Akihiro, slumping himself down heavily into the chair. 'Well, I've thought about this moment, and this is something special.'

'Whisky?' Natsuo said, turning the bottle of amber over in his hands. '"Young Seven"...'

'Limited release, from Nisshin Shurui. They make sake and shochu over in Tokushima. Good stuff. But they had a go at whisky. Nobody bought it, they barely publicised it, no idea how to, but it was amazing. I got a few bottles back in the day when my friend told me they had made it. I kept a bottle back. The idea was to drink it with you when you were eighteen. But of course, when you were eighteen...'

'Well, come on then, old man.'

An approving grunt. Akihiro popped the cork stopper and sloshed out two large pours of the local whisky.

'Mmm,' he purred. 'Smell that? Toasted vanilla, sweet cereal and cinnamon apple.' Natsuo smelled it and winced, causing his father to chuckle knowingly. 'And that'll be the 45% alcohol. Don't sniff too deep.'

'It's nice.'

'It is,' answered his father, sighing mournfully. 'I'll miss this. The little human moments. Where I'm from nobody sits out under the stars.'

'I met a strange creature that made sake in a valley of meteors.'

'You met Hozaki! That old haradashi is legendary. I used to drink gallons of his stuff after a fight. It is a shame I shan't taste his brews again.'

A gentle and soft silence settled between the two men and they were left with the scratching of the cicadas and the rustling leaves of the bushes. Then a light; a warm glowing light. A cockerel with a bright red comb and fine scarlet and green plumage appeared on the fence, its light blue tail feathers quivering. It stared at Natsuo and Akihiro. As it squawked orange fire licked out of its beak, its head twitched fretfully, and it flew away.

'How about that...'

'Basan.'

'I've seen one before,' Natsuo smiled. 'It was the night before my birthday, and I was sleeping in a temple. Can you imagine?'

His father laughed-grunted.

'They eat charred wood and embers, you know,' Akihiro said, straining tipsily, as he tried to call up distant facts from the crevices of his mind. 'And they usually stay clear of humans. So I guess this is good luck.'

'Though I should imagine this might be the norm from now on.' Mused Natsuo. 'Yōkai showing up here and there, becoming part of the daily humdrum of life.'

'I should think so. At least for your lifetime.'

'My brain is too fuzzy to think about the new world order awaiting us. That's for tomorrow. There's always a tomorrow...'

Again, the comfortable whisky-soaked blanket of silence was pulled over father and son for a while; their last conversation occurring in small random bursts as each fought to stay awake in the sultry night air.

'Tomorrow, I want you to say this to your mother.' Akihiro creaked onto his side so he could look directly into Natsuo's eyes. 'Itai doushin. Okay? Itai doushin, that's what you need to tell her.'

'Two bodies, one heart.'

'Sou desu.' And he smiled a ruddy-cheeked happy smile and fell back into position on the deck chair. 'Kampai.' They brought their glasses together and sipped, watching the stars twinkle in the eastern sky whilst the white noise fuzz of the summer cicadas danced in their ears.

Akihiro then winced suddenly, his eyes scrunching in on themselves, and a pained moan slid out against his will. His free arm instinctively covered his stomach.

'Are you OK?'

'Yes, yes...'

They both knew what was happening. What was starting. The cicadas clicked, the stars continued to sparkle and the air flirted with a breeze.

The sound of someone being punched in the gut, a guttural groan. His father coughed, and crimson pearls landed in his whisky, while blood seeped out the side of his mouth like a scarlet tear.

'Otousan...'

'I think we had better call it a night.'

Natsuo thought about fighting back, about staying, remaining in the chair next to father. But then he thought better of it. The only result would be horror.

'Tsss, ah!' His father looked at his hand. A scabrous red patch appeared on the centre of his palm. It was as if someone had taken a pairing knife to his flesh and flicked off a chunk of meat. It soon swelled pink to red to leaking with blood. 'Please, son...'

Natsuo looked into his father's eyes and understood everything. To have his child watch him wrenched from reality piece by piece would be torture for the both of them. Getting to his feet, Natsuo finished his whisky, and simply squeezed his father's shoulder and briefly looked into his eyes.

The cries pained Natsuo right to his core, his bones and his marrow. It seemed like every few minutes, few moments, a deathly moan would drift in from the garden. He couldn't help but think of those sad scenes from nature documentaries; the last groans of some elephant or wildebeest, left by the herd to die after its ankle broke.

And each time he heard his father cry and whelp he would bury his face more into his pillow and duvet until it was wet with tears, trying to disappear inside the tatami mat, trying not to think about his organs, his muscles and meat, his very essence, being ripped away bit by bit.

He hoped, if hoped was the right word, that it would be quiet and unseen; like a dandelion losing its grey seeds to the wind. Instead, the death throes were deep and broke Natsuo's heart again and again and again.

He didn't know at what exact point during the night, or the morning, he finally fell asleep, the power of slumber managing to overtake the waking nightmare that was his father's demise, but when Natsuo came to in the morning, with the fat summer sun humming into the sky as white-throated needletails and leaf warblers flittered and twittered above, he noticed his father was no longer in the chair as he sat on the veranda looking out at the garden.

When he rubbed his eyes and got to his be-slippered feet there was also the unmistakable sound of seagulls as well as the very unmistakable presence of a hangover.

'*Ohaio*!' called his mother from the living room, the sliding doors fully opening onto the veranda and the garden.

'Morning, Mother.'

'Your father?'

'Is he not inside?'

Why ask? You know he's not...

She shook her head and Natsuo looked at the chair. Locking eyes again with his mother they both understood. They shared a quiet breakfast of steamed rice, omelette and *umeboshi*, as well as some melonpan that Yui had picked up the day before.

A mother had lost, again, her husband, and a son had lost, again, his father. But this time it didn't hurt so much. This time it was bittersweet. Natsuo felt closure, that he finally got to meet the man that Ōtakemaru had given up being a demon to be.

His life as a Hikikomori was officially over; that much was true. And, despite the madness and chaos of recent months, he felt now, in his thirtieth year, that he was finally able to start living the life his parents had given him.

As Natsuo bit into the sweet cantaloupe-shaped buns he looked at his mum, gracefully sipping at a cup of homemade coffee.

'Okaasan...' She looked up and smiled expectantly. 'It all begins now.'

Chapter Twelve: Ketsuron
結論

Conclusion.

He washed his hands, purifying both the left and right with care, before filing up the small pail and walking up into the forest of stone pillars. He was followed by a shuffling old lady, her hands clasped in front of her as she looked at the ground. Arriving at the family gravestone they bowed and joined their hands in prayer. Religion wasn't really the point; it was about respect and remembrance. Another small bow.

Slowly and methodically, he used the ladle to bring up water to the top of the grave pillar and poured it over, bit by bit washing and cleansing every part of the inscribed granite. The Buddhist names of his ancestors, on one family side at least, dripping and gleaming, droplets hanging off the edge of kanjis before giving in to gravity and zig zagging down the rock to the earth below.

After he finished washing, the old lady took out a small bottle of sake, some onigiri and chocolate and placed them together with a small bouquet of Chrysanthemum at the base of the grave.

The man then lit a candle and some incense and the two once again brought their hands together, closed their eyes, and stood in silence a while.

The ritual visiting of the family grave, *ohakamairi*, was a time to think about past generations and send souls off to their final resting place. Natsuo wondered how his mother's ancestors would feel about being joined by a demon.

'I hope Father is at peace.'

Yui squeezed his arm and then mother and son left the cemetery, heading into town to see the festivities of this year's Obon festival.

The last two summers had been free of typhoons and life was adjusting to its new reality. A few days after his thirty-second birthday Natsuo had nonetheless decided to restock the Tosashimizu home with a typhoon survival kit. Just in case. Perhaps more than anyone in Japan, he would need a little more time to let the events of back then just blow over or be considered normal.

It was amazing how quickly humanity could adapt. It takes just one pandemic and countries all over the world start to wear masks as a daily habit, almost forgetting the times when they didn't. One hijacked plane and the prohibition of liquids and the removal of shoes just becomes another part of a process.

The appearance of fabled beasts also becomes commonplace. Like going on the same big rollercoaster three times in a row; it loses its thrill as it becomes familiar.

In the old town streets and on the little fisherman houses lanterns had been strung out. Later in the evening the lanes would glow warm orange. Families would release candle-lit lantern floats out into the bay under the young moonlight and people would dance through the streets in kimonos. Then, each family would drink sake into the night and sing and laugh and toast to their forebears.

Natsuo and his mother, being the sole remnants of their family heritage, decided to hold a more relaxed and personal affair; lighting a small bonfire in the garden and enjoying a summer dinner of cold somen noodles with a soy sauce-wasabi dipping sauce, some ayu set up on makeshift wooden stick-skewers stuck into the garden and leaning over the embers to grill, and kakigori shaved ice smothered in strawberry syrup.

'Mmm, umai!'

'You like the sweetfish?'

'It's great. Reminds me of when I was really little.' Natsuo was delicately nibbling the meaty grilled flesh off the fish bones.

'Masaru-san; he always gets the best ones. I've been buying from him since before you were born. He must be older than me! He used to keep some of the catch aside for me, knowing I'd be passing by on Saturday mornings. Now he texts me on my mobile phone, can you believe it!' She clucked like a contented hen before picking at a little plate of crunchy summer pickles.

The unfinished bottle of Lucky Seven whisky sat on the trestle table as a silent reminder.

'Why don't you finish it?' Yui asked softly. 'I know it reminds you of him, but why not drink it?'

'I will. I probably will in time. Maybe a sip here and a sip here. But it's not just a reminder; it's a physical representation of our last moment together.' Natsuo smiled at his mother. 'Also, who knows, maybe one day he and I will finish it together. Stranger things have happened.'

In the years after the event Natsuo had reconnected with the man from Kochi who had tried to help coax Hikikomori out of their cages with the alluring temptation of oranges and mochi. He had since learned the man was called Eiji, whose meaning 'eternal peace', Natsuo thought quite apt.

When they had met for the second time, the first being back when Natsuo was a recluse, Eiji had joked about his surname being a problem, Ezaki. Eiji Ezaki was a mask-wearing professional wrestler whose stage name was Hayabusa, 'Falcon'. As a consequence, for the last twenty years Eiji had been called 'the falcon' by his friends. He used this fact as part of his way of starting conversations with the Hikikomori; given the likelihood that they watched wrestling in their homes.

'I remember you,' Eiji had said the day Natsuo, a thirty-two-year-old man, entered the recluse centre with a bag of oranges.

'You do?'

'I never forget a face.' He smiled. 'Even less likely to if it's one I've failed.'

Natsuo was a thirty-two-year-old man. One with no job and little prospects on paper. One who had spent his adult life sponging off his ageing parents, hidden away in his room, selfish and clueless to his actions. A universe of one. Having broken that cycle, he intended to help others.

His actions in Tokyo hadn't gone unnoticed. The power of the modern era of phones and the internet, had meant that, amongst all the monstrous faces and celestial beings, his human Japanese features had stood out. One man against the masses.

Natsuo was quickly able to set himself up a charity organisation and had government offices and companies, for glory or altruism — he didn't care which — falling over themselves to shower him with grants and free money.

There were times when the last tendrils of his Hikikomori existence still licked at his soul when he was called upon to talk to groups, to speak with salarymen, needing to convince and cajole. These were skills he never honed. But he managed, and within the first year after the incident, founded “Hikikomoranai” with its Yin-Yang logo of a tengu and a tanuki.

His charity was based out of Takamatsu, on the Sea of Japan, on the northern part of his island, but he still lived in the Kochi house. He quipped to his mother that he felt it high time he made use of the rest of the rooms. She had moved in with him and this time he doted over her; though she refused to let him cook.

'Once a month you can order us a pizza.'

Despite the earlier dark thoughts he had attributed to his Hikikomori house, vowing never to be back there, pragmatism easily won out. It was now a house of light. It smelled clean, he bought perfume sticks and always burned incense at the weekend. The house in Tosashimizu became the weekend away holiday home. Status quo.

Another quirk of fate and good fortune also fell in Natsuo's lap in the spring following what the papers had called the “Battle for the Nation”. An award ceremony for 'Outstanding Contributions to Local Society' in Osaka. He had found himself in a group of seven other recipients who were, in his eyes anyway, far more impressive than he.

I'm not even from Osaka, he had thought to himself.

A local priest in Kimino who had sheltered a whole busload of children during the typhoons.

The chief doctor of a hospital in Amagasaki who had set up a free clinic in the local sports stadium.

A lady from Kaminotaishi who prepared bento boxes and packed meals for elderly people living alone and who delivered them herself.

The owner of the Orix Theater in downtown Osaka who offered free concerts and musicals to anyone wanting diversion during the leisure-bereft summer months.

An owner of a construction company in the midst of a large project who paid his employees double to make them stay home and stay safe.

A chef in Kobe who made his way through the middle of a typhoon to help a farmer collect his prized cattle worth millions of yen.

A woman in Yoshino who took it upon herself every day to spend her free hours as a freelance aid-giver to anyone in need in the local mountain villages.

And Natsuo, who felt like he didn't deserve to be there.

The woman handing out the award stood out for two reasons. Firstly, she was a beacon of warmth and humanity in a sea of suits and bespectacled officials.

Secondly, because Natsuo knew very well who she was: Machiko Satonaka, one of the most important, influential and forward-thinking *mangaka* in the country; especially for girls and marginalised groups.

Natsuo had read most of her works, with a special fondness for the manga *Tomorrow Will Shine* and *Constellation of the Hunter.* The frog in his throat and the explosion of butterflies took a while to subside but her calm nature soon put him at ease. She was in her seventies and acted with the grace of someone contented with their lot and, perhaps, happy to have nothing pressing left to do.

'Natsuo-san.' She had approached him at the canapé social after the ceremony. 'I see in your story something for me to draw.'

A year later and the upcoming announcement of the new manga *Hikikomori* from the Kodansha award-winning author would be hitting the shelves by Christmas. Machiuko had visited him many times to both his house in Kochi and the family home in Tosashimizu, also with a notebook and soft pencils. She wanted as much detail as possible. Not just what he saw, what he lived through, where he went and what he ate. But the inner turmoil. She wanted this to be an important work, something meaningful, as well as a piece of artistic entertainment.

Natsuo often mused on the irony that his now whirlwind life had itself started with a summer filled with whirlwinds of a different kind.

The green was almost unreal. The saturation turned up to the max. The grass an artist would paint as if commissioned to create the Japanese idyll. The summer rice paddies had recovered from the storms of two years ago and were bursting with excess life.

The flooded fields shimmered between the leaves. An orderly curated marshland. Little birds whipped through the air catching the damselflies and fireflies that were dancing as dusk drew near.

Laughter and childish screeches ricocheted over the paddies followed by the cries of an angry farmer. The local kids were chasing each other about, splashing through the rice crops, stirring up the bugs and pestering the villagers. However, it was still nice to hear the squeals of happy youth.

But it was when you paid attention to the finer details that you realised some of the gallivanting young people were claw-toed boys with one eye, lolling tongues and little trays of tofu. Tōfu-kozō.

The young were always the quickest in accepting the different and strange as normal.

Kids also love tofu.

A strange balance had been created in the world since the rupture. The first thing was that the denizens of both heaven and hell returned to their realms. However, the yōkai worked in the shadows of the middle-world. Some had disappeared, feeling their role defunct now. The element of otherworldly surprise gone. Others seemed to take to living alongside humanity peacefully. Enjoying their new-found freedom, as shaky as it was.

The mischievous kappa and kawatarō of the rivers, as well as the rare otter-like kawauso, had continued their tricks, but had found themselves becoming symbols of nature preservation, humans treating them as they would other endangered species. They became logos and mascots for eco-friendly groups. No longer unknowable monsters.

The last era when the yōkai were out in such numbers was one of arrows and swords, of wooden houses, when the capital was called Edo and other countries functionally didn't exist for the people of Japan. Now was a time of technology, a world online, guns and drones.

Things like magic and monsters held not the same power as before. If you were to come across a mukade centipede, a Sasquatche-esque ijū, or were unlucky enough to stumble upon the cave of the tsuchigumo earth spider, the likely next response was to call pest control, not live in fear and create fables. Strange and beautiful women with long taloned hair beckoning men to their deaths like sirens or the futakuchi onna with ravenous chomping mouths hiding under prehensile hair on the back of their heads were more likely to have themselves reported to the local koban police boxes than strike utter fear and myth into their prey.

The larger and more destructive yōkai were increasingly finding themselves ousted by the military. Oni, Godzilla-shaped hōnengyo, harmful roaming giants called hitotsume ōnyūdō, strange one-eyed, one-horned, red-headed demons with terrifying serrated grins called shunobon, all had their claws and their teeth, but recoiled in the presence of Howa Type 20 assault rifles, Sumitomo MINIMI 5.56mm machine guns and, if needed, Type 10 battle tanks.

Contrary to what Natsuo expected, the sudden appearance of yōkai in the world actually helped the country's Hikikomori situation. People who had been shut up away from the world for years suddenly had their childish, fantasist wonder awakened. All the myths that had filled their eyes and heads. All that was printed and animated. It was coming to life. The modern era had documented at length the concept of 'fear of missing out', something that rarely bothered the shutaways. But it did now.

Whether it was destructive or productive, many people were leaving their homes in search of contact. Natsuo used this to his advantage when helping Hikikomori going through exactly what he had.

In turn those recluses looked to Natsuo as a beacon of hope, an ideal, a goal. Knowing what he had been through, how he had lived, and seeing themselves in him, it spurred them on.

We could save the world. We could have adventures. We could be the heroes of our own stories.

The Floating World woodblocks of centuries past found their images a reality. As annoying as it was, it would no longer be considered uncommon for an old pair of unloved slippers to sprout eyes and legs and bounce out of the house.

Interestingly this encouraged the average person to take more care of their belongings. Some out of fear that they would awaken to see their pots and pans dancing about the kitchen, but also partly because they got the message that this was only a possibility if and when one's unwanted items were badly treated and forgotten.

The stories and morals attached to the ideas behind the yōkai were starting to rub off on the world.

The ukiyo-e of today were the Instagram artists and the online forum communities. This new world would create the images and pieces of art that in centuries' time might also be looked upon as whimsical fantasies of days long past. How then would the world of the future account for the videos and the photos, selfies and TikToks?

Only time would tell.

Another sighting today of the Akaei. The titanic island-sized fish was spotted off the northern coast of Hokkaido. It surfaced next to Rishiri-tō and for a while just remained there looking at the volcanic island. Locals came out to stare and take photos. Then, a couple of hours later, it sank back beneath the waters. In other news, wagyu kudan. Can we really eat yōkai or is it –.

Natsuo turned off the television. He was sat in the Kochi house living room with a beer and a pizza. An accidental homage to his days as a Hikikomori. This time however it wasn't fast food delivery pizza through a faceless transaction. He had picked up a Margarita from Pizzeria Loredana, his new favourite, as well as a pack of Italian lagers, and was enjoying a light-filled late summer evening while his mother was fast asleep upstairs. A far cry from the dim and fetid days of yesteryear.

It had taken thirteen years of being a recluse and a couple more years after the events in Meido, Osaka and Tokyo, to finally feel some form of peace. That peace was him sitting on his old sofa in an Akira t-shirt, grey jogging bottoms and sporting a two-day old shadow on his face.

On the cushion next to him lay the pre-release copy of the *Hikikomori* manga. He had urged Machiko to stay away from the classic, handsome hero features so commonplace in most comics. He wanted to look normal, common, everyday. Like himself. Not the perfectly coiffed, spiky-haired protagonist with the big eyes. It needed to be real.

The irony of the word “real” was not lost on him as he flicked through the pages seeing images of flying tanuki, fighting gods, demons and monsters in neat ink lines.

The first cooling tongues of the October autumn had begun to lick the heat off the days as summer yielded finally to easier daytimes and more comfortable nights. Natsuo intended to enjoy his weekend, as for the first time in his life he found himself actually busy. Monday to Friday his phone was aflame with texts and emails. The weekends were for living. Perhaps he'd go hiking in the trails on Mt Miune or maybe he would finally get around to visiting the relaxing hot black sands of Kagoshima.

His phone pinged.

Natsuo had his mobile on mute and his messages set to dormant on the weekends. It was automatic. So how had a message come through?

It was a name he hadn't thought about for a while. Not since back then.

Abe no Seimei:

Natsuo-san. You are well, I trust. You seem to be. Forgive the intrusion. But we may need your help again. Something has...come up. Please write back at your earliest convenience. It is a mission that would do well with your involvement.

Mission. Help. Abe.

Natsuo sighed deeply and closed his eyes. He thought about his elderly mother, his charity, his upcoming comic appearance. He enjoyed the last few bites of the pizza and looked at his bottle of beer, stood up, stretched and rubbed his neck.

Kssk!

He finished the half bottle of Moretti and picked up his phone.

Dearest Abe...

Owari
終り

The End.

Acknowledgements

There are a couple people who deserve some thanks, as writing a book is rarely a solo endeavour unless you are disgracefully talented or every so slightly egomaniacal.

To my great friends Fabio and Heather and my girlfriend Laura for reading the first drafts.

Fabio for his brutal humour, devil in the detail attention and eye for spotting grammatical errors.

Heather for her teacher's vision, clinical brilliance and colourful Post-it notes.

Laura, both for reading it and putting up with me blathering on about it and either whinging or bouncing ideas off her whether she liked it or not.

To my Japanese teacher Nao for helping me with language points even past the point I had stopped classes. He is himself a class act and with whom I one day hope to retake the linguistic reins.

And, I guess, thanks to Japan, for being bonkers and brilliant.

Glossary

Ame - rain
Amenonuhoko - legendary bejewelled land-forming spear
Anime - literally, Japanese animation
Anoo... - Um...
Arigato (gozaimasu) - thank you (very much)
Butsudan - family memorial shrine found in the home
Chaya - traditional tea house
Chirashi - bowl of rice usually covered in sashimi and vegetables
Chotto mate - wait a moment
Chozuya - ceremonial hand cleaning area at a temple
Daijoubu - it's fine
Dashi - stock, for soups and various dishes, usually with ingredients like soy sauce, mirin etc
Dōzo - multi use word, can mean 'there you go', 'please', 'after you'
Ganbatte! - a popular exclamation of encouragement
Genkan - small entrance area to a house for removal of shoes
Geigi - another word for geisha, often used in the provinces
Geiko - west Japan term for geisha, especially in Kanazawa and Kyoto
Hafu - Japanese mixed race person, literally 'half'
Hajimemashite yoroshiku onegaishimasu - typical polite introductory greeting similar to 'nice to meet you'
Hai - yes
Haikyo - abandoned buildings
Hanami - cherry blossom viewing festival
Happi - traditional robe shirt, prevalent in festivals and restaurants
Hiragana - Japanese phonetic script
Honjozo - style of sake that also includes distilled alcohol during production
Hyakki yagyō - night parade of a hundred demons
Ie - no
Ijime - bullying
Ikai - the spirit world
Irasshaimase! - a chant of welcome when you enter a shop or business

Irezumi - traditional Japanese tattooing. Note: in Japan tattoos are often connected to the idea of yakuza, with many bathing areas prohibiting entry to anyone with body ink
Irori - a sunken hearth usually located in the centre of the main living room around which people can cook and eat and keep themselves warm
Itadakimasu - phrase said before eating, denoting respect to the food and the cook
Itako - shamanistic medium
Jigoku - hell
Junmai - sake only made from rice, water, and koji
Kami - gods
Kanji - traditional Japanese script, based off logographic Chinese symbols
Katakana - Japanese script for loan words and foreign imported language
Katsuoboshi - dried tuna flakes
Kijin - a particularly large and fierce demon or spirit
Kirei - beautiful
Kitsune - Japanese fox spirits
Kobun - apprentices in a Yakuza family
Koji - a green spore used in sake production
Komainu - lion-dog statues found at the entrance to religious complexes
Konbanwa - good evening
Kondo - main hall at a temple
Konjac/konnyaku - a type of yam often to make jelly or a semi-solid gel used in cooking
Koshiki - traditional wooden rice cooker used in sake production
Koshu - aged sake
Kudasai - please
Kura - sake brewery
Kusanagi-no-Tsurugi - legendary sword
Kuso! - shit!
Manga - Japanese comics and graphic novels

Mangaka - manga artist or writer
Matcha - Japanese green tea
Matsuri - festival
Meido - afterlife or purgatory
Mirin - a form of sweetened cooking sake
Miso - a fermented bean paste commonly used to make miso soup
Mochi - squishy, pounded rice cakes
Mochiron - of course
Nama - fresh, unpasteurised sake
Namahage - demon popular for scaring kids into being well behaved
Ne? - right?
Neko - cat
Nihonshu - actual name for 'sake', translates as 'Japanese alcohol'
Obaachan - grandmother
Obon - August festival honouring the spirits of one's ancestors
Ofuro - tall, sit-in Japanese bath tub
Ohaio gozaimasu! - good morning!
Ohakamairi - the ritual visiting and tending to family graves
Oishii/umai - tasty/delicious
Okaasan *diminiutive okan - mother
Okaeri! - welcome home, response to tadaima
Okonomyaki - fried, multi-layered batter mixture comprised of meat, vegetable and anything else
Omamori - little charms on sale at most temples and shrines
Omoshiroi - interesting
Oni - demon
Onigiri - rice balls usually with a filling and semi-wrapped in seaweed
Onna - woman
Onsen - hot springs, usually used as communal baths
Otousan - father
Oyabun - head of a Yakuza family
Ryokan - traditional Japanese inn
Sakura - cherry blossom
-sama - a suffix denoting respect to somebody of greater age or status

-san - a suffix that proceeds a first name *in lieu of Mr. Mrs. Ms. Etc
Sanmon -entrance gates to a temple
Sekai - the human world
Senbei - rice cakes
Sentō - public baths
Shide - zig zag shaped paper streamers found at holy sites
Shimenawa - Shinto straw rope found at holy sites often wrapped around trees or hung above doorways to temples and shrines
Shitsurei shimasu - phrase said on entering a room where people are, similar to 'sorry for intruding'
Shōchū - a distilled rice beverage
Shogi - traditional board game similar to western chess
Shojin ryori - Buddhist cuisine, exclusively vegetarian
Shōnen - young man
Sou desu - that's right
Sou ka? - is that right?
Sumimasen - excuse me or sorry
Tadaima! - I'm back! Called when entering a house
Taiyaki - grilled stuffed sweet pancakes in the shape of a fish
Takamagahara - Shinto heaven
Takoyaki - popular street food, like a deep fried octopus croquette
Tamago - Japanese omelette
Tanuki - raccoon dog, depicted often in folklore carrying sake and having huge testicles
Taoism - ancient Chinese religious and philosophical tradition
Tatami - mats used as flooring. Note: instead of by square metres or feet, traditional the size of a room or house was measured in number of tatami.
Tengoku - heaven
Tengu - long-nosed Japanese goblins, often red, sometimes with the ability to fly
Tōji - the chief sake brewer of a kura
Tsukemono - Japanese pickles
Uchide no kozuchi - legendary magical hammer than makes wishes come true

Umeboshi - pickled plum
Unagi - eel, usually soy-glazed and grilled
Wakarimasu/Wakata - I understand/understood
Yakitori - grilled soy-lacquered chicken (and every part of said chicken) skewers
Yōkai - creatures and beasts of Japanese folklore
Yomi-no-kuni - Shinto realm of the dead
Yukata - house robe, a kind of Japanese dressing gown
Yūrei - ghosts
Yuzu - a citrus fruit akin to lemon
Zazen - Buddhist meditation